Lasting Word

ANNABELLE OF ANCHONY SERIES BOOK IV

Ruth Apollonia

THE APOLLONIAN
ARTS COMPANY

IN MEMORIAM

When I started working on *Lasting Word* eight years ago, I wondered to whom I would dedicate it. My mom was not ill at the time. She fought well for five years and passed away in 2022.

Though she was gone before *Kingdom's Call* was published, I didn't have strength to put it in writing and to change the dedication already written in that book.

Though it hurts to have your heart ripped from you, it is with faith in the Good News that I have hope I will see her again. Because she received the sacrament of Anointing of the Sick a few days before her death, died enrolled in the Brown Scapular, and had Gregorian Masses said for her soul, it is with as much confidence as one can have—short of being added to the canon of the saints—that I trust she is in Heaven.

And now, along with Our Lady, I have two mothers beyond the veil.

My mom was my biggest supporter. She would take the hand of people she knew and pull them to my table or casually walk up to strangers at my book signings and say "My daughter wrote a book." And so I dedicate *Lasting Word* to the memory of my mom, Rose Ann Anderson. Besides life, the greatest gift she gave to me was the Catholic faith.

The faith she instilled in me plays out on the pages of my books.

NEW CHARACTERS OF IMPORTANCE
FROM KINGDOM'S CALL

In Anchony

Queen Camrina of the Sockor Islands: King Francis's sister, who tried to steal the Anchonian throne from him by working with Prince Howercus. She is currently imprisoned in the dungeon in Aboly.

Sir Halptus of Sutherland: The knight who, in an effort to regain the good graces of his father (after leading his father's knights to defeat in battle against the Demolites and the sovereignty of Anchony), stole Prince Eduard and then sought out Queen Camrina.

Sir Hugo: The Baltamian knight charged with assisting the Anchonian knights with the prisoners in Aboly. He is to remain in Aboly while being in charge of the Baltamian knights until King Henricus returns to Anchony.

Sir Altus: The knight who released Princess Anastacia when held by Lord Rackus, returned the grave robber's makings to the Sethelian graves, and assisted Sirs Melvon, Jacobus, and Frankus in finding Queen Mona. He has now joined with the king's knights.

Eunisia: A worker at Lathrop Castle, where Queen Clara was a servant prior to her servitude at the Abolian Castle. She provided information to the Sethelians, which led to Queen Clara's taking.

Father Mycus: A missionary priest from Sethel. He and his companions brought Annabelle back to Anchony.

In Baltam

Sir Harkus: A Baltamian knight who was charged with leading the knights to find King Henricus while in Anchony.

In Sethel

Lord Cortell, duke of Summerton: Appearing to be on Prince Howercus's side, the duke is the prince's second-in-command. Friends with the late Prince Phillipus and informed of the brewing plans to steal the crown, he covertly wants the crown to be returned to Princess Anastacia. He and his wife, Lady Alana, made it appear as though they hanged King Francis of Anchony.

Lady Alana, duchess of Summerton: Wife to Lord Cortell, she secretly hid King Francis away from Prince Howercus as she assisted the king in his recovery from the wounds he had obtained by the Demolites.

On Trader Island

Kyphosis: A disfigured man who rescued Princess Annabelle from Snake Island.

On the Seas

Captain Anguis: Captain of a pirate ship, he paid the captain of a merchant ship to rescue Annabelle from Oro Island.

Captain Vitalis: The captain of the merchant ship who was paid to rescue Annabelle of Anchony from Oro Island.

MAP

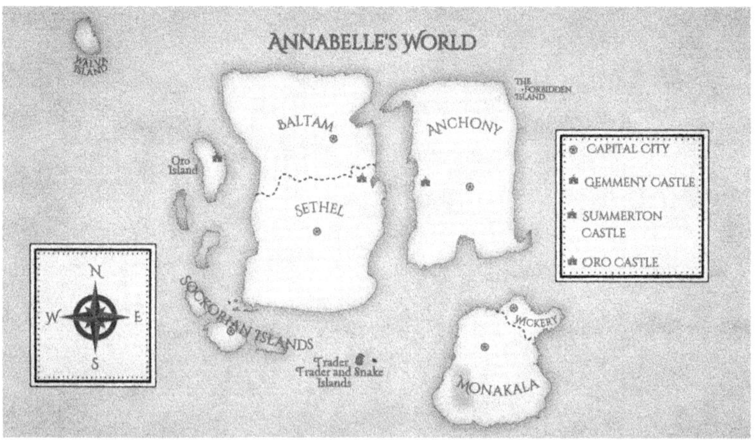

To view a larger image of this map, visit RuthApollonia.com.

CONTENTS

GLOOMY CLOUDS

Nicholaus, we're off the island! As Oro Island faded from her view, Princess Annabelle turned her eyes to the menacing storm clouds rolling above it and drawing ever nearer to the wooden vessel transporting her to her beloved husband. Lowering her gaze, she looked to her growing abdomen. With a gentle smile, she whispered a prayer in her heart. *With Your care, Father, we will make it home to him. But I want nothing but Your will.*

Beside her, Melody gasped as a bright fork of lightning lit the sky and struck a tree in the distant land.

The princess moved her hand from her stomach to the shoulder of the nearly twelve-year-old girl. "Don't fret, Melody. It is still far a—" A crash of thunder that followed the lightning flash interrupted her words.

Annabelle of Anchony, second daughter of King Francis and Queen Clara of Anchony and wife to Sir Nicholaus Hunts, was, sadly, accustomed to being far from her loved ones. Taken from her parents and siblings as a young child and later returned to them, she was again separated from her family and left for dead upon the distant Snake Island by her own aunt, Queen Camrina of the Sockor Islands. Rescued by a disfigured man named Kyphosis, she was transported to Oro Island by Sethelians following orders from their murderous prince, Howercus, who was in league with the villainous queen.

"Annabelle, Melody, come in here," Captain Vitalis called.

As her breath was nearly stolen by a strong wind, the princess turned toward the cabin while leading her friend toward the opening. "Come along, Melody. The captain wishes us to go in."

"The storm is coming closer," the girl noted with a tremble in her voice.

"Yes, I know. We need to make certain we're not in the way of the mariners."

Melody nodded as they walked toward the shelter.

A peasant girl from southern Anchony whose family was slaughtered by the terrorizing political group known as the Demolites, Melody Picker had no one left in the world but the princess. Together they had found themselves trapped on Oro Island after being forced into slavery by Queen Camrina, who had freed Anchonians from the enslavement she had created in a failed effort to win the people's support.

"It's getting rough out there. Come in, come in." Captain Vitalis, who'd been paid by a pirate, Captain Anguis, to deliver the two females to Anchony, waved them inside.

Stepping inside, Melody jumped and her eyes grew wide when another overpowering thunderclap seemed nearly to shake the ship itself apart.

"Oh, don't you worry," the captain said calmly. "It shall pass, and then it will be smooth seas." Turning toward the door, his smile faded into a worried countenance.

"How long?" Annabelle asked him. "How long shall it be until we're back in Anchony?"

Glancing at the door, he quickly walked to the table and pulled out a crude map. His finger slid over the lines and markings. "This is Oro Island. Over here are the western lands of Baltam. It will take a day or so, depending upon the weather, to get there." His finger ran across the page as he quickly glanced again at the door. "The quickest route to Anchony would be to go north around Baltam. But with the seasons changing, that would not be wise. So south it shall be, around Baltam and Sethel." Annabelle watched his finger slide down around the curves. "To the western lands of Anchony. That route will take a few weeks."

Weeks. Moving closer to view the map better, Annabelle leaned over the table and fingered the letters. *Port Arlus. Gemmel of Gemmeny.* "I know these names." *Nicholaus, we'll be home soon!* She smiled as she looked up at the captain.

He returned her smile and then stepped away. "We must first anchor in Baltam, though, to drop off our goods."

"But you will take us all the way to Anchony?" the princess asked.

"Yes, I gave my word." He looked to the floor. "To a *pirate*, of all people."

A mariner stuck his head inside the cabin. "Captain, you are wanted on deck."

"Excuse me." Bowing his head, Vitalis left.

"A pirate?" Melody asked. "Do you think that was Captain Anguis?"

Annabelle shook her head in amazement. "I know of no other pirate. Do you?"

"Only the others that were with him."

"It is odd. Why would a pirate pay for me to make it back to Anchony? He could have used me as ransom."

Melody shrugged. "It was the right thing to do."

"Since when do pirates abide by what is right?" She shook her head. "There's more to that man than a pirate."

"What do you mean?"

"I don't know. But a true pirate would have ransomed me."

Melody, perplexed, stared at the western edge of Anchony on the map. "If he's not a pirate, what is he?"

Princess Anastacia, the true heir to the Sethelian throne, rose from her hands and knees and looked desperately around her locked room in the Sockorian castle in Callum. *Where'd it go? It was right here last evening. Where is my letter?* She turned around. *Did it somehow fall into the fireplace?* The door rattled as a key turned in the lock. She approached it. *Will Nakala know what has become of it?*

As the door opened, a gasp escaped her lips and she took a step backward, alarmed at the presence of a strange man with dusty blond hair and around a decade her senior. "Who are you?"

The man entering the room surveyed the chamber and found her to be the lone occupant. "You are a prisoner of the Sockor Kingdom?" he asked.

Swallowing her fright, she backed away until she ran into the bed post. "What do you want with me?"

He closed the door behind him and stepped closer. "You're the niece to Prince Howercus, the true heir to the throne of Sethel?"

Fright paralyzed any speech she might utter.

"Queen Camrina has some gold, and I'm here to take it," the invading visitor said.

She shook her head as he approached. Finally, able to muster a sound, she whispered, "I . . . I don't know where it is. Please! I know nothing! I've been locked in—"

"Shhh!" His hand covered her mouth and, leaning toward her ear, he whispered, "I didn't ask you if you knew."

In the growing light of the sunrise, Nakala, Princess Anastacia's servant, stood with her brother in the cemetery of the vandalized church next to the Sockorian castle, preparing to begin lauds. She handed folded pieces of paper to him as he held the prayer book. "She's been working on this for a while."

"What is it?" Narkalus asked.

Nakala frowned. "Her story. It tells of all that has taken place in Sethel—that poor girl. I believe King Marcus shall find it of use."

"Very good. Very good." Folding the paper, he tucked it into his tunic and then opened his prayer book.

They both stopped suddenly as the village's warning bell rang out. They stepped into the sunlight and scanned the castle and sea. Nakala gasped. "Thieves from the sea! I hope she is alright."

From the distance of about 400 yards, they watched as seven chests were placed upon rowboats along the seashore and taken to the awaiting ship. She glanced at her brother, the knight. "Why do the castle wards not stop them?"

Sir Narkalus unsheathed his sword. "Because they're likely dead already."

Nakala took a breath as she approached the door. "It's still locked. The princess should be safe."

"Make certain," her brother said as he looked down the corridor.

Reaching for the lock, she halted. Turning around, she looked at her brother. "What will we do with her? All have fled the castle."

"We will take her back with us to Monakala."

Nodding, Nakala unlocked the door and pushed it open.

"Princess? Princess Anastacia?" Turning around the room, she looked at her brother. "She's gone."

Nodding as he looked inside the vacant chamber and then the empty hall, Sir Narkalus found his sister's glance. "The pirates must have taken her. We can't avail her now. But there is no one here. Now is our time to do what must be done."

Nakala lowered her head and spoke before walking past him into the hall. "Let's do it with haste then."

"That chest I want placed in my cabin," the leader of the looters commanded. He followed the men as they carried the chest to his sleeping quarters. He watched as they dropped it roughly in the middle of the floor, then waited until they left to step inside. Shutting the door, he took out a key and unlocked the chest.

With a tear-streaked face, the gagged princess looked up at him.

"Pledge to me you will not scream. Do you pledge it?"

Seeing a nod in response, he removed her gag and then freed her wrists. Sitting up, she scooted to the corner of the chest, hugging her legs. Somehow, she managed to whisper, "What are you going to do with me?"

He stood. "Stay in here and stay quiet."

"Please," she begged as he turned toward the door. "Who are you? What do you want with me?"

"I'm Captain Anguis. I'm on my way to Sethel with Queen Camrina's gold."

Shutting the cabin door out on the deck, he looked at the few pirates standing around.

"You placed a chest in there?" one ventured.

He stared at the man. "What's it to you?"

"It was lighter than the others," the man observed.

Captain Anguis, stepping closer, gripped at his dagger as he repeated more sternly, "What is it to you?"

The pirate lowered his head and backed away.

Inside the broken church next to the castle in Callum, Nakala knelt before the earthen hole, looking down at her brother. She shook her head as rough stones bit into her knees. "No body at all?"

Sir Narkalus looked up at her. "You were right." Climbing out from the grave, he joined his sister as they stared at the empty tomb. "Was he never interred here?"

"All those years ago. It was not right! Nothing about it was right!" Disgust filled her as she remembered Queen Camrina's dismissive remark: *"He's buried in the church. There's a stone. Go see it, if you don't trust my words."*

Shaking her head with passion, Nakala rose. "What did she do with his body?!"

"We will go to King Marcus," Sir Narkalus said as he stood.

Looking around the dilapidated church, Nakala pulled the letter from her pouch and gave it to her brother. "You give this to him. I'm staying here."

"Why?"

"I deem more can be learned here than anywhere else."

ABOLY

In the royal seat of Anchony, Princess Cristine stood round a fire with Rossa, a villager from Stonton in the northern part of the country, some trusted servants, and other villagers. Nearby was the large hut that served as the temporary royal residence while the castle was being rebuilt. They watched the youngest princess, Elizabeth, leap over puddles. "Your sister is having fun," Rossa said.

"Oh, to be that young again," said Avilina, the wife of the master mason rebuilding the destroyed castle, with a smile. "Not a care in the world and to see life for all its majesties."

Majesties? Cristine's shoulders lowered as she looked around at the villagers busy with their late morning tasks and the masons rebuilding the Abolian castle. *Annie is dead, Edus is still missing, Sir Nicholaus has yet to return.* With a sad countenance, she stood back from the overwhelming heat of the fire in the fall air. *The number of bound Demolites is greater than the number of our knights, our evil aunt is in the dungeon along with her best friend, the despicable Queen Mona of Sethel . . . but, oh, the majesties!* She shook her head at the sarcastic, negative remarks jumping through her mind.

"What's wrong, my lady?" Avilina asked.

The princess looked back at the older villager. "She's dulled by life. That's why she leaps puddles. Liza, come here."

Princess Elizabeth came at her sister's call, always wanting to be helpful. "Crisa?"

Cristine handed the stick with the cooked fowl impaled upon it to her sister. "Take this to Isa and Lord Symon."

"And Emma?" Elizabeth asked.

Cristine could not help but give a slight smile. "And Emma, too."

"With haste!" The youngest princess gleefully took the stick.

"I can do that, Your Highness," one of the servants said as she stood from the fire.

"She needs something to do. You may take this one, Alicia." She handed another cooked fowl to the servant.

"Oh, no." Rossa squatted down next to the fire as if it could conceal her as the young princess ran toward the blacksmith shop with the servant following. "That woman is back."

"What woman?" Cristine followed her gaze.

Rossa nodded in the direction of a peasant woman, dressed in drab clothes that matched her demeanor. "She is from the southern lands. She searches fiercely for her children. I wish I could help her, but I can't." Looking at the princess, Rossa gave up hope of being saved from the peasant as the woman made her way closer.

"Most do," Rachel, the servant from Gemmel, said as she rotated the other cooking birds over the fire.

"I have told her before that I haven't seen them, but yet she comes back looking—*every* day," Rossa explained further.

Cristine watched the woman, from a distance, bend down at every fire to converse with those gathered round and then rise and move on. "What are her children's names?"

"There are many that search," Avilina stated as she recalled the numerous times she had been asked about missing children. "So many."

Rossa rubbed her head. "I've forgotten. All the names stir together when you hear so many of them."

"Why don't you make a record and write them down?"

The two villagers and servants looked at one another. "We would," Rachel answered, "if we knew the letters."

"Here she comes." Rossa, taking a deep breath, smiled at the woman. "I fear we haven't seen them today."

"Tilus and Kara. Tilus is my boy and Kara my girl. They have brown hair, brown eyes. They are this—"

Rossa shook her head. "I'm sorry."

The woman dropped her hand from the prescribed height, and as it fell, so, too, did her head.

Standing in the doorway of their temporary hut looking toward the campfire, Queen Clara's emerald eyes watched her youngest daughter jump joyously around the puddles and then take off toward the blacksmith's shop, her mind was miles away and months behind, fretting over the last sight she'd had of Annabelle as the Sethelians faithful to Howercus rowed her daughter toward Snake Island—rowed toward what was surely her demise. Her memory then sprinted to weeks prior, when she discovered her pregnant daughter had survived the Demolitic attack upon Aboly, which had left the castle and city in its present wreckage. They had been reunited at Gemmeny Castle, when Lord Cortell tried to free Clara from Prince Howercus's grasp, but his efforts had merely resulted in both Annabelle and the queen being taken.

"Clara?" She felt her husband's hand upon her shoulder. "There you are."

Looking distantly, she shook her head. "Annabelle could

have hidden. They weren't looking for her." She turned to look into Francis's eyes. "She wouldn't. She said . . . she saw you die before her eyes . . . as if the fault was hers. As if you died because she left you." Clara's solemn expression turned downward as she fought back the tears. "She said she wouldn't leave me, too."

He gripped her shoulder for comfort; she gladly accepted it as she leaned onto his arm and wept. "And it's I," she said, "who left her! I . . . I watched them take her to that awful island!"

"Shhh, Clara." He rubbed her back. "There was nothing you could do."

"To lose her yet again . . . I'm not sure I can bear it."

"Shhh. Yes you can, my queen. You bore it before, when she was five, with patience and prayer, and you are bearing it again."

"But it's not the same this time." She gently touched his chest as a tear ran down her cheek. "It wasn't only her life but the child's, too."

"Yes." Francis took a deep breath as he fought back his own tears.

The queen looked at her husband with desperation, unable to pose the real question upon her heart: *Is there any hope she could have lived?* "Have you heard from Sir Nicholaus?" was all she could speak.

He gently rubbed her back as she leaned into him. "No."

Pulling back, she looked into his eyes. "That's good? He still searches for her?"

Caressing her face, he held it with both of his hands. "Clara, you're the one who told me she couldn't have lived."

"I know. I know!" Her head landed back upon him. "But I don't want it to be true!"

His voice tightened. "Did Camrina know she was with child?"

"Yes," she said sadly.

He closed his eyes in disdain of his evil sister's actions.

❄

"She will not speak!" Prince William, the heir to the throne of Anchony, said with agitation as he sharpened his sword with a rock. He and his brother, Prince Thomas, sat upon some rubble within the fortress wall. "How are we to ever find Edus if she will not tell us anything?"

Thomas, the second eldest, shook his head as he looked across the bailey, watching the masons and captives move the heavy stones. "It is likely that she knows nothing. The man that Sir Michael was chasing, Sir Halptus—we *know* he had Edus. We need to find him! If only we knew *where* to find him."

William shook his head. "I'm telling you—Camrina knows something!" Sparks flew from the metal as he rubbed with passion.

"He couldn't vanish." Thomas shook his head. "Someone has to know something! There are no tidings from the south, and I have searched the western lands myself to no avail."

"It wouldn't be out of her character—she has killed Grand-mamá and Annie. We know she took Princess Anastacia, so I'm certain she's behind Edus's taking as well!"

Thomas glanced at his brother before looking down at the broken link in the chain mail he was mending. "But we know a Sir Halptus had him."

"Wherever he is from is still a mystery. I know Camrina, and I know where to find her!" William threw the rock down in frustration.

Thomas took a deep breath. "But not how to make her talk." He shook his head. "If only Papá could get the truth from her."

"I doubt that will ever come to be," William said with a near grunt. "She's not right, Thom. Not right at all. She thinks her savage ways are . . . a rightful duty."

As his older brother spoke his dismay of their aunt, Thomas looked toward the bailey wall, remembering how his sisters had found the young Prince Eduard hiding nearly three years prior, when Princess Elizabeth had been snatched away.

"Thom," Cristine dropped her arms after getting his attention and then pointed. "We found him under the wain, but he won't come out!"

Following his sister's finger, he walked over to the cart to hear Isabella beg, "Please, Edus, won't you come out?"

"No!"

"Why not?" Isabella asked in confusion.

Cristine folded her arms. "Thom, pull him out and end this folly!"

Thomas, glancing at Cristine, knelt down next to Isabella and touched her shoulder. "I'll get him."

Isabella took a breath. "I've tried for a while—he won't come. He clings fiercely."

"She's being too gentle!" Cristine insisted.

Ignoring her comment, Thomas asked, "Did you tell Mamá that you found him?"

"You're the first one I saw," Cristine said as Isabella stood.

"She must be so worried," Isabella said with concern. "We'll go in haste." Taking a few steps away, the next comment was directed at Cristine: "I was hoping he would come out on his own."

Watching his sisters jog toward the castle, Thomas sat down next to the wheel and spoke over his shoulder. "They're gone. It's only me here now, Edus. Won't you come out?"

"No!"

"Why not?" Thomas looked at the ground as he waited for a reply.

Finally, the little boy yelled, "It's not safe!"

Thomas slowly nodded his head. "So, it is fear that hides you? You are afraid someone will take you like Liza was taken?" He waited for a reply, and when he received none, he turned around toward the dark lump hiding in the shadows. "Edus, you can't live your life afraid of what might come to pass."

"You're grown," the boy said. "No one will try to take you. You don't need to be afraid!"

"There are times when we need to be cautious, but we can't be *ruled by fear." He released a breath. "Truth be told, I am afraid for Liza right now." He shook his head. "And I'm galled that Papá forbade me from searching for her. I would much rather be out there looking for her than being here, doing nothing."*

The little boy crept forward a few inches. "You would search for her like Will is?"

"Without question."

Eduard lowered his head and then looked up at him sheepishly. "What if it was me? Would you look for me?"

Thomas tilted his head. "Why would I not?" He lowered his head closer to his five-year-old brother. "Prince Eduard of Anchony, I give you my word now: If ever you are taken, I will seek you out and search until I can no more! Now come out of there so I can speak it to your face!"

"What shall be done with her?" Prince William continued the tirade against his aunt.

Thomas, finding the eyes of his older brother, shook his head. "I have to find him, Will. I pledged to him I would if he was ever taken." He looked back to the broken wall at the spot where his sisters found Edus. "In this very bailey, I spoke my word to him." His eyes caught the form of Cristine walking toward the library rubble. "What are we to do, Will? How are we to find him and how are we to make certain the rest are safe?"

William, looking over at the training recruits, frowned. "I don't know, but I'm certain we won't be able to count upon the new men." He watched his brother stand. "Where are you going?"

"To see what Crisa's doing."

Catching up to his sister before she scaled the broken stones to enter what remained of the library, he touched her arm.

"Thom!" She took a quick breath. "You scared me."

"I'm sorry. I didn't mean to." He looked at the broken stones covering the scattered books. "What are you doing?"

"I want to find some paper and ink to help the commoners."

Cristine turned her head, and Thomas followed her gaze. Their parents were passing by quickly, heading toward the dungeon. Neither the king nor the queen even noticed their two children standing nearby, so intent were they upon their mission. Cristine looked to her brother. "Do you think Papá is finally going to let Aunt Camrina know he lives?"

Clara's heart fell as she looked at her sister-in-law chained inside her cell. *What has become of you, Camrina?* Looking over her shoulder, Clara spoke softly, "Sir Melvon, will you remove Queen Mona for the moment? I want to speak with Queen Camrina alone."

"Yes, Your Majesty," the knight mumbled as he walked past her and into the cell. He took Mona by the arm and led her to the door. Clara watched them exit as Mona vociferated her objections to the perceived ill treatment.

Walking out of the shadows, Camrina tilted her head. "Clara, you have come yet again? Do you come to crow? Oh, how your visits tire me."

Clara shook her head at the sadness before her. "Do you think I take joy in what has become of your life?" She gripped the bars. "You have but one life to live, and yours has been for nothing but crime."

Rage boiled in the Sockorian queen's blood as she stepped forward. "Do not speak to me, commoner!"

"You may call me what you like, Camrina. I will never claim I was not your servant. I will never claim I was born of noble blood. But I also will *never* claim I am not married to the king. I would never choose any other path despite all you could say or do to me." She shook her head as she took a deep breath. "It was God's will that we wed."

Camrina's eyes flashed with anger. "Why do you come here?"

Clara's tone was more forceful as she stiffened. "Where is he?"

"Who?" The word was spoken with disgust.

"My son, Prince Eduard. Your nephew."

The prisoner, briefly lowering her eyes, looked back into the emerald hue with a new resolve. "I don't know."

Clara's chin stiffened as she gripped the bars tighter. "You're lying. You know something. Tell me where he is."

Camrina smirked. "Why ever would I do that?"

Clara, noting an inhuman look, lowered her hands as she moved backward. "Why can't you speak the truth?"

The chained queen lurched forward. "The truth?" She sinisterly laughed. "I'll tell you the truth: I will find my freedom and I will take what is mine by birth!"

Clara tried to look into her eyes. "Is there any virtue in your heart? Can't you see that in God's eyes no one is better than—"

"Do not speak to me of God!"

Clara stepped back toward the stairwell, knowing her husband was but a few feet away. "I'm sorry, Camrina, that you have come to be in such a way."

The bound queen, with nostrils flaring, stared through the bars. "I'm only sorry my brother had not! That his sons have not!"

Clara gasped in exasperation as she shook her head. "Your brother, Francis, is the best man I know. He sees past the wretchedness of the person and sees them as—"

A guttural laugh escaped Camrina's core as a smirk slid across her face. "Thanks to me, my brother is dead!"

Raising her head to meet the Sockorian's challenge, Clara stepped closer to the bars. "What a pity it would be for you if he weren't." Tapping her fingers against the bars for a moment, she then gripped the roughness that scraped at the delicacy of her skin. "You would still be seventh in line. I avow to you, Camrina, that my children will *never* let you take the throne."

Thrashing forward with all her might, Camrina bled where the rough iron cut against her wrists as she boiled in her passion. "They don't have the right! Your churlish blood runs through them, servant!" She flung herself forward with more fury. "I'm sorry I didn't kill you and your offspring long ago!"

"That's enough out of you!" King Francis's voice echoed against the walls as he rushed down the stairs.

Camrina recoiled in recognition of the voice and fell to her knees, aghast. As she saw her ploys unravel before her, she said, "No! It can't be!" Camrina's eyes enlarged inside her shaking head as her brother emerged from the spiral staircase. "You . . . are . . . dead."

"No. Camrina, your feint failed—all of it." He touched his wife's face. "Clara, I could stand no more."

Clara swallowed with difficulty as she caught the image of her bewildered sister-in-law from the corner of her eye. "She knows something of Eduard."

Glancing quickly at his sister, the king kissed his wife. Camrina, disgusted, moved back into the shadows. "William awaits at the steps," he said.

Nodding, she turned toward the stairwell.

Hearing his wife's footsteps ascend the stones, Francis stepped closer to the bars as the heavier footstep of Sir Peter Josephus the Lion descended. "Jous, open the door."

Stepping inside, Francis knelt down and shook his head. "Camrina, what have you done?"

Looking at him with disgust, she replied, "All that I was taught to do."

"To plot your brother's death? To force others into slavery?" He rose. "You are the only slave here."

She rose to meet his challenge. "I am a slave to no one!"

He eyed the blood upon her wrists where the rough shackles had torn at her skin. It soaked into the sleeves of her dress. "By your lust for pride and authority, it has swarmed your body and you can't even see it."

"The only thing that holds me bound are these chains." Countenance changing, she attempted to smile. "Francis, will you take them off?"

"Your cunning will not be rewarded here."

Her smile faded. "To hell with you then! Your servant wife calls you the greatest man she knows, yet you will not aid your own sister."

Francis's head shook in anger. "Did you do it? Did you kill Mamá?!"

Her eyes drifted to the corner of the room as she remembered that fateful evening in the forest.

"Mamá . . . you came . . . and alone as I asked." She could not hide her grin—all was going as planned.

"Camrina, dear, I beg of you." Queen Katerina's eyes pleaded with her. "Let this pass. Your brother loves his wife."

Turning her back to her mother, Camrina spoke over her shoulder, "Mamá . . ." Her eyes looked coldly to the dark forest. "You know this is your doing, right?" Turning around, she walked closer to the mother queen. "You spoke to Papá. You pressed him to make amends with Francis before Papá's death." She stared past her mother's shoulder to the darkness all around, slightly turning away. "If it was not for you, this kingdom would be mine."

Queen Katerina shook her head adamantly. "I'm not sorrowful, Camrina. What I did, I did for Anchony."

"I see." Camrina turned toward her completely, dagger lurking at her side. "I have been banished from Anchony. My own brother

banished me! I fear this is the last time we shall meet." She opened her left arm toward her mother for a hug. *"Let us depart with an embrace."*

"Yes, I killed her."

"Why?" Francis pounded his fist into his other hand. "Answer me, Camrina! Why did you kill Mamá!"

Tears falling in rage, Camrina bit back: "Why did you marry a servant? *My* servant!"

"Are you truly so . . . prideful . . . that you can't be glad that I found love?"

"You don't deserve it," she said through clenched teeth.

"What?" Francis looked at her in disbelief.

"You left it. You forsook Papá! You forsook Anchony! You ran from the throne! It was in my grasp."

"I ran toward love!" His voice spoke fury. "I had to do what was in my heart. I had to do what God asked of me! I would have joyfully lived out my life with Clara and our children in some nameless town."

"You should have!" Her face twitched in anger. "If it hadn't been for Mamá, you would have!"

Francis stepped away with the revelation. "You killed Mamá because she got Papá to take me back?"

"She did more than that! She pressed *her* to marry you! I was there—on the other side of the door. I heard her words spoken in that chapel. I heard what she said of me: 'My daughter can't be queen.'" Swallowing with great difficulty, she stood straight. "She chose Clara over me! A servant! A servant over her own blood! And you! You have soiled the throne of Anchony by your marriage to that churl! Yes, I killed her! I knifed her in the heart as she knifed me!" Pulling against the chains, she screamed like an injured feral animal.

Francis leaned against the bars for support. "Camrina . . . you are not well." Looking at Peter, he walked out of the cell as she continued to scream and rage in fury. In disbelief, he stared at her as fresh blood trickled down her wrists from the resistance of her movement against the iron.

When she finally settled upon the floor, exhausted by her own passion, she hunched over upon the stone ground, shaking in fury. The king looked back at her. "I want to know where my son is."

She released a deep chuckle as she looked up at him from the tops of her eyes. "Why ever would I tell you anything?"

Sir Josephus Peter the Lion, the man who raised Annabelle upon the Forbidden Island and the father to her husband, walked up the stairwell behind the king. Nearby, Grand Sir Michael Doey was working on training the new recruits while Prince William, dismayed, stared at the hopeless efforts within the training boundary. Peter halted beside the white rocks of the training area to observe. As he watched, yet another wooden sword was flung away from a recruit's grasp by one hit of Sir Doey's weapon. Closing his eyes, Peter rubbed his face in despair.

Spotting Prince Thomas climbing out of the castle rubble with paper in his hand, he despairingly approached him. "I fear I have failed you, Prince Thomas. You won't get good protection out of these men."

"We're aware," William answered back as he walked away from the hopeless trainees. "You, Sir Altus, and Sir Doey are all that we have."

Thomas's eyes looked toward the Sethelian knight who was returning from imprisoning the young queen once again. "What of Sir Melvon?"

"He sees it as his duty to make certain Queen Mona stays where she should," Prince William answered. "He doesn't stand there on watch for Anchony; he gives protection to the true throne of Sethel, and since she has threatened it . . ."

"At least we know his fealty is not toward Prince Howercus." Thomas stepped away from the stone wreckage. "When Sir Hugo and the Baltamian knights leave—whenever that will be—we'll have too few." His eyes looked at the prisoners forced to work on the castle as he released a puff of air. "There is a traitor amongst the castle servants who should arrive any day with the Anchelian commoners. How are we to stop it all from taking place again? If that one man—whoever he may be—chooses to act—"

"We shall have to find him out!" William declared adamantly.

"How?" Thomas turned toward his brother. "How are we to do it, Will?"

"Sir Victorus?" the eldest prince suggested.

Peter shook his head. "He doesn't know. He knows there was a castle servant working with Lord Rackus, but not the name."

"Then we shall ask Lord Rackus himself!" William declared.

Peter glanced over at the prisoner. "He will not speak the truth. I have asked a number of times. Each time he gives me a new name. His word can't be trusted."

Sighing heavily, Prince Thomas walked toward the forest, easily seen through the broken bailey wall. If he could not solve that problem, he could at least help Cristine with hers.

Thomas placed the quills upon the table as he set down the other needed particulars. "From the castle and the woods."

"Thank you," Cristine said with a smile, eager to help out the frantic parents in whatever way she could.

"Do you have everything you need?" her brother asked as she sat at a table in the empty market.

"One at a time!" Elizabeth spoke with her hands as if it

would make up for her shortness in stature as she attempted to direct the crowd with aid from the servants, Alicia and Ida. "Form a line."

They both looked away from their youngest sister as Cristine suggested, "Ruling the crowd?"

Nodding, he walked to his youngest sister. "Liza, join Crisa at the table."

Disappointment veiled her face. "But I want to help her. Crisa said my letters aren't good enough. What am I to do, then?"

"Make certain the ink is full," Thomas suggested.

Looking from the table to her brother, she shook her head. "You filled it, didn't you?"

"Liza, I don't want you to be harmed."

She lowered her head when he looked away, knowing he was searching desperately for some way she could be useful. "I'm not big enough to help her." Moping, she walked over to her sister.

Cristine looked at her sister's downcast glance. "Liza—"

"Milla," said the first peasant who stepped to the table, with an urgency in her voice. "My daughter is Milla."

"Oh, um . . ." Cristine looked to the woman. "And from where do you hail?" Glancing at her sister out of the corner of her eye, she watched the youngest princess sit down with a frown upon her face.

Northwest of Aboly, within the walls of the Cavern of the Hunted weeks prior, Clare, daughter to Sir Josephus Peter the Lion, studied the carvings upon the cave wall. As her fingers nearly touched the rough rock, she lowered her hand. "Tha ha Mass hare?"

Samus turned toward his sister's voice after checking to ensure all Demolitic bodies had been removed from the gigantic cavern. "Yes, this is where they had Mass when they were assailed."

"Every last body is out and ready to be buried," said Stephanus, the reformed Demolite—an Anewlite—addressing him. "Father Mycus is about to begin."

Samus tapped his sister's shoulder. She peeled her eyes from the carvings. "It is starting," he said.

Clare immediately walked down the wing toward the opening of the hidden haven as Stephanus stepped closer to Samus.

"I have tried to find the Demolite whom Sir Victorus spoke about," Stephanus said. "But the servants offer no aid. I don't think they know. Whoever he is, he is well hidden." He shook his head. "At least we know it's no one from Anchelo."

"Can we delay our return to Aboly?" Samus pondered out loud.

"After the funeral, we have no more reasons to delay leaving."

"What if we go to Anchelo first? Give the servants the choice of staying there or returning to the destroyed Aboly?"

Stephanus shook his head. "So the traitor will either get away or return to Aboly to do more harm?"

Samus stared at him for a moment as he thought about the two options. "Either way, it could give more time to Aboly."

"Time for what?"

Samus released a breath. "I don't know. To ready themselves for his coming?"

Clare turned around. "Ya camin'?" They hurried down the wing to help her down.

FATES ACROSS THE SEAS

Lady Alana, duchess of Summerton in Sethel and wife of Lord Cortell, rubbed the giant ruby within her fingers as if it was the most precious gift, containing a million secrets and a million questions. With a tear rolling down her cheek, Lady Alana closed her hands around the ruby as she took a deep breath while standing in her castle chamber.

"You cling to it tightly, my lady."

Alana looked at Luna, her servant. "I do, don't I?"

"Why? That's the jewel that the princess had, is it not?"

"Annabelle of Anchony, yes." Alana nodded once and then turned toward the servant. "But it has great meaning to me."

"How did the princess come to have it?"

Alana looked down at the redness as she shook her head. "She said she was told where to find it, but I don't truly know at all."

A knock upon the door took her attention. A male servant entered and said, "My lady, there are men here. Come quickly, please."

"Men? Who?" Glancing over her shoulder at the man, who

had already disappeared into the hallway, she briskly turned and walked after him.

"A Sir Marthelus. He claims he is a king's knight."

Watching the men invade the Summerton Great Hall, Alana walked forward with determination. "What is the meaning of this? I demand that you stop this intrusion of my home!"

Sir Marthelus smirked. "Demand?" He snickered. "You? Tell me, where is your husband?"

"*Lord Cortell* is with Prince Howercus."

Sir Marthelus put up his hand. "Stop," he told his men. All motion ceased. He looked back at the woman. "Your husband is Lord Cortell?"

"Yes! I am Lady Alana, the duchess of Summerton." She placed her hands upon her hips. "My husband is Prince Howercus's second-in-command. I demand to know why you are here."

"Lord Cortell is your husband?" the man asked again with a friendlier tone. "I wish pardon, my lady." He moved uncomfortably. "I was in search of some outlaws. I was told Summerton might know something of them." He lowered his head. "I did not know you were the wife of Lord Cortell."

"That I am." She stood straight. "Your counsel on these outlaws was wrong." She took a deep breath as she stood straighter. "Of what was Summerton accused?"

He lowered his head, ashamed to speak the words: "Hiding them."

"Hiding outlaws?" She stared at him with a stern face. "Summerton is not hiding anything. You are free to look, if you think that is needed. And I will make certain my husband hears of it."

He stared at her for a moment. "No, my lady. I do not wish

Prince Howercus to hear of my folly." He bowed his head. "We will leave at once."

Watching them exit from the Great Hall, Alana took a quick breath as Luna quietly walked across the stone floor toward her. "Are they leaving, my lady?"

"Yes." When the door closed, she released her breath and looked to the floor.

"What did they want?"

"They accuse Summerton of harboring outlaws."

"So, they are not to search the place, my lady?" the servant asked with a concerned face.

Glancing at her servant, she smiled. "No fretting, Luna. They are on their way back to Salone."

Sitting cross-legged upon the floor in the cabin of the ship in the late afternoon, Melody skidded a few inches across the wood as each wave crashed against the vessel in the sea west of Baltam. Annabelle, seeing the terror in the girl's face, sat down beside her.

"Melody, there's nothing of which to be frightened. It's a tempest that shall pass," she said. The boat suddenly lurched to the left. It seemed to groan and bellow in rejection of the movement. Suddenly the room itself turned, and everything that was not nailed down flung to the port side, including Melody and Annabelle.

Water was suddenly pouring in through the cracks of the door. Melody, dazed and confused, shrieked in horror. She tried to stand. "Princess! Princess!"

Annabelle, opening her eyes after being flung to the wall and having a lantern crash into her, saw a blurry image of Melody's panicked face screaming at her. She pushed herself up, disoriented. As her vision slowly returned to its previous acuity, she saw that the ship was on its side and taking in water through every crevice.

"Princess! There's water coming in!" She pointed all around in a panic.

Annabelle swept her hand across her head and looked at it. Warm crimson colored her fingers. She felt her extended stomach with her other hand as she stood. Looking at the panicked girl, she pointed. "To the door." Stumbling toward the only entrance as they walked upon the wall, a gush of water pushed the door open.

"We're going to drown!" Melody called out as she was swept off her feet toward the back of the cabin by the power of the salty sea.

Annabelle grabbed for her. "Stand up!" Squatting down, as the room began to fill, Annabelle looked into the girl's eyes. "Melody! Melody! I shall swim for you. Now, get up!" She turned back toward the door. "Take my hand!"

Melody, compelled by the look in Annabelle's emerald eyes, reached for her hand and was yanked out of her stupor. Pulled against the rushing water, her feet tried to grip the floor, but soon the water was too high. "Ahhh!" She gurgled as her face went below the waterline. Just as quickly as she went under, she was pushed to the top again.

"Hold your breath!"

Without question as to why, the girl gasped and Annabelle pulled her under the water, having to dive down to pass through the doorway. Soon they were grasping on to the bulwark of the starboard side of the ship. Chin quivering with fright and cold, Melody watched water envelop the cabin. "Princess, it's going under! The ship is going under!"

Annabelle held tight to her and the ship. "But we're alive, Melody."

The girl looked at the sinking ship and the vast sea.

"Annabelle!" A voice called from their right. They looked to see the captain and a few crew members, struggling to overturn the rowboat as the bulwarks continued to sink.

As Annabelle glanced over the fading wreckage, Melody began to scream. The wooden vessel she was desperately clinging to was disappearing beneath the surface. "It's going! It's going!"

Grabbing the terrified girl under her arm, she assured her, "I've got you."

With her large belly and Melody's weight, Annabelle fought against the waves to get to the men. As the waves, with help from the violent wind, splashed her in the face, she closed her eyes and thought of her battle against the salty sea when she was younger. She had just been wounded by a bear and had a fresh claw mark upon her shoulder. As her training from her time on the Forbidden Island took over, the bittersweet struggle reminded her of how she dearly loved to swim.

Opening her eyes, she watched as the small boat finally was righted and the mariners' heads emerged above the water. They gasped for breath and spat seawater.

"Annabelle!" The captain waved to her.

"Take her." Annabelle placed Melody into his arm as he, still in the water, gripped the rowboat with his other hand. "She can't swim."

As the waves pushed violently against her, she looked to where the ship once was. *It's gone.* Spotting nothing but water, her way to Anchony had disappeared into the sea. *How quickly things vanish that once were. Is this Your will, Father?* Water dripped from her face. *You have allowed it.*

"Annabelle!" Turning back to the rowboat, all the mariners except for the captain were inside. As Captain Vitalis hoisted her up from the water, her arms were grabbed by the mariners. Three men helped to pull her inside.

"How long will we be out here?" Melody asked sadly as they drifted on the night sea. Annabelle did her best to comfort her with a loving pat, but it was the captain's words that gave encouragement as he looked at the now-clearing sky. The light of the stars was beginning to peek through the thinning clouds.

"The waters take us north. We will certainly be to the beaches of Baltam in a few hours or so."

Baltam. Annabelle placed her right arm around the girl. *That's better than Sethel.*

"I'm so cold," Melody said.

Annabelle reached her other arm around the girl and held her tighter. "We'll keep each other warm."

Captain Vitalis, rubbing his core, moved over on the other side of Melody. "We have to make it to sunrise. Then our clothes will be dried by the warmth."

"You see?" Annabelle said to Melody. "It will all be better in the morning. We only have to wait for the sun." She was so terribly miserable herself. She began to tremble. *Oh, Father, please! Don't let us freeze to death! After all we've endured, that can't be Your will.*

"Give him the seal."

Annabelle, confused, looked between St. Celestria and Princess Anastacia's pleading face. "I did."

She was suddenly in the Gemmenian castle, pulling the seal from the darkened corner, walking up the steps, opening the castle door, placing the precious metal into Lord Cortell's hand.

"Anna, what has become of you?"

At the sound of Nicholaus's voice, the princess awoke to find she was still in the rowboat, lost upon the sea.

Melody, snuggling closely, opened her eyes with the princess's movement. Looking around in the dim light of the stars and moon, she frowned. "Do you know how close we are now?"

St. Celestria? The Father knows where we are. Annabelle squeezed the girl's hand as she answered with an amazed wonder, "No."

Melody turned to look at her. "Are you smiling?"

The princess looked to the stars. "I am."

"Why?" Melody asked in puzzlement.

"Because it could always be worse. We could be stuck out in the sea without a rowboat. Or worse yet, alone in the sea." Releasing a breath, a bigger smile crested her face.

"How are you so calm?" the girl asked sullenly.

"Because I'm beginning to see how blessed I've been my entire life—how blessed we all are. We will never be forsaken by God."

"Weren't you taken from your family as a child?"

"Yes, but that's how I met Peter. I enjoyed my childhood upon the Forbidden Island." She could dimly see Melody's face in the moonlight. "There was a time I found myself upon a boulder abutting the island in the sea. St. Celestria was there."

As the memory of the saint treading upon the sea came to her mind, so, too, did the new disturbing dream. *I gave the ring to Lord Cortell as my dreams had asked, Father. Why is my mind still burdened?* She looked up at the night sky.

"So, when you say God will not forsake us, it's because you know He's never forsaken you?" Melody pondered.

Annabelle found the girl's eyes the best she could with the limited light. "I deem it is."

Melody looked down at her hands as she rubbed them. "So where was He when the Demolites came after my family? When they slaughtered my father, my brothers, and my mother? When Bethania and Maxus were killed? Where was He when the Sethelians took me as a slave?"

The princess squeezed Melody's hand again. "The evil that

is done in this world is a lack of God's love—people choosing not to love. Bad things come to pass in everyone's life, but He is with us through it all. Look at what came to pass upon Him. Look at all that He endured—the savagery, the betrayal—so we might live forever with Him and the Father. Do you think He was not there with you when your family was slain? When Bethania and Maxus were killed in front of us? When you were taken by the Demolites? And then the Sethelians?" Annabelle touched her cheek. "You have endured much. And in all that comes to pass, that is God calling you closer to Him."

Melody thought hard upon the princess's words. "To trust more in Him and less in myself?"

"Yes." Annabelle nodded. "Vile things come to pass in this world, but it's only *this* world. The evermore is what matters. It is what's lasting."

Melody released a breath. "I am not to be angered that my family was killed before me?"

"It should change you, but the change in your heart should be that you draw closer to God. Seeing the evil that some people do—doesn't that make you more grateful for the good? Make you treasure kindness more?" Annabelle took a deep breath as she thought of another girl she once comforted after her family was killed before her eyes. "Is it any comfort to know you are not the only one that has seen their family killed before their eyes?"

"Of whom do you speak?"

"Princess Anastacia of Sethel." Annabelle gazed at the moving reflections of the stars that seemed to be floating on the surface of the water. "She watched her father and sister slain before her and then she, too, was taken by the Demolites."

Stacia, where are you? Is she safe, Father? Did she make it away from the Demolites? Or did they drag her to death through the forests of Anchony?

Sticking her finger through one of the many airholes in the chest, Princess Anastacia then pulled her finger out to gaze through. *He told me I could get out as long as I don't leave the cabin. Do I want to leave the chest?* Seeing an empty room, she pushed open the lid. Cautiously looking around, she remained in the chest, for it was her safety.

How long must I endure this?

Sitting in the dark hull of that same ship, the pirate Captain Anguis stared at the apple in his hand as a memory from several years in the past came upon him:

An apple extended through the iron bars, offered by the small hand of a young Princess Anastacia. Stepping forward, he cautiously took it. Biting into the juiciness, he looked into the young eyes as the hand dropped and the girl stepped away from the bars, called away by her brother's voice.

With his bitten apple in his right hand, Captain Anguis sat upon a barrel as his attention returned to the present. Behind him, some of the crew gaily teased each other while snacking upon the fruits of the Sockorian kingdom. His mood did not match those of the other pirates as he remembered the kind offer from the young girl made many years past.

Taking another bite from his apple, he grabbed a second one with his other hand then climbed up the ladder. The sun's rays warmed him as he stepped onto the deck. He tossed the apple core over the side and proceeded into his cabin.

Anastacia, having ventured out of the chest, heard steps approaching the door. She quickly jumped into her wooden box of safety, closing the lid.

She stays in there all day? Staring at the chest for a moment, Anguis finally squatted down and lifted the lid. He extended his hand toward her, offering the apple; she recoiled immediately.

"Take it."

Her reddened eyes looked from the apple to his tight countenance.

"Take it," he repeated. "You have to be hungry."

Her right hand slowly advanced forward and then suddenly she pounced upon the apple just to sink back into the corner of the chest. Looking at him from the tops of her eyes, she slowly brought the fruit to her lips and bit into the sweetness.

He sat down next to her confined area, speaking softly. "I wish you didn't have to hide in here. But nobody knows you are here but me."

Anastacia halted her chewing for a moment to stare at him. Her eyes drifted away as she swallowed just to find them again while she dared to ask, "You are captain of this ship. Why does it matter what the men under you think?"

"Their fealty doesn't lie with me."

"Then with whom does it lie?" she whispered back with contempt.

"It lies with gold. It lies with our makings. It can change at any time." He leaned in closer. "If they found you here and realized who you are—" His head shook as he looked away.

Looking across the room, she asked tensely, "What are you going to do with me?"

Tilting his head, he looked back at her. "What do you want

me to do with you? You don't truly have any choices, do you? If you go back to Sethel, your uncle will get you there."

"Anchony," she said with hope.

"Oh, Anchony. Of course, the kingdom now ruled by the queen who took you." He looked into her eyes. "So that is where you want to go?"

A whimper escaped her lips as she tried to physically hold it back with her hands.

A knock upon the door ended their conversation. He quickly closed the lid and stood.

"Are you speaking to someone in there, Captain?"

Exiting the cabin, he closed the door behind him. "Only to myself." Walking toward the bow of the ship, he noticed the others leaning close to each other, whispering. Taking a deep breath, he turned toward all of them. "The gold is not to be opened on this ship."

"Does that include the chest in your cabin?" one man asked sternly.

Anguis raised his finger. "Hear the words of your captain again: No chest of gold is to be opened upon this ship. Am I understood?" Looking around, all the heads nodded.

East of the Sockor Islands and south of Anchony was the large kingdom of Monakala and its bordering neighbor, Wickery. Inside the Monakalian castle, the king gazed upon the crucifix in the chapel as he had done daily for nearly three decades. Swallowing the lump in his throat, the disgust he felt was not transferred to God—he took full responsibility for his own failings. Family meant everything to King Marcus of Monakala and, having no children of his own, he took his duties as uncle to his sisters' children seriously. An unfulfilled promise he made to his young nephew haunted him to this day.

Holding the small prince of the Sockor Kingdom in his arms, he vowed to the boy: "Leo, if ever you need me, I'm here for you. I give you my word." *He looked at the boy's father.* "My sister might be dead, but our alliance is sound. If ever you need anything, Monakala is here for you." *He shook King Barthelmus's arm.*

He shook his head in disgust. *The first vow I was not able to keep.* "But I will see that justice is done! If there is a hand that took his life, that hand shall see justice, no matter how many years in the wait or what kingdoms took part!" Taking a deep breath, he thought, *Nothing good comes from Anchony.* He looked intensely up at the crucifix. "That is my vow to You, O God!"

REUNION

Cristine looked sadly at the sheet, yet another one filled with the names of lost children. Shaking her head slowly, she placed it to the right for her sister to stack. Catching a glimpse of the back, Elizabeth's head tilted as Cristine turned to question the next bereaved parent. Elizabeth's eyebrows furrowed as she turned the paper over.

Cristine, spotting her sister's countenance, asked, "What's wrong, Liza?"

"There are numbers on this side. They don't add."

Cristine, busily spelling the names spoken to her, glanced at the serf in front of her. "Numbers? From what?"

Elizabeth shrugged and placed the paper on the pile. "I don't know."

As the woman stepped away, Cristine grabbed the stack. "Let me see." Flipping over the paper, she curiously looked at the numbers. *She's right. They don't add.* She shook her head in confusion and she pushed the papers aside as a man stepped forward. "Your name please."

"Iaredus."

"And you were taken as a slave?"

"Yes."

"Whom do you seek?" She watched Elizabeth gather the papers into a straighter stack.

"My wife and children. But I pray they got away."

"Their names?"

"Bethania, Maxus, and Emma."

Emma? Cristine froze as her heart began to pound swiftly.

Elizabeth looked up at the sound of the name. "We know an Emma!" the youngest princess said with a smile as she glanced at her sister for confirmation.

"Ages?" Cristine asked quickly as she held her breath.

"My son is five. My girl is younger—around two years by now."

Elizabeth, looking at her sister, tilted her head. "Why do you not write it?"

Cristine, ignoring her sister, looked into the man's face. "You say Bethania is your wife?"

"Yes."

Cristine glanced at Elizabeth and then back at the man. "Wait here." He nodded as the princess stood, grabbed her sister's hand, and pulled her away, calling to a servant, "Alicia, tell Sir Altus we'll be back!"

The servant looked over to watch her disappear as the knight and prince ran over. "Where does she go?"

Cristine breathlessly sprinted down the old, empty marketplace, with her sister Elizabeth struggling to keep up. Finally she stopped next to the blacksmith's fence.

"Symon!" she called.

Catching up, Elizabeth nearly collapsed beside her.

"Crisa!" the girl cried in exasperation.

"Princess Cristine?" Symon set down his hammer. "Something troubles you?"

"Emma . . . Who . . . What is her mother's name?" She slowly recovered from her sprint.

"Her mother—the one that gave her to your sister?"

The princess enthusiastically nodded.

"Bethania."

Cristine leaned against the post as she released a deep breath and closed her eyes, slightly shaking her head.

"What is it, Princess?"

"Her papá is here."

Behind the blacksmith shop, sitting in the green grass, Isabella took the leaf from Emma's outstretched hand. "Thank you."

Noticing figures in her periphery, she turned to find her sisters staring at her. Her smile slowly faded as she noted their sullen faces.

"What is it?" She turned toward them as she stood with the toddler in her arms. "What's wrong?"

"Emma's papá is here," Cristine said.

Isabella smiled. "Sir Nicholaus?"

"No." Cristine took a deep breath. "Her sire."

Isabella looked down at the child and felt her world begin to crumble. She whispered, "Are you certain?" Squeezing the little girl just a bit tighter, she walked nearer to her sisters. "Are you certain it is him?"

Cristine nodded as Elizabeth elaborated, "He spoke of her brother, Maxus."

Isabella looked at her younger sister. "She has a brother?"

"She did." Cristine's shoulders dropped with the wretched news. "Symon told us Maxus and her mother, Bethania, both died trying to free Annie."

Isabella took a ragged breath. "Free Annie? From what?"

"Isabella." She looked to her left to see her husband and brother standing there with an unknown man.

"Emma!" the man cried out. He tried to step forward but was halted by the prince's hand. The toddler turned toward the voice and smiled.

Isabella, looking at all the faces and then down at the little one in her arms, gently stroked Emma's hair away from her forehead and then walked forward. "You . . . are her papá?"

The man nodded.

Turning away for a moment, she pressed her cheek into the child's head. "Stay safe, little one. Know that you're loved." Kissing her on the forehead, she turned around with watery eyes and handed the toddler to her father.

Kissing her on the cheek, the man hugged his child and looked at the princess with gratitude. "Thank you for tending to her. I never thought I'd find any of my family alive."

Standing there empty-handed, Isabella felt like she was missing something. All she could do was nod. As her chin began to quiver, she watched the man turn around and the child disappear from her sight.

She felt Symon step next to her. "Isabella."

Swallowing with great difficulty, she looked up at her husband. "She was all I had left of Annie." Feeling his arm around her, she was soon smothered with a hug.

Cristine's touch was soon upon her shoulder. "You did the right thing. She should be with her papá." Cristine shook her head as she looked into the distance, and Thomas watched the man walk down the abandoned marketplace. "Very likely, she's safer with him."

Elizabeth's weight pressed against her waist. "I miss Annie, too. And now Emma."

The king watched his wife stand as their daughters entered into the hut.

"Girls?" Clara's smile faded. "What's wrong?" She looked at Isabella. "Where's Emma?"

"Her papá took her," Cristine revealed when she realized Isabella would not speak the words.

Francis stood up. "Is Sir Nicholaus here?"

Clara tilted her head as all eyes fell upon the princesses. "You don't mean Sir Nicholaus."

"Her *true* papá," Elizabeth stated as she walked to her mother.

"It seems he was one of them taken to be a slave," Cristine added as she sat down carelessly.

Clara held out her hand. "Isabella, are you alright?"

Isabella nodded slightly. "It is as it should be. She is with her family now." Her chin quivered again as she fought the tears that wanted to fall.

"Isabella . . ."

Hearing her name upon her mother's lips released the tears, and she fell into the queen's arms. "Everything is taken away! Edus is gone! Annie's gone! Now the one thing she left behind is gone, too! I've tried to be strong, Mamá, but I—"

"Shhh . . ." The queen caressed her daughter's face. "Life can seem unfair, but we mustn't forget: Nothing is ever truly lost to us. With God's mercy, we shall meet your sister again. The love you have for Annabelle will stay in your heart. The love of God will never fade away. Of all that changes, there is one thing that is constant: His Word. There will be a day with no more suffering and no more tears, that is His vow to us. That is why Christ became man and died for us! He is the only constant we have in this world. His words are lasting and true—don't live for this world, but for the next." She laid her cheek upon her daughter's head. "Trust that you will see her again. Don't let this steal your joy."

Francis, watching his wife comfort his eldest daughter, was enveloped again with the fright that struck him to his core: What of his sister? *One must accept the words of God. Where will she go when she takes her final breath? Will she choose Christ's mercy, or will she reject Him as she does now, with her heart full of hate?* The fear invaded his being. His sister, if she did not accept Christ's mercy, would go to hell. And, in her present state, she would gladly choose it over His forgiveness. An unsettling illness overcame his stomach. *O Lord! What can I do? How can I help her to see that she needs You?*

Taking a deep breath, Isabella said, "Emma was my way to amend my failings with Annie. She was my grace from God. Tending to her was my way of helping Annie, you see. My way to be there for Annie since I failed her all those years ago." She looked desperately up at her mother, a bit lost. "Was I so wrong? I thought God wanted it of me. What am I to do now?"

"For Annabelle? Pray for her and keep your joy." The queen smiled radiantly at her eldest daughter. "He did ask it of you, Isabella, but only for that short time. What you are to do next will be shown to you, if you have the eyes to see. My daughter, you have such a sweet soul! Always let God's graces flow through you."

Glancing over at her husband, the queen's smile faded into a concerned countenance. "Francis?"

The king backed away as he stammered, "I . . . I . . . must tend to my sister."

"You have come for another visit, Francis?" Camrina said coldly to her brother as he looked through the bars at her. "Will this call for Mona leaving yet again?"

Francis eyed the dark shadow in the corner. "What I have to say to you is as true for her."

"Have you come to beg truth from us for the workings of Prince Howercus?" Camrina said with an eyeroll.

"No." He nodded his head at Sir Michael, who unlocked the bars. Entering, he knelt down to look at his sister sitting upon the stone floor. The chains that held her wrists rattled with her every move. "Of all the things I have said to you, Camrina, these are the only words I wish for you to truly heed: No matter what you've done—whether I know about it or I don't—God will forgive you of everything, if only you are repentant and you ask. Receive His merciful sacrament, Camrina!"

A voice from the opposite corner arose: "Why do you say these words are for me? I did not knife my own mother. I did not try to kill you." Queen Mona stepped forward into the light. "Don't speak to me as if I'm on the same level as her."

Camrina chuckled. "Of course, you are far better than I."

Francis stood. "It doesn't matter who has sinned more! That only means He will be more merciful to you!" Shaking his head, he looked at the woman close to the age of his daughters. "All that matters is that you ask for His mercy."

Despairingly, Cristine sat back down at the table. *What am I doing?* She looked at the pages and pages of names. *Out of all that have come, Emma is the only one who has found her parent. Emma!*" Shaking her head, she looked to the clouds. "Is this some cruel wile? I try to do a kind deed, and all I feel is sorrow!"

Catching the castle in her glance, she followed it downward and then scanned the gray stones. Her focus turned to the deep blue tabards of the Baltamian knights and her thoughts to the king behind the kingdom. *Where is King Henricus? He won't come back now that he knows we're found.* She released a breath with her admission.

"Are there any more?" Elizabeth interrupted her thoughts as she walked up with Isabella.

"Not today." She turned back toward her sister.

"Princess Cristine." Avilina came toward her with a smile. "My lady, we wanted to thank you for all of your hard work. We are not besieged every moment now."

Cristine gave her best smile, though there was a hidden sadness behind it. "I'm glad I could help *someone.*"

A sea away from Anchony, in Baltam, Sir Ragus, the former lead council to the former king, addressed the now-crowned king of Baltam. "Sire, why do you insist upon going back when we have word that they are found?"

"Sir Ragus, what I choose to do is up to me," King Henricus said. "Tell me, do the Ruffatons keep to themselves in their town?" He tilted his head and squinted while looking across the chamber at the floor.

"We have had no new tidings. The 'Wanted' posters were sent out weeks ago." Sir Ragus replied. He watched as the king rose from his chair, walked across the room, and descended to his hands and knees before the head of his bed. He reached silently toward the wall.

"What is it, Sire?" Ragus asked.

"Did my father take messages while ill?"

"He demanded he read all of them. When he couldn't get out of bed, yes, they were brought to him. Why do you—"

King Henricus held up a small scroll he found on the floor under the bed. "So how long has this been here?"

Ragus shook his head. "Sire, I—"

Breaking the wax seal with a sigh, King Henricus scanned the document. His mouth slowly opened.

"What is it, Sire?"

"There's been a change in what is pressing. I won't be going to Anchony—not yet, anyway."

"And the knights that are there?"

The king hurried to the door and spoke over his shoulder. "They shall stay until I make it there myself."

"Captain Anguis?" South of Anchony in Monakala, King Marcus looked up from his table, surrounded by members of his council, at the informant. "So, this prideful pirate declares his name when he besieges Monakalian merchant ships?"

"And he flies the flag of Sethel," the informant said quickly.

"What? The Sethelian flag?" Marcus flew to his feet. "Does King Henrard know of this?!" He looked around at the men on his council. "I will have it made known to him. Fetch me my scribe. If the king of Sethel will not put a stop to this, then Monakala will!"

HOPE AND DESPAIR

"The Sethelians took us as slaves! What is King Francis going to do about it?" A southern villager with crooked teeth asked indignantly as he sat near a fire on the periphery of the Abolian village as the sun set.

"It was the queen's doing, though, and she is bound in the prison," another answered as he tried to relax after his day of work.

"But the Sethelians were working with her, and they go free!"

"Free? They are forced to work." They both watched as an armed man squatted down next to the fire to warm his hands.

"Who are you?" the crooked-teeth man asked.

"The queen of the Sockor Islands is in prison, you say?"

"Aye."

The armed man looked toward the once bustling city. "Pray tell, who all is here?"

The second man eyed him. "Well, the king of course."

"I have seen no knights."

The first man chortled, "That's 'cause they have none!" He

shook his head. "It's rather a sight." He looked to his fellow villager. "Did you see Cassian Tiller disciplining with the weapon? I think the sword left his hand before the knight even touched it."

"And he thinks he can give protection to the family?"

"Who wouldn't want to with the king's dau—"

The newly arrived man shot up from where he squatted and suddenly the crooked-teeth villager found himself pinned against the log he was leaning against, with the man's dagger against his throat. "Be careful your words—you don't know who you might offend!"

Crooked teeth threw up his hands, scared for his life. "I meant no malice. Honest!"

"Why do you speak of the princesses?"

The villager looked around desperately for help from the other villager. Seeing that the fellow serf would offer no aid, his eyes returned to his attacker. "Who wouldn't want to give them protection?"

The armed man released his grasp and stepped away. "Forgive me. I thought the worst of you."

"Who are you?" The man watched him walk into the forest. He emerged a moment later, leading a horse.

"I am Sir Nicholaus Hunts. And they are no longer without a knight."

"Well, Sir Nicholaus, you have returned to us, I see," said Sir Michael, standing guard outside the king's hut, as he watched the knight dismount. "What tidings do you bring?"

Nicholaus shook his head. "None. I couldn't find her body."

Michael nodded. "Go get some sleep. It seems you are in dire need." He pointed to a small hut. "Your father is there. He's to take watch in a few hours."

"And the family?"

Michael pointed to the extra-large wattle and daub structure. "Sleeping at present."

Nicholaus looked at the building with its walls of woven sticks and plaster. "All in there?"

"All but Princess Isabella." Michael pointed to a structure close by. "She is with her husband, Lord Symon, in the blacksmith shop."

Nicholaus looked to the ground and spoke quietly, "They wed. That's good."

"And Prince Eduard." Nicholaus's sullen countenance looked up as Michael shook his head. "He's still missing. Queen Clara believes Queen Camrina knows something, but she will not talk."

"I heard she was held here," Nicholaus said without vigor.

Michael nodded. "In the dungeon."

"Who watches her?"

Sir Michael placed his hand upon the younger knight's shoulder. "Sir Nicholaus, all this can wait 'til morning. Find rest."

Rest? I don't think I shall ever rest again. He shook his head. "Sir Michael, the commoners know that there are so few to give protection."

"I know they know. We are trying to teach sword skills to some more men, but it's not going well. Until morning's light, Sir Nicholaus." Michael watched him turn toward the castle fortress. "Where are you going?"

"To tend to my horse."

Sitting on the floor of Cinny's stall, with the smells of hay and horses bombarding his nose, Nicholaus rested against the wall with bent knees as he pondered his predicament. *How can I face*

them? The king and queen's countenances flashed before his eyes and then those of his wife's siblings and his father. He shook his head in disgust of himself. *And Prince Eduard is still missing!* He closed his eyes. *Father, what do You want of me?*

With fatigued eyes, a disoriented stare, and the sound of Cinny munching on straw lulling him to sleep, the surroundings of the stall faded into the image of the vacant Gemmeny Castle that he had desperately searched through five days prior. *Why couldn't you have been there? Oh, Anna!*

Remembering the emptiness of the cold, abandoned stones, the hollowness inside him seemed to expand deeper and deeper into his being until an uncomfortable irritation rattled his core. He fought sleep with all his might—for he knew, in his sweet dreams, his wife would be there to greet him, but he would only wake to the bitter reality that she was gone.

Cinny's neigh alerted him to his present location. He released a deep-held breath as he realized that here in Aboly, he would be constantly reminded of his loss and his failure to protect his wife and their child within her. Truly, he did not wish to set his eyes upon her family. But his oath as a king's knight had propelled him to his present place.

He swallowed with difficulty as his head bobbled against its own weight and his stinging eyes cried out for mercy—relief—if only for a moment. He could no longer fight it. Giving in to fatigue, he leaned over and fell asleep.

Inside the temporary royal residence, the golden hue of the sun's light touched Cristine's eyelids as it slipped through the cracks in the shutters. While fighting the coming of the morning, Cristine recognized Thomas's voice from across the large, one-room structure: "Did you hear?"

Cristine, slowly opening her eyes, turned over next to her

sister and pushed herself up as she heard her mother reply, "Hear what?"

"Sir Nicholaus is back. He came in the night. Though we're not quite certain where he is right now. He went to—" His voice changed as he seemed to interrupt himself with his own conclusion. "He likely didn't make it from the stables."

He's back? Sir Nicholaus is back. Anxiety suddenly enveloped the princess. *Oh, no!* Scrambling from the bed, she was surprised when Elizabeth did not wake.

Pulling the dividing curtain back, she rushed into the first section of the temporary residence.

"Cristine?" her mother called in shock at the hurried movement.

"Is it true? Sir Nicholaus is in Aboly?"

"Yes. Thomas went to check on him. Where are you going?"

As Cristine rushed out of the wattle and daub hut and sprinted across the mud in her bare feet to pound upon the door of the blacksmith shop where Symon and Isabella slept, Peter—on watch—curiously observed her movement.

"Cristine?" Symon asked, still half asleep as he opened the door.

"Symon!" Without waiting for a reply, she pushed her way inside. "I need to speak with Isa!"

"Crisa, what is it?" Isabella said as she pushed herself up from the bed.

"Sir Nicholaus is here!" It came out with a near cry as she covered her mouth.

Isabella looked down as she slightly whispered, "Oh, no."

Symon looked between the two sisters, clueless as to why they were so bothered by his arrival. "That's a good thing that he's back. One more knight."

Cristine turned to him, ready to cry. He cautiously stepped

back as Isabella scrambled from the bed to hug her sister. "It's alright. We did the right thing."

Symon, shaking his head, shrugged his shoulders when his wife looked up at him.

"Is everything alright in here?" Peter asked as he looked through the open door.

Symon turned around, answering, "I'm not certain." He moved to show the Lion the two princesses clinging to one another. "Isabella, please, what's so wrong about Sir Nicholaus being here?"

"Symon, we gave away his child." She placed her hand upon her chest. "If she meant so much to me because I knew she was Annie's . . ."

Symon's eyes diverted away from his wife's saddened countenance as he said, "If it's any solace, I don't think he even knew you had her."

Peter took a deep breath as he nodded. "He will come to see that she is better off with her true father."

Dismounting at the side entrance of Gemmeny Castle, he pushed open the door of the desolate castle. The silent bailey and gray stones of the high walls matched the gray of the clouds and the dullness within him.

"Anna?" he called. A stream of light broke through the clouds, lighting the stairwell to the second floor and the entrance to the chambers. A smile crested across his face as Annabelle stood under the arches, waving with her bountiful smile, long, auburn hair, and emerald eyes.

"Nicholaus!" Running down the stairs with all happiness, she rushed into his open arms and pressed her warm body into him, squeezing him tightly with a hug.

"Anna!" He hugged her back as his heart filled with joy, wanting to hold on to her forever.

Heart racing at the startling noise, Nicholaus scrambled to his feet as he pulled out his dagger, still disoriented from sleep.

"Sir Nicholaus?"

Prince Thomas? The prince's voice cued him to his current location: He *had* made it back to Aboly. He had been to Gemmeny Castle, and she was not there. Rubbing his aching muscles, he lowered his dagger as he called out, "Here. I'm in here."

Opening the gate, Thomas looked at the knight's current condition. "Did you choose to sleep in here with your horse?"

"I suppose so." Clearing his throat, he sheathed his dagger. "I couldn't keep my eyes open."

Thomas offered him his hand. "It is good to have you back."

Nicholaus shook his head as he gripped the prince's arm quickly and released it. "I searched for her but . . . the snakes must have . . ."

Thomas touched Cinny's nose as he listened to the knight's words, tilting his head. "How large were they?"

Nicholaus closed his eyes for a moment. "What?"

"Are they big enough to eat a person?"

Nicholaus, not wanting to follow the current conversation, shook his head. "I . . . There were lots of them . . . and venomous. It doesn't matter if they couldn't. . . . The venom would kill her first."

Thomas, noting the knight's discomfort, changed subjects as he looked to the stall's floor. "Did you find something? Your bag is larger than it often is."

Nicholaus, swallowing the lump in his throat, picked up the bag. "It's nothing. I shouldn't have . . ."

"Sir Nicholaus, are you in here?" It was Michael's voice.

"Yes, sir. I am here," he happily answered to get away from the prince and his questioning. He left the stall and went out to greet Sir Michael.

Thomas, watching Nicholaus leave, looked back at the horse.

Petting the horse's red hair, he spoke to her. "Tell me, Cinny, how would snakes tear my sister into pieces? I don't believe snakes do that. It is likely that if she fell apart, they could then, but what amount of time would that take?" Petting Cinny's neck, he shook his head. "Good thing, you are a horse and aren't burdened with such questions."

Isabella and Cristine, holding one another's hands, watched their youngest sister joyfully run up to their brother-in-law who was walking toward the training square with Michael.

"Sir Nicholaus!" Elizabeth called.

Turning around, he bowed and then hugged her when she would not release him. Isabella and Cristine looked at one another and then cautiously approached.

"Princesses." He bowed to them as he released Elizabeth.

"It's my fault!" Cristine blurted out, unable to hold it in any longer.

Nicholaus, rising from his bow, looked at her and then quickly glanced at Isabella. "What?"

"Sir Nicholaus . . ." Isabella suddenly found herself speechless when he looked at her.

Cristine looked at her sister and then toward the knight. "Emma . . . was here."

His eyes dashed around, hope rising. "Emma's here?"

"Was. Was, was, was." Cristine bit her lip and whispered, "I'm so sorry."

Trepidation passed over his face as his voice tightened and his stomach suddenly rolled. "Where is she?" He held his breath.

Isabella put up her hands as if it would stop his morbid thoughts. "She's not harmed. Or at least she wasn't." Her arms slowly lowered. "She's with her papá."

Her papá? "Her sire? He's alive? He found her?" He felt lightheaded. If only he could have such a fortuitous uniting with the child that was lost to him.

"Are you angry?" Cristine's very worried face stared at him.

He did not know how he felt. He shook his head. "I thought . . . I thought she was dead . . . that I'd never see her again anyway . . . as I will never . . ." Shaking his head, he turned away, unable to finish his sentence.

Cristine held her breath. "So, you forgive us?"

He looked between the two of them. *Forgive?* He swallowed with difficulty, thinking of the babe he lost whom he would never get to hold. He shook away his thoughts as he cleared his throat. "You gave her to her sire. You did nothing wrong to forgive."

The sisters, looking at one another, took a collective breath as a massive burden was lifted from them. "Thank you, Sir Nicholaus."

Nodding quickly, he turned away from their relieved faces to see Queen Clara's emerald eyes staring at him. The king was at her side. He immediately bowed.

"Sir Nicholaus," Clara greeted him.

"Your Majesties." Rising from his bow, his eyes immediately bypassed the queen's.

"Michael told me you didn't find her," the king said.

"No, Sire." He slowly looked at the king's face.

Francis placed his hand upon Nicholaus's shoulder. "You tried. That's what matters."

"Yes, Sire." He turned his gaze toward the training recruits and nodded in their direction. "Sire, if you would allow me."

"Yes, of course." The king pulled back his hand. The royals watched him jog away, eager to escape their presence.

A hand landed upon Nicholaus's shoulder as he uncomfortably watched the prospective guards fight their own weaponry. "There you are."

"Papá." He quickly greeted his father with a hug and turned back to the trainees, afraid his father would think poorly of him returning without Annabelle's body. "Do you have word on Samus and Clare?"

"Victorus saw them south of the hidden haven. They should arrive any day," Peter said.

Taking a quick breath, Nicholaus nodded to watch the show before him; he was soon shaking his head. "They are a sorry sight."

"Indeed," Peter said with a bow of the head. He stepped inside the training ground and picked up a shield. "They don't know how to handle a weapon. Should we show them?"

Nicholaus hesitantly unsheathed his sword, pausing to feel the weight of it. The sword—with a lion on the hilt—was of the highest quality. He had inherited it when his father abandoned Anchony for the Forbidden Island. The weight now seemed too heavy to carry. It was made for Anchony's top knight. How did he dare to hold it when he could not protect his wife and child?

Exhaling deeply, Nicholaus chose a shield.

Peter positioned his hand inside the straps of the shield with a bit of concern for the young knight before him. "Then let's dance."

Knowing his son was not going to make the first move, the Lion attacked. Nicholaus caught the strike with his shield and swung back; Peter rotated out of the way and shoved Nicholaus with his shield. Peter and Michael glanced at one another as Nicholaus swung back around to have every one of his predictable attacks answered back.

Peter stepped away with a resolved concern upon his face. *What is wrong with you, Nic?*

Nicholaus looked at him. "Had enough?"

Peter eyed his son. "When are you going to start?"

Nicholaus shook his head. "What do you mean?"

Peter, walking closer to him, pointed toward the dungeon entrance with his sword. "Queen Camrina, who killed your wife, is right down there. Doesn't that make you angry?"

Nicholaus, looking toward the entrance, spotted Sir Melvon standing guard. He lowered his head. "How is anger going to avail me?"

"Anger without control helps nothing, but anger is due." He pressed his son, "Are you going to get angry?"

Nicholaus lowered his shield. "There's no point." His head followed his shield. "There's no point in anything." Shaking his head, he looked at the sword in his grasp. "I thought I could do this, but I can't."

To Peter's surprise—and profound worry—his son suddenly stabbed the sword into the ground, dropped the shield, and jogged out of the training area.

A recruit spoke up. "So that's how we're to handle a sword!"

Michael and Peter both looked at the villager as other comments were added: "That was fast!" and "Did you see those moves?"

Michael, shaking his head in disgust of the comments and the pitiful state of the young knight, approached Peter. "What's wrong with him?"

"His grief is so deep he doesn't feel anything—not even anger."

Queen Clara, watching Elizabeth make a gloomy face as Nicholaus bolted away, wandered away from her present relations to think of those relations that had passed. *Father, shield her heart from too deep of a wound. Make her whole. Losing a sister at such a young age takes a piece of one's heart.*

Finding herself along the Barstow River on the eastern edge of the castle grounds, she turned away from her daughters to watch the swift current push the crisp, fall water south. *It was not by water.* An inner chill invaded her body while she crossed her arms in response to the frigidity in the memory.

"It moves so fast!" Little Clara, beaming with a smile, watched the stick disappear downstream, and then turned to look at her sister, Murion.

"Clara, don't get so—" The older sister was a few seconds too late for the warning. Clara screamed as the earth gave way and she fell into the river. Under the shocking water she fell, deeper and deeper until a plunge and a mass fell beside her and soon, she was rising to the crest.

Clara placed her fingers upon her mouth as she recalled how she scrambled up the bank with help from her sister but was unable to return the favor.

Her hand stretched as far as she could reach as her sister lost her grip and was pulled downstream. "Murion!" Standing, she began to shiver as she screamed. "Murion!"

"Clara, there you are," her father said as he ran over.

"Papa!" Her little finger pointed as it quivered in its wetness and she desperately watched the ever-changing river.

"Clara, what are you doing here? Why are you wet?" Her mother fell down beside her. "You know you are not to go to the river by yourself!"

"But Murion—"

Her father's eyes scanned from the pointing finger to the river's rage. "Where is she?"

"It took her!"

"Murion?" Her mother stood as her father dived into the near iciness. Pulling Clara into her side, her mother prayed for the safety of her loved ones as Clara shivered next to her.

"Mamá? You're thinking about Aunt Murion?"

Clara turned toward her daughter's voice. Cristine stepped

closer as she recalled her mother's collapse inside the castle when she had thought Annabelle had drowned in the Angler River after finding out she had survived her first kidnapping. "You got your wish—Annie's death wasn't by water."

Clara pathetically shook her head. "But snakebite instead."

"At least . . ." Cristine shook her head. "At least no one else died like Grandpapá did from the cold when he tried to save Aunt Murion. How long did it take before his passing again?"

"A few days." The queen shook her head. "He searched for so long. The cold got to him. When he came home . . ." A special sadness overcame her as she remembered the last days with her father. "He coughed and coughed. He tried to be so strong. But once he went to bed, he never got up."

"So, then you and Grandmamá went to Lathrop Castle?"

"The guild tried to help us. But there were no battles. No one was buying their arrows at the time." She nodded. "We ended up servants at Lathrop Castle."

Cristine looked across the bailey at the Demolitic creator. "And that is when Sir Victorus chased you here?"

"Yes," the queen said without much emotion.

Cristine's eyes searched the torrent of the water. "I wonder how your life would have turned out if you had not fallen into the river. How would you have met Papá?"

Clara looked at her daughter. "I don't know." Glancing over her shoulder, the queen looked at where she last saw Nicholaus before he exited the bailey. "Annabelle's death did take the life of another." She looked into the princess's eyes. "Your sister was with child."

"With child?" Cristine's mouth opened in shock. "A niece or nephew." She shook her head in rejection of the thought as a gloomy cloud came upon her. "Does Sir Nicholaus know?"

Clara glanced at the last position where she saw the knight. "Yes." She looked back at her daughter. "I fear her death is taking his life, too."

Cristine turned around to search for her brother-in-law. "Surely it is expected that he is to be sad with his wife's passing?"

Clara slowly released a breath. "It is more than sadness but guilt because he couldn't stop it."

"How can you tell?"

Clara returned her gaze to her daughter. "He won't look at me in the eyes."

"He can't face you?" Cristine looked at the recruits in the training square. "Shall he ever heal?"

Clara, placing her arm around her daughter's shoulder, took a deep breath. "If he wants it. Time is a great healer of the heart. Our Father can heal all brokenness—if one wants it to be healed."

The princess lowered her head as she thought about the spark within her heart lit by King Henricus.

Her mother gave her a tight squeeze. "Give him time, Cristine, and he will come for you."

Cristine blushed. "How do you know my thoughts, Mamá?"

Clara smiled as she lifted her daughter's chin. "I don't. I know *you*." She dropped her finger. "I've learned to watch others carefully." She glanced at the captives, from Lord Rackus—vociferating his resistance to the Baltamian knights—to Sir Victorus, who was wiping his brow after placing a large stone onto the wall being rebuilt. "Very carefully."

Eunisia, the servant who had once worked beside Clara and her mother, looked at the silver piece within her grasp. Such was the payment for her betrayal of the queen of Anchony to Prince Howercus. Tucking the coin away in the coin pouch attached to her belt, she picked up a small bag full of bread and scurried away from Lathrop Castle.

I will leave this place and no longer be tormented. Clara, I shall finally be rid of you!

With hope in her thoughts, she headed west—away from the only life she had ever known.

Nicholaus sat upon the cathedral steps as the hilt of the sword was offered to him by his father.

"You dropped this."

A savage and strong lion. The hollow within was numbing all his senses. He shook his head in rejection. "I don't want it anymore."

"Nic."

"It's your sword anyway." Shaking his head, he removed his belt with the sheath and offered it to his father. "I don't *deserve* to have it! I couldn't even find my wife . . . or my child!" When his father would not take the sheath and belt, Nicholaus dropped it on the step.

"Is that the way it is to be?" Nodding, Peter removed his belt and weapon and insistently handed it to his son. "You need a sword."

Nicholaus begrudgingly took the inferior sword as the Lion sheathed the sword with the lion on the hilt and belted it around himself. "I failed her in every way," Nicholaus said as he held on to the belt given to him.

Peter, taking a deep breath, sat down upon the steps next to him. "And I your mamá . . . and Samus, and Clare, and you."

"We lived!" Nicholaus stood, not wanting to hear more. To think of his murdered child made the numbness worse. He knew he should be furious, but he did not feel it and that worried him even more. Cinching the belt with irritation, he spoke quickly. "I'm a king's knight. I gave my oath. I will not stray from my duty. I'm here, aren't I?"

Peter, shaking his head, descended the few steps. "You're here in Aboly, but her family is in there."

"I . . . I had to get away for a moment."

"A moment? It seems to me even when you are in there, you aren't truly there."

Nicholaus looked at his feet. "What do you want me to do? I tried to find her. I looked and looked."

Peter shook his head. "Nic, no one blames you for not finding her—"

The younger knight straightened with passion. "I blame myself!" Turning around for a moment, he rubbed his face. "I can't look at them without knowing how I failed! How I failed her! How I failed our child!"

"You need more time, Nic."

"I'm here now!"

"No, you're not *truly* here."

Nicholaus shook his head in rejection of his father's words, but Peter continued, "In your present state, you are a danger to them."

"Danger?" Nicholaus asked in disbelief.

The Lion shook his head. "It is perilous to fight without your head. Eventually, you'll have to let go and yield to what has come to be."

Nicholaus felt his stomach churn. *Yield to it?* The illness deepened, for, paradoxically, the thought of not being hollow within was just as upsetting, and—for the first time in a while—he felt anger. "You're one to speak these words! Did you? When Mamá was killed? You ran away! I'm here, aren't I?! I'm not like you—I'm doing my duty. I haven't run away from all people to a forsaken island!"

Peter, taking a deep breath, stepped back. "You haven't, Nic. But you're not here either." He grabbed his own belt with both hands. "Another princess could die because you have such sorrow invading your soul and clouding your mind."

Nicholaus lashed out, "You forgot about your word! You ran! I came back. How badly I wanted to lie down upon that island and let the snakes bite me and take me out of this world! But I came back because I gave my word to defend the king! I didn't forsake *everyone* like you did!"

Peter, nodding his head, looked at his son. "You speak truth. I did run away. But I ran away because I was afraid of myself. Not because I wanted to die but because I wanted to kill! I wanted vengeance on every last Demolite." With profound humility, he lowered his head and admitted, "You have returned to do your duty; you are a better man than I. But I'm fearful you can't do your best duty at present." Looking up at his son, he nodded. "Nic, I'm proud of you for returning, but now you need God's grace to help you through this."

Descending the steps all the way, he turned back to his son. "I will pray for you."

Watching the grasses waving among the gentle, sloping hills south of the castle grounds, Nicholaus stared at the movement. Wanting to think of nothing, he remembered how he had looked at the same sloping lands—seasons ago—believing he would never see his wife again. When he had thought her dead, he found her alive; that fact was further distressing.

"There you are, love. I'd heard you'd returned," Avilina, the master mason's wife, said.

Nicholaus turned to the voice to see a friendly smile. Descending the steps, he held out his arms. "Avilina. I saw Roland working and wondered if you were here."

She returned his embrace then pulled away. "Yes, all of Stonton is here. When we heard Lord Rackus bragging that he had destroyed Aboly, we knew we must aid in the mending of the castle." She glanced at the wicker basket in her arm. "We're taking lunch to them."

Nicholaus looked over her left shoulder at Rossa.

When she spotted him eyeing her, she felt compelled to speak. "I'm sorry for your loss."

He nodded his head once in acknowledgement.

Glancing at Avilina, Rossa took a step closer. "Princess Cristine told me you had wed her sister. I was glad for you and the princess. She asked me to pray for her sister and for you." She lowered her head. "And I did as she asked."

He gave no response, and it frightened both of the women.

"Well." Avilina looked at the basket as Rachel and Alicia went around them with their arms full of food for the captives in the prison and their guard. "We'd better hurry along. There are hungry men waiting."

Following the older woman a few steps, Rossa looked back at Nicholaus. "I think now, Sir Nicholaus, you should pray for yourself." She slowly nodded. "She would want you to do that."

Glancing at the women as they walked away, Rossa's words were like fire within his brain, for he knew the truth of them.

Turning toward the cathedral entrance, he looked at the top stairs—the very spot where he had stood and professed his vows to his wife. Slowly climbing the stairs, the memory invaded his entire being. He saw her face, her smile, her eyes. He felt her hands he had held in his.

Reaching the top, he closed his eyes and stood where he had stood on his wedding day, feeling her touch, her warmth, her happiness. And for the briefest moment, he felt the happiness within him, too, and he dared to smile.

Opening his eyes, any happiness faded away as he was greeted with the void of all humanity and the numbness crept back into his heart. He felt worse than he did before, being so awakened by the memory of contentment he had once found.

Despairingly, Nicholaus hung his head as he pushed the

cathedral door open. He was overwhelmed by the calming presence of the Eucharist—remnants of his uncle's last visit—waiting silently in the tabernacle for all to adore. It was as if he was pulled forward by an unseen force, compelled to wander closer, summoned by the Holy Spirit. He found himself kneeling at the Communion rail, but he could not find words to speak, so he knelt silently. The silence was unsettling. As it began to cause irritation within, he finally spoke forth words from his heart. "Help me, Father!"

He lowered his head and rested it upon his folded hands. "I cry out to You: heal me! I know we are not made for this world, so help me to let her go! And the child . . . *my* child! They are both in Your hands, as we all are. I do believe all things work for Your greater glory for those who know and love You. Use my emptiness as a prayer for her soul. This hollow pain I feel—may it be used for good, for the good of her soul! I add it to the emptiness You felt, forsaken upon the cross."

Taking a deep breath, a tear fell down his cheek. "In all things, Father, may Your will be done. When it pleases You, for me to move on, I shall try. But I can't do it without Your grace! Aid me, O Lord!" He slowly nodded as he looked up at the crucifix. "I know that You will because You always hear the cries of Your children. You have given Your Word and Your words can't be silenced. Your Word put all things into being. You are the Word made Flesh!"

Relying completely upon his faith, Nicholaus dared to smile. "I thank You in advance for helping me throughout this time." His fists gripped each other harder. "Your will. Your will in all things!"

Nodding, he closed his eyes in contentment. A fleeting image of his wife flashed before his eye, but different from his dream. She was morose as she cradled her large stomach. Heart-racing, he pushed himself up and looked around at the altar. *She was larger than I last saw her. Much larger.* Utterly confused, his breaths came quickly as he tried to discern the meaning. *She's not with child now.*

"Sir Nicholaus," the queen called out.

He turned toward the voice, swallowing hard as the figure approached him. "Your Majesty." He diverted his eyes away from the emerald hue.

Clara studied him. "Are you alright, Sir Nicholaus?"

"I . . . I came to pray for . . ."

Clara looked toward the tabernacle. "I pray for her, too. And also for you."

He lowered his head. "Thank you, my queen."

Clara took a deep breath. "The men don't appear very skilled, do they?"

"No, my lady."

"I worry about my daughters." Looking to the tabernacle, she smiled. "But I know, all that matters in this life is that we live our lives in a way that we will be with Him in the next."

Nicholaus nodded with his head still lowered.

Clara smiled briefly and then looked over at the downcast head. "Sir Nicholaus, will you look at me please?"

He forced his head up and his eyes slowly followed to find hers.

She took his hand with both of hers. "Thrice now I have thought Annabelle dead."

Nicholaus tilted his head. *What are these words from the queen's mouth? Does she deem this time like the last two? She was the last one to see her.* His mouth slightly opened in hope.

"She has had many prayers for her soul," she continued. "Let's hope she has already reaped their rewards."

His head lowered again. *No, she thinks Anna dead.* Taking a deep breath, he nodded as he looked up at her. "I would like it if she were to greet me in Paradise."

"If God wills it, I pray she greets us all." She smiled again at the tabernacle. "She goes before us and, thanks to the merciful

Christ, will make it home before we do, we hope. It is the one solace I have to fill the sadness in my heart. May it mend yours, too." She squeezed his hand and let it go.

"Thank you, my lady." After bowing, he began to walk away.

"Sir Nicholaus," she called back.

"Yes, Your Majesty?" He turned back around.

"Could you check on Elizabeth and Thomas? My youngest daughter wants to be of use, but I fear she might be getting in his way."

"Yes, Your Majesty."

"With child?" Isabella looked at Cristine.

Cristine, standing in front of the blacksmith's fence with her sister beside her, shook her head in sadness. "I feel such pity for Sir Nicholaus. He lost a child he didn't even get to know."

"And we gave away the one he did." Isabella lowered her head. "I wish we could help him somehow."

"Or you could leave him be—not make it so he thinks about his loss," Symon said as he wiped his brow and set down the hammer behind the wooden fence. "He'll get over it. It will only take time."

Cristine stared at her brother-in-law as she spoke to both of them. "But what if that's what he needs?"

"What do you mean?" Isabella asked.

Cristine turned to her sister. "What if he needs to think upon what he's missing?"

Symon cautiously shook his head. "No, I—"

"Emma!" Cristine backed away from the fence, looking at both faces.

Isabella shook her head. "What about her?"

"I don't think he's so sad because Annie's dead. I think he's sad because he couldn't help her. But Emma's still alive. He could aid her—do *something* for her."

Isabella looked at her sister as she leaned upon one of the posts at the blacksmith shop. "Do you think it would help him?"

Symon, shaking his head, took up his hammer. "I think you should let it rest. He will come around with time."

Cristine touched her sister's arm as she nodded toward the knight. "He comes now." Isabella turned to stand next to her as Symon began to pound away behind them. "What else is going to help him?"

Nicholaus shook his head at himself. *Why would I think there's any chance she's alive? Why would I allow myself to think such a thing?*

"Sir Nicholaus," the younger princess called.

Looking at the princesses, he took a deep breath as he walked over. "Your Highnesses," Nicholaus said without much enthusiasm. "I come at the queen's—"

"We were wondering if you could do something for us," Cristine interrupted.

He looked at both of them as he caught a glimpse of Elizabeth following Thomas into their home, both burdened with books from the library. "What is your wish?"

"Could you check on Emma?" Cristine spoke quickly.

"Emma?" He shook his head, not understanding and not wanting such a mission.

"Could you make certain she's safe?"

His jaw stiffened for a moment as he thought of Cristine's words. "You didn't trust him?"

Isabella made a face. "It's not that."

"What is it, then?"

"We deem you should," Cristine blurted out in her blunt fashion.

"You *deem* I should?"

Isabella lowered her gaze for a moment and then made it rise and find his. "Don't you want to know if she's alright?"

He felt as if he was hit in the chest with a very large object. "I . . ." He knew he should, but he was afraid he would regret it.

Cristine watched him take a step away. "If you don't want to do it for us or for yourself, will you do it for Annie?" Her eyes lowered when he finally looked up at her.

"For Anna?" He spoke the words weakly. *For Anna.* He felt his head nod.

SEA AND LAND

Annabelle watched the rowboat be pulled upon the rocky shore by the mariners. Looking to Melody, she smiled and hugged the girl's shoulder. "We made it."

"So we're in Baltam?" Melody asked with a wearied face as she studied how the grey stones of the shore were intersperse with trees that accumulated into a forest a distance away.

Captain Vitalis nodded. "We are." His eyes inquisitively looked between the trees in the distance and then lowered. "I hope we are not too far north in Baltam."

"Too far north?" Annabelle asked as she took a mariner's hand to step out of the wooden, lifesaving vessel against the wishes of her cramped muscles. "What's in northern Baltam?" She looked at the man. Hesitant to answer, he shook his head, but she would not let it be left a mystery. "What is in northern Baltam, Captain?"

"Ruffatons," he finally admitted.

"Who are they?"

He shook his head. "A group of commoners who don't like to abide by the king's laws."

Annabelle tilted her head. "They don't hold him as their king?"

Shrugging his shoulders, he lifted his hands. "We don't trade with them because we don't trust them." The mariners all looked at one another.

"Are they trying to usurp the monarchy?" She tried to ascertain if the Ruffatons in Baltam were the equivalent of the Demolites in Anchony.

"No." The captain shook his head. "They don't want to follow the king, but they know he is the monarch."

Releasing a breath, she looked around at the rocky soil and the woods. "Which way is it to your king's castle?"

Vitalis turned around to look at her. "*The* Baltam castle? Why?"

Looking from Melody to Vitalis, she slowly nodded her head. "Unlike the Ruffatons, I shall follow King Henricus." Vitalis eyed her oddly as she added, "And he, I."

Vitalis, disbelieving the words from her mouth, put his hands upon his hips. "You claim to know the king? You claim the king knows *you*?"

Annabelle's attention was skirted away from the conversation to distant sounds of rustling from the forest floor. Pulling Melody behind her, she backed up toward the boat.

"How on earth would he— What are you doing? What's wrong?"

"There are people—"

Shouts erupted from the woods as peasants jumped out with makeshift weapons.

Standing behind the mariners, at the edge of the ocean, Annabelle listened intently to the tense words between her companions and the villagers. Vitalis had already convinced them that they had no weapons.

"Then what are you doing here?" A gruff man with a faded rag over his left eye, demanded with anger.

"Our ship sank. We arrived just this moment," the captain said.

She heard the leader's voice come closer. "At this moment, you claim?" He looked around the mariners to their vessel and, finding Annabelle and Melody, tilted his head. "You have women?"

"They were lost. We were taking them home."

The leader, who, heavily burdened by the cares of his harsh life, appeared older than his age, looked back at the captain, saying with contempt, "Lost? Did you pick them up in the sea?"

"On Oro Island."

The leader straightened. "Oro Island, you say?" Looking back around from the mariners, he addressed Annabelle. "Is it as he says?"

Standing straight, Annabelle looked at the villager and the captain. "It is."

Vitalis stepped closer. "I am Captain Vitalis, and I care to know your name."

The villager looked away from the princess and back to the captain. "I am Ruffatus."

Ruffatus? Of the Ruffatons? Annabelle closed her eyes. *Please, Father, let them let us go!*

"You are the leader of the Ruffatons?" Vitalis asked.

Ruffatus tilted his head the other direction. "I am. What's it to you?"

"A man that has no fealty can't be trusted!"

Annabelle shook her head. *Oh, no!*

Ruffatus stepped closer with the challenge. "We have fealty where it is needed. But it does not extend to monarchs who leave us without protection!"

"I am from Anchony." All eyes turned toward the princess as the mariners around her moved to look at her. Taking Melody's hand, she stepped forward. "We are from Anchony. Whatever lies between King Henricus and the Ruffatons has nothing to do with us or the mariners. We simply . . . came ashore here. And I . . ." Her voice cracked with her emotions. "I only want to get back to Anchony!"

The mariners stepped away as a tear rolled down her cheek. Ruffatus noticed her enlarged abdomen for the first time. Looking around silently, he finally nodded. "Come along then. I'm certain you're hungry being at sea."

"Thank you." Taking the offered squirrel meat from Ruffatus as they sat around a campfire that was a day's journey away from the beach, Annabelle pulled it apart and gave some to Melody.

Melody looked cautiously at the dirty, faded red cloth covering the man's injured eye before her. "Did you fight someone?"

"Melody," Annabelle said nearly inaudibly. Melody lowered her gaze.

Ruffatus looked at the girl's face as he squatted down next to the fire. "I had a daughter once, younger than you, and a wife—" he glanced at Annabelle "—who was with child." He pointed to his left eye. "This is the *gift* I was given the day they were taken from me!"

"Who took them?" Captain Vitalis asked.

Standing, Ruffatus sneered at him, leaving the question unanswered.

With Melody resting beside her, Annabelle looked across the fire toward the cold leader, once he had time to simmer from the captain's question. "I'm sorry for your loss."

He looked away.

"I had a wound such as yours," Annabelle continued. "I think you have fared better than I would have." She shook her head, certain her words were making no sense. "I was healed by God. That's the only reason I can—"

"When will the baby come?"

The princess gently shook her head. "It's my first."

"We will take you east to what is left of our woman folk. There are midwives there."

Annabelle looked into his eye. "Thank you." Shaking her head, she turned it away. "But I was hoping to be back in Anchony. Back to my husband before one is needed."

He tilted his head. "Your husband remained in Anchony while you were taken?"

Annabelle, looking down, said, "He thought I was safe in the castle."

"Castle?" The man gave her his full attention. "What castle?"

Closing her eyes, she remembered the Gemmenian door closing with Nicholaus on the other side. *"Go, Nicholaus."* Taking a deep breath, she shook away the memory. "Gemmeny. It gave me good protection until . . ."

"Until what?"

She remembered the fright she felt as she clung to her mother and they watched the axe make its way through the burning castle door. "Until men came."

"And they took you to Oro Island?"

She shook her head. "It's a long story."

Glancing at her quickly, he turned away. "Well, you won't make it to Anchony—you are too large. It looks like it could come at any day."

Looking at her swollen abdomen, she shook her head, "That

soon? I've known for some time, but the quickening was not so long ago. I thought it took longer."

"It was the Seafurs," Ruffatus said quietly to the captain as they stood around the campfire the next night, making their way to the village.

Annabelle, awakened by the voice behind her, opened her eyes as she lay next to Melody.

"The Seafurs?" The captain's voice was utterly surprised to hear the word. "They are only stories."

"Does this look like a story?!" Annabelle could imagine Ruffatus pointing to his eye. "Can I make my wife and daughter come back, since you deem them only tales?" She heard the man march away.

Turning over, she watched the captain sit down next to the dying fire. "Who are they, Captain?"

He shook his head. "A legend of fiends from the sea."

"Fiends?" She sat up and looked around cautiously; Ruffatus had stomped off toward the woods to get away from the captain. "What do you mean?"

"Heathen mariners that assault upon the coast and vanish as quickly as they come."

She looked to the back of Ruffatus—*That's from whom they need their protection?*—then back upon the captain. "Why is it a legend?"

"It's as if they are ghosts. Nobody knows from where they come. If they appear, you are at their mercy, so the stories go."

She looked again at Ruffatus's back as he squatted down to collect firewood. "He has seen them, though. He knows them not to be a legend."

The captain shrugged his shoulders.

With the morning birds singing in the Baltam woods the next day, Annabelle silently approached Ruffatus. "You are against your king because of the Seafurs?"

Ruffatus jumped in surprise when he found Annabelle before him, looking around frantically. "Where did you come from?"

"The Seafurs are the reason you don't have fealty toward your king?"

Heart pounding, he willed himself to calm down. "That is none of your—"

"Does he know? Does King Henricus know about the Seafurs?"

"Of course he knows!"

Annabelle shook her head as she looked to the forest floor. "I don't believe that."

He tilted his head as he stepped closer. "And what would you know of it?"

Her emerald eyes looked up at him. "I have met King Henricus. He is an honorable man."

"You, one from Anchony, have met the king of Baltam?" He shook his head. "I have lived in Baltam my entire life and have never set eyes upon any monarch."

Should I trust him? Swallowing with difficulty, she moved a step closer. "I *have* met him. But it wasn't in Baltam. It was in Anchony. He was looking for Princess Anastacia of Sethel."

"Sethel? In Anchony?" He shook his head with a smile. "This keeps getting better."

Staring at him for a moment, she finally announced, "I am Annabelle of Anchony, sister to King William, daughter to King Francis of Anchony, who was hanged in Sethel as of late."

He stepped back awkwardly. "A princess?" His brow elevated. "The king of Anchony was hanged?"

She nodded with all sincerity. "By Sethel."

His smile faded. "That is the truth?"

She quickly tossed aside his comment with a flick of her wrist, to address the more pressing conversation. "I have met King Henricus. If he knew of your strife, he would help you." Lowering her head, she turned to walk away, but quickly looked back at him. "There are many troubles in this world, Ruffatus. Don't add to them."

Walking back to the camp of mariners and traveling Ruffatonians, Annabelle watched Melody, kneeling on the ground, studying the gold coin sealed with the Anchonian crest. "Melody, you should put that away."

Frowning, she stuffed it back into her pouch. "How do you think it got onto Oro Island?"

"I deem we'll never know."

"Let's move east," Ruffatus announced as he marched back into the camp.

Annabelle turned around to see Ruffatus staring at her.

"In haste now?" Vitalis said in surprise. "First, you wanted to kill us, now you wish to take us to safety?" He shook his head. "Have you forgotten that we don't trust you?"

Ruffatus looked at the captain. "I don't trust you either." He nodded toward Annabelle. "She is the one I want to get away from the coast."

Upon their horses in the northeastern lands of Baltam, Sir Ragus spoke to King Henricus: "Sire, the monastery from where the note came is over there." Neither the king nor Sir Novus looked toward the distant buildings.

King Henricus said, "I'm not interested in who wrote the words, but the one who had them scribed."

King Henricus looked around at the desolate village in northern Baltam as Sir Novus dismounted his horse to investigate. The main street on which they and their horses stood was overcome with weeds. The king shook his head. "It looks as if it has been a very long time since anyone has lived here."

Sir Novus disappeared between a hut and the village church, to reappear moments later. "Sire, there's a large mound in the back. I fear it is a mass grave."

Henricus quickly spurred his horse forward and then dismounted to study the elevated ground within the churchyard closer. Kneeling down next to the grassy mound, he looked at his knight. "Were there tidings of illness?"

"No, Sire. I've heard of none," Sir Novus said.

"Sir Ragus?"

"I've heard no tidings of an illness, Sire."

Novus looked at the village and back to the grave. "I think the village too large for the size of this grave."

"Someone had to bury them." The king rose. "Where did the rest go?" Shaking his head, he walked back to his horse. "I deem I shall stop at that monastery after all, Sir Ragus."

"Yes, yes, I have not forgotten," the hunched monk in his habit spoke as he scratched his head trying to recall all the details as they stood within the Scriptorium of the monastery, where the scribes worked. "It was quite a while ago. He was ill at ease. It seems his child had died."

"And how did that come to be?" King Henricus asked as he looked back at the note. "He said he needed aid. How can the king of Baltam avail a town against an illness?"

"No, no. It wasn't an illness. It was an assault. Men came

from the sea. Or that's what he claimed, at least." The monk nodded as he looked across the room at the other monks diligently copying manuscripts.

"From the sea?" Sir Novus asked incredulously as he looked at the king. "Who could it be? Sethel? Anchony?"

Henricus shook his head with confusion. "Did he say anything more?"

"He said he would wait for a response. He came back several times to see if there was a message. After six months, when I told him there was no word, he took off. I've not seen him again. That was a couple of years ago."

"Two years?!" Henricus slumped his shoulders as he looked at his knight. "This man asked for help, and Baltam replies by making him an outlaw?" He stared at Sir Ragus in disbelief.

"What is your will, My Lord?" Sir Novus asked.

"Find him. I need to speak with him. I need to know who it is that assaulted us." He looked at the monk. "Thank you kindly for your time."

The man nodded his head and turned back to his table.

"Ruffatus has been gone for a while. Do you deem that's a bad sign?" Melody asked the princess as she sat upon a rock. Ruffatus had left several hours ago, saying he wanted to check upon the town of Bartell.

"I fear it will not lead to good tidings for Bartell." Looking into the trees around them, Annabelle quickly stood.

"What's wrong?" the girl asked with immediate concern.

Annabelle scanned the tree line. "There's something in the woods!" Holding her belly, she turned around. "They're everywhere!" Before she could take three swift steps, her legs were tangled with a bola—a weapon of two heavy balls corded together used to stop animals from running—and she fell to the ground.

Falling to the earth in her utter fright, Melody attempted to crawl away from the large, burly man covered in furs. Her pouch lodged upon a stick and, as she struggled to free it, she found herself being turned over. She was too scared to scream or even breathe. The husky man reached down for her. He diverted his attention to the gold coin peeking through the ripped pouch. Reaching for the gold with his right hand, his left removed itself from her shoulder. Briefly looking at her, he spoke words she could not understand and then turned away as he took the coin.

She released the air held inside her. *He's leaving? He's leaving me! But what of the others?* Her eyes wandered to where she last saw Annabelle. *The princess?* Finding her feet, she hid behind a tree as she watched the huge men exit from the woods toward their awaiting boats that were taking the mariners. Two of them held Annabelle by the arms, leading her away.

Melody gasped. "No!" She pushed herself away from the tree. "No!" Looking at the blood-saturated earth, she shook her head in protest and screamed with all her might: "*Noooo!*"

With all fury, she ran toward the men. "Let her go! Let her go!"

One of the men turned around and caught Melody in her hopeless attack. As he picked her up to take her, the one with the gold coin spoke to him. She was released and pushed down as the last man pushed the rowboat into the water and then climbed inside. "No! Princess! Princess!" Weeping violently, she ran out into the sea. There was no chance of keeping up with the Seafurian rowboats.

Turning back toward the rocky beach, she spotted one

mariner laboring to breathe. Weighted down by her wet dress, she ran to him the best she could. Kneeling down next to his head, she lifted it up to place upon her knees. "You're not alone. You're not alone." Her tears fell upon his face as she gave whatever comfort she could.

He grasped her hand as a thank you while blood oozed out of his wounds. Her shaking hand tried to stop the flow, but it was fruitless.

"You'll be before God in a moment." Looking up to the sky, she said, "Have mercy on him, Father." When she felt him stop moving, she glanced down. Seeing his pallid face, she knew he was gone.

With shaking hands, she gently placed his head upon the ground as she backed away and stood. Gazing upon her blood-covered hands, she felt as if she was living someone else's life. As if she was in a nightmare. As she looked from her bloodied hands to the ghastly scene of the blood-soaked earth, she released a deep wail and fell to her knees. *I am the one who is alone!* She glanced to the sea—as if there was some hope of the rowboats returning, of the princess being there with her—the Seafurian ships were still within sight, but only dots in the distance moving farther and farther away. *Where are they taking the princess?*

Why didn't they take me? Why didn't they take me?

Sitting on her knees upon the rocky beach, Melody looked out into the ocean as she rhythmically rocked herself, a quarter of an hour after the ships disappeared from her sight. *They took the princess. They took the captain. They took the other mariners. Why didn't they take me?*

"Melody? Melody, what came to pass?" It was Ruffatus's

voice, but she did not turn to look at him approach. "Did they come? Were they here?"

You're too late. She had no more tears to shed. *Too late. She's gone. They're all gone.*

"Were they here, Melody?" He looked from her to the sea. "Did they come here? Was it the Seafurs?" He turned back around, eyes searching the ground for any clues. "The mariners are either dead or gone. Where's Princess Annabelle?" He went to the one body left behind. "Is she among them?"

They're gone. They're all gone.

Running back to the girl, he fell upon his knees and shook her shoulders. "Where's the princess?!"

Melody, lifting her shaking, bloody finger, pointed at the vast sea as a salty breeze seemed to blow through her body and send a chill to her soul, reminding her of how alone she really was.

Ruffatus searched the horizon, but there was nothing but endless ocean fading into an eternal sky. Looking desperately at the water, Ruffatus shook his head. Closing his eyes, he looked down and glanced at Melody. "She's gone, then. If they took her, she's gone." Slowly standing, he turned away from the reminder of all he had lost in the years past. "I'll take you east to the women. There's nothing else that can be done for her now. She's lost to you."

Melody, entirely distraught, only stared at the vast expanse that had taken away her princess.

COME WHAT MAY

In the northern-most ocean of all the waters of the world lay a massive island occupied by a village with an expansive community of language, culture, and "religion" that thrived despite its distant position. Because of its location, where the summers were pleasantly crisp and the winters were horridly frigid, no other kingdom had set eyes upon it. But isolated from others the people of this land were not, for the seas were their highway upon which they were in command. When setting sail, they were pagan pillagers who would do anything for gold. At home, they were fishers, hunters, and ranchers who toiled against wolves to sustain their sheep herd, whose wool was desperately needed for their sails in order to keep their status as the legendary, fearful, and dreaded sea people who came from nowhere and disappeared just as quickly —the Seafurs.

Amongst the villagers there was one that called Walva Island her home, not out of want but out of survival. For two decades she had studied her captors, learned their ways— though she did not accept them—and their language. At first resistant to interact with them, she had come to see that learning from them was the only way to survive and, by some miracle, one day to return to the kingdom from which she was taken. The natives called her Lina, the Seafurian word for female slave.

As Lina sat in her simple hut consisting of a cot, a firepit and a table with stools, a village woman set another large pile of dyed wool upon her floor. She did not need to ask its purpose—fashioning it into yarn had become her job and, though mundane and repetitive, it gave her something to do. After decades of such toil, she was proficient and the best skilled of any upon the island.

Her ears were caught by the sound of young voices, crying out in fear. Looking outside the door, her heart sank as she set eyes upon the captive children. "Where are they from?" she asked in the native tongue.

"Trader Island," the woman answered back in the same language of the people.

Lina closed her eyes in disgust. *More.* Her stomach grumbled in sickness. "When?" she asked as she stared at the crying children. "It's coming soon, isn't it?"

"Yes," the woman answered.

"How many this time?" Lina cautiously asked.

The village woman looked at her with a stoic face. "As many as is needed," she said and walked out of the hut.

Lina, shaking her head, closed the door. *Why? Why!* Sinking back against the wood, she followed it to the floor. *And am I only to keep spinning wool?* With wet eyes, she dishearteningly stood up to get to work. *There is nothing else for me to do.*

"Annabelle! Annabelle!"

Slowly opening her eyes to a pounding head, it took a moment for her eyes to focus. When she was able, she saw an arm desperately reaching through the bars across from her cage. "Captain?"

"Yes! You're alive!" Captain Vitalis breathed a sigh of relief as he pulled his arm back inside. "Thank God you're alive!"

She looked around the chilly, dark hull that smelled of leather, wood and dirty. "Where are we?"

"We were taken. It must be those Seafurs of whom Ruffatus spoke. We're on their ship."

Annabelle looked around through the near darkness. "Melody? Melody?"

"I don't think they got her."

She's safe. She closed her eyes in gratitude. *Thank You, Father.* Slowly, she pushed herself up. "Where are they taking us?"

"I don't know. To their home?"

"Where's that?" She touched her head to find it was bleeding.

"No one knows. No one has ever known. They have only been stories!"

Wiping her bloody fingers with the hem of her skirt, she shook her head once. "We've learned today that that is not the truth."

Captain Vitalis despairingly looked to the planks of the boat. "Are we better off now for knowing this truth? I would rather be without truth than to be here."

Setting her head against the boards behind her, Annabelle thought upon the captain's words. "How can you say as such? It is always better to know the truth. They were true even when you didn't know about them or thought them false. Now we know."

"And what good will it do us?" a mariner asked from within the captain's cage.

Swallowing with difficulty as she rubbed her stomach, she replied, "We can pray for them. Prayer always helps someone." Whispering, she added, "This must be God's will. That must be what He wants."

"God's will?" another captured mariner, one of the eight that were taken alive, asked incredulously. "God's will is for us to be taken by these people?"

Vitalis stared across the hull at the caged princess. "I wish I had your faith."

"All things work together for good, for those that love the Lord. So, yes, this is God's will. He has allowed it to take place," she replied to the mariner, speaking with faith, unsure of the whole plan. Hearing the man grumble in protest of her words, she added, "This is not the first time I've been taken. I've seen that it's true. Time and time again, I have seen the truth of it. God never forsakes us. He loves us so deeply, we can't even fathom it."

"Is your faith enough to move mountains? To move this ship back to Baltam?" the second mariner asked.

"You have faith that you will be saved from these people?" another voice asked from across the hull.

"I have faith that God is allowing this. So I will yield to His foresight and trust that He can bring good from it, if we obey Him, and follow where He leads."

Closing her eyes, she tried to remember how she ended up on the boat. All she could recall was the plethora of noises and then she fell to the ground. *Nicholaus? Nicholaus, where are you? Come for me. Come find us!*

Opening her eyes, she whispered to herself, "He will come when God wills it."

Peering through the foliage southwest of Aboly, Nicholaus froze as he looked upon the toddler beside her father, who was kneeling next to a fire, skinning a hare. *For Anna. Do it for Anna.* He convinced himself to move out of the hidden shadows.

"Who's there?" Iaredus turned toward the noise as he grabbed Emma.

Nicholaus stepped forward with his eyes glued to the little girl. *Emma.*

Iaredus took note of the man's stare. "Who are you? What do you want?"

"I am Sir Nicholaus Hunts. Your wife gave Emma to mine."

Iaredus lowered his eyes. "Oh. Thank her again for taking care of my Emma."

"I would." Nicholaus lowered his head. "If she were alive."

The peasant's head tilted. "I'm sorry." Confusion came upon him as he looked in the direction of the distant city. "Did something take place in Aboly as of late?"

"No."

"But she was there a week or so ago."

Nicholaus closed his eyes. "That was her sister."

"Oh." Iaredus looked at him. "I'm sorry for your loss." He looked to his fire. "Do you want to sit? To warm yourself?"

"Papa," Emma babbled, and Nicholaus's eyes swung to her.

"She knows you. Do you want to hold her?"

"No!" He took a step backward as he extended his arms in protest.

"Oh, well . . ." Looking around, Iaredus sat her down and continued skinning the rabbit he had recently caught.

Nicholaus studied the man kneeling before the fire. "Where were you taken?"

Iaredus shook his head. "I don't know to where."

"From what county do you come?"

"In the south."

Nicholaus looked to the child. He watched her pudgy feet walk toward him, and his mind went to the first steps the child had taken.

"Look at you, Emma!" Annabelle looked up at him. "Did you see?"

"I did, indeed." He squatted down. *"Emma, come."* She eagerly walked to his open arms.

As the memory passed before him and the peasant talked away, the knight knelt before the toddler and held out his hand. "Emma, come."

Smiling, the child was happy to oblige with much more coordination and steadiness than he remembered.

As the little girl came into his arms, he scooped her up. Looking at her smiling face, he could not help but smile in return. "Emma!" He pressed her head into his neck as he gasped when he began to feel the love he held for her within his heart. *Anna!* Tears stung his eyes as he held the child. *Emma is safe, but you're gone. And the child—the one I will never hold—not even given a chance to live, because of Camrina.* Anger slowly boiled up within him until he could take no more. He suddenly stood. *Oh, Father, help me!*

Iaredus, noticing the movement, stood too. Fear gripped him when he saw the look upon the knight's face. He held out his hands. "Please, sir, give her back."

Iaredus's disturbed countenance alerted Nicholaus to his own inner state. He took a step backward as if he could distance himself from the raging anger that wanted to burst forth. Emma's hand reached for his face. "Papa."

As the little girl's voice rang in his ears, his father's voice reverberated in his mind: *You are a better man than I.* Nicholaus lowered his head. *Father, let Your graces fill me. I don't want to seek revenge!*

"Sir, I beg of you!" Iaredus stepped forward in desperation.

Looking from the pleading man to the sweet face of the child in his arm, he kissed her head and stepped forward. "Give me your word you will tend to her with the utmost care."

He nodded. "She's my daughter. Why would I not?"

Nodding, Nicholaus released her and looked away, empty-handed. "Well, I . . . I need to get back to Aboly." Walking toward Cinny, he looked back for one more glance and then swiftly mounted his mare.

Nearly numb, Lina opened her eyes to see the color drained from the child's face. As the bowl of collected blood was taken to the sacrificial stone high above the outskirts of the Searfurian village, she looked up at the sky. *How much longer must I endure their need for bloody sacrifices?*

"It is done," Acwa, the leader, spoke in his native tongue once the golden stone was painted crimson.

Turning away from the demonic practice, Lina looked over the land from the top of the sacrificial hill. *Any beauty upon this land has been darkened by the death brought about for their fiends.* She had long ago stopped offering any resistance to the intolerable acts, for, after years of attempts, she knew there was nothing she could do to stop the evil practice. As she silently walked down to her hut, the screams of the children calling out for help from all her years upon the island reverberated in her mind. She pondered why she still lived. *It would have been better if they had killed me years ago. Why do they keep me alive? Why do they let me live?* She looked to the sky. *Why don't You take me, Father? I don't want to be around this any longer!*

Within the stillness of her mind, she heard a reply: *Why have you given up?*

Disturbed, she halted outside her hut. *Given up? There's nothing I can do about it!*

There is always something that can be done: prayer. Why do you doubt that I AM?

They're children! Why would You allow such evil?!

Lina lowered her head. She knew she should not have such a

thought but could not help but think it. Stumbling into her hut, she quickly closed the door as a tear rolled down her face.

Help me! I fear I have given up on You, too!

PLANS

Standing guard outside the dungeon in Aboly, Sir Melvon shifted his weight, preparing for a verbal lashing, as Rachel approached. Still stewing upon words the servant had spoken to him weeks prior, he asked, "So, it is your turn now to bring the food?"

"It is," she replied as she handed him the basket. "Here is yours. I'll take the others down." She watched him move awkwardly. "Is there something you wish to say to me, sir?"

He spoke in a quieted tone, "How can you think I'm anything like *her*?"

"Queen Mona? The same arrogance I see in her, I see in you."

"Arrogance?"

"Yes. You think you're better than everybody else!"

"I don't think that!" he protested.

Rachel looked at him in surprise and asked, "Truly?" Watching him turn away, she nodded her head. "And now you shall deny my words because you think them foolish. I deem there is one difference. You, at least, gave me the chance to speak, whereas Queen Mona would deny my words before I spoke them, simply because of my service."

His hands thrust forward. "Give me the food. I'll take it down."

"You may think me a fool, sir, but I can do my duty."

"I—" He turned toward the stairwell as he grabbed at the keys. "Do your duty then."

Descending into the near darkness, Mona's voice wrecked the silence between them, "Are you trying to starve us to death?"

Watching the door open, Rachel stepped inside and set the food down. As Mona sneered at her, she responded, "If I were trying to starve you to death, I would not come at all."

Queen Camrina sat quietly in the corner, watching the interaction.

Stepping out, Rachel heard the iron bars crash closed. "No one would, if we wanted you dead." She glanced at the queen of the Sockor Islands before saying, "You should be thankful that we bring you food."

Mona approached the bars. "Thankful? I suppose you think I should be thankful that I'm locked up in here, too!"

"I am," Sir Melvon said. "If you're in here, that means you're not out there plotting the death of other Sethelian sovereigns."

Head jerking in anger, Mona grabbed the bars. "I didn't—"

"Mona," Queen Camrina spoke, silencing the younger.

Rachel turned and ascended the steps. Outside again, she felt the warmth from the sun upon her face. Melvon tugged at her arm gently. "You still think I'm like her?"

Looking over her shoulder, Rachel slightly shook her head in perplexity. "Why does it matter to you if I do?"

Lowering his head, he returned to his post.

"The woman responsible for your wife's death is down there. Doesn't that make you angry?" Nicholaus winced as he heard his father's words again in his mind.

His journey back to Aboly had been a mixture of agitation from the black hollowness within him, a fiery anger, and a willful determination not to let it overcome him.

"You are a better man than I."

I want to be that man. I want to.

Just outside of Aboly, he could take no more. Dismounting from Cinny, he stared at the city and fell to his knees as his will sought grace to spare him from the overpowering emotions eating at him, seeking revenge. "Father, I yield it all to You. Fill me with Your grace! I can't do this by myself!" Stretching out his arms, he pleaded with faith: "You said, 'Seek and you shall find; ask and the door shall be opened.' Here I am, Lord, seeking and asking for Your grace to wash over me." Silently, he waited while he knelt in the cold mud. "Help me! I give it all to You!"

As the older village woman stepped away, Cristine finished writing the information with Elizabeth next to her and requested the next person to advance forward. "For whom do you search?"

A large shadow fell upon her table as a man's voice came closer and closer. "There wouldn't be a need for a name if it wasn't for your family!"

Suddenly the man reached across the table for her. But Thomas, who had been standing near the wall behind her, was quicker, pulling her backward. Elizabeth yelled out in fright and jumped away from her seated position, hiding behind her brother.

The man suddenly cried out in pain as his arm was twisted behind him. "You will maintain your manners for the princess," said the voice of the man who'd grabbed him as Thomas unsheathed his sword.

"Sir Nicholaus!" Cristine and Elizabeth cried out in unison.

The knight nodded as he shoved the man away from the table then watched him quickly scurry off.

"You're here!" Thomas cried out.

"That I am."

Elizabeth, emerging from behind the protection of her brother as Cristine reached for her, joyfully asked, "Did you find Emma?"

"I did, Princess Elizabeth. She is well."

Nodding, Thomas looked at his sisters. "Let's call this a day, Crisa and Liza."

Nicholaus looked to the training ground as everyone turned his way. Glancing at the stables, he spotted Cinny being led inside by a villager. He walked to his father.

"You're back?"

"It appears so," he stated calmly as he stepped inside the training area, unsheathing his sword and donning a shield.

Peter picked up his own protection as Nicholaus walked closer. "So, you're ready to dance?"

Nicholaus tilted his head. "Are you?"

Peter smiled as he donned a helmet. "Then let's dance." The recruits stepped outside the boundary stones.

The clink of the swords and indiscernible movements that ensued drew the attention of every eye in the bailey. A wonder to watch, the movements were blocked and answered as quickly as they came for nearly a half hour.

Falling to the ground with Nicholaus upon him, Peter forced both of them over and returned the predicament. Looking into his son's eyes, he smiled as he, breathing heavily and nearly exhausted, let go and held out his hand. "You're back indeed!"

The crowd stepped back, exhausted themselves from just watching the long tussle.

Michael nodded his head as he turned to the wide-eyed recruits. "Now *that* is how you handle a sword!"

Watching the two knights walk to the periphery of the bailey to cool down, Thomas spoke to himself as his ever-creative mind turned quickly, "He came from Snake Island." As his brother affirmed his statement as if it was a question, he looked at Prince William beside him. A smile crept across his countenance.

"Oh, no. I know that face, Thom. What is it?" William asked with hesitancy, for his brother's brilliant concoctions, though always well-prepared and thorough, could be challenging to all involved.

"I think I know how we can make Camrina talk."

With their clothes wet and faces dripping with perspiration, the two knights sat down along the wall of the bailey. "How was Emma?" Peter removed his helmet.

"Walking better than when I last saw her." Nicholaus pulled down his chain mail from around his head.

"And her papá? Is he a good man?"

"As far as I can tell."

Peter looked at his son's profile, still panting in the fall air. "Do you feel better now?"

"A bit. I needed that."

"Time. Time, Nicholaus." He tapped his son on his arm.

"Time cannot bring them back. But that's what I want."

"They have gone to their true home."

Nicholaus closed his eyes as he continued to catch up with

his needed breath. "I know that, but I wanted her to be with me for longer. I wanted to meet our child."

Peter nodded. "Cherish the memories. The memories will keep you going when the sadness comes."

Nicholaus shook his head. "They are all I have left of her now. And I have none of the babe."

They both looked up as they noticed the princes approaching. Peter tilted his head as he stood. "You have a look about you. What are you plotting?"

William smiled. "It is clever indeed." Both the knights turned to look at the younger prince, following the example of the older.

"I don't know if Papá will consent to it." Thomas looked at the younger knight. "Sir Nicholaus, you play the main part."

FRIGHT AT SEA, UNEASE ON LAND

Sir Narkalus, after giving Princess Anastacia's letter to King Marcus of Monakala and telling him all the tidings of the princess and the missing body of Prince Leonardus, watched the king—after a moment—gain composure and rise from his knees. Upon hearing the news, the king's sorrow overcame any strength he had, and his legs gave way. "What would you have me do, Sire?"

King Marcus read the letter written by the princess telling the events surrounding her family's death at the hand of her uncle, Prince Howercus, and Queen Camrina so her uncle could acquire the throne. Turning around, he slapped Princess Anastacia's letter against the knight's chest. "Once already I sent a message to Sethel, but have heard nothing. You shall be my messenger this time. You will go to Sethel. You will find this Captain Anguis that assaults my people's ships. While at the castle in Salone, look for the princess. Anyone who works with Camrina must lack all virtue and should not rule anything."

Sir Narkalus nodded in agreement but remained where he was.

"You do not move?"

"What about Queen Camrina of the Sockor Islands, Sire?"

Resolutely, the king took a deep breath. "I will have her watched keenly as I ready my soldiers. When all is right, she shall be met with such might she will rue the day she took reign!"

"In Anchony? You would assail Anchony?" Sir Narkalus asked cautiously.

King Marcus pointed his finger at his knight. "Nothing good comes from Anchony! Now find men to go with you to Sethel!"

"Aye, Sire." Nodding, Sir Narkalus backed out of the room and hurried down the hall.

Captain Anguis eyed his mariners before closing his cabin door. He knew they were growing suspicious of him and the chest within his room as day after day he spent more time hidden away behind the wooden door. Turning around, he opened the lid to spot the princess huddled in the corner. Glancing away, he picked up the fish and handed it to her.

Looking at the offered food, Anastacia wiped away her tears, stood, and climbed out of the wooden box to stand against the wall. A fresh tear rolled down her cheek, which she defiantly rubbed away as she sniffled. "I have had plenty of days to think about it, and I deem that you want all the reward yourself." She looked out the port window.

"Shhh!" His hand landed upon her mouth as he pressed her against the wall, whispering, "Keep your voice down." His lips moved closer to her ear, and he whispered even quieter, "If you haven't figured it out, I don't intend to give you to your uncle."

Looking at him out of the corner of her eye, she saw him move away as she felt the pressure release from her mouth. Glancing around the cabin, she finally found his eyes. "Then what do you intend to do with me?"

With a look of agitation, Anguis shook his head. "I'm not certain."

She looked at the cabin, her prison. "Why?"

He leaned against the door. "Why what?"

Anastacia shook her head as she thought quickly. "You think you can get more gold from someone else?"

Looking at her with near disgust, he shook his head. "Why do you think I'm only after treasure?"

"You said so yourself—gold and your makings, that is where your fealty lies!"

Staring at her for a moment, he finally spoke. "Sometimes we are forced into the lives we live." Looking out the small window, one of the memories of a moment that changed his life flooded his mind.

Hearing the muffled cries of the mariners, the young Anguis listened intently to all the noises coming from the deck. When all quieted, he bravely climbed up the ladder to see who had overcome the ship.

"What have we here?" a man's voice asked as the boy climbed out into view. The man looked at the captured mariners. "Did you know about this one?" The mariner shook his head.

Little Anguis looked around in surprise. "Did you take the ship?" he asked.

"What's it to you?" The leader approached the boy as he pulled out his dagger.

"You did it with haste," the young Anguis replied with fascination.

The pirate walked closer to the boy. "Did you run away from your parents, boy?"

"My parents are dead. I have nowhere to go. Can I go with you?"

Tilting his head, the pirate knelt down in front of him. "We are pirates, boy. Do you know what we do?"

Looking around, the boy nodded.

The pirate heartily laughed as he stood. "So, you're out for an adventure, aye? What do they call you?"

Studying the men, he said, "Anguis."

Anguis shook his head as he looked at the princess before him. "One is not born into piracy."

"It's what you chose," she spoke adamantly.

He looked into her eyes. "It was a forced choice."

Her eyes darted around the small cabin. "Is anyone forcing you now? Choose another path!"

Lowering his head, he looked at her from the tops of his eyes. "It's not that easy."

"Ask God to avail you," she said matter-of-factly.

"God?" Anguis nearly laughed. "God has not cared about me in quite a while."

Nodding, she leaned against the wall as she swallowed a lump in her throat with her own memory. "I watched my sister and father be killed in front of me. I was bitter toward God for taking them away." She found his eyes. "But it was God who healed me."

"Healed you?" He tilted his head. "Were you broken?"

"In a way, yes." Anastacia turned to look out the window. "I see how He was there with me, the whole time. I didn't see Him then. And for the longest time I refused to see Him." She slowly nodded. "Now, He asks of me to help my people. But I don't know how, locked up on a ship going to I-don't-know-where. I was . . ." She looked back at him. "I was writing a letter telling of my family's strife, my uncle killing my papá with help from Queen Mona and Queen Camrina."

His attention was piqued as he thought about her words. "Who is Queen Mona?"

"My awful stepmother. She is only a few years older than my sister, Rissa, was. We never liked her." Sitting down upon his cot, she met his eyes. "Please, Captain, what will you do with me?"

Staring at her, his mind went to another place, a few years in the past.

"Will you help me?" Anastacia's brother, Prince Phillipus, asked with desperation.

"This has nothing to do with me!" Anguis looked around the room with agitation. "Why do you tell me these things?"

Prince Phillipus shook his head, not believing the words he was hearing. "You have to do something!"

"No, I don't!" he defiantly challenged. "I am a pirate!"

Coming to the present, he looked into her eyes. "I know where you must go."

"Where?"

A sudden pounding startled them and shook the door. "We know someone's in there!" an angry voice called from the other side. "Come out! Show us who you're hiding!"

Anastacia's mouth lowered in fright. "What are you to do?"

Anguis shook his head. "If I don't go out, they'll break the door down."

"They're your men!"

"Gold is not the only hunger they have."

Backing against the wall, her face began to quiver in fright. "What are you to do?"

He shook his head. "There's nothing we can do. We must go out." He turned toward the door and yelled. "I'm coming out!" He gestured for her to come forward.

She adamantly shook her head. "I don't want to go out there with them!"

"You're coming!" Grabbing her arm, he pulled her forward.

"No!" She struggled against him in vain.

Opening the door, he stepped out, pulling her forward. She froze in her struggle as the six pirates stared at her.

"Is that what you've been hiding in there?"

"Who is she?" another asked.

"She's no one!" Anguis yelled.

"Then why do you hide her?"

Another pointed. "Did she come from the Sockorian castle?" The pirates looked at one another.

"A captive of Queen Camrina? She could bring much money!"

"She could," Anguis agreed. The princess's face showed trepidation and disdain as she breathed shallowly. "If she were a hostage of the Sockorian Kingdom."

"Then who is she?"

"I picked her up in the castle, but she is only a servant."

A couple of men stepped closer. "Why did you hide her?"

"Because I want her for myself!"

She struggled against his grasp. "Let go of me!"

He looked at her from his periphery with agitation.

"Release me!" Tears streamed down her face as she struggled with a new vigor. Grabbing her with his other arm, he picked her up and took her back into the cabin, slamming the door and locking it. Scrambling to get the farthest away from him, she tripped over the chest and landed upon the edge. Pulling herself over, she turned around in fright to see him leaning against the door. "What are you going to do?"

He looked over at her. "What did you want me to tell them? The truth? That you are the true heir of the throne of Sethel? That you would be worth more than all the gold upon this ship to your uncle—dead or alive? With death being his grand desire!"

Backing against the wall, she looked at him in fright. "I want off this ship."

"You *need* off this ship!"

Tears poured from her eyes as she leaned her head against her palm. "I want Rissa!"

He stood up all the way. "There is no point in wanting what you can't have."

Swallowing with difficulty, she looked at him. "How am I to get off this ship, Captain?"

"We are coming closer to Sethel every moment."

"Sethel?" She shook her head.

He looked over at her, annoyed. "I am not going to give you to your uncle!" He looked back at the door, lowering his voice. "Why will you not believe me?"

"Because you're one of them!"

Shaking his head, he slid down the door to sit upon the floor. Supporting his head with his thumbs, he confided, "I don't know what I am anymore."

Anguis watched Anastacia's head nod as she struggled to stay awake, until she finally gave in and leaned over to sleep on the floor. Shaking his head, he picked her up and placed her upon his cot. He pulled the blanket up to her chin. Looking down at his belt, he unsheathed his dagger. Staring at the glimmer of the dim light from the oil lamp off the metal, he placed it under the blanket beside her. Moving her hair out of her face, he whispered, "I'm sorry, Princess, I got you into this. Can you find it within you to forgive me?"

Rising, he took a deep breath and went out on to the deck.

"Who is she?" one of the pirates asked as Anguis left the princess alone in the cabin.

With the sound of the door flying open, Anastacia startled awake, sitting up in the bed unsure for a moment where she was. "There she is," one of the pirates called out as another followed him into the cabin.

Struggling against the concavity of the mattress, the princess kicked back the blankets and, noticing the dagger for the first time, grabbed it as she scrambled from the cot. "Stay back!" She slashed the man as he came forward.

The man grabbed at his core as the blood seeped through his tunic. "She cut me!"

The other pirate pressed forward, grabbing at her.

"Don't touch me!" She jabbed the metal into his core and pulled the bloody dagger out, arms shaking with fright.

The first man reached for her yet again. She slashed at him and ran for the door where she was promptly grabbed by another pirate.

Hearing her scream as she was pulled out of the cabin, Anguis, on his hands and knees from his own tussle with his men, turned around toward the door. "No!" Seeing her kicking and raging against the man's grip, he pushed himself up and ran forward but was quickly knocked across the deck by an insubordinate pirate.

"We heard you talking! Is Prince Howercus her uncle?"

The pirate with the slashed stomach stumbled from the cabin. "She's got to die! I don't care who she is!"

Anguis scrambled to his feet as they pulled her roughly to the edge of the ship. "Don't!" he commanded.

"Tell us who she is. If she's his niece, she'll live. If she's no one, she'll drown!"

Anastacia struggled the best she could, but she could not get away from the man holding her.

"We want the truth!" another pirate yelled.

Anguis nervously looked toward the coast in the east as the sun slowly began to rise before him. "She is no one. Let her drown!"

"No!" Anastacia screamed as the pirate gripping her arm lifted her off her feet and threw her overboard.

The pirates looked back at the captain. "She is taken care of. Now for you!"

Anguis, without delay, sprinted across the deck and, scrambling over the edge, launched himself into the ocean.

Coughing, Anastacia fell upon the wet sand. Pushing herself over, she looked at her rescuer in the morning twilight. "I don't understand you!"

"You're alive, aren't you?" He pushed himself up to his knees, as the dripping seawater puddled on the sand beneath him.

She looked back at the sea and the ship in the distance. "They threw me over because you lied! They threw me over! I nearly drowned because of *you*."

He crawled closer to her. "If I had not, if I had told them they were right, they would have taken you to him." He shook his head. "This was your only escape."

Closing her eyes, she began to cry as she set her head in the wet sand, thinking of the dagger she'd been forced to push into another person. *Did I kill him? I don't want to have killed him!*

"Oh, stop crying!" Shaking his head, he turned away. "I can't take it any longer!"

Turning toward him, she watched him stand. "You are heartless!"

"Heartless?" He turned back toward her, pointing at the distant boat. "I gave up everything for you! The gold, my ship! So tell me, how am *I* heartless?!"

Swallowing with difficulty, she shook her head as she thought of his words. "Your heart is . . . chained by . . . I don't know what. Pride? My brother would always say that there is a good heart inside every man, but sometimes it needs help being unshackled." Closing her eyes, she rolled over and set her forehead upon the sand, shaking with nerves.

Swallowing hard, he placed his hands upon his hips. "Your brother was a good man," he said.

A new anger bubbled up inside of her as her eyebrows furrowed. "How dare you say that as if you knew him! You've never met my brother. He wasn't a thief! He was an honorable man, unlike you!" Her wet hair whipped around, splashing him, as she scrambled to her feet.

Anguis grabbed her arm.

"Release me!" she cried out.

Grabbing her other arm, he pulled her closer as she fought against him. He whispered into her ear, "I did know your brother."

She looked up at him as he released her. "What . . . what do you mean?" She watched water drip from his hair and roll down his face as the morning light slowly expanded. "You met my brother?"

Grabbing a handful of his tunic, he wrung it out as he admitted, "Prince Phillipus set me free."

"What do you mean?" She watched him release the cloth and start to walk up the shore. "Wait! What do you mean? Set you free from what?" He walked toward an embankment. "Where are you going?"

The captain turned around. "Do you want to stay here in Sethel?"

She looked around at the beach around her. "No!"

"Then come along!"

She cautiously caught up with him. "This doesn't mean I trust you. I have no other choice is all!"

"Fair enough."

She shook her head as she blindly followed. "Where are we going? When did you meet my brother?"

"You are full of questions, aren't you?"

She stopped walking as disgust flashed across her countenance. "I have been taken four times now. Four!" Her voice grew in tone as other voices from a village close by became louder. "I have been dragged across the ground, locked in a room, closed inside of a chest, forced to stab a man, and then flung over the side of a ship and nearly drowned in the ocean! Don't you think I deserve some answers?"

Glancing around, he walked back to her and took her elbow, forcing her to keep moving as he whispered into her ear. "Not here. Not now."

Stepping under a rock overhang, he finally released her arm. She immediately turned around, determination smeared across her face as she folded her arms.

He lowered his head. "I was once bound by your father's men when I was young. I met your brother when they took me to your castle."

"My castle?" She dropped her arms. "You were in Salone?"

Remembering the young hand with the apple, he looked up at her. "Yes. I have even met you before."

She shook her head in disbelief.

"You were very little. I was in the dungeon."

"How did you get out?"

He looked toward the north. "I told you already—your brother let me go."

She folded her arms in dismay of the comment. "Why would he do that?"

His eyes studied the dark outline of the terrain of the western coast of Sethel in the morning light. "I don't know. I was younger. He thought he could set me on a right course."

"And you did not cease your thievery after he granted you mercy?"

Glancing back at her, he walked forward. "It's this way to Baltam."

❄

"Ruffatus?" a woman spoke in north central Baltam as she stepped away from the few huts of the relocated village. "Who do you have?"

"The village of Bartell was slaughtered. I came upon some mariners. The Seafurs got them, too, all but this one. This is Melody." They walked into the middle of the village. "Tend to her." He turned around.

Melody watched his movement. After walking with him for a week, he was leaving so unexpectedly. "Wait. Where are you going?"

Looking back at her, he slightly shook his head. "I have to get back with my men. We have to see what men are left. They have to be stopped, somehow."

"You're going to leave me here?"

Ruffatus did not reply, he only kept walking until he disappeared into the woods. She turned around to look at the female villagers, about twenty she could see. A younger woman walked up to her. "You look so frightened." The woman's arm went around her shoulder. "I am Kinna. Let me show you everyone."

Though physically there, Melody was anything but present as she pondered upon the fate of her friend, stolen away from her several days prior. When she could take no more of the smiles and cordial greetings, she blurted, "My friend was taken! I need to tell someone," Melody looked around in desperation as she stood between the few huts where the relocated female villagers stayed.

An older woman approached. "If the Seafurs took her, there's nothing that can be done about it."

Melody gasped in exasperation. *How could I do nothing? Who could help her? Prince Thomas? Lord Symon? Does Sir Nicholaus live? I'd have to get to Anchony.* She looked upon the landlocked village. *How can I get to Anchony from here?!*

"I have to do something! She's my only friend!" she cried out.

"You'll be safe here, if you stay with us," Kinna offered with a pat upon her shoulder.

"No one can stop the Seafurs." Eda squatted down next to Melody. "I say this with all kindness: Forget about your friend—there is nothing that can be done now. Once they're taken, they're never seen again."

"No." Melody insistently shook her head. "What about the king of Baltam? He could—"

"The king does not care." This from another woman.

Melody turned to the woman. "What do you mean?"

"We hide from him."

The girl looked at Eda. "Hide? From your king? Why?"

"*We* are the outlaws. He doesn't defend us from those fiends."

Melody looked around in desperation. "How can he?" A cold wind blowing in from the north brought a new chill to her lonesome frame as she stood, surrounded by the Ruffatonian women, utterly alone.

SALONE OF SETHEL

Dismounting from his horse, Lord Cortell walked toward the agitated Prince Howercus, pacing on the second step from the top outside the Sethelian castle as Sir Arkel stood stoically behind him.

"Did you find Sir Tratus?" the murderous prince was quick to ask.

Cortell shook his head. "I have searched far and wide. No one has seen him or heard from him."

Howercus, speaking to anyone who would listen, tilted his annoyed head. "Has he betrayed me? Has everyone betrayed me? How am I to take the throne?" Looking no where in particular as his eyes moved randomly, he said to himself, "Is this what I get for killing the babe? But if I hadn't, Camrina would have! So it makes no difference. It makes no difference, you see?"

Sir Arkel and Lord Cortell stared at the distraught man.

Noticing Arkel's stare, Howercus turned to him and asked, "Why do you look at me like that?" Before the knight could respond, the prince quickly changed subjects. "What of Captain Anguis? Have we heard from him? Or has he betrayed me, too?!"

"No, Your Highness, we haven't had any word," Sir Arkel answered.

"The merchants say he says his name with every ship he takes and flies the Sethelian flag. I told him to stop, and he doesn't! And now there are threats from Monakala. Threats!" He held up the message from King Markus. "And the gold?" he asked frantically. "Did he take my gold?"

"We know nothing of it," Arkel responded as Cortell walked up the steps toward the prince.

"He needs to be found. He's betraying me. I know he is! Where are the knights? Why are the knights not looking for him?!"

"The knights have been in search of the outlaws, Your Highness." Sir Arkel stared at Lord Cortell when he added, "They've been to Summerton."

Lord Cortell looked at Sir Arkel quickly.

"The outlaws, yes, those trying to take my throne. What did they find?" Howercus asked.

Cortell's eyes turned toward Howercus. "Summerton is my dukedom, Sire."

"Oh, that's right," the royal said quickly.

"A truth Lady Alana was quick to point out, I hear," Sir Arkel revealed as he took a step down. "They did not search the castle."

"I would certainly hope not," Cortell said indignantly. "It is, after all, *my* castle, and the very castle where a *certain man* was hanged."

Sir Arkel sneered. "Of course, how could we forget that you hanged King Francis? You mention it so much."

Cortell ascended a step. "I don't abide by your knights bothering my wife."

"Certainly it was an accident. When they realized their folly, they left. Folly, folly, only folly," Howercus said, looking from one man to the other. "Lord Cortell, tell me, have I been betrayed?"

Cortell looked at the prince. "Your Highness?"

"Captain Anguis and his pirates, have they betrayed me? Sir Arkel, I want you to find them!"

"And the outlaws, Sire?" Sir Arkel asked.

"The outlaws? The outlaws?" Howercus looked to Cortell for assistance.

Cortell shook his head as he looked to his feet. "Have there been any new tidings of the outlaws? Are they causing any more trouble?"

Howercus looked at the knight. "New tidings?"

"None," Arkel answered quickly.

"Then it is up to you," Cortell said to the prince. "Is it the missing gold or punishment for the outlaws that is more pressing?"

"Gold or the outlaws? Gold or the outlaws?" Howercus's eyes danced around as he came to a decision. "The gold is Camrina's. I want the gold. Camrina must pay! She must pay!" He looked to the knight. "Find that Captain Anguis. I will put a price upon his head if I must! A high price!"

"Yes, Sire." Sir Arkel eyed the duke as he descended past him toward the stable.

Watching the knight descend the steps, Cortell listened to the frantic prince ask, "Does he not like me? Does he not like you? And you? Do you not like him?"

The duke looked at the royal. "I have no ill will with him, Sire. I think he has an ill will with me."

"Why? Why? Why would that be?" Howercus asked quickly.

Because he's rightfully less trusting than you. "I don't know, Sire. Perhaps you should ask him." Cortell looked at the agitated man before him. "Sire, are you alright?"

"Alright? Alright? How can I be alright? The outlaws betrayed me, Captain Anguis has betrayed me, and Sir Tratus—

Sir Tratus is not to be found!" Shaking his head, Howercus turned toward the castle door and ascended a step. "You're certain there's been no sight, no word of him in all of Sethel?"

I'm certain there's been no sight of the person for whom I've truly been searching—Princess Anastacia—in all of Sethel. If he does not know she lived when her family was killed, she'll be safe. But what of Sethel? There is no one to stop this mad traitor before me from taking the crown.

"No sight and no word, Sire."

"Odd. Odd, indeed. Where's he gone? Did he betray me? Do I deserve to be betrayed? She was with child—the child!" Shaking his head as his eyes darted around for a moment, he gave out a slight moan as he turned to walk into the darkness of the castle, but no matter where he went, he could not hide himself from all that he had done. Besides working with the Demolites and Queen Camrina to ensure the death of his brother, King Henrard, and all of his heirs, Howercus ordered Princess Annabelle to be left on Two Breath Island. He and Camrina were certain the princess—and the child within her—would find her demise. He had never been so present to a death he had ordered. He had never been so haunted by the decision to send to death a life that had never had the chance to breathe. It pressed heavily upon his mind and soul. Talking to himself, he added, "And where is the bishop? Does he betray me, too? I should be crowned—crowned already! I am the heir. The only heir! Where is the bishop?"

Watching Howercus enter the castle, Cortell looked away. *The bishop? I don't know, but Sir Tratus—that traitor—won't ever be found. He was hanged before your eyes before he could tell you that Prince Phillipus told me all about your feint.*

At the castle stable, a man, full of mud, climbed from the pig pen, where the pigs were rooting in the mud. "Sir Arkel, what do you do here?"

Turning up his nose to the overwhelming odoriferousness, the knight quickly looked away to take a breath. "Lucious, do you want to make something of yourself?"

"What do you mean? I tend to the castle hogs."

"I will be away for a while. I need your eyes."

"What do you mean, brother?"

Stepping closer, Arkel tilted his head. "Do not call me that here." Stepping back, he said, "Duke Cortell of Summerton—watch him and watch him well."

"I am a servant of the castle. I have my duties of which I am to attend."

Arkel stepped forward, grabbing Lucious's shoulder. "This is your new duty."

"But what of the animals?"

"Do both." Pulling his brother close, he whispered into his ear. "This is dire. If Howercus loses power, it will be back to the fields for the both of us."

The man shrugged his shoulders. "I didn't mind the fields."

"Lucious!" Sir Arkel exclaimed. He did not understand his brother's lack of ambition. "I will make certain that your wife and children are well cared for. Wouldn't it be better for them to live in the castle than in that woeful, little hut?"

"I like my—"

"Will you do it? Will you do it for me, brother?"

"Lord Cortell, you say?"

"Yes." The knight nodded enthusiastically.

"I have seen him. I know his face."

"Good!" He slapped his brother on the shoulder. "Then you consent to it?"

Lucious shrugged his shoulders. "I suppose I do."

THE PIT

In the dungeon in Aboly, the eldest princess walked down the spiral staircase, followed by Lord Symon. "Aunt Camrina, we've not yet met. I am Princess Isabella. And this is my husband, Lord Symon."

"Be aware: She has trickery in her blood." Queen Mona stepped forward to hold the bars. "That is the only way she got a duke to marry her." Isabella called off Symon with a shake of her head. "You see that! He does her bidding!" Mona said as she pointed.

"Mona, she didn't come here to speak to you. Go away." Camrina watched the younger queen return to the corner with a dejected face as her own chains jingled when she walked forward. "My brother now sends his eldest daughter. How low is he willing to fall?"

"My papá did not send me," Isabella said quickly, irritated that her aunt was attacking her father.

"Truly?" Camrina nearly laughed. "Then why ever did you come?"

"I come on your behalf." Quickly glancing at Symon, Isabella stepped closer. "I came to plead with you. Please, Aunt Camrina, tell me where my brother is. That is all I ask."

Camrina sneered with a scowl. "I will tell you nothing."

"If you don't tell me, then the knights . . ." Shaking her head, she looked down for a moment. "They are contriving, Aunt Camrina. Please, for your sake, tell me something! Anything!"

"That's enough," Michael's voice boomed and only strengthened in intensity as the footsteps descended. "If she has not told you anything yet, she will not!"

Isabella stepped aside to watch Sirs Melvon and Michael charge down the steps. She whispered to her husband, "I tried."

Placing his hand upon her shoulder, he nodded. "You did."

The princess and duke ascended the steps while the iron door of the cell opened behind them.

As their heads were graced with the brightness of the sun streaming in from the top of the stairwell, Isabella heard Sir Michael speak forcefully, "She asked nicely. I won't."

Camrina stepped back as Sir Melvon forced Queen Mona into the corner and Sir Michael charged forward at her. "Where is Prince Eduard?"

"I won't tell you any—"

"You will speak!" He roughly grabbed her arms and unlocked the chains from the wall. "Your day of reckoning has come."

Worried, she watched him move with passion. "What? What are you doing?"

"Finding the truth."

As he pushed her toward the door, Peter descended the stairs and approached. She met his eyes. "What is this?" she asked.

Peter halted a foot in front of her. "Queen Clara tells me you sent Princess Annabelle to die on Snake Island." His stern face held no compassion. "And you knew she was with child." He quickly took a breath. "Did you know I am the one who raised her since she was five years old? Did you know it is my grandchild that you killed before he had a chance to breathe?"

She weakly laughed. "You can't do anything to me. Francis won't let you."

"And if I've changed my mind?" She turned to her brother's voice as Peter, stepping to her side, grabbed her other arm. Her eyes slowly found her brother's. "I will ask you one more time: Where is my son?"

"And I . . . will tell you nothing." She smiled. "You won't do anything to me."

Francis straightened as his nostrils flared. "No, I won't. But Annabelle's husband . . . that's another story." He looked at the knights. "Sirs, take her to the pit."

"Francis? Francis, what is this? What's the pit? What are you going to do? You can't let them do anything to me. Francis, I am your sister!"

He followed the knights and their captive up the steps. "You have grown too at ease with my kindness."

Walking toward the newly dug hole between the training area and the orchard, he watched his two friends lower his sister into the six-foot pit as the princes stood close by. "You see it as a weakness."

Looking up at her brother from inside the pit, she watched a younger knight step forward with a leather bag. Her brother knelt down.

"I don't know if you ever met Sir Nicholaus Hunts," he said. "But he was Annabelle's husband." Francis stood. "He has been in search of her. He has been to your beloved Snake Island." He stepped aside as the cover was brought forward. "And has returned with a gift for you."

"What are you going to do?" Worried, she adamantly shook her head. "I don't know where Edus is. Honest! Francis, please!" Shadows fell across her face as the slotted lattice of sticks was placed over the hole.

"You lie." He looked to Nicholaus. "Release the snake."

Opening the bag, Nicholaus, with a forked stick, forced the head of the slithery creature with slit eyes through one of the holes.

"Francis! Francis, don't let him do this!"

"Tell me where my son is."

"Don't do this! Don't do this!" She pushed herself into the side, distancing herself the best she could from the four-foot descending snake.

"He will take it away if you tell us where he is. Camrina, don't let it bite you!"

Clawing at the dirt on the wall of the pit, she watched the forked tongue move closer and closer. Turning around, she screamed out in fright. "He's with the hostage! He is with her! Ahh!" She sunk down to the bottom, collapsing in her weakness to withstand their plans. She cried in her loss of power.

Francis looked at his sons and knights. "Her? She speaks of Princess Anastacia?"

Thomas knelt down. "Where is the princess?"

Opening her eyes, she looked around the dark hole as the hissing neared. "She is at my castle. At the Sockorian castle." Backing up against the wall, she begged, "Please! Please! Take it away!"

The king looked at his son-in-law, who was still grasping the tail end of the snake, as his sister cried for her life. "Nicholaus, that's enough."

Enough? Hesitating for a moment, the bereaved husband pulled the snake back up and bagged it. *That wasn't enough.*

Taking a deep breath, he shook his head. *Father, save me from myself!*

William turned toward his father. "At the Sockoriá castle? But we looked there!"

"Could she have moved them there?" Thomas suggested.

"She says he's there now?" William asked in distress.

Thomas shook his head. "I'm certain he's not in Anchony. Where else could she have taken him? Wherever he is, Princess Anastacia will be with him."

Shaking and crying, Camrina stumbled into the prison cell. As the chains rattled around her and the head knight bound her back to the wall, Sir Michael spoke softly, "This would have been less distressing had you told us what we wanted from the start."

As his footsteps and those of Sir Melvon exited the dungeon and ascended the steps, Mona approached her. "Camrina?"

Breathing in quickly, bitterness flew from her mouth: "Do not address me so commonly!"

Mona, with disgust, looked at the wretched lady before her. "Then you should not address me so commonly! I was the queen of Sethel, after all!"

Camrina's head rose to meet the challenge. "Don't you forget who made certain you got such a title!"

King Francis, turning away from his sons inside the wattle and daub structure, looked at Grand Sir Michael Doey. "I want Eduard to be found, but I can't spare anyone."

Prince Thomas nodded his head. "I will go, Papá. I will search for Edus."

"No." William stepped forward. "I will go."

Thomas turned toward him. "I gave my word to him, Will, that I would search for him! It has to be me! Besides, you are a more skilled fighter than I—everyone knows it. You are needed here."

"You, Thom, are the thinker. If anyone can figure out who the traitor is when the castle servants come, it's you."

"I don't want to send either of you!" They both turned to the king as he lowered his head. "But I know I must." He sighed as he made up his mind. "Thomas, I will not send you alone."

The prince could not help but grin. "Are you going to send one of your new castle wards with me?"

The king pathetically shook his head as he looked to Michael. "I don't know yet."

"Papá," William stepped forward. "When the traitor is amongst us, we'll need extra men on the Demolites and Aunt Camrina."

Thomas looked between his eldest brother and the king. "What about Sir Victorus, Papá?"

The king placed his hands upon his hips. "What do you mean?"

"It seems a waste of his skill to be with the other Demolites building the castle."

William looked at his brother incredulously. "You think we should set him free?"

"Papá, he fought for me. He fought *against* Aunt Camrina."

Michael lowered his head. "It is true, Sire. In the woods, I don't think I would have lived if it had not been for him, and I believe he did the same for Jous. When the Demolites took you, he tracked you. He released the Demolites' horses. We might not know all he has done for us."

The king tilted his head as he looked between the men before him. "You think he is to be trusted?"

Thomas, quickly glancing around at the other faces, stepped

forward. "I think he has proved himself thus far." He shook his head. "Countless times he could have died, defending Anchony."

William shook his head. "It could be trickery. What if he did all he did to make you trust him? To make you think this way? To make you let him go?"

Francis, shaking his head, leaned upon the table. "No matter how badly I need knights, I can't let him go. He is what started this in the first place!" He looked into his son's eyes. "I'm sorry, Thomas."

Squatting down, Nicholaus reached into the sack and pulled the snake out. Looking into its eyes, he could not help but smirk. "What cruel trickery, but so well deserved." Setting it down, he watched it slither away. "Someday I may come for you or your fellow serpents again to scare the wits out of Camrina. Make her think she is to be poisoned."

Gasping, he put his hand over his mouth. *Anna! Was it painful? Did it last long?* He pounded upon his chest as he looked to the sun peeking through what remained of the leaves. *Why couldn't it have been me? I would have gladly taken her place, Father.* He fell to his knees as his head sank toward the ground. *Anna, why did I leave you alone in the castle?*

Pulling his dagger, he jumped to his feet and swung around.

Peter put out his hands. "It's only me, Nic."

Sheathing his dagger, Nicholaus looked to where the snake disappeared into the woods. "Part of me wanted it to be venomous. I wanted Camrina to die the same terrible death."

Peter nodded as he walked closer. "I understand. And as long as the other part of you knows to let God's love come upon you —to let it cool the bitter flames enticing you—you'll be alright."

Nodding at the memory of Annabelle cowering in the cave upon the Forbidden Island the day of her arrival, Peter said with a smile, "No matter how awful you feel, you must be open to God's love. It took me many years to understand that. And it was your wife—that sweet child—that finally made my heart begin to love again."

Nicholaus took a deep breath to hold back his emotion. "Papá, I miss her so."

"We all do. We all do."

From the distant woods came crunching noises. Nicholaus and Peter simultaneously turned in their direction.

"Who's out there?" Nicholaus called out.

Peter looked back at him, having caught a glimpse of the visitors. "It's Dominicus and the Sethelian knights."

"You know where your princess is now? You will be off to find her?" Rachel, having heard the talk, asked Sir Melvon as he took the offered food. "Are you going to be leaving soon?"

"You'd like nothing better, wouldn't you?"

She lowered her head.

He released a deep breath. "To your regret, not yet." He looked around the bailey as he said with a lowered voice, "How I wish to be free of this place."

"You don't like Anchony?" Rachel asked in all seriousness as she adjusted the basket in her arms.

His eyes found hers with the change in tone. "Anchony is not my home. Sethel is my home. That's where I belong."

She shrugged her shoulders. "My home was Gemmel, but now it's here. You can always make your home somewhere else."

"I have an oath to uphold to my kingdom!"

"But Sethel won't be the same, will it?" she asked as she looked to the orchard trees in the northwest corner of the bailey.

He tilted his head. "Your meaning?"

"The king you served is dead. If what I hear is right, the man that killed him has taken his throne. When you go back to Sethel, will you not have to serve him?"

His tone turned stern. "Prince Howercus is *not* my king and *never* shall he be! Princess Anastacia is the rightful ruler. I will find her in the Sockorian Castle, and I will make certain she rules!"

Rachel tilted her head. "Single-handedly? You would go it alone, if that were the only way?" She nodded as she studied the man before her. "Yes, I dare say you would."

He lowered his head. "Leave me be. I do not wish to be chastised for fulfilling my word."

She stared at the knight before him. *He is honorable, I'll give him that. His oath is what moves him forward. His oath to the true king of Sethel. He will not forsake his homeland though it may be in ruins.* Her stance softened as she opened her mouth.

He looked back at her. "You wish to say something? You've never stopped yourself before."

Although snide in nature, his words held truth. She lowered her head in humility. Unable to speak her newfound realization and respect, she forced out in a quiet manner, "I'm sorry."

"Sorry for what?" he asked gruffly.

She spoke quickly, "My words to you." Then she walked away without giving him a chance to reply.

He watched her walk toward the dungeon at a slower pace than she arrived, as if her mind was preoccupied from the task of walking.

UNCERTAINTY IN BALTAM

Captain Anguis halted as he looked ahead, standing upon a hill. "That's it."

"What is it?" Princess Anastacia asked as she looked forward.

"Those hills far away. That is the Port of Brotherton in Baltam."

Baltam. "When will we be out of Sethel?"

He turned around, studying the landscape. "I believe we've crossed over."

Princess Anastacia took a relieved breath. "I never thought I would be so happy to get out of my own kingdom."

"The end of one kingdom and the beginning of another holds little value when a man is enticed by what his heart seeks."

Her mouth dropped open. "You think my uncle would have Sethelians storm into Baltam to find me?"

"The edge is wide and the king of Baltam lives far away." He glanced at her. "How badly does he want you dead?"

Dread came down upon her. *I'll never be safe no matter where I am, is that it?*

Princess Anastacia looked around at the filthy market, with its stone walls and four tables saturated with juices from the wild catches of the sea, as her nose was overwhelmed by the smell of fish.

"How many would you like?" the vendor asked the pirate as he cut the head off the game of the sea.

Anguis eyed him and then looked around at the other venders in the seaside market. "I didn't come here for fish."

"Fish is all we have to offer. The other market is down the street," the man said with a dour tone as he scraped fish guts into a wicker basket.

The pirate stepped closer. "I've come looking for a man that goes by Fulco. Do you know of him?"

The fishmonger hesitated for a moment and then grabbed another fish. "What do you want with him?"

"Here's the next catch."

The fisherman placed another basket full of fish onto the saturated table. Anastacia noticed that the other cleaners had momentarily paused from their occupation.

Anguis, watching the fisherman walk away, stepped closer. "I was told by a man—a Phillipus of Sethel—that I would find him in the Port of Brotherton cleaning fish." He turned his head and spoke louder. "So, it is one of you."

My brother told *him? What did my brother say to him?* Anastacia stared at the pirate in complete confusion.

The man, standing tall, looked into the pirate's eyes as he leaned closer. "Are you Anguis?"

"I am."

"Then I am Fulco. What tidings do you bring?"

Anguis quickly looked back at the princess. "I'm not here on that matter."

The man's voice became irritated. "Then what matter brings you to Baltam?" He angrily chopped down upon the fish.

"I need to beg a favor." Lowering his voice, he said, "A favor on behalf of the prince." He moved the princess forward. "This is Stacia. She needs a home."

Anastacia opened her mouth in disbelief. *What's he doing? Leaving me with a stranger?!*

Fulco looked at her and then Anguis. "Phillipus? Who is she? Why does Phillipus wish for her to be my ward?"

Anastacia defiantly crossed her arms. "Prince Phillipus is dead." She looked around the market as a deafening quietness seemed to suddenly blanket the place.

"Dead?" Fulco asked as he moved his jaw laterally and glanced over his shoulder just to look back upon the pirate. "Is it true?"

Anguis lowered his gaze. "It is."

"Were you . . . going to tell me?" The fishmonger's nostrils flared as he threw the filleted fish into a basket and hurriedly picked it up to take it to a cart.

Anastacia watched as three other men gathered around the angry man. She silently followed Anguis as he walked closer.

The four men turned around to look at him. Anguis, shaking his head, said, "I deem you owe this to him."

Anastacia looked between the pirate and the vendors. *What is this about?* Unable to take any more of the secrecy, she stepped beside the pirate and pulled on his arm. "Owe what? I demand you tell me!"

Moving his arm away, he looked over his shoulder. "Not now!"

The princess moved away.

"Who is she? Why do you wish for us to tend to her?" Fulco asked.

Anastacia, about to cry, backed away. *I don't!* She looked

around for anyone who might be able to assist her. *Where can I go? Who can I truly trust?* She suddenly took off running.

She was out of the market, and the wattle and daub buildings passed by on her right. On her left far below, the powerful ocean crashed upon the edge of land as she ran along the cliff.

"Anastacia!" She could hear Anguis calling her name.

Where can I be safe? The tears finally fell as she breathed excessively hard with her fright. *Father, You want me to help my people? How can I? How can I as I'm left with strangers in Baltam?*

A protesting scream escaped her lips as she felt a strong arm around her core and she was raised off her feet.

"Let me go!"

The pirate's hand pressed firmly over her mouth, and he whispered into her ear. "Princess, this is for your good." She struggled against him. "Your brother trusted them."

Did he truly? Fishmongers from the western Baltam coast—why ever would he?! How did he come to know them?

But Anguis knew they were here. Does he speak the truth? She slowly calmed her thrashing.

Setting her back down, he turned her around. "Did you trust your brother? Did you?"

"Yes," she said weakly as she looked at the pirate before her.

"Well, he trusted me, and he trusted them."

She looked back at the market. "Who are they?"

He shook his head. "I don't know."

He doesn't even know? "Do they know you're a pirate?"

"I deem not."

She took a step backward. "So . . . you're going to leave me here with them?"

He looked down. "Yes."

"Why?"

"I can't help you. I shouldn't . . ."

"Shouldn't what?" she said, annoyed.

"I shouldn't have taken you from the castle in the first place."

Taking a quick breath, she looked up at him. "Well, why did you?"

"I . . . I don't know." He turned away.

"I think you do!" She folded her arms. "You did it for my brother? For letting you go free, you freed me?"

Staring at her, he looked down, uncertain what to say. Perhaps that was it. He was not quite sure himself.

"How long am I to stay here with these fishmongers?"

He shook his head. "I don't know. Until it's safe for you to go to Sethel."

"It will only be safe for me to go to Sethel when my uncle is dead. And who knows when that will be, if ever. It might never be safe for me to go to Sethel!"

Anguis moved nervously. "Take heart, you'll be safe here. Camrina doesn't know where you are. Let your brother's trust in them give you hope."

"You claim he trusted you, too, yet you're forsaking me!" Looking around, she placed her hands upon her head. She wondered aloud, "How am I to help my people when I'm hidden away in Baltam?"

Stepping away, he lowered his head. "I can't help you anymore. I . . . I'm *only* a pirate." She followed him a few steps as he continued, "You must stay here. You must be Stacia the servant. You were rescued from the castle."

"Rescued from whom?"

"Prince Howercus."

"And what did he ask of Stacia the servant?"

"To kill Phillipus."

She shook her head. "But they know he's dead. They'll think I killed him!"

"You warned him, and he gave you to me to bring you here."

She shook her head. "It's all lies. Why not the truth? I'd rather not speak than to tell lies!"

"Where would the truth lead you?"

"But if Phillip could trust them, why can't I tell them who I am?"

Anguis looked at the people passing by. "He trusted them, but I know nothing of the people of Brotherton. Are they truly loyal to Baltam? Or have Sethelians loyal to your uncle moved in? You are not so far from the Sethel kingdom. They are only fishmongers; they are not like your knights at home."

She looked at him pathetically. "So you leave me with people that can't defend me if my uncle comes?"

He shook his head. "I can't offer any further protection either."

"Why not? You did—from the other pirates."

Shaking his head, he backed away. "I can't. This is what needs to be done. To leave you here." Taking a breath, he looked up. "You know where you need to go. I've done what Prince Phillipus asked of me."

"Wait!" her face pleaded. "Who says we are to be 'safe' in life? What if going to Sethel is what God wants of me!"

Shaking his head, he turned around. "No, you can't."

"Why?"

"Because he will kill you!" He lowered his head. "You can't help your people if you are dead!"

"Well, I can't help my people in a Baltamian fish market either!" she screamed at him.

Shaking his head, he realized there were no words he could say that would ease her. So he left her without another word, sprinting away toward Sethel.

As the distance increased between them, he heard her yell: "At least I felt safe in the castle! Why didn't you leave me be?!"

"Amana, this is Stacia. We are to tend to her. She was a servant in the Sethelian castle. I'll say more later," Fulco said as he dropped his new ward off with his wife.

Princess Anastacia watched the fishmonger walk down the path toward the seaside market. Amana, brushing the dirt off her dress, stood in the garden to watch her husband walk away. Turning her eyes toward the girl, she briefly smiled. "Stacia? I'm Fulco's wife. Amana. Would you like to help me?" In her early thirties with a comely face, Amana's beauty was slightly obscured by the dirt she toiled in and the brown garb she wore.

Anastacia, feeling abandoned by everyone, moved forward with a downcast glance. "I'll do whatever you want of me. Tell me what I'm to do."

Amana looked at her with the greatest concern. "Are you alright?"

The princess ventured, "Can you tell me how Fulco knew Prince Phillipus?"

Amana, quickly taking a breath, kneeled back down. "The pumpkins are ripe."

She will tell me nothing. With her head sinking even farther, she entered the garden. "What do I do?"

ISLANDS IN THE NORTHERN SEA

Shoved over the side of the rowboat with her feet chained together, Annabelle landed in a few inches of chilly water. Gasping in utter surprise, she pushed herself up against the weight of her extended abdomen. Her fear increased when she felt a minor contraction of her womb.

"Leave her alone!" Captain Vitalis yelled. "Can't you see she's with child?" He was immediately hit by a Seafur and fell backward into the boat.

"Captain." A couple of the mariners tried to help him up, but one of the Seafurs pushed them aside, then picked him up in his arms and dropped him into a foot of water. The captain gasped at the shocking coldness of the northern sea, and then, recovering, he scrambled to his feet.

"Annabelle!" Shoved from behind, the captain landed upon the rocky soil as the other mariners were forced out of the boat behind them by the captors.

The princess, being ushered up the bank, looked back at him. "I'm alright, Captain."

Turning around, she gasped at the large man who stood in

front of her. The man beside him spoke in a broken sentence, "When baby come?"

Annabelle shook her head.

The interpreter, Ecwab, stepped closer. "When baby come?"

"I don't know!" She shook her head as she fought back the tears that wanted to fall. Looking over her shoulders, she spotted the captain and the other mariners being forced up the rocky coast, too.

After climbing the summit of the hill, Annabelle looked upon a village of several huts—three were very large—and two prison yards sprawled out in a valley. She watched the mariners be forced toward an enclosure with its perimeter made of metal and wood as she rubbed her arms in the cold climate.

The largest man and the leader, Acwa, spoke as he tilted his head toward the other enclosure, filled with girls. Annabelle was forced forward.

The iron door slammed closed in front of her. Through the stick slits, she saw the captain shoved behind the bars of the other enclosure across the way. Resting her head upon the door, she took a deep breath as she felt the sharpest pain yet in her abdomen. When it subsided, she turned around to see young eyes upon her. "Good day?" She could see her breath before her.

Huddled in a corner under a small, three-sided structure—the only protection from the elements the captives were allotted—behind a small fire, was a large group of girls, perhaps twenty in all. The princess approached them. "I won't hurt you. I'm Annabelle. What are your names?"

They were reluctant to give any answers, but one girl finally ventured, "Nila."

"Nila? And where are you from?"

"Baltam."

Transporting her basket full of dyed yarn across the village, Lina glanced at the captor's female prison enclosure. Seeing a grown woman in it, she took a double glance. The woman, tired but determined, looked at her. Lina looked away. *Keep walking.* She was listening to herself when she watched Annabelle turn away and her extended abdomen was revealed. Horror overcame Lina.

Oh, no! Father, no! You want me to trust You? Why did You send another one?

She quickened her pace toward her destination.

"I'm not," another girl answered shyly within the female prisoner camp.

Annabelle looked back at the girl addressing her. "Not from Baltam?"

The girl shook her head.

"From where do you hail?"

The girl looked at the others around her until a bigger girl spoke up. "Salisburg."

"Salisburg? In Anchony?"

The girls nodded.

Oh, no! She pulled the closest girl into a hug. *How did they get them?* She suddenly grimaced as she felt an uncomfortable pain. *Oh, Father! Did you send me here for them?*

"I want to go home," a small girl called out. "They took the other girls, and they haven't come back."

"We heard screams," another offered. "It came from that hill."

Annabelle knelt next to the crying child. "What?" Glancing through the metal bars weaved with sticks, trying to find the hill, her eyes suddenly caught sight of the woman who stared at her moments before, staring yet again, as if conflicted. The woman looked around cautiously, then suddenly ran over and knelt down on the opposite side of the metal and wooden wall, waving her over.

Annabelle warily approached her.

"I have to warn you."

The princess looked at her in surprise. "You speak my tongue."

Lina, mesmerized by the color of her eyes for a moment, tapped upon the bar to shake away her distracting thoughts. "You must listen. They will take the child."

"Which child?" She looked to the girls huddled together.

"*Your* child." Lina looked at her stomach.

"What?" Annabelle grabbed her abdomen.

The woman looked into her eyes. "They will sacrifice it."

"What?!" Annabelle shook her head as she stood in defiance. "No!"

Lina looked down, unable to offer any good advice. "That's what they do."

"No! I won't let them!" Annabelle adamantly declared as she felt a sharper pain.

Lina shook her head as she slowly stood. "You can't stop them."

"I will fight them." The princess gripped the bars until her fingers turned white. "Or I will die trying if I must!" A tear of fear rolled down her cheek as she stared into the woman's eyes.

The woman touched her hand. "Is it your first?"

Annabelle nervously nodded as her chin began to quiver.

"I have had seven of my own." Lina looked into the distance as she remembered happier times gone by. "It takes a lot from you. You won't be able to stop them."

Annabelle covered her mouth as she watched a Seafur storm over. *Nicholaus! Nicholaus, where are you?*

"Lina!" the man yelled in his language, pulling the woman's

wrist away from the prison. "Don't talk to them! What did you say to her?"

Lina pulled her wrist away and rubbed it as she stood straight to meet his challenge. She answered back in the native tongue, "That woman is going to give birth very soon. If you want that baby, you'll need me to calm her unless Ecwab would like to try!"

He stared at her. "Get to your hut!"

Annabelle, nearly hyperventilating, watched the woman named Lina walk away.

They can't take my child. They can't take it. Father, don't let them take it! Nicholaus! Nicholaus, I need you here! I need you here now! Sitting down, she began to rock herself. *Father, this can't be Your will! This can't be Your will!* Tears streamed down her face. *Whatever You allow, I will trust You. I will trust You!*

Leaning against the door, Lina looked at the back wall. *Prayers? What are prayers going to do when they kill the babe? I've seen too many die. I need to help. Could I steal it away? They'll catch me . . . certainly they will.* She shook her head. *I don't care. I can't stand to see more blood be spilled for their fiends!* Her eyes darted around the room. *If I ran into the woods . . . they'd find me.*

"But I can't sit idle any longer!" she said angrily to the empty room.

"Ahhh!" The princess, hours later, could no longer bear the contractions silently. Backing against the bars, she braced herself as she tried not to incite attention.

The girls backed away nervously. "The baby comes?" one asked. They had nothing but fright upon their countenances.

Another wave of pain hit her as she watched the villagers open the bars. Shaking her perspiring head, she bent forward with the pain as they grabbed her by her arms and dragged her from the prison. "No! No!" she cried.

The men pulled her along the road of the village. When the contraction subsided, she slapped the man's arm away from her, but as she was preparing her next physical assault she was hit by a new wave of agony. "You can't have my baby! You can't!" she screamed, her face red and sweating, though it was frigid.

As they neared the edge of the village, the road turned into a path and ascended up a hill. They half-led and half-dragged her up, her feet and sometimes her knees dragging in the soil. At the top, they came to a clearing, and in the center of the clearing were five, flat stones, stained in messy dark splotches. The men stopped and looked at the stones with a strange and frightening reverence. Again a contraction contorted Annabelle's body in pain.

In the village, she heard a deep bellow from a ram's horn, the call to the offering. Looking down the hill, she saw villagers emerge from their warm huts to watch the event.

The men released her next to the stones. Annabelle rolled onto her back, pushing herself away from the captors. The man signaled to two Seafurian women standing nearby. They stepped forward and freed Annabelle from her ankle shackles, then intrusively moved her dress away.

"Breathe. You need to breathe." Lina knelt down beside her.

"They can't have my baby!" Annabelle screamed out as she grabbed Lina's arm. As a contraction hit her, the two midwives by her feet started talking.

"They see the head," Lina informed her.

"No!" As much as she wished to resist, her body forced her to push. "My baby! My baby! No!"

"Push again. It's almost out!" Lina encouraged.

With a scream of pain and utter fright, her hair plastered with sweat to her straining, reddened face, Annabelle pushed a final time.

"It's out!" Lina looked at the princess as she heard the women speaking. "It's a boy."

Annabelle reached for him as they wiped him down.

"Lie still. The afterbirth must come," Lina said. She looked at Acwa, who stood next to the offering stone. He was preparing his dagger. She secretly fingered her own, hiding within the folds of her dress.

"Give him to me!" Annabelle cried desperately. "No! Bring him back!" She watched the women clean the baby as he wailed his rejection to the cold environment. "No! Give him back! I'm here! I'm here!" She attempted to get up but was promptly pushed back down.

One of the women handed the baby to Ecwab. He examined the newborn as if to ensure there were no defects. As he did, Lina stood. Found acceptable, the baby boy was passed to the leader. Acwa performed his own assessment and then set the crying newborn upon the stone. As Lina slowly crept up behind Acwa, gripping her knife, he raised his dagger.

Suddenly Annabelle felt another contraction grip her body and she released another scream of agony. Confusion overcame her—were the labor pains supposed to return? All eyes turned back toward her. The midwives beside her knelt down, felt Annabelle's abdomen, and began arguing with one another. Acwa turned to see why she had screamed.

Lina loosened the dagger in her grasp. *Twins?* Lina looked between Annabelle and the chieftain.

Annabelle released another cry as she watched the Seafurian women move away from her as if she were poison.

Acwa and Ecwab began to argue. Acwa, disgusted, gesticulated wildly. Lina, seeing that the native women were not going to help the birthing captive, knelt down in front of the princess and covertly hid her knife.

"What's . . . going . . . on?" Annabelle asked through her pain.

Lina felt Annabelle's abdomen and looked at her with hope. "There's another!"

Annabelle closed her eyes with her despair. "No!"

"No, that's good. Very good. They won't offer them to their gods!" She looked at the chieftain and spoke in the Seafurian tongue, "It is twins!"

Everyone backed away from the crying baby lying on the sacrificial stone.

"Make certain!" Acwa spoke in his tongue.

"Certain?" She pointed to Annabelle. "Can you not see she is still in labor?" Turning back toward the princess, she looked in her eyes. "It will be alright. It will all be alright! Give it time. Give it time."

The Seafurian villagers began whispering in fear of the babe and the woman who brought evil to their island.

"Stay away!" Acwa ordered his people as he impatiently waited to make certain it truly was another babe.

Lina looked into Annabelle's eyes. "You can do this. This child will save the life of its brother. Now, push!"

When the sound of another crying baby filled the evening air, Lina burst into a smile as she held up the babe. "This one's a girl!" Lina was quickly pushed over and the baby stolen from her grasp. The umbilical cord was severed, and she heard Acwa speak. Her smile faded away.

"Give them to me!" Annabelle yelled at the woman who was now holding both of her children. As she reached for them, her wrists were shackled. "No!" She resisted the attempts but, still weak, her struggle was minimal.

The woman with her babies turned and headed toward the woods.

"Come back!" she yelled at the woman.

With tears rolling down her face, she looked to Lina. "Where is she taking them?"

Lina, swallowing hard, lowered her head. "To the woods to freeze to death."

"No!" Annabelle pulled against her shackles as new waves of contractions, much weaker than the labor pains, hit her.

"Lie still. The afterbirth must come," Lina spoke in a quiet voice as she looked over Annabelle's head at the woman disappearing into the woods with the newborns.

"My babies!" Annabelle's face was full of tears as she pushed yet again to dispel the second placenta. Feeling much relief, she relaxed for the slightest moment and then looked at Lina. "Where are they?" Impassioned, she found a bit more strength and scrambled her way to her knees as Lina looked upon her helplessly. "I want my babies!"

At that moment she felt a sharp burst of pain on the back of her head, and the world went dark.

INTO THE WOODS

The Seafurian villagers watched in confusion as the babe, intended to be a sacrifice, was placed into the midwife's arms along with its twin and promptly taken into the woods. Acwa looked at his people and spoke in the native tongue, "Dafod!" meaning, "They're evil!"

One of the village children, Katara, a curious twelve-year-old, was momentarily distracted by the racket coming from the male slave quarters down below. After glancing in that direction, she turned back toward the shackled mother next to the sacrificial stones and saw that Acwa had approached her from behind. Suddenly he swung his beefy arm and hit her in the back of her head with his fist. The woman fell immediately to the ground and lay there unmoving.

"She brings evil. Stay away from her!" Acwa's voice boomed in the Seafurian tongue. The villagers obediently stepped away.

Turning to Lina, he ordered, "Back to the hut!" Lina quickly turned and ran down the hill.

"What are you going to do with her?" one voice yelled out.

"That is a question for the gods," Acwa said matter-of-factly, then turned and began descending the hill. The villagers who had gathered around the clearing followed behind him.

As Katara followed the crowd down to the village and watched Lina running into the hut, she once again heard the voices of the male slaves.

"Annabelle! Annabelle! Where did she go?" Captain Vitalis rattled the iron bars in frustration, fright, and anger. "What have you done to her? You'll pay for this!" The intensity of his dismay increased as the other mariners began to remove the sticks weaved between the bars to increase their chances of seeing something that would provide an answer.

Katara's eyes enlarged as she watched the wall of sticks go up into flames by the mariners' hands and Ecwab and the other Seafurian men rushed toward the encampment. "What you do?" Ecwab shook his head. "You make bad for self! Wind blow through."

"Where is she? Let us out!" Captain Vitalis yelled on the other side of the flames.

"She slave. No matter!" Ecwab stated as if it was the end of the conversation. Turning away from the burning compound, he spotted Katara observing the whole scene. "Go to your hut!" he ordered in the native tongue.

Pulling her fur closer around her neck, she glanced at the sacrificial hill before turning to the warm dwelling awaiting her.

Coming to consciousness, Annabelle slowly opened her eyes. She was still in the clearing, laying on the cold ground where she'd given birth. How long had she been unconscious?

Attempting to focus on the dying fire from the male compound below, she pushed herself up. *What came to pass?* Pulling the fur closer to her neck, she looked at it oddly. *What is this? How did it get here?* Closing her eyes, she remembered the woman walking into the woods. "My babies!"

As a piercing headache reminded her of the blow she had received, she reached for the back of her head. When her fingers touched her skin, something nearly fell out of her grasp—halted only by the leather strap hanging around her fingers. She pulled her hand away from her head and looked at the object in her palm. It was a key.

Where did this come from? Finding guards standing far away with their backs to her—scared of the one who brought evil to their island—she wondered if it would work on her shackles. With hope, she quietly inserted the key into the hole on her fetters. It went smoothly. Turning the key, it fell open. With excitement, she unlocked her other wrist. The shackles fell off. Bending over, she fit the key into the hole on her shackles around her ankles as well. As they too unlocked, she no longer cared about the answer to her questions. Working quickly, she freed her ankles from the metal and crawled toward the forest. Aided by the shadows from the setting sun, she was able to slip into the woods unseen.

Once in the forest—the last place she'd set eyes upon her children—she leaned against a tree. *Father, please let them be alive! How long has it been?* Her breath billowed out in front of her as her throat felt raw with the cold and emotion.

Falling to the ground, she searched for footprints. *Let me find them!* Locating a suspicious indention, she pushed herself up and forced herself forward, her head still pounding. *Father, please! I don't hear crying. Why aren't they crying?*

She ran as quickly as she could, scanning the ground and the trees ahead. *Where are they?* Tears began to rush down her cheeks as the trees dashed past her. *I have to find them! I have to find them! They'll be so cold! So cold!* The quicker she ran, the more emotional she became until she could take no more; she fell to her knees in her distress. *Father, why? Why?*

Attempting to control her hysterical state, she focused on breathing calmly. She hung her head, and her tears fell upon her knees. *Did You allow them to be spared from sacrifice only to freeze to death in the woods?*

Suddenly she felt a hand upon her head. Freezing in fear, she turned her eyes up and saw wavy, blonde hair. "Why do you fret?" a serene voice said. "Does the Father not know exactly where they are? They are, after all, a part of the Body of Christ."

Celesa? The princess looked up to find no one there. Standing with a new invigoration, she nodded her head. "They are God's gift to me! He loves them more than I ever could!"

Looking around at the trees, she spotted a villager in the distance, slowly rising from the cold ground. Hiding behind a tree, she watched the woman—the midwife that ran away with her children—search the area and, not finding what she wanted, stumble back toward the village with a bleeding head.

She can't find them?

As the woman disappeared, Annabelle emerged from her hidden location and searched the scene herself. Slowly kneeling, she felt the ground for any signs that her eyes could not easily discern. Finding a large branch, her fingers slid over the wood until she felt an unusual wetness. Bringing her fingers to her eyes, she could see they were darkened. *Blood?*

She looked back to where the woman had disappeared. *She was hit?* Annabelle arose. *Who took my children from her?* Closing her eyes, she heard St. Celestria's words again: *They are, after all, a part of the Body of Christ.* Opening her eyes, she nodded. "The water! Where is there water?" She bolted toward the sound of a distant river.

"Oh, shh, shh, shh, shh, shh!" Lina held both of them in one arm as she climbed up from the riverbank. "I know it's cold, but please don't make a sound! You'll only give yourself away. And they mustn't find you! They mustn't!" Swaddled in a woolen blanket, she pressed them tightly against herself. "I must keep you safe! God wants me to keep you safe! How am I to do it?"

Rising from the riverbank, she looked around into the near darkness as she heard a sound. *No! They're already here!* Hearing the forest alive with sounds, she jumped as she looked frantically in every direction. *I've failed!*

"Stop!"

Lina froze when she heard her own language amongst the babies' crying. *That wasn't Ecwab. That was a woman.* With her heart beating uncontrollably, she turned toward the voice in the darkness. "Who's out there?"

The princess stepped out from behind a tree as she looked at the bundle in the woman's arms. "You took them from the woman?"

"You're alive!" Lina gasped with great relief. "I thought they killed you!"

"My babies!" Annabelle, staring at the woolen blanket, walked forward to meet her children, feeling as if she was in a dream—or a nightmare. Her chin quivered uncontrollably.

Lina graciously handed them over. "They're hungry. They need you."

Annabelle took the newborns from Lina's arms. So overcome with love when she looked upon the precious faces, she lowered herself to the cold ground with her children as tears poured from her eyes. "What beauty!"

Lina looked nervously at the woods behind the princess. "They will come for them. They think them evil." Licking her lips, she glanced back down at the new mother. "They were baptized."

"I know," Annabelle said with a smile as she stared at the great gifts within her arms.

Lina tilted her head. "You know? You saw it then? I don't know who—"

"'They are, after all, a part of the Body of Christ!'" Smiling radiantly, Annabelle looked away from the lady to gaze back upon their sweet, sinless countenances as she warmed them between herself and the blanket.

Lina, not sure how to respond to the mother's statement, shook her head. "I . . . I don't quite know . . ." She looked to the village. "Are we safe to light a fire here? Are we far enough away?"

Peeling her eyes away from the pristine skin, Annabelle shook her head. "We're not. We need to go deeper into the woods. The woman you hit—she went back to the huts. It's only a matter of time until they come."

Lina faltered for a moment. "Oh, no. I'm not safe there any longer."

The princess thought quickly as she stood, holding both babes in one arm. "You hit her from behind?"

"Yes."

"Did she see you at all?"

"I don't know."

Annabelle nodded. "You can be safe. They'll know I'm gone —they could blame me. If you go now, before they see that you're gone."

Lina shook her head. "I can't leave you here. What would you do?"

The princess could not help but smile. "This is not my first time in a forest. We'll be alright."

"I . . . I can't leave you. Or them. They are—"

Annabelle grabbed her hand. "You are the only hands of Christ that those people know. You must return."

Struck by the conviction in Annabelle's voice, Lina was speechless for a moment. She lowered her gaze in shame. "I saved your babies but . . . there have been too many that I haven't, and I haven't even—"

"You can always start anew. That is why Christ came."

Lina, looking into the emerald hue, pulled away from the princess's grasp, with a multitude of emotions running through her. "It has been years since I've heard the Son's name spoken. I think I have failed Him in every way."

"That's what mercy is for."

Lina stepped away more, looking around nervously. "I have to make sure they live—that's how I will not fail Him. That's what He wants me to do, you see?" Taking a deep breath, she shook her head. "They can't know they're alive. If they ever find them, they'll kill them. They think them evil because they're twins. I don't know what we'll do. The winters are bitterly cold here—you won't stay alive on your own with two babes."

"My twins are evil, but *they* kill babies?" Annabelle could not help but smirk at the ridiculousness of the irony. She shook her head. "They are my gifts from God! I shall tend to them the best that I can, and what I can't do, He shall do for us."

"Well, I can't . . . I won't leave you here." Looking around in the night air with her breath bellowing before her, Lina nervously shifted her weight. "I will find some sticks for you— to warm them."

They'll see a fire. Annabelle held the babies tightly as she, looking around, heard the helpful woman walk away in her search. *It will only tell them of our whereabouts.* Gently shaking her babies in both arms, Annabelle's eyes scoured the land in the moonlight, from the rolling stream westward to its more turbulent beginnings where it welled up from the earth, to the darkened outline of the hills surrounding it, dotted by evergreens and the skeletal remains of the deciduous arbors. She shook her head. *No, there can't be a fire—not here, not in the open.*

Her eyes scanned the humble beginnings of the spring in the moonlight, examining how it was able to maneuver its way through the foliage. *It comes from the earth.* She dared to approach with hope as she gently bounced the babes within her arms. "If it comes from the earth, that means there is water under the ground."

Her eyes looked to the stony hills, and she spoke again to her children, "And if there are streams in the earth, there too could be a cave." Her vision focused upon a certain section of the stony structure jutting out from the hill. "Oh, Father, let there be a cave to keep us warm, and if there is a cave there, help me to find it."

Moving in the limited light, she transferred both wee babes to one arm and outstretched her other as she neared to let her hand begin searching. Sliding her hand across the roughness, she felt the subtle slope of the rockiness inward. *Could it be?* Stepping closer, she leaned the left side of her body against the stone wall and extended her arm. Sweeping her appendage back and forth, she nearly cried when her arm perceived the cavernous opening. *Father, thank You for this! Please, let it be deep enough.* Raising her hand, she could feel the warmth of the earth emanating from within the rock hole.

"Is anything here?" Hearing no response, she shouted louder, "Any animal?" She then released a burst of a scream to scare anything away that might be lingering in the cave's warmth. Not yet fully satisfied, she found a stick and threw it within the four-foot opening and listened intently. Looking down at her children, she could not help but smile. "I deem it vacant."

Switching the babes to her left arm, she slid her back against the stone and carefully pushed herself up the sloping, four-foot cliff wall to the first small terrace. Once secured in the sitting position, she elevated her feet against the cold stone and pushed again in the same fashion. She repeated her movement until she had inched her way up the incline and safely found the platform.

"Do you feel that? It's already getting warmer." Backing up

until she could no more with her legs five feet from the opening, she closed her eyes in relief. *Thank You, Father.* Opening her eyes, she looked at the spot where she had last seen the helpful woman. "I'm sorry, Lina, but you'll be safer and we'll be safer if you don't know where we are. You need to go back to your hut."

Turning back to the cave, she stuck her arm out to begin another search. *How far over does it go?* Moving deeper into the hidden side, she nodded with all hope. "They won't see the flames from within here."

Lina turned around in a circle with the sticks in her arms. *Where'd she go? Oh, no! Did they find her?* She looked around desperately. *I wasn't gone for very long. How could they? I didn't hear them.* "Good day? Good day!" *I don't even know her name!* Gasping, she gazed through the trees. *What if they find me here— what would I say? Was she right? Will they think it was she that hit the midwife? Do I still have a chance of returning without them knowing my part? Do I keep them alive by going back? Or did the Seafurs take them?* Her eyes scanned the area again for any answers to where the young mother ran. Finding none, she dropped the sticks and quickly dashed back toward the huts.

At the edge of the village, she slowed. *Do they know I was gone?* Walking to her dwelling, she stared at the female prison yard. *Is she there?* Not spotting the figure of a grown woman within the compound, she was not sure if she should be elated or sorrowful. *Where did they go?* With a downward glance, she walked into her home.

"Where did the mother go?" one Seafurian asked Acwa, the

leader, in the native tongue as he walked to the front of the meeting hut before he had a chance to speak.

"The mother? What do you mean?"

"She's gone."

Yet another said, "Malaya was hit in the woods. She must have gone after her babies."

"She's gone?" Acwa asked again for clarification. As he stared at his people, his face reddened in anger. "She escaped? We must make certain she and her children are dead!"

"And what of the god of winter?" another asked. "Was the sacrifice of the young linas enough?"

Acwa shook his head. "The gods say all must be given to them to make up for the evil the green-eyed one has brought to our land." He looked at all the faces. "And the green-eyed one must be found and given!"

Heart racing, Annabelle sat up and cried out as pain suddenly pulsated from the side of her head after contacting the cavernous ceiling. "Ohhh." Swallowing her nerves, her eyes swung to the opening as she heard the origins of her discontent: wolves. Extending her hand toward her children sleeping near the warm wall, her other touched her head to find a large goose-egg forming. Laying her head down upon her arm, she momentarily closed her eyes. *Nicholaus? Nicholaus, where are you?* Turning her head to the opening, she crawled forward just a bit to see more clearly as a pack of wolves answered each other near the stream below. "Nicholaus, we're alive. Come find us!"

REVELATION

Bishop Dominicus, hugging his knightly nephew for a second time, tapped him on the shoulder. "Nicholaus, could you tend to my horse?"

"Certainly." Nicholaus nodded and then bowed to the monarchs before leaving the house.

Watching him walk out the door, the bishop turned around to look at his brother, Sir Josephus Peter the Lion, and King Francis and Queen Clara. "I didn't wish to speak these words in front of him—not yet, anyway. There is a Sister Gabriella at the convent who has the gift of seeing angels. She is the one who told Annabelle she was with child." Swallowing hard, he shook his head. "What she didn't get to tell her is that there were two."

Clara gasped, moving her hand to her mouth. "Two babies?" She looked at her husband, who wrapped his comforting arm around her.

Peter shook his head as he swallowed with difficulty. "Yet another life she took that we didn't know about."

The bishop looked at his brother. "You speak of Camrina?"

Peter nodded. "There's something not right with her."

"Is she here?"

"Yes. She's in the dungeon with Queen Mona," the king answered.

"I would like to see her."

Francis shook his head. "She won't like your visit. She doesn't want to see anyone."

"Is that so?" He slowly nodded his head. "Take me there."

Peter glanced at the king. "I'll take you."

Sir Jacobus, with Sir Frankus at his side, approached his brother knight, Sir Melvon. "I see, sir, you yet live tending to Queen Mona," he said.

"I've lived through more than her," Sir Melvon said as he turned to his fellow Sethelian knights who had returned with the bishop. "I couldn't get word to you that Queen Camrina took Princess Anastacia. She made known that the princess is in her castle." He slowly nodded. "Prince Thomas is going to the Sockor Islands to get his brother back." He eyed his brother knights. "Anyone want to go along and get our princess?"

"What of Queen Mona?" Frankus asked. "Should we leave her here?"

"Leave her here to rot. I want to be rid of that woman." Turning away in disgust, Sir Melvon watched the bishop, king, and Anchonian knights descend the spiral staircase.

Camrina sighed as if just hearing footsteps descending the stairwell created a great exhaustion. "Haven't you done enough with me today?" she called out.

As the figures of Bishop Dominicus and Peter emerged, her discomfort grew. Looking upon the bishop, she shrunk farther away from the bars. "What do you want?"

Bishop Dominicus glanced at his brother. "I want to go into the cell."

"Don't come closer!" Camrina demanded.

Queen Mona, shrinking back into her corner, silently observed the oddity of the other queen's behavior. Peter pointed at her. "Stay there."

"Torch," the bishop said as he held out his hand.

"What do you want?" Camrina screamed as if the proximity of the man physically injured her.

Dominicus squatted down to her level. He looked her in the eyes, shook his head, and then looked up at Peter. "I've seen all I need to see."

Camrina began to gutturally laugh as the bishop and Peter left the dungeon. "That's right. You run, bishop! You run!"

Mona looked at Camrina in utter fright. "What's wrong with you?!" She looked to the spiral staircase. "I don't want to be in here with her any longer! Someone, let me out!"

"Oh stop yelling! Are you so frightened of me?" Camrina tilted her head as she smirked at Queen Mona.

Mona whispered in truth, "You're not right."

"Not right. Not right?" She walked toward the younger woman as far as her chains would allow. "Would you like to know what is not right? You."

Mona looked at her queerly and shook her head. "I don't want to hear anything you have—"

"Well, I'm going to tell you anyway."

The bishop chose his words carefully as he looked at the king, queen, and their offspring in the fall light. "There is a battle for her body. I see it in her eyes." The bishop shook his head. "And she is on the wrong side. Nothing can help her if she doesn't want to be helped."

"Is there anything that can be done for her?" Clara pleaded.

"Everyone is given free will—free will to either choose to serve Him or to go against Him and be taken by Satan."

"But can't—"

Dominicus shook his head. "No. She doesn't want it. If she wanted to be free, then I could. But she doesn't want it."

"We can pray that she will change," Elizabeth suggested with all seriousness.

The bishop, sighing, knelt in front of her and shook his head. "That would be praying against her will, wouldn't it?"

Cristine shook her head. "So, she's hopeless?"

Clara shook her head. "There's always hope. Certainly there's something we can do?"

"I won't give up on my sister."

William shook his head. "The sacraments can't help her, because she's in a state of mortal sin and she will not go to Penance." He looked to the dungeon entrance, wondering if he was hearing yelling from deep within.

Nodding, the bishop added, "She can only be helped if she turns to God—and for that she will have to *want* to turn to God."

Isabella's mouth dropped open. "Can we pray that she wants to turn to God or wants to want to turn to God? That she wants to change? That's not going against her will, is it?" She slowly nodded as she looked at the ground. "It's praying that her will will be open to change." She looked back at the bishop. "Is that safe?"

The bishop slowly nodded. "That is likely the most effective prayer." He watched William walk toward the dungeon entrance.

"No doubt, this calls for fasting," Clara stated as she looked at her daughters.

"I will fast for her," Elizabeth said.

"I, too," Isabella agreed as she took her youngest sister's hand.

Cristine, sighing, looked at her sisters and then the bishop. "I am not as willing, but what if that means I need to do it the most?"

Elizabeth grabbed Cristine's hand with her free one. "We'll help you, Crisa."

"We'll all help one another," Clara said as she put her arm around Cristine.

Moved by the love of his family, Francis shook his head as he watched his son and knights run toward the dungeon, called by unknown noises. "You are all so willing to help your aunt even after all the evil things she's done?"

Elizabeth tilted her head as she looked at her father. "Isn't that what we're supposed to do?" She looked up at Cristine. "Why would we do anything else?"

Isabella stared across the bailey as she spoke the turnings of her mind: "I deem I feel sorry for her." Everyone looked at her. "Satan battles all of us, but she fell to him." She looked at the bishop. "Even if it was her choice, she chose him because he enticed her." She shook her head. "I mean, it is grace, isn't it? Grace is what keeps us from not falling?"

The bishop nodded. "Humility is the key to everything. If one is humble enough to accept the grace of God, then one shall not fall."

The king looked down. "Pride has always been her downfall." He shook his head. "I wish I could've done more when I was younger to help her."

"Stop. You can't blame yourself for your sister's deeds." Dominicus looked toward the sky. "If it was a fault from her childhood and if anyone is culpable beyond her, the fault lies with your parents, not you." The king lowered his head. The bishop's hand landed on his shoulder. "You have done what you can for her."

The bishop turned and walked toward the gatehouse, toward the cathedral. After watching him go, King Francis walked toward the training square. There he stood with Michael and watched with satisfaction as Nicholaus trained. "Sir Nicholaus trains with vigor now," he said.

"He does, indeed." Michael, taking a deep breath, suggested, "Sire, I think Sir Nicholaus should go with Prince Thomas. It's not good for him to be around things that make him think of her." The head knight slowly nodded. "He makes me think of myself when my family died."

"You got better." Francis looked at his friend with incredulity.

"I got better because I had a job to do—to defend your family, to go after the Demolites."

"So does Sir Nicholaus."

"He is a huntsman. He finds things," Michael said as he looked at his friend. "All he finds here are memories of what he will never have again." He looked back at the young knight. "He fights with passion now because he feels he must. If he is as I was, he wants to keep moving so he has less time to think of his loss. His heart needs to heal." The head knight shook his head. "It won't take place here. There is nowhere he can turn that there's not a memory of her." With a deep breath and a nod, he concluded, "Time heals all, but his time needs to be spent elsewhere. Let him do what he does best—find things. Let him find your son."

Setting his hands upon his hips, Francis stated, "We'll be back to three knights. Is that what you are asking?"

"Wouldn't you rather have a knight go with Prince Thomas than for Thomas to go alone?"

Francis lowered his hands as the image of Thomas, beaten by the Demolites, presented itself before him. He could not help but nod. "Send him to me."

❄

Mona's head shook in discombobulation as she knelt on her hands and knees, staring at the floor. "You lie!"

Camrina stood stoically. "I do not."

Infuriated and perplexed, she looked up at the chained prisoner. "For some reason, you are only *trying* to make me angry."

Camrina chuckled. "How you wish that were true." Squatting back down next to the distraught woman, she tilted her head. "Don't you see? You are of *my* making."

"No!" Shaking in fury, Mona pounced upon her like an animal with claws sharp and strong.

Camrina, pushed backward, bounced back with a more ferocious response. The young queen cried out in agony as Camrina thrust her upon the stones and pounded upon her. Unable to get away from the length of the chains, the older queen's fingers wrapped themselves around the younger's throat.

"What are you doing?" Peter called out as he rushed for the door, grabbing at the keys, followed by the prince and Sethelian knights.

"She's choking her!" William called out as he peered through the bars. "Open the door!"

Pulling the door open, Peter flew into the cell and ripped Camrina off her victim.

William glanced at his aunt in disgust as he pulled Mona away and then knelt down beside the abused and disoriented queen. "She's bleeding. It's above her eye." He looked at the queen in the corner. "What were you doing to her?"

Camrina focused upon Peter with frigid eyes containing a depravity of all things decent; he was forced to lower his gaze in humility—the only answer to the prideful bask of sinful premeditation in her eyes. Her delight revealed itself as it crept across her face into a smirk with an accompanying snicker. He shook his head in rejection of the vileness and turned away.

Sir Jacobus knelt down next to Prince Thomas. "How bad is it?"

"I don't know. I can't see very well." The prince looked at Sir Jacobus. "Let's take her into the light."

Shaking her throbbing head in her dazed state, Queen Mona was assisted up the stairs by Sir Jacobus and Sir Frankus.

Locking the prison bars, Peter glanced at the queen one last time before leaving her in the lonely darkness.

"What took place?" Elizabeth asked in astonishment as she watched the Sethelian knights help Mona onto a stone to sit.

Cristine, beside her sister, spotted the crimson and turned her head away as a lightheaded feeling came upon her. "Oh! There's blood."

"There was only one other person in the dungeon with her," William answered.

Isabella, mouth dropping open, rushed to the queen's side, as she pulled out a handkerchief and applied it to the bleeding eyebrow. "Aunt Camrina did this?"

"Well," Cristine spoke with her head turned, "if she could kill Grandmamá and Annie, harming Mona is nothing."

Elizabeth, stepping closer, pointed. "What's on her neck?"

"Liza," Isabella chided.

"She was choking her," Thomas said.

"They're bruises?" Elizabeth said with near amazement.

Isabella looked at her sister. "The blood is covered now, Crisa. You may look."

Turning her head toward the queen, Cristine studied Mona's whole stature. "Mona?" She knelt next to her sisters. "She must be harmed more than we know—she's not screaming to get away from your corrupted hands."

"Mona?" Isabella gently called.

Mona's eyes wandered around sporadically as her mind swirled with the information, pondering whether the revelations were true or false. *They touch me. They are nothing. But I? I am . . . nothing?* Anger bubbled up inside of her as she rejected her own thoughts. *I have to get away from here! I have to get away from these people—all of them!* Her eyes suddenly focused on the gatehouse. In her disorientation, she barreled through the princesses and swiftly fell, unaware of her own dizziness.

The world spun as she was lifted up, and a voice grew louder: "You're not going anywhere!"

Sir Melvon looked at Prince William. "What am I to do with her?"

"She can't go back with Camrina," Isabella insisted as she, picking up the bloody cloth, stood to place it on the queen's forehead. "She won't live."

William shook his head. "There is nowhere else to put her."

"We can rid you of her trouble." All eyes turned toward Sir Frankus. "We could take her when we go to the Sockorian Castle."

Jacobus nodded. "Yes, that is the only answer." He looked at Sir Melvon. "I'm sorry, my friend, but you are not rid of her yet."

Elizabeth tilted her head as she looked at her sister. "I thought Queen Mona was friends with Aunt Camrina." She looked up at Cristine. "Why would they fight each other?"

Cristine shook her head as she touched her sister's shoulder. "True friends they must not be."

"Until we leave, she'll have to be chained," Jacobus said.

"There are no more chains. Symon will have to make more," Thomas said.

"He's been working on some." Isabella looked around as she continued to press the cloth to Mona's face.

Cristine's fingers landed next to hers. "You go. I will hold it."

"Are you certain?"

Cristine, swallowing with difficulty, spotted a bit of crimson. "Be quick about it." She turned her head away.

"Are you certain you're alright?" William asked as he touched his sister on the shoulder.

"As long as she stands still and the cloth covers the blood." She looked at Sir Melvon. "Hold her tightly if you can."

William sighed heavily. "I must inform Papá."

Elizabeth raised her hand. "I will do it for you, Crisa."

Cristine smiled. "Thank you for the offer, but it must be pressed."

Elizabeth lowered her arm and her head. "You mean I'm too little?" She turned away.

"Liza," Cristine called her back. "You shall grow in time."

"Sir Nicholaus," King Francis said outside the temporary living quarters of the royal family.

The young knight approached the hut as the king's voice summoned him.

"Nicholaus, it's good to have you back." Lowering his head, Nicholaus felt the pressure of the king's hand upon it. "But I'm not so certain it's good for you to be here."

Nicholaus raised his gaze. "Sire, I will do my duty to—"

The king's hand halted him. "I know, Nicholaus." Taking a deep breath, the king looked to the evening sky. "You are true to your word. But I have another duty for you now: Prince Eduard. Thomas insists upon the duty himself, but I want you to go with him."

"But what of—"

"Your new duty is to find my son." A royal hand landed upon a knightly shoulder. "Annabelle's gone, but Eduard could still be alive. I pray he's alive at Camrina's castle." Gripping the knight's shoulder, he looked into his eyes. "Find him . . . and come back to us with a new strength for life."

As the party of three Sethelian knights, one disgruntled queen, the young Anchonian knight, and the second-in-line to the Anchonian throne mounted their horses, one servant stepped forward. "You are leaving now to find your princess?"

Everyone turned toward her, but it was Sir Melvon to whom she had addressed the question. "Rachel?" he asked with great surprise. "What are you doing here?"

"I . . ." She lowered her head. "I thought about your words and . . ." She glanced at the awaiting members of the convoy. "I wanted to say . . ." Seeing her difficulty getting her words out, the others took off toward the west.

Melvon looked at her from his horse as it danced in anticipation, wanting to run, too. "What?"

Slowly nodding, she looked at the horse's saddle. "You can be rough in your speech, but you have a quality of the highest value that I refused to see before." She shook her head as she admitted, "Your duty to your land and to your people is truly honorable." She lowered her gaze. "I am ashamed of the way I treated you and I beg your forgiveness." Taking a deep breath, she found his eyes. "I wish you well and I hope you find your princess and restore the Sethel crown to what it was meant to be." She quickly smiled. "With hope that there will be others to help, so you will come out alive." Returning to a serious face, she added, "If you were to die, it would be a loss for the world." Nodding her head in agreement with herself, she quickly bowed and stepped away.

"Sir Melvon, are you coming?" Sir Frankus had stopped his horse to call back to his fellow knight.

Melvon looked from Frankus back to where Rachel previously stood; she was hastening away into the crowd of villagers. With perplexity, he watched her disappear and, ruminating on her words, he forced his horse westward. *A loss for the world? Truly honorable?* Perplexed by the spoken words of respect, he spurred his horse to a quicker pace to catch up with the party.

WALVA ISLAND

Opening her eyes, Lina sat up, awakened by the screaming somewhere outside her hut. *What's going on?* Startling when her door opened, she scrambled to her feet. It was Ecwab, the interpreter.

"What do you want?" she yelled in the native tongue, fearful they had found out her treachery.

"You come!" Ecwab said as he grabbed her arm and yanked her from the warmth as she reached for her fur cloak. Pulling her toward the prison, he pointed at the agitated men. "You calm!" He shoved her forward.

"Where is she? What did you do with her?" the mariners yelled out in fury.

Wrapping the fur around her, she looked at the men. "What upsets you?"

Hearing the words without an accent, every eye turned toward her as one, stepping forward, grabbed the bars.

"We want to know what became of Annabelle," the captain said through gritted teeth. "Where is she?"

Annabelle? Is that her name? Lina cautiously looked at Ecwab through her periphery, not wanting to reveal too much. "She had her babies."

"Babies?" Captain Vitalis gripped the bars tighter. "More than one?"

"Twins." Her eyes quickly glanced at the Seafur.

Vitalis looked down and said with a calmer tone, "What became of her?"

"She ran into the woods." Lina shook her head. "I don't know anything past that."

"And the babies?"

"They were taken into the woods . . . to die."

"To die?" Face tightening, his eyes veered to the Seafur. "What have you done?" He shook the bars as the other mariners stepped forward, offering their dismay.

Heart beginning to race, Lina looked nervously from Acwa to Ecwab as he spoke in his tongue: "We've had enough out of them! We will kill them all now if you don't calm them."

"Spare them! They knew the woman. They wished to know where she is. Do you know?" she asked in the Seafurian tongue, for herself as much as for the men.

"She gone," the interpreter spoke.

Gone? Lina became sick to her stomach.

There was a moment of silence from the men and then an uproar. "They killed her!" Vitalis declared as he turned around to the mariners.

Ecwab stepped closer, pointing his finger. "She kill self when run to woods."

The men fell silent.

Killed herself? Lina looked at the Seafurs. "And the babies?" she spoke in their language.

"They don't cry. The wolves must have gotten them," the leader replied in his tongue. "You tell them. You calm them. They can't do anything. She's dead. Tell them."

Is it the truth? Turning back to the men, Lina said cautiously, "There . . . is no more crying now in the woods." She put up her hand. "Nothing can be done. If you do not calm yourselves, they will kill you all."

"Calm ourselves? After they killed her?"

Glancing at Acwa, she stepped closer and barely whispered: "They are heathens. Not only will they kill you, but they will offer you to their fiends." She looked into Vitalis's eyes. "Calm your men unless you want all of them to die."

As the frigid wind blew over them, Vitalis turned around. "She's gone. We can't help her any longer but by our prayers." He lowered his head as the last whisps of smoke rose from the charred remains of the wooden pieces they'd ripped from between their cage's bars.

Katara watched the Seafurian men arm themselves with spears and blunt objects. Looking at another resident of her hut, she questioned in her tongue, "Do they need all that to find one woman and her babies?"

"Yocht, pa lay dafod," the woman answered back, meaning, "Yes, for the evil."

"Why did they tell the slaves she was already dead?"

The woman, tilting her head, looked at her. "Because it will all be true by the end of the day, after the sacrifices are made."

Setting her feet upon the earth, Annabelle turned back to the small cave after stretching her arms and picked up her babies. "We have to find a safer place." She glanced over her shoulder. "It must be much farther from the huts." With light from the sun and more warmth than the previous evening, she set out on her journey with her babies wrapped tightly in the wool blanket and fur.

Walking deeper into the woods, she was nervously aware of every sound. If it were just her, she would have no fear, but since she had two defenseless babies depending upon her, there was a hypervigilance arising from within. She had to stay alive so they would live. She paused when she heard the same call from the horn as was blown when her baby boy was intended to be a sacrifice. *Who do they kill now? Did they find out the lady helped me? Is it the girls? Is it the mariners?* With a new determination, she gripped her dear babies stronger and quickened her pace away from the village.

Watching the herd of men take to the forest with their weapons after the last bowl of blood was poured out on the sacrificial stone, Katara stepped away from the pile of smoking small bodies as the rest of the villagers descended to their huts. Turning back around, she looked at the lifeless remains being consumed with fire. Glancing back at the trees, all the men had disappeared into the forest on their hunt for the green-eyed one. Taking a quick breath, she ran down the hill and through the village at her fastest pace and only slowed when she neared the northeastern bluffs overlooking the huts. Coming to the bluffs, she silently slipped to the northern side and went through the natural tunnels only known by a handful of people throughout time.

Twisting her way through the dark maze, she stepped out of the tunnel on the southern side of the bluffs high above the sea and village. Closing her eyes, she felt the biting wind taking her breath away. Pressing forward, she opened her eyes and carefully followed the ridge westward until she had a grand view of the island. From her position, much higher than the trees, she gazed over the acres of woods and grasslands, streams and caves, prey and predators.

Deep into the forest after hours of searching, Annabelle came upon another stone wall, much larger than the first, rising from the hills around it. Nearly exhausted, she made her way to the structure to investigate the solidness. Tilting her head, she approached a darkness that appeared, from a distance, to only be a shadow of the stones around. Placing her hand in front of the small hole at the base of the stones, she felt the rush of warm air. *What's in it? Has some creature claimed it as its home? Father, should I go in?* She leaned against the stone as she closed her eyes. *I'm so tired and hungry.* She pushed herself away from the wall. "I don't have time to eat."

When a flock of birds flew to the heavens, Annabelle's focus turned to the forest and the noises now emanating from a distance away but drawing nearer. As she intently listened, she heard voices from the strange language of the Seafurian people upon the wind. *Oh, no! This far away, they still search?* As one baby began to cry, she gently bounced them both. Lowering her head to their faces, she whispered to them, "If ever I needed you quiet, I need it now." Turning back to the cave, she scooted herself through the cave feet-first, contorting her way through the tightness that skinned her extended abdomen, as she pulled her babies toward her. If there was an animal inside, she wanted it to greet her first.

Turning around inside the cave, she was welcomed by darkness but for a thin stream of light from up above. Hearing the voices outside, she swiftly found her way to a corner.

Pressed up against the cavern wall, Annabelle hid in the darkness as she fed her children, silently praying the village men would give up on their search. *Can they think me dead? Please, can they think us dead?* With a pounding heart, she heard their voices growing louder. When a Seafur stopped outside the opening, she froze. As more and more light was blocked through the little opening by his feet, she pushed herself into the wall, wishing it could somehow consume her so, at that moment, she was the wall.

The voice turned in the opposite direction as words were spoken and more light appeared. Just as she was beginning to release the stale air within her, torchlight painted the cavern opening with visibility as an arm extended through the hole. "Lina, sidinta?" She watched in horror as the large, buff man tried to squeeze through the tight slot. "Lina, sidinta?"

Go away. Go away. Go away! Father, I cry out to You for help! She squeezed her babies so tightly, she was surprised they did not cry, but the light from the distant torch revealed weakly that they were both soundly asleep after their feeding. Glancing back at the glow, she watched an ember shake free and fall upon the man's hand. Reacting quickly to the heat, he dropped the torch and could not retrieve it as it rolled away, his body too large to squeeze farther through the opening.

"Lina sidinla?" another man's voice spoke, and the searcher's hand pulled out of view.

"Nacht," the searcher replied as he turned away from the cave completely and the original light from the opening bathed the cavernous innards as much as it possibly could.

As she heard their voices quieting by the distance, she put her hand over her mouth to conceal her cries. *Father, You have spared us from being found! Thank You!* Closing her eyes for a moment, a tear of relief released and rolled down her cheek. Looking down at her babies, she spoke to them quietly. "We're going to be alright. The Father is tending to us."

Taking a deep breath, Annabelle pushed herself up and retrieved the torch. Rising from the ground with her babies in her right arm, she watched as the light from the fire revealed a spacious, beautiful creation full of stalagmites and stalactites. Carefully stepping down the layers of rock, she could not help but think of the first cave into which she ventured with Peter upon the Forbidden Island.

"How tall do you think this cave is?"

"I don't know."

"Truly right."

So consumed with the majesty of God from the marvel of His creation, she dropped to her knees. "Do you see, Auggie and Claudi, even in this land filled with such evil, God is with us? He reveals Himself through His creation!" She could not help but smile. "It will all be alright. He is with us, and He will never leave us alone! He never forsakes His people—He has given His Word! He calls us all to Himself, and everything that takes place is His call for us to come closer to Him! That must be what He wants of me—complete trust in Him! I will trust in You, Father. Help me to trust in You."

Annabelle walked deeper into the cave with the torch in her hand. A moment later, her mouth dropped open as she beheld a pond hidden in the shadows. She curiously watched as light began to paint the farthest wall toward the ceiling of the cave. "How odd." Moving to the side, she followed the path of the light to its source. "There must be another opening up there. But how to get to it?"

Walking toward the side with the upper level, she studied the wall with the light from the torch. "It could be climbed if I had both arms to use." She gently shook her babies. "It shall have to wait." Sitting down near the cave pond, she watched as more and more light streamed in from the upper level and lit the pond to reveal the bluest water she had ever seen. She hardly noticed when the torch burned out.

WHITE WOLF

Carefully scanning the northern part of Walva Island from her perch high above the village, Katara caught the quick movement of a tiny, white speck below. Moving with haste, she ran to the cave opening and snaked her way through the inner passages until she arrived at the foot of the bluffs. "Sna? Sna? Ditsidida?" she called out to the woods. As a white wolf appeared, she knelt down with a smile. The albino animal gladly came to her call.

Rubbing the wolf's head, she pulled out a small piece of wool soaked in blood. "Esa lina. Forgumla? Forgumla lina?"

The wolf smelled the wool and then, walking backwards with a whine, she turned toward the woods and took off. "Sna?"

Smiling, Katara stood and followed after.

Annabelle held her stomach as it grumbled fiercely, and her babies began to fuss. Looking around cautiously, what she really wanted to do was collapse. Instead, she tried to calm her babes.

"Shh, shh, shh. I know it's cold out here, but I have to find something to eat."

Finding a rock, she knelt down to pick it up. Once down, she took a moment's respite. "I have to make a knife, you see. We will get nowhere without something sharp." Switching her children to her left arm, she grasped the rock in her right. With a burst of energy, she stood and hurled it against the cave wall, quickly turning around to protect her babies from any shards that might fly their way. *Was I wrong to leave Lina? Should I have let her stay with us and risk her life? It would have been much easier; she at least could have watched you two so I could have two arms to hunt.*

Turning around, she found the biggest hunk of broken rock and investigated its sharpness. Broken in half, one edge was as sharp as a razor, though there was no tip. *Will it do? It shall have to.* Hearing a noise, she turned around quickly and looked to the forest. *Have they come back looking for us?* Staring into the darkness, she knew someone was there. Not wanting to give away the entrance to the cave, she ran to the edge to see who was in search of her.

Hiding behind the wall, she closed her eyes for a moment. *Father, I trust in You. You are allowing this for the salvation of my soul and Your greater glory.* She pressed her stomach as it grumbled more. *I'm so hungry. Why can't this place be like the Forbidden Island with plenty of berries?* She shook her head at the irony of plenty when satisfied and scarcity when in dire need. *Father, I need Nicholaus!*

As she heard a creature draw closer, she peeked around the rock to see a white wolf sticking out amongst the gray of the rocky formation. Gripping the broken rock, she brought it closer to her body, preparing for its release if needed.

"Sna? Forgumla?"

It's a Seafur! But it sounded like the voice of a child. She pressed herself against the rock. *How many are here?* Closing her eyes, she listened intently. *Not many.* Opening her eyes, she turned to look around the rock.

She watched in wonder as a girl searched around the opening of the cave. *Only one girl and a wolf?*

"Canoodo? Sna, lina a canoodo?" the girl said. The wolf whined as the canine sniffed the entrance and around it. As she made her way toward the princess, Annabelle stood and backed against the wall, readying her rock.

"Sna?" Katara followed the wolf over. When it started to yelp, Katara touched her back and walked forward. "Lina?" Shaking her head, Katara looked to the rock and said awkwardly, "An-na-bell?"

She knows my name?! Hidden behind the rock, the princess froze, unsure if that was a good or a bad thing. Pushing herself into the wall, she shook her head. *Please, Father, make her go away! I don't want my children to become sacrifices!*

"An-na-bell?" the girl repeated.

As Annabell's stomach growled even louder, she sunk down to the ground. *Your will, Father. Nothing but Your will.* Hearing the noises dissipating, the princess cautiously peeked around the rock to see that the girl walking into the woods.

Releasing a sigh of relief once the animal and Seafur were no longer around, Annabelle stood up, shaking with nerves and hunger. "You have spared us yet again, Father!" About to cry from happiness and stress, she retreated back to the cave opening with a dash.

Watching the light slowly fade from the opening in the upper terrace, Annabelle sat in the cave pondering how she was to survive. She scraped at the end of a stick with her makeshift half-arrowhead as her stomach still angrily growled. "Father, I see now: I can't do this by myself. I was full of pride. If You want me to find food, You need to help me." Closing her eyes, she shook her head at herself. "I trust in You. I do. But it's hard when I'm so hungry and it's so cold!" Opening her eyes, she placed more sticks on her fire. "You two need to stay nice and warm!" *If it is this cold now, how will it be in winter?* Looking to the stalactites, she said, "I will trust it You."

"An-na-bell, sidinta?"

Panic arising within her, the princess grabbed her sleeping children and fled to the protective corner as the light from the small entrance was blocked.

"An-na-bell? There?"

Annabelle held her breath. *Who is this girl? Is she speaking* my *tongue now?* She shook her head in disbelief. *It can't be!*

"Sna, legaswe." She heard the whine of a wolf with the girl's sounds.

Holding her breath, Annabelle listened intently until she heard no more sounds. Looking at the entrance, she curiously approached it, for the light was still blocked. Upon her hands and knees, she looked through the hole. *There's something there.*

Crawling partly through, she reached her hand out and touched fur. Her heart pounded uncontrollably as she backed out from the entrance and looked at the dead rabbit in her grasp. She cried in shock and relief. "It's a hare! Auggie, Claudi, that girl brought us food!"

Shaking her head, she looked back to the hole to see if there were any signs of the girl. "Why would she do that? Father, thank You for her! But please don't let her tell her people where I am! Bless her, Father. Bless her abundantly!"

Watching the hand that extended from the cave entrance drag the body of the hare inside the cave, Katara petted the wolf beside her. "Sna, forgumla!"

Turning to the forest, she stood as she heard men's voices a distance away. Gasping, she picked up the other dead hare beside her. "Vermasla?" She shook her head. "Nocht vermasla!" She dashed into the forest.

MOVEMENT

Nicholaus looked at the bag of coins in Thomas's hand as they stood with the Sethelian knights and their captive, Queen Mona, in Port Salisburg. It had been a few weeks since they had left Aboly.

"Do you think that will be enough to get us a ship and crew daring enough to go to the Sockor Islands?" he asked the prince.

Thomas tilted his head. "I deem we shall find who's brave enough and faithful to the crown." Scanning the port, his mouth opened when he spotted an uncommon ship anchored in the port. "Look at that strange ship. What do you make of it?"

Nicholaus shrugged his shoulders. "It's not like any I've ever seen."

Thomas, looking into the distance, tilted his head. "Could that be Camrina's?" He slowly smiled as he nodded. "The *Sockortale*."

Nicholaus looked at the prince from his periphery. "What are you thinking?"

Thomas held up the coins. "We might not need this after all. Who wouldn't want to be a mariner on the quickest ship of the sea?"

"Her mariners might not take too kindly to the intrusion," one of the Sethelian knights, Sir Jacobus, stated.

Thomas looked at all of the knights. "Are her mariners a larger issue than you can handle? They are, after all, the men that took your wife and your princess."

Nicholaus swallowed hard as he took a deep breath. "They won't be trouble at all."

"Who are you?" a mariner called out as he freely surrendered to the armed knights before him.

"I am Sir Nicholaus Hunts, and you all are being arrested by the crown of Anchony."

All of the mariners but the one who spoke looked at one another in a panic.

"That's right," Thomas said as he stepped aboard from the rowboat, pulling Queen Mona alongside him. "Your queen is not ruling anything."

The mariner knelt before the knights, offering his arms to be tied. "You speak truth?"

Thomas, walking toward the man, looked at him. "Who are you?"

"My name is Warinus."

Another man, walking past the one surrendering, demanded, "I am the captain of this ship. If you speak, you speak to me!"

Thomas looked at the captain. "Alright, Captain, where does your fealty lie?" He stepped away to address all the men. "You see, we are taking this ship—"

"You will not—" the captain began, but was forced on to his knees when Sir Melvon kicked the back of his leg and drew his dagger.

"You don't understand. You don't have a choice," Prince Thomas said. Taking a deep breath, he glanced out at the ocean and then back to the mariners. "It was you that killed my sister and took my brother and the princess of Sethel."

"We were following the queen's orders," the captain insisted, scared of the knife next to his throat.

Thomas looked at him in disgust. "Following the queen's orders? You are so obedient that you do what is wrong and say that it is right because you are following orders?" Thomas turned away in disgust. "Get them off of this ship."

"What do you want us to do with them once they are off?" Sir Jacobus asked as he bound the captain's hands and pulled him up.

"They shall be yoked and marched to Aboly!" Prince Thomas declared.

"Is the queen there? In Aboly?" Warinus asked as he dared to look at the prince.

"Captured—as you are," Nicholaus said as he pulled him up.

"Who is to march them to Aboly?" Frankus asked as he bound a mariner and pulled him up.

"We shall find someone trustworthy."

Elizabeth sighed heavily. "How long will Thom be gone?"

"As long as it takes to get to the Sockorian castle and back with Edus," Cristine said, carrying a pile of papers. They were walking toward the blacksmith shop after another long day of writing names. Word had spread outside of Aboly, and people were coming from all directions to tell them of their missing children.

"I wish they were here already."

Cristine, smiling, looked at her sister. "Am I truly *that* dull?" She sighed, too, as she looked at the busy villagers and servants. "It's only been a few weeks—they're probably not even out of Anchony yet."

"Princess! Princess!" Cristine and Elizabeth turned toward the woman's voice as she struggled to curtsy in front of them with a child on her hip.

"Yes?" Cristine asked cautiously.

The woman jogged forward, tapping on the child's leg she held at her side. "You are the one taking names?"

Cristine looked at the toddler in the woman's grasp. "Are you missing a child?"

"No. I have too many." Cristine tilted her head as the woman, stepping closer, presented the child in her arms to the princess. "This is Mabel. I thought maybe you would know of someone who would want her."

"You don't want your daughter?" Elizabeth asked in shock as she looked at the little girl.

The woman shook away the question as if it was silly. "She's not mine." She looked over her shoulder at a man surrounded by children. "I have three of my own. We don't know how we will tend to them." She held Mabel out to the princess.

Cristine hesitantly took her. "Whose child is this, then?"

"Her mother was young. She died giving birth."

"And her father?"

"A Demolite." The woman looked down as if it caused pain to speak the words.

"Oh." Cristine looked into the dirty face of the girl in her arms.

"Can you find parents for her? I thought maybe with the names . . ."

"But they want to find *their* children," Elizabeth said as she looked between her sister and the woman.

"Certainly if they are in want of their child, they will take *a* child," the woman said with all hope. "I was her wet nurse. She is weaned now. Our town is scattered. I don't know where any of the girl's family is. Can you help?" She offered the child toward Cristine.

Cristine looked into the woman's pleading face and then cautiously stepped forward to take the little girl. "I will . . . try."

"Thank you! Thank you dearly!" The woman graciously smiled and, after squeezing Mabel's hand, backed away as she bowed. "I do wish I could keep her, but I can't!" She eagerly scurried to her husband, and they quickly left the empty marketplace.

Cristine looked into the eyes of the child she held. "Mabel?"

The little girl looked up at her with big brown eyes.

The youngest princess took the little girl's hand. "I'm Liza." The big, brown eyes turned her way. Elizabeth looked up at her sister. "Does she smile?"

Cristine grimaced. "Her face is so dirty, I deem we couldn't tell if she did."

"So, this woman left her with you?" Isabella asked as she knelt down next to Cristine.

Nodding, Cristine looked to her eldest sister. "Isa, you wouldn't want her, would you?"

"Crisa . . ." Isabella watched Elizabeth struggle over to them with a bucket of water. After she'd nearly spilled all of it halfway to her destination, Symon picked it up easily from her. ". . . she can't take Emma's place."

Cristine shook her head. "I don't want her to take Emma's place. I want Mabel to be loved for who she is."

Symon set the bucket down. "If you can't find a home for her, we'll take her."

Isabella nodded. "Yes. Ask the others first, though." She turned her head. "Tending to Emma was what God wanted of me, but now I know, I am to spend my time praying for Aunt Camrina."

Taking a breath, Cristine wet the cloth and wiped the dirt

from the child's precious skin. "Well," she said, "no one would take *this* child from you since her mother is dead and her father is an unknown Demolite."

Isabella looked back at her sister's busy hands. "Ask around, please." She rose to stand next to her husband.

Working busily, Cristine eyed her sister as she spoke her mind in a lowered tone: "You shouldn't have tried to use another for Annie's place."

Isabella, hearing her sister's comment, took a ragged breath. "Crisa, it wasn't like that. It was my chance to—"

All of them turned to look toward the north as a flock of birds flew noisily out of the trees. They could hear distant murmurings from within the arbors, and then as they watched, a group of thirty or so people emerged from the woods.

"Who are they?" Elizabeth asked as Cristine placed the child upon her hip and she stood to watch the figures draw near.

Elizabeth's mouth dropped open in excitement as she looked at her sisters. "It's Clare!" She ran toward her long-lost friend, the daughter of the Lion.

Isabella looked with concern at the crowd. "It's the servants from south of the hidden haven."

Cristine nodded as she sighed. "And with them comes the traitor."

While walking into the bailey, the mouths of the castle's servants dropped as they beheld the destruction. The multitude of eyes looked from the village masons to the Demolites forced to labor with the cleanup and construction to the trainees attempting to hone what little skills they had to the broken castle. Cleaner than it once appeared in its damaged state, the fallen stones had been gathered into strategic piles, and the walls of the castle were beginning to rise higher.

"Watch them keenly. See if one approaches Lord Rackus or if he attempts to speak with any of them. This traitor will be found out," Francis said to his childhood friends.

There were whisperings within the crowd as Sir Michael, the Lion, and the king approached. One servant finally shouted out in glee, "He lives! King Francis lives!"

Smiles broke forth as the throng began to bow to their monarch.

The three men eyed them all cautiously, but no one stood out from the crowd. No one gave away his treacherous tendencies.

Ikus the head butler, stepping beside Prince William, looked at the destroyed castle and shook his head. "I can't believe it. To think something so strong could be in so many pieces."

William glanced at him. "This looks far better than it did before." He pointed with his hands. "The walls are twice the height they were a couple weeks ago."

Silus the Steward stepped forward, looking at what was left of the library. "What became of the books from Anchelo?"

"Prince Thomas couldn't help himself—my brother had to save them from the conditions of being in a broken castle."

Ikus nodded.

"That's good." The steward smiled. "After the Demolites attacked Anchelo, not many books are left up there."

William glanced at him. "You've been to Anchelo since the Demolites sacked it?"

Ikus nodded. "Yes. It is a pitiful sight. The hospital and university are in shambles now. The monks lived only by hiding under the monastery."

Silus, staring at the broken castle, looked at the prince from his periphery. "Where did he place them?"

"Place what?" Prince William asked.

"The books."

"They are in our home."

The steward's eyes studied the curvature of the rising fortress wall. "Ah. Very good."

Ikus shook his head as he released a deep breath. "I can't believe this is the castle."

Tilting his head, Francis squatted down and dug at the shimmer in the ground. Pulling out a pence coin, he rubbed it with his thumb, noticing the "F" he had carved into it, as he remembered the first time he had held it.

A smile crested the prince's young face as he looked at the shiny coin resting in his hand. His countenance spoke nothing but gratitude as he eyed the vendor before him whose vegetables he had just helped save from some escaped pigs at the market. "Thank you."

"No. Thanks is to you and your friends."

There was a tug upon his sleeve. "Francis, let's go."

Closing his hand, he glanced at the younger Jous and Michael before looking back at the vendor. "I shall treasure it always!"

"You still have that?" Michael asked as he walked up beside him. "You carried it with you through all you suffered with the Demolites?"

"No." He shook his head in amazement. "I found it here." Taking a deep breath, he looked up at his friend. "We have to bring it back—the market, the city, all of Aboly. It needs to return to what it once was."

"I agree—without the Demolites, of course." Michael tilted his head. "What are your thoughts?"

Staring at the coin, he nodded his head. "All things are better when you have your own part in it, are they not?" He stood. "We let the people work."

Michael nodded with hesitation. "There are many people, Sire. If everyone does his own part, there will be many parts and not a whole."

Francis looked across the bailey at the master mason. "One needs to be in charge." His eyes found their way to his friend. "The steward?" He slowly nodded, agreeing with himself. "I'll place him in charge of it all."

Sir Narkalus of Monakala, dressed not as a knight but as a noble emissary, stood at the gatehouse in Salone in Sethel with King Marcus's note in hand. "I have a message from King Marcus of Monakala."

A guard, walking forward, stuck out his hand to receive it.

"He demands I deliver in person."

The guard glanced at his fellow guard and said, "Then your protection stays out here."

"I assent," Sir Narkalus said. As the gate opened, he nodded quickly at the two other Monakalian knights, standing to his left and right.

"Your Highness, Monakala sends another message," a guard informed Prince Howercus inside the Great Hall. "This time it's in person."

Howercus glanced at Lord Cortell with panic. "King Marcus sends a messenger, not a bird!" He looked around frantically. "He wants Captain Anguis, but Anguis is mine! He can't have him!"

"It is good, then, that we don't know where Captain Anguis is," Lord Cortell whispered in reply as he looked upon the messenger standing in the doorway. "You should not deny Monakala what she wants. You do not want her as a foe."

Sir Narkalus assessed the room and then looked at the prince. "King Henrard?"

Howercus nervously looked at Cortell and then said, "My brother perished in Anchony."

"Prince Phillipus?" Sir Narkalus asked as he walked farther into the room.

"He too—all of them. All dead. All gone."

"Hmm," Narkalus said as he offered the scroll, which Cortell retrieved and handed to the prince. "King Marcus sent a message earlier. Was it received?"

"Message? Message? What message? No, there's not been any message from Monakala," Prince Howercus looked at Lord Cortell to back up his lie. Lord Cortell remained silent.

"Well, I shall get to the point of that message and this one. A Captain Anguis, while flying the Sethelian flag, has taken many Monakalian merchant ships. King Marcus has placed a bounty on his head. The knights are here to bring him back to Monakala to face justice."

"You can't have him!" Howercus said in a panic as he jumped up from the throne.

Cortell blocked the royal from attacking the man. "Your Highness, this is a Monakalian messenger! King Marcus will not take lightly any harm to one of his men." As Howercus stepped back, Cortell added in a whisper, "Don't start a war that Sethel can't win! Sit down . . . Your Highness."

Howercus reluctantly complied.

Narkalus, watching the interaction, flared his nostrils when Lord Cortell turned back around. "So a pirate was working for Sethel? Working to assault Monakalian merchant ships?"

Cortell shook his head. "Sethel, too, has a price upon the pirate's head. Prince Howercus is angry at the pirate and wishes to find him to give him justice."

"Justice is due to the people of Monakala," Sir Narkalus insisted.

"You can't have him! He is mine! That traitor!" Howercus yelled out from the throne.

Cortell looked between the two men. "Well, he's not here and he's not been found. Justice—for all—shall have to wait."

Sir Narkalus folded his arms. "Then I will wait, for Monakala shall get her man."

BOOK OF ACCOUNTS

Clare, with arms loaded with sticks she had gathered, walked from the forest to the path in front of the royal house. She stopped in her path as a person she had not heard approaching passed in front of her. She glanced up in time to see a man carrying something thick within his arms, mostly covered by furs. Looking at his previous path, she noted his journey had to begin from the wattle and daub house in which the royal family temporarily resided; the door was ajar.

"Clare?" Samus, carrying sticks in his right arm, asked as he came up the path behind her, along with Stephanus, who brought two freshly killed squirrels with their front legs tied together with thin rope. Continuing on in her original task, Clare walked to the campfire and dropped the sticks, and then turned to track the man with her eyes. Samus noted her strange behavior. "Clare? What's wrong?"

She watched the back of the man quickly walking away. "Tha man staward, righd?" She nodded in his direction.

Samus, turning to where she pointed, viewed no one, as the

man had just disappeared around a hut. "I don't see anyone. What about him?" he asked as he set down the sticks he carried.

She shook her head. "I da knaw." She sat down on the ground, looking at the area in which he'd disappeared.

"Here you go." Stephanus offered once the dead squirrels were untied.

Samus stood to take one of the squirrels from Stephanus. As Samus knelt back down to prepare it, Clare stood up. "Clare? What are you doing?"

Not hearing him, she wandered the direction the man had gone.

"Where's she going?" Stephanus asked.

Samus shook his head. He pulled the dagger out of the animal, stood up, and began following his sister.

Having followed his sister as she weaved between the huts to the west of the market, he found her staring at one of the communal campfires for the Abolian residents. In the middle of the day, this firepit was abandoned except for one person. "Clare?"

His sister's eyes were fixated upon the steward and the item the man had just placed within the flames. When Samus touched her, her heart nearly pounded out of her chest as she turned around in fright.

"What are you doing?" Samus asked his sister as she appeared to be concealing herself behind a hut.

Clare's eyes were caught by the sight of the prince approaching the man.

"Silus?" Prince William addressed the man as the steward threw more wood on the fire.

Hearing his name spoken, the steward, standing beside the fire, turned around and awkwardly bowed to Prince William. "Your Highness. To what do I owe this visit?"

William tilted his head as he stepped closer to the fire, looking around the man. "Are you burning something?"

"No." The man, moving quickly, bent down to pick up some sticks and threw them on to the fire. "I am building the fire larger, that's all. The days are getting colder."

"That they are." William stepped closer. "I thought it looked like fur."

"No." The steward shook his head. "Why would I burn fur? It is only sticks."

The prince, looking cautiously at him, cleared his throat. "The king wishes for Aboly to be what it once was, with the market and people. He places you in charge of this. Do you assent?"

Moving hesitantly, Silus stepped forward. "Of course, whatever the king wishes."

Clare looked at her brother. "Whad tha say?"

"Who?"

She looked at the prince and the steward. "Tha man and prance."

Samus looked toward the two men and shook his head. "Prince William was asking him to lead the city being built." He shook his head. "We shouldn't be listening to their—"

"Prance poin ta fir. Wha hay say abou fir?"

"Prince William asked if the steward was burning the fur. We shouldn't be listening to their words to each other." He took her arm. "Let's go."

Refusing to move, she looked back at the two men. "Whad hay say?"

"He said it's only sticks."

Clare's mouth dropped open as she shook her head. Her glance turned back to the prince as he walked away from the steward. "Na! Hay lie!"

Samus shook his head. "Who lied? Clare, I don't have time for this. I have to help Stephanus with the squirrels."

She tapped her brother on his chest. "Ya tell ham."

"Tell who what?"

"Tha prance. Tha man lied."

"About what?"

"At was-ant stacs."

Samus shook his head. "I don't have time right now, Clare. I will later."

"Ga naw!"

"So he's not burning sticks?" He shook his head, not under-standing why she was burdened by what she perceived. "Look, Clare, if you think it's a pressing matter, you tell him."

She stepped back at the preposterous idea. "Na ma."

"Why not? You're the one who saw it. Do you think he won't listen?"

"Na," she said softly and then looked toward the path the prince took. "Hay man."

Nervously entering the bailey, Clare bit her lip and lowered her head as she looked at the large gathering of men there. *Do I truly need to say something? Yes, I must! The steward lied to him.* Swallowing the massive lump in her throat, she moved to the most intact stone wall and cautiously walked to the training area. *If Papá is here, he will tell him for me.* She looked around eagerly for her father. *I don't see him!* She pushed her perspiring palm against the rough stone as she neared the white boundary of the training area.

Mustering courage from somewhere within, after several minutes of internal dialogue, she pushed herself away from the wall and walked with her head down toward the periphery of the training square. Stopping behind the prince, it took several more seconds of self-encouragement to speak his name.

Turning toward her, he looked at her in astonishment. "Clare! It's good to see you. So good." Shaking his head, he cleared his throat. "You're much better than the last time I saw you."

She stood, froze in fright, with her head lowered.

"Can I help you?" He looked around in shock as his heart beat quickly, realizing she did not hear a word he spoke. "Do you need something?" He glanced around to see if the Lion was in need. "Does Sir Josephus need something? Or Samus?" His eyes returned to her, desperately wanting her to look up at him.

"I nad say . . ." She could not finish her sentence. Shaking her head nervously, she stared at his feet.

He looked at her cautiously. "What do you need to tell me?" Stepping closer, he dared to touch her on the side of her arm.

She slowly looked up. Fright plastered across her face.

A mix of emotions swept over him as he whispered, "You can trust me, Clare. You know that, right?"

"I knaw." She immediately lowered her gaze.

"I won't hurt you," he pleaded for her to truly understand. Standing there, waiting for her to speak, he gently moved his hand to her elbow as he stepped closer, wanting her to look up.

Feeling the strength of his hand upon her arm, she was suddenly reminded that this was the man who had carried her through the northern woods of Aboly to Anchelo when they had to flee from the castle. He was the reason she stood safely where she was. An overwhelming peace came down upon her, and for a moment, she forgot the reason she stood there.

He slightly lifted her elbow as if to prompt her to lift her head. "Clare, what is it? Will you tell me what's wrong?"

Suddenly remembering the steward, she slightly looked up and said, "Hay lied ta ya." Her head promptly lowered.

William shook his head. "Who? Who lied to me?" Fidgeting, he prompted, "Clare?"

Looking up at him and finding true concern in his eyes, she revealed, "Tha sta-ward." Heart beating wildly, she looked away, for the intensity of his eyes were too much to bear.

Tilting his head, his voice turned stern. "Lied about what?"

Breathing heavily, she stepped away at the strained tone in the prince's voice.

He shook his head and offered his hand as an apology. "I'm sorry. I'm so sorry!" Clearing his throat, he used a calmer voice. "What was the lie?"

"Hay tak bak. Hay burn bak."

"He was burning a book? I thought I saw fur."

Nodding, she added, "Tha bak wa in fir."

He slightly gasped when he understood her meaning. "The book was wrapped in fur?"

She nodded, barely looking at him.

Shaking his head, he placed his hands upon his hips. "You saw him?" Grabbing her hand, he squeezed it. "Thank you, Clare."

Watching him sprint away, she found her way to the castle wall, away from others, and rested against it. She had never felt such safety and such peace; she did not know what to do about it. She wanted to cry. She wanted to marvel. *Why?* Needing to get away from all the other eyes within the bailey, she awkwardly tried to hide her face with her raven hair as she hurried back to her brother.

❄

Dumping the water upon the fire, nothing but smoke filled Prince William's vision for several moments. Wafting it away with his left hand, he used his right to dig through the ashes and charred wood with his sword. There was no sign of a book or of animal skins. If they had been there before, the flames had completely consumed them.

Hearing movement, he turned to see the steward approaching. "What were you burning?" he asked.

"Sticks, Your Highness, like I said before."

William, shaking his head, stepped closer. "No. I was told you were burning a book. I want to know what you burned."

"A book?" he asked, as though William were playing. He shook his head as he slightly laughed. "Whomever told you that mistook what he saw. I think highly of books. I would not burn one." His face turned serious. "Do you think I'm hiding something?"

William looked directly into his eyes. "So, you aren't?"

"No."

"Give me your word."

"I give you my word." He shook his head as he looked the prince in the eyes. "I'm not hiding anything."

"Prince William?" Samus called as he watched the royal walk toward the rising wattle and daub home.

With a distraught face, William looked at the Lion's son. "Samus, I want to speak to your sister."

Clare, catching his figure and still stewing over the peace she had felt, looked at him in wonder from across the living quarters being constructed.

"She's over there." Samus nodded in the direction of the far wall.

William walked inside. Waiting until he was close enough for her to see his lips, he said, "I didn't find a book."

"It born," she answered quickly.

William shook his head. "There wasn't a book, Clare. He gave me his word."

"But I sa bak." Her mouth dropped open as she declared, "Hay a liar!"

William, taking a deep breath, searched for the right words. Stepping closer, pleading for understanding, he said, "Are you certain you didn't see wrong?"

"Na!" she insisted. "Hay burn bak! Hay tar up and pot on far. I say ham."

"Clare, maybe it only looked like a book," Samus offered as he stepped up next to the prince.

Clare's mouth dropped open at the betraying words. "Ya dan't bay-lave may eitha?" Shaking her head, she turned away from both of them as tears of anger began to roll down her cheeks.

"Could it have been a branch that looked like a book?" Stephanus offered from his position across the room as he looked at Clare.

"Yes, perhaps it was a branch that looked like a book," Samus repeated for his sister to hear after tapping her on the shoulder.

With a reddened face, she swung her head around. "Na branch! Ita bak!" Looking between her brother, Stephanus, and the prince, she jumped over the wall being built, needing to get away from the suffocating stares that did not think her capable of correctly seeing.

"Clare!" She moved her arm away when her brother tried to grab her.

Prince William swallowed with difficulty as he watched her run away. *What have I done? Am I to believe her or the steward that gave his word? She's angry with me.*

But what if he's the traitor? He was disgusted by his own thought. *Silus?* His heart began to race.

Elizabeth, spotting Clare run away from the future shelter toward the woods , followed her over. "Clare?"

Clare, having collapsed at the base of the tree in distress, looked up when she saw movement. "Leeza, ga way."

The youngest princess sat down beside her. "What's wrong?"

Clare, with her reddened eyes, looked up toward the home. "Tha daunt bay-lave may."

Elizabeth looked to the wattle and daub structure to see her brother and Clare's looking at them. "Will and Samus?"

Her tears turned from anger to pain. "Tha daunt thank I say." Shaking her head, she looked at the princess. "Cause I daunt hare well?" Clare was confused.

With a concerned countenance, Elizabeth looked into her eyes. "What didn't you see?"

"I did say! Tha thank I daunt! I did!"

"What?"

"Tha sta-ward—hay barn bak. Ya bor-dare na say in far, so hay thank it na thare." She looked over at her brother. "An Sam-mas na bay-lave may!"

Elizabeth touched her arm. "I know how you feel. When I met Annie, she fought the Demolites in the woods, but no one believed me when I told them." The princess, taking a deep breath, looked into the trees. "It's like I'm too young for them to believe. I'm too young to help with a lot of things."

Clare shook her head. "I na a lil' garl." A fresh tear graced her pale skin. "Tha thank I am." She looked at Elizabeth's profile. "Ya'll graw ap. Tha'll al-ways thank may lil' garl."

Elizabeth looked back at the woman. "Clare, I'm sorry." The princess was not quite sure what to say; she felt selfish at the moment as she realized the truth in Clare's words: One day she would be grown and would be believed, but Clare would always be looked upon as a child.

"Liza." She turned to see Cristine approaching. "I didn't know where you went. Will told me—he seems to be in anguish." Seeing Clare's wet cheeks, she asked, "What's wrong?"

Clare shook her head, not wanting to divulge the aching of her heart yet again.

"Clare?" Cristine asked more insistently.

Elizabeth frowned. "She's sad because everyone treats her like a child." The princess lowered her head. "They do me, too, but that's because I'm not grown."

Cristine looked at Clare. "How's that?"

"They don't believe her."

Taking a deep breath, Cristine sat down on the opposite side of Clare and touched her hand. "They might think you're a child, but you can change their minds. You can show them that your word is to be trusted." She slowly nodded. "You have to make your word mean something." She slowly shook her head as she remembered the bruises upon Isabella's neck from Symon's Demolitic cousin. "Papá didn't believe me when I said Arnaldus shouldn't be trusted. I hope he believes my word now, but what a price for trust."

"He believes Mamá," Elizabeth said. "Whatever she says."

"Yes, he knows her word is to be trusted." Cristine squeezed Clare's hand, and Clare turned to look at her. "No matter what age you are or what age people believe you to be, always speak truth and your word will always be trusted."

Clare shook her head as fresh tears poured from her face. "I've neva lied . . . but still tha daunt bay-lave may."

Cristine patted her arm and then hugged her.

Elizabeth suddenly gasped. "I know where he could've gotten a book!"

Elizabeth's mouth dropped open as she looked at the stack of books. "There's one missing!" Inside the royal hut, Elizabeth, Clare and Cristine looked upon the five stacks of books that were all about the same height.

Cristine kneeled down beside her. "Are you certain?"

The younger princess enthusiastically nodded. "I counted them. There were ten in each."

Cristine quickly went to work counting the books within the multiple stacks, using her fingers to help guide her on her quest. Looking at her sister, she glanced at Clare. "There is eleven in this one and eight in this one, though they are the same height."

"At wa a thackar bak." Clare held her thumb and finger three inches apart, visually describing the thickness of which she spoke.

Cristine looked at her fingers and then to her sister. "Someone took a book and then tried to make it look as if it is not missing."

Elizabeth's eyes enlarged. "We've got to tell Will!" She ran for the door.

"Wait." Standing, Cristine turned toward her companions and then veered around toward the beds in the back of the hut. "The paper."

Elizabeth tilted her head. "What paper?"

"That the names are written on!" She searched quickly through the stack. "Do you remember, Liza, when you asked me what was on the other side? I didn't pay much heed to it, but the numbers didn't seem to add." Finding the paper, she pulled it out and turned it around to find the numerical markings. Scanning the paper again, she slowly nodded. "They don't add at all." She turned toward Clare and her sister. "The steward wrote these numbers. He was burning the book, trying to hide something!"

Should I tell Papá? I have no proof of anything. Is he the traitor? What would it mean if he is? What would it mean if I call him such, and he isn't? Distressed, William leaned against the castle wall across from the royal hut. *But it was Clare! It was Clare who told me. She spoke to me. And I didn't believe her and now she cries!* He went from distressed to horrified. *How could I have done that?!* He followed the wall down to the ground, grabbing his hair as if it would help him to sort everything out.

"Will?" Cristine, with Elizabeth at her side, walked toward her brother as he looked up at her.

"How's Clare?" The words slipped out.

"There's a book missing," Cristine said as she shoved the paper toward her brother.

"What's that?" Standing, he took the paper and then quickly glanced up at her, just processing what she had said. "A book missing?"

"One from the library that Thom collected."

"How do you know?"

"I helped him stack them," Elizabeth said with certitude.

Cristine pointed to the paper. "The numbers don't add. Silus is trying to hide something."

Elizabeth placed her hands upon her hips as she defended her friend. "Clare saw what she saw!" Crossing her arms, she declared, "You should be sorrowful for your words to her!"

"I already am," he said as he looked from the figures on the page to his two staring sisters. He walked away to think with better clarity. *Crisa is right—these don't add. What has the steward done? He is the traitor?* He shook his head at himself. *This is only one page. He could've corrected his numbers. Was it the book of his entries? Did he burn it?* Jogging into the large hut, he searched through the stack of books.

With the books scattered everywhere, William looked up when Cristine and Elizabeth walked through the door. "What did you find?"

"The book of Anchony's accounts is gone." Standing with agitation, he shook his head as his teeth clenched. "That man lied to me! Directly to my face! And because of that I didn't believe Clare." As his anger began to boil, he paced, and his mind began to muddle. Shaking away his anger, he attempted to think rationally. *I have to tell Papá!* He looked at the lone paper in his hand. *But this is all that remains. He burned what he was trying to hide!* He suddenly paused his pace. *What of the money?*

Not saying anything else to his sisters, he ran out of the house.

"Will?" he heard Cristine calling behind him.

Jabbing the torch into the soil, William pulled upon the chest with both hands. In the near darkness of the secret passageway leading to the northern woods, he fumbled for the iron lock on the strongbox and stuck the key inside.

Opening the lid, he moved the torch in front of the golden coins. Nothing seemed out of place. Digging into the precious metal, his fingers pushed around the minted metals until he felt something odd. Pushing his hand deeper into the chest, he pulled forth a large stone and heard the coins fall into the void. Tilting his head, he set it down and investigated further as he shook his head.

You traitor! What've you done?

"Papá, we've been too trusting." William entered their home where his parents and Sir Michael were.

"What do you mean?"

"A gift from Silus the Steward." William set the rock upon the table before his father.

The king looked up from the stone. "What is this?"

"I only looked at one strongbox, but I found six of these in it."

Francis stood. "It was missing gold?"

"Half full," William said as he took a deep breath, trying to quell his rage.

"So, the steward is the traitor?" Michael asked but did not wait for an answer. Shaking his head in disgust, he ran out of the hut.

William tilted his head in anger. "Among other things."

"He's gone. The villagers haven't seen him since earlier today," Sir Michael informed the king and prince inside the bailey.

The king shook his head as he stared at the Barstow River. "And so he has escaped."

"Do you wish one of us to go after him, Sire?" Sir Michael asked.

Francis glanced over his shoulder at his friend as he took a deep breath. "I wish to know for what he used it." He looked back at the river. "Were the Demolites able to do what they did because of Anchony? Did the stolen gold pay for the war against *us*?" He shook his head. "There are too few knights here." He looked down at the ground. "He can't get to the gold now." He looked back at his friend. "Likely it's better that he stays away from Aboly—away from Lord Rackus and Camrina." Turning back to the river, he sighed heavily. "I can't believe it. Silus is a Demolite?"

"Papá, I will go. I will find him!" William said with agitation.

Francis shook his head. "We need you here, William."

"He is a traitor and a liar!"

The king nodded enthusiastically. "Yes, and now we know it!"

William stood there, mouth agape, shocked by his father's lack of fervor. "You are to let him go? To do nothing!"

The king turned to face his son. "Sometimes it is wiser to do nothing than to act when grasped with passion!"

William shook his head in disbelief. "Doing nothing will only help him to get farther and farther away!"

"Yes, farther and farther from Aboly!" Francis stated with an increased tone to his son's challenge. "Farther from the gold." He shook his head. "He is no use to the Demolites now. He is no use to us. What would we do with him? He can't help the castle to rise; he is only good with numerals and trickery."

"We can't let him get away! He lied to me, Papá! Lied to my face! I didn't believe Clare because of him!"

"So it's injury to yourself that fuels such passion?"

"Justice for Anchony!" William shook his boiling head.

"And to you?"

"He gave me his word, Papá!" William took a step away. "I can't let him get away!" He rushed across the bailey, impassioned by his bruised ego.

"Anchony is better off with him gone. We know who the traitor is now, William—"

He was too far away to hear the rest of his father's words.

"Prince William?"

"Don't try to stop me, Michael." The prince shook his head

as he quickly readied the horse inside the stable. "He can't get away!"

"We can't spare the men."

"*I* am going! He can spare me! Do not follow."

Michael watched him mount the horse and replied calmly, "He told me not to."

William glanced at him quickly and replied, "Good." He rushed out of the stable.

"He's gone?" Elizabeth's mouth dropped open in shock.

"Papá, why did you let him go by himself?" Cristine asked with a face marked by concern as they sat around the table. "Why don't you send Grand Sir Doey after him?"

Clara looked at the range of emotions upon her family's faces. "Cristine, your papá can't spare the knights," she said with a calm voice and watched her husband's face lose a bit of tension.

"When will he come back?" Elizabeth asked through a saddened countenance. "Why does everyone leave?"

Cristine, sighing heavily, said through tight lips, "I wish to speak with Isa about finding parents for Mabel. May I go?"

Clara looked at her husband then nodded her head to her daughter's request. Cristine approached Alicia and the wee girl, who were playing together in the corner, and lifted the child into her own arms. Then she exited the home.

Sighing with Mabel in her arms, Cristine stopped outside the blacksmith shop. She did not really want to speak with Isabella—she wanted to get away. She looked up at the evening sky as her breath spread before her, trying not to succumb to the anxiety over the fate of yet another brother.

"Princess Cristine, you are ill at ease?"

Looking down she forced a smile. "Grand Sir Doey, I a—" Releasing a breath, she nodded. "Yes, I am."

"Is it about the child?" He looked at Mabel.

"In a way. I have a whole list of names of parents who might want her, and I thought . . . I thought Will could help me ask. But now he has taken off into the wilds of Anchony, and who knows what shall become of him!" She looked toward the campfire between her parents' house and the blacksmith shop. "I am worried for him yet mad at him at the same time!" She bounced Mabel in her arms with agitation.

"And you are worried you won't find parents for the child?"

"I've asked around Aboly, and nobody wants her. How could nobody want this child?" She shook her head as she glanced at the blacksmith shop behind her. "Isa will only take her if I've asked everyone, and no one wants her." She shook her head. "Why won't she just take her?"

Michael eyed the blacksmith shop. "Your sister has been through a lot."

"But she is married now—she could give her a good home with a mother and a father. I don't understand!"

Michael slowly nodded. "There have been many times in my life when I have said, 'I don't understand.' But I tell you now, it usually works itself out in the end for the better."

Cristine closed her eyes. "I deem God gave me this task, but I have no way of searching for parents for her. How am I to do God's will, if I can't? I know you, Sir Altus, and Sir Josephus are needed here and there is no one else. Will was my one hope, and he up and left!" Sighing, she shook her head. "I'm sorry to bother you with this, Michael." She shrugged her shoulders. "Maybe Isa and Symon will change their mind . . . or help me find a way to search? But Symon can't leave—he's needed here."

Shaking her head, she turned around and knocked on the door of the blacksmith shop.

Caressing Elizabeth's sleeping face, Clara studied her daughter's reddened eyes. Looking over from the cot, she watched her husband sitting against the wall, holding his head with his hands. Rising, she sat down next to him, taking his arm. "He made his choice."

He looked into his wife's emerald eyes. "You are not upset with me?"

She squeezed his arm. "You did what you thought was right for Anchony. As did our son. How can I be upset with that?"

He took a deep breath as he tried to explain further. "No one saw him leave, there is no trail. He could be anywhere." He shook his head. "How long will he search until he finds it is trifling?"

Clara squeezed his hand. "We'll have to trust in God that He will keep him safe."

Francis shook his head. "It is his hurt pride that took flight. He is so quick to act and think later!"

Clara could not help but smile. "I can't forget another prince who was quick to take flight when he had words with his papá."

Closing his eyes, the king tensed with the memory of the argument. "I was not going to be forced to marry a woman I did not love." He pulled her closer. "No matter how much he wanted it."

"And William does not wish to let a traitor go, no matter how much you tell him to."

The king kissed her head. "He is too much like his papá."

She touched his face as she looked up at him. "Time shall make him into the man God wants him to be." Leaning on his shoulder, she took a worried breath. "I only hope he returns safely and soon."

"You know if I had more knights, I would send them after him. But he made his choice when told not to go." Caressing her arm, he shook his head. "What am I to do when I haven't any knights?"

Clara, looking across the dark dwelling as she leaned upon him, said, "You could have one more."

"What do you mean?" He looked down at her profile when she did not answer promptly.

Slowly pulling herself away from him, she met the gaze of her husband. "Sir Victorus."

You, too, Clara?, Francis found himself thinking.

"I do believe he has truly changed," Clara continued. Turning her head away, she remembered her observations as the former king's knight worked on the castle.

He shook his head in distress. "I can't release a Demolite."

"Truly? You let one go free."

Francis sighed. "The times in which we live."

Turning around to face him, she gently touched his chin. "Are the times for which you were born." She smiled. "I shall continue my prayers for our son . . . and for the steward."

He could not help but smile back. "My queen." He kissed her. "Where would Anchony be without you?"

HIDDEN

In Brotherton, Princess Anastacia stared out the back window of Fulco's wattle and daub home as she thought, *Is there any way to find King Henricus? To get a message to him? I've not found a way yet. I suppose God wants me here. Until a way comes to me, I'll have to stay here with Amana and Fulco.*

Glancing at Fulco's wife, she asked, "Can I ask you something, Amana?"

"You can always ask; I might not answer." The woman had grown accustomed to Anastacia's probing questions in the weeks she had been with them.

Anastacia turned away from the window as the Sunday rain gently fell. "Why do you not have children?"

Holding her breath for a moment, Amana then spoke quickly, "I've had four children, but none of them have made it past the age of three."

"Oh. I'm sorry to hear that." She glanced back at the window and then squinted. *Is that Fulco? Where is he going?* "What of Huebertus and Ienna?" she asked, referring to Fulco's brother and sister-in-law.

"They've never had any."

The princess's mouth dropped open as she watched Aricus and Martelus, Fulco's other two brothers—who were both fish vendors—take the same path into the forest. "Do the brothers meet in the woods?"

"What?" Amana gave the princess her full attention as she walked over and closed the shutters. "They like going for walks is all."

Anastacia looked through the cracks of the shutters. *A walk? In the woods? Why?*

In Sethel, Anguis's mind was haunted by Anastacia's voice.

"Why won't you believe me?"

"You're a pirate! You said it yourself—all you want are your makings!"

Her voice could not be extinguished from his thoughts while his feet splashed on the muddy path and the cold, fall rain soaked into his inner being as he trudged deeper and deeper into the unsettling Sethelian lands, unsure where he was really headed.

"My brother always said there was a good heart in every man, it only needs help being unshackled."

"You're going to leave me here? Why did you take me?"

Her pleading face could not be erased from his memory as he tried to rationalize away his actions. *I took her to Brotherton. I did my duty. That's what Prince Phillipus wanted. I don't need to do more. I've done enough!*

"Have you?"

His footsteps froze while the rain continued to assault him. As a group of villagers passed by him on all sides, he suddenly felt entirely lost while he looked at the muddy ground. Closing his eyes, he heard more of Anastacia's voice: *"God wants me to help my people. How am I to do that by hiding in Baltam?"*

Anguis's mouth dropped open as he suddenly realized what drove Anastacia. *It's God's will. After all she's been through—her family killed before her eyes, being taken many times—all she wants is to do God's will!* He fell to his knees in the puddled path as he suddenly succumbed to a self-loathing sickness. "All I want . . . is to be free . . . free to do anything I want without recourse to anyone."

As he looked at the mud, more convicting conversations from days gone by bombarded his mind, this time from a green-eyed princess upon Oro Island.

"If you spend your life stealing gold, what good will it do you in the next? . . . I don't know you or what's in your heart, but God does, and there is nowhere you can go to get away from Him. Let that be in your head the next ship you conquer, the next town you take."

Hearing the toll of distant bells, he looked toward the noise. Rising, he walked closer and closer to the stone church, drawn by the deep knell of the metal. Staring at the building, he yelled out, "You were there for them! Where were You for me?"

He shuttered as a long-forgotten memory exploded into his awareness.

From the dark corner of the cathedral, little Anguis jumped when the candelabra crashed to the floor. His heart rate tripled as he squatted to get away from the booming voice of the horrid queen: "Destroy it all!"

"What is the meaning of this?" Father Hartus spoke as he approached Queen Camrina.

"You're still here? I gave you time to get away."

"I will not abandon my flock!" Fr. Hartus said with passion.

"I am ruler now, and I say there is no more flock."

"No more?" Anguis watched her guards seize the priest. "You may burn our churches, you may burn our bodies, but you can't burn the faith out of the hearts of the people! You can't burn away God!"

Nervously turning his little, frightened eyes toward the queen, Anguis watched a smirk spread across her face. "Watch me."

Breathing deeply, Anguis stared at the gray structure in the middle of the village. "Why did You not defend the Sockorian people from Camrina?" Momentarily defeated, he fell to his knees. "What do You want from me?"

More of Annabelle's words came to his awareness.

"How can you lead others when you are not an honest man your-self? I have known true leaders, kings and knights. They bow humbly toward God. That is the sign of a great leader."

"Bow humbly?" he whispered aloud. *I vowed long ago I would be indebted to no one!* A new wave of defiance overtaking him, he jumped to his feet and ran down the path, fleeing from all the words that haunted him. He hoped his speed would clear his mind, but the opposite was true: the faster he ran the quicker the memories came.

Prince Phillipus stood in front of him along the coast of Sethel. "Learn some humility."

"You speak about humility? You who order people around and—"

"Pride seethes from you!" Prince Phillipus challenged as he stepped closer with passion. "You find pride in answering to no one! You find pride in being unfettered to anyone or any place! There is nothing humble about what you do!"

The trees began to thin as Anguis neared the ocean, and the truth of the prince's words seeped into his mind.

"You don't know me at all!" he responded to Annabelle's piercing words upon Oro Island.

"You are a pirate. You chose the life you live."

"And if I was forced into it? What if a pirate is all I can be?"

Her emerald eyes stared into his. "Because you can't live being an honest mariner?"

Seeing the expansive sea before him, Anastacia's challenging words upon his ship rolled in his mind next as thunder echoed over the water: *"No one is forcing you now. Choose another path."*

Falling to his knees upon the beach, he looked to the vast, troubled sea as a wind cut through his soaked clothing. Shivering from the weather and the truth revealed about the prideful proclivities of his soul, he lowered his head. *It's all true! Pride has had its grasp upon me and turned me blind to my ways, but I did do what was asked of me!*

As the rain turned to a drizzle that diminished to near nothing, he heard the squawk of a seagull. Raising his head, he watched it glide across the gray sky as it screeched at its distant height.

"There you are." Father Hartus, a couple months prior to the sacking of the churches by royal decree, climbed down the rocks. "What are you doing down here?" The young Anguis did not remove his gaze from the flying creatures as he shrugged his shoulders. "Your uncle is looking for you," the priest said calmly.

Anguis, taking a breath, looked at the man. "Why can I not be a bird and fly wherever I want?"

"They do seem free, don't they? But even they must do as nature tells them—south for the winter, returning in the spring. Yet even the least of these, God cares for. And how much more does God care for those with lasting souls than the birds in the air? If you were a bird, you wouldn't be made in His image with free will and all. There is nothing better than to choose to seek Him out, to choose to yield to His love."

Looking upon the bird, a tiny speck against the background of the heavens, he was overwhelmed with the realization that it, being a creature of God, was entirely cared for and loved by the Father. Watching the bird land, Anguis stood. "I have lied to myself for far too long. I *did* choose to be a pirate. Could I be more? Could I be an honest mariner as the princesses asked of me? Is that what I'm to be—a mariner?"

Watching Fulco exit from the tree line in Baltam, Anastacia covertly hid as he entered into his home. Hearing the door close, she wandered into the woods. Hiding behind a tree, she watched Martelus place leaves down upon the ground.

"Stacia?" She jumped as her heart nearly pounded out of her chest. "Stacia, what are you doing here?" Aricus asked from behind her.

"I . . . I . . ." Not finding any words, she sprinted back to the house, wishing she had not been caught.

Lowering herself against the side of the structure, she watched in fright as Aricus and Martelus came from the path to knock upon their brother's door.

Shaking in fright, she heard the door creak open. *Who are these men? Father, what am I to do?*

"Stacia?"

Her heart seemed to pound in her throat as she opened her eyes. *Fulco calls for me.* Slowly rising, she walked around the house, her right hand touching the wood frame as if it would ensure her some safety. *If he turns me away, where will I go?* "Phillip trusted them. Phillip trusted them." Swallowing with difficulty, she rounded the last corner and spoke softly, "I am here."

Fulco stepped toward her with his brothers, glaring at her. "Were you in the woods?"

She nodded with fright.

He crossed his arms. "What were you doing there?"

She looked at the brothers and spoke in a near whisper, "What were you?"

He tilted his head in disbelief. "That is none of your business." Her eyes descended. "You are not to go there. Do you understand?"

Swallowing with difficulty, she found strength within her and looked up at him. "How did Prince Phillipus know you?"

He cleared his throat as if he was searching for an answer.

As she watched his brothers walk away, she added, "He had never been to the western side of Baltam as far as I know."

Fulco chuckled in disbelief that she would make such a statement. "You are a servant. How would you know where your prince went?"

She lowered her gaze as she spoke truthfully, "He was very kind to the servants."

Fulco, taking a deep breath, stepped forward. "Does that mean he told his servants everywhere he went?"

She shook her head.

Nodding, he placed his hands on his hips. "Then in the same way, think of yourself as a servant here: I don't have to tell you where I go or why. Understood?"

She nodded. As he turned to go in, she looked up at him. "Are you truly a fishmonger?"

Glancing at her, he tilted his head. "How can you ask me that? You have seen me day after day for weeks go to the market. So, you tell me, am I a fishmonger?"

"You want to appear as one."

"Appear?" Grimacing, he stepped away from the door, closer to her. "You don't think me one?" He watched her look away, fighting the words she wished to say. "Speak your mind."

"I don't know why Prince Phillipus would trust a fishmonger from the western side of Baltam."

"Well . . . I deem that is something you shall never know."

She looked up at him with a pleading face. "I would know, if you told me."

He shook his head as he walked back to the door, waving his hand—dismissing such an idea.

She leaned against the wattle and daub home. *Phillip, why did you trust them?* Looking out at the vast sea, she spotted the small church at the bottom of the hill. Pushing herself away from the house, she dashed to it.

❆

Father, I want to do Your will. But I'm here with strangers who I'm certain are hiding things from me. I don't understand anything! She looked up at the crucifix hanging above the tabernacle on the stone wall. With stone walls and a stone floor, it was the one building in the port of Brotherton built to last. "But I will trust in You in all things. I don't know why my brother trusted them, but I will trust You. I place my whole life into Your hands. My fate—whatever it may be—I offer to You." She nodded her head. "I want to help my people." She smiled as she whispered, "You know the best way I can do that."

Rising from her time of adoration, she had no more answers than when she entered, but she was assured that her life was in God's hands—and there was no better place for it to be.

"Here you go." As Fulco pushed the bucket of fish guts into Anastacia's arms a few days later, she looked to her right as a small creature let out a scream. "Take it to the sea," Fulco ordered, completely ignoring his brothers.

As he moved away, she watched Martelus retrieve the dagger that had caught the unsuspecting rat by surprise. *He hit it from so far away? How did he learn that selling fish?* When he spotted her staring at him, she quickly turned away. *They don't want me to know any answers.* Adjusting the basket in her arms, she walked toward the sea pondering upon the men with whom she had been placed. "They can't be fishmongers at all." *I have to see what they hide in the woods!* Dumping the guts quickly, she hurried back to the market. "May I go back home to help Amana?"

Fulco looked up at her. "Alright. We're about done here."

Setting the basket down, she hurried up the hill toward the house. Approaching it quietly, she looked for any signs of Fulco's wife outside. Not seeing her, she dashed into the forest to the forbidden, secret area.

Turning in a circle, she investigated the designated spot where Martelus had dropped the leaves, moving her foot across the leafage to find what it would uncover. Seeing what looked like a door, she fell to her knees and hurriedly wiped away the fallen foliage. *A hidden door? It must be their hiding spot!*

Struggling to move the heavy door, she moved it enough to find a buried chest. Pushing the door open with the weight of her body, she the opened the chest enough for light to stream onto the contents. When the gleam of the metal reflected back into her eyes, she dropped the lid and scooted away from the secret. *Swords? What does it mean? Are they knights? Or did they steal them? If they are knights, why do they cut up fish all day? Why would they hide that they are knights?* Her eyes searched around as she conjectured more. *They aren't king's knights—I know that for certain! Did they steal them for my brother? Are they pirates, too? Why did Phillip trust pirates?!*

"Stacia, there you are. Where have you been?" Amana asked as she tied the goat to the fence post and watched the teenager walk up the path.

The princess looked over her shoulder toward the bottom of the hill. "At the church—praying."

"Fulco said you left early to help me. This is the first I've seen of you," Amana said as she sat down upon a stool.

"I needed . . ." Her eyes dashed around.

"What is it?" Amana asked as she rubbed her hands together to warm them before touching the goat's teats.

"Answers."

"Answers? Answers to what?" Amanda began milking the goat.

Princess Anastacia momentarily bit her lip. "How well do you know your husband and his brothers?"

"Well, I've been married to him for longer than you've been alive."

"And what did he do before you were married?"

Amana looked at her oddly. "What kind of question is that?"

"Was he ever a pirate?"

The lady looked at her queerly. "A pirate?" The woman could not help but smile at the suggestion.

"Would you have known if he was?" Anastacia moved awkwardly.

Amana looked to the view of the ocean west of her house. "Did you see some pirates today down by the sea?"

The princess released an extended breath. "No." She moved uncomfortably as she posed another question, "How did you end up in Baltam?"

Amana looked up at her from the goat. "What makes you think I wasn't born in Baltam?"

"Well, Fulco knew Prince Phillipus. I deemed you were from Sethel." Anastacia watched the squirts land along the clay pot and roll down the sides to collect with the growing whiteness.

Amana nodded her head. "You're correct."

The truth—for once. The princess's countenance changed. "How did you come to live in Baltam?" Anastacia asked with hope that more might be revealed to her.

"Oh, that is a long story."

Anastacia shrugged her shoulders. "I have time."

Amana smiled. "That wasn't an offer to tell."

Any hope of the truth faded. Downtrodden once again, Anastacia admitted, "I'm from Sethel, too."

"Yes, a servant in the sovereign castle. Tell me, what is the castle like?"

"Large and cold, even with all the fires lit." She shook her head to shake away the memories. "But it doesn't matter now— it shall never be the same again with everyone dead."

Amana turned back toward the goat. "Not everyone's dead; I hear Prince Howercus is alive."

"Yes. I'm certain he's claimed the throne," Anastacia said without much emotion.

"Claimed? From whom is he to claim it? He was given the throne, that is the nature of succession with his brother, nephew, and nieces dead. There was no one else." She looked at Anastacia when she did not respond.

The princess lowered her gaze. "Yes, the nature of succession."

"Are you alright?"

"Yes." She handed Amana the next bowl. "It's . . . what if he wasn't?" She bit her lip. *I shouldn't have said anything! I shouldn't say anymore.*

Amana looked up at her. "What do you mean? Is there someone else that nobody knows about?"

"I . . . forget it." Shaking her head, the girl turned to walk away.

Amana caught her arm. "Wait. What is it? You worked in the sovereign castle. Is there something you know that no one else knows?"

She looked into Amana's eyes. "Who is your husband?"

The woman stiffened and then turned back to the goat. "You know Fulco. He's a fishmonger."

"Is that all he is?"

Amana took a deep breath. "What? What is this questioning? You have not answered me: Is there something you know from being in the sovereign castle?"

"Nothing I want to share with a fishmonger's wife."

Amana turned toward the goat fully. "If not Prince Howercus, who do you deem should be king of Sethel?"

King? Anastacia stared at her for a moment and then, shaking her head, gave no reply as she began to walk away.

The woman spoke again, "There are some things, Stacia, that

must not be made known." She turned to see if the girl was listening.

The princess nodded her head. "Yes, some things that must not be made known."

Watching the third mariner lean over the rowboat and spill the contents of his stomach, Anguis heard the leader in distress, "Oh no, not you, too! Get out of the boat, we don't want you going with us." As the man stumbled onto the rocky beach to sit next to two other ill men, the captain stepped out of the small vessel shaking his head in discontent. "I wouldn't get too close if I were you," he said to Anguis. "It seems to be spreading." Shaking his head, the captain looked at the sky. "What am I to do? What am I to do?"

Anguis took a quick breath as he stepped closer. "You're in need of a mariner?"

The captain, with his white hair and beard and leathered skin, looked back at him. "Indeed I am. I have goods that need to be delivered soon, sick men, and the unease in the seas."

"Unease?"

The man shook his head. "Pirates."

Anguis lowered his head and slowly nodded. "I am a mariner. I will sail with you if you will allow it."

"Are you truly? You are an answer to my prayers! Do you think you can do the work of three?"

He looked at the ill men. "Yes, I know I can."

"And you have knowledge of the seas?"

"I deem I know the seas better than I know land."

"Is that so?"

Anguis nodded once.

"Well, payment comes when goods are delivered, we divide among all. You agree to it?"

"Yes."

"Then welcome! I'm Captain Harmonus." He looked at the ship anchored in the ocean. "Likely we'll be able to leave today now."

"Where are the goods to go?"

"Langston in Sethel and then to Callum of the Sockor Islands." The captain tilted his head at Anguis when he took a quick breath. "Does this give you distress? Do you change your mind?"

"I'll go. I said I would," he said as he climbed into the rowboat.

TRAITORS

Thirty miles from Aboly, Silus the Steward sat down next to a tree to rest for the night.

I shouldn't have burnt it. I should have made everything known, he scolded himself.

No, it will only be my downfall.

My downfall was to do it in the first place! I must go back!

But I've already fallen. I can't go back.

I shouldn't have left in the first place!

I am the traitor. They will rightly put me to death!

Looking into the woods, his distressed internal debate was too much to take. Standing, as if the change in stature would clear his mind, he yelled out, "What am I to do?" His eyes bolted toward the canopy. "Father, what should I do?" He fell to his knees; prayer was the only hope he had.

"You're not well." Opening his eyes and looking to his right, Silas moved away in shock at the proximity of the woman three-feet away.

"You are distressed," she said.

Fear overcame him as he recognized the figure with wavy blonde hair from the portrait placed outside the Great Hall for every St. Celestria's feast day. With a celestial glow lighting her countenance, hair, and dress, he lowered his eyes to the ground.

"You know who I am?"

"Yes," he said with shame. "Why do you bother with me? I am a sinner."

"Everyone is a sinner. That is why the King came." Her ethereal appearance seemed to reveal the amount of grace he needed at that moment.

He slowly looked up at her. "I'm afraid to go back. I can't face him. I can't face the king—he'll kill me."

Tilting her head, she kneeled down in front of him. Along with her glow, came a warmth he could feel. A warmth lit by the charity of God. "Isn't that what you deserve?" Her eyes wandered to the canopy then returned to him. "God has heard the cries of the Anchonian people—cries for their children."

"Children?"

She leaned in closer. "Tell me this: Why did you agree to it in the first place?"

Thinking back to years in the past, he suddenly gasped. Looking up, he was greeted by escaping birds as the warmth disappeared. He turned in every direction to find her nowhere. He adamantly stood. "I have to go back!"

"So this is Mabel?" the bishop said as he smiled at the little girl in Cristine's arms as the princess sat at the table inside the royal home.

"Yes," Cristine said to the bishop without much enthusiasm as she gave the girl a small piece of bread.

"Sir Michael has told me of your distress. It's maddening when one hears the call of God but can't follow it." He looked down at the table as he sat across from her. "Do you have the list of names with you?"

"Oh, it's over there," she answered, nodding toward the thin sheaf of papers lying on a table across the hut. The bishop stared at her. "Oh, you want me to get it?" She hopped up, and the bishop held out his hands to take the child. Passing her to him, she retrieved the papers and placed them on the table as she took the child back.

Spreading the papers across the table, he nodded his head. "This is indeed a lot of names."

"*Someone* has to be willing to take her, though no one in Aboly is." Cristine shook her head. "It's so sad."

Gathering the papers together in a stack, he nodded as he looked at every scribed name. He shuffled the papers, then tapped them as he set them down on the table. "This one. Conlee. This is the place you need to go."

Cristine's brow furrowed. "Why there?"

"I don't know this name; only a New Conlee."

She sat down on the stool and said sorrowfully, "I wish it were that easy—that I could take her there, but now with—" She stopped midsentence when the bishop raised his hand.

"I am aware. That's why I shall take you."

Her mouth dropped open as her face lit. "You'll help me find a home for her?"

"Yes. And I want to know about this town—they don't have a priest."

"Truly? Thank you!" She nearly laughed. "Thank you so much!" She graciously hugged him with her free arm. Pausing for a moment, she pulled away. "Will Papá let me?"

"I already asked him."

"He agreed? That's good, indeed!"

"It's your turn, Ida," Rachel said adamantly, standing next to the oven outside.

"But I don't want to!" Ida replied in desperation. "She scares me. Alicia?"

"It is your turn," Alicia said meekly.

Isabella, hearing the formations of an argument, walked to the servants standing around the stone structure. "What are you speaking of?"

"We're taking turns bringing Queen Camrina her food. It's Ida's turn this week, but she doesn't want to," Rachel said.

"I'm scared of her, Your Highness! Please don't make me."

"None of us want to, but we do it anyway!" Rachel countered.

"That was before she attacked Queen Mona!" Ida looked desperately at Isabella.

Isabella looked curiously at Rachel. "You, too, are scared of her?"

Rachel looked the princess in the eyes. "I don't care about her words toward me. Queen Camrina is not the reason I don't want to take the food."

"Then what is it?"

Releasing a deep breath, she admitted, "Every time I go there, I can't forget how poorly I treated Sir Melvon. I am ashamed of the words I spoke to him, Your Highness."

Isabella, slightly smiling, asked, "Do you miss him?"

"I . . ." Rachel moved uncomfortably as she glanced at Ida. "I'm sorrowful for my words."

Isabella touched her arm. "Don't be too hard upon yourself. We've all made mistakes. And now you know better for next time."

"Next time?" Rachel looked around a bit perplexed. "Do you think he'll ever come back to Anchony?"

Isabella pulled her hand away. "I don't know. I thought not, but I mean . . . with others. We all have to learn from our faults. We can't carry them around as a burden upon us—I did that for too many years. Trust me: Forgive yourself of your folly, for God does. Let His grace, His joy overcome you." Looking at the other servants, the princess nodded her head as she smiled. "I'll ease you all. I'll bring Queen Camrina her food."

"Bless you!" Alicia said with all gratitude.

Princess Isabella grabbed Alicia's hand, giving it a squeeze. "You've been through enough. You all have." Alicia lowered her head as she tried to forget the encounters with Arnaldus and his men, which left wounds upon her body.

"Truly?" Ida nearly cried in relief as all the servants looked at the princess with the utmost gratitude.

"Truly," Isabella said. She let go of Alicia's hand and looked at all the servants. "Does she speak poorly to you?" They all either nodded or turned their heads away. Isabella held out her hands for the bread. "I shall take it now."

"Thank you, my lady!" Ida said in great relief.

As Isabella turned around, she heard Alicia ask Rachel, "You want Sir Melvon to come back, don't you?"

"Only to tell him of my sorrow."

"Well, if I had a choice, I would want him back, too," Ida said, nodding in agreement with her words. "I felt safer with him there."

Alicia slowly nodded.

"You too, Alicia?" Rachel asked in surprise.

"He never truly spoke to me, but that means he didn't speak harshly." Looking down, Alicia added, "And he never harmed me."

"So it is Princess Isabella that now serves me my food?"

Squatting down next to the bars, Isabella pushed the bread forward. "Although you act like a fiend, you are still my aunt."

Camrina tilted her head. "Are you to be *my* servant now?"

She looked to the wall, chuckling to herself. "It is in your blood, after all."

The princess stood. "I serve you because the servants won't. If I did not bring you your food, you would certainly starve." When she heard no reply, she turned to leave.

"Why? Why do you stoop so low as to serve another?"

Isabella turned around toward the bars. "Because Christ asks it of us. He didn't come to lead His people in victory against the Romans as everyone thought, but to be a humble servant." Looking to the figure in the darkness, a smile crept across her face. "You know? I would much rather be like Him than you."

"Humble servant?" The words rushed out of the queen's mouth as if the ridiculousness would muddle her mind if she kept them inside.

"Yes." Turning to the staircase, Isabella spoke over her shoulder before ascending, "But I fear you wouldn't know anything about that."

Camrina's shackles rattled as she jetted forward, not allowing her niece to get the last word. "Humility is nothing but weakness!"

The princess paused, then turned around to meet the eyes of the queen through the bars. "No, Aunt Camrina. It's because you are weak that you are not humble." The princess only lingered long enough for her countenance to show the sincerity of her words. If her aunt offered a rebuttal, she did not hear it, nor did she care to.

Wiping his perspiring brow, Sir Victorus glanced at the entrance to the dungeon as he placed the next stone where the mason directed. "What was its purpose?" he spoke to himself.

"If you will not join me, then I beg one request." Victorus watched

Queen Camrina doff a necklace with a monstrance jewel. "I want you to give this to that servant."

Victorus queerly eyed the ruby. "Why?"

She placed the heavy necklace in his hand. "It's hers now."

"You stole it from Queen Clara?"

Camrina's smile faded. "I know no one by that name."

"You ask the purpose of this stone?" the mason asked with incredulity.

"No." Turning around to retrieve another rock, he looked at the mason. "Do you know anything of rare stones?"

"Jewels?"

"Aye." Victorus stood with a new piece of limestone in his grasp.

"Only that I deem I shall never see one. These stones are the only ones I know. Why do you ask?"

As he set the stone on the wall, he glanced across the river. "I have come across one of rarity. It was as red as blood."

"A ruby?"

"Aye."

"You didn't steal it, did you?" The mason stared at him with a stern face.

"Sir Victorus? Which one of you is Sir Victorus?" a Baltamian knight called.

Victorus turned around. "I am he."

The knight unlocked his chains from the other captives. "King Francis wishes to speak with you."

Victorus dusted off his clothes as he looked at the mason. "I think it was already stolen."

Sir Victorus bowed before King Francis as he stood in the bailey, next to the northern entrance to the keep. "Your Majesty."

The king looked at the Baltamian knight. "You may leave."

"Yes, Your Majesty." He bowed his head before returning to his post assigned to him weeks before by Sir Hugo, representing King Henricus.

The king stared at Victorus for a moment and then finally spoke. "I have been told how you helped Prince Thomas, the Lion, and Grand Sir Michael Doey. How you aided them in their distress, fought bravely next to them. They might not have made it without you." He shook his head as Victorus lowered his. "But their words are not enough to free you."

"I do not ask for freedom. I deserve far worse than has been my lot here. If it was any other king, I certainly would have been—"

Francis put up his hand to halt the man's speech. Then, stepping closer, he pulled out the keys. "It is only my wife's words that cause me to take this action. Hands."

The captive lifted his shackled hands and watched in surprise as the chains fell from his wrists. "Sire?"

"You took an oath, once, to be a king's knight. You did not fulfill it. Fulfill your word now." Francis looked directly into Victorus's eyes. "Queen Clara believes you would, if given the chance. My wife is never wrong about people. Don't make her into a liar."

Victorus shook his head as he realized he was being given a second chance. "I wouldn't dare to." Looking up, he spotted Sir Michael walking toward him.

Offering a sheathed sword, Michael held it until Sir Victorus looked into his eyes. "Don't make us wish we had not made this choice."

"I give you my word, I will not."

"There are some men to train." He pointed with his head to the training square.

"Yes, sir." Victorus eagerly jogged over.

"Grip it tighter." Peter squeezed the man's hand around the sword. "Don't let it go!" He turned to all the men. "Your sword will be your only means of defending yourself—hold tightly!" Catching Victorus approaching, he walked toward the white stones that marked the boundary of the training area. "Trust you?" he said quietly.

"Yes, trust me," Victorus said as he exchanged his weapon with a wooden sword.

Peter slowly nodded and then turned back toward the men, announcing loudly, "This is Sir Victorus, founder of the Demolites. He shall help you train."

Victorus watched as the faces of the men gathered before him grew momentarily puzzled and then angry. Glancing at Peter, he muttered, "Thanks."

Peter smiled. "You might be the one thing they need."

"You started the Demolites?" one of the recruits asked in disbelief.

"I did," Victorus said as he stepped out in front of them all.

"What are you doing here?" The second recruit pointed. "You should be dead or at least locked away with that vile queen!"

Victorus slowly nodded. "King Francis thinks I can help you train." He beckoned them forward. "So let's see what you've got. Everything you've ever wanted to do to a Demolite." He extended his arm. "I am here. Do your worst."

The prospective guards looked at one another, gripping their wooden practice swords. One, seething in anger, raised his sword above his head and ran at Victorus as he released a long-held grunt of frustration. Victorus easily knocked the sword out of the man's hands and brought him to his knees, his own sword at the man's neck.

"You have heart but no form," Victorus said. Pulling away, he retrieved the man's sword and handed it back to him. "Try again."

The man, seething with more anger from a deep hatred, grabbed the sword and as Victorus was walking away, lunged at him. Victorus moved out of the way and watched the man fall to the ground. The knight stepped upon the sword as he knelt down next to the man. "Rule number one: Don't go on the assault without a clear head." He looked at the other recruits. "If you haven't plotted your next move, you don't make a move."

"I will not listen to this! I will not listen to you!" the man upon the ground said, spitting on the knight's boot.

The Lion stepped back into the training area. "Sir Victorus is a king's knight. If you do not trust your king, then we don't trust you, and your presence is not wanted here." He held up his hand. "Now is the time to be in accord. You either stay and train to be wards of the castle by whomever the king assigns, or you leave now." He stared at all of the men.

The man upon the ground stood up and shook his head. "I'll not be trained by a Demolite!"

"That is your choice," Peter said sternly. As the man stepped outside the white stone border, he turned back to the other recruits. "I think the first lesson today is in humility—to see that we are all weak. We all need the Savior." He looked at Victorus. "And the Savior can change hearts and minds." He looked back at the recruits. "You may not like the fact that Sir Victorus is training you, but he trained the Demolites. So if it is the Demolites whom you fear, why not learn what they have been taught?" He straightened his stance as he stepped forward. "Are the rest of you with us? Are the rest of you willing to trust your king? To stand for something other than yourself? To live for your king? To die for your king, if need be?"

He watched heads nod. He yelled louder, "Are you with us?"

"Yea!" the recruits' voices joined as one in a yell.

"Then begin!" Looking at Victorus, Peter pointed his hand to the assembly of men. "They are all ears!"

"Nice speech," Michael said as Peter stepped beside him outside the training area.

The Lion shook his head. "They needed something to push them to give it their all."

Michael sighed. "I only hope their all is good enough."

Peter looked at his friend. "For a ward, likely—not for a knight. If it is knights that the king desires, what we need are boys—to train them properly as pages, squires, then knights. We need boys that are raised to swing a sword, to react quickly, to ride a horse, to be in battle."

"Hmm," Michael said. "So many children are missing. Who would be willing to send away their sons for learning?"

"Word should be spread that we are in need." Peter looked at the head knight.

Michael slowly nodded. "I'll speak with Francis."

"Silus the Steward—have you heard the name?" William looked at the tavern keeper in Peddleton and was only answered with a shake of the head.

Offering a drink, the tavern keeper leaned in closer. "Take heed, there is one that would do you ill." He pointed with his head. "He just walked out the door." Standing straighter, he took a breath. "Been here for days, he hasn't stopped talking—or drinking, for that matter."

"Who does he claim to be?"

"A Sir Halptus from somewhere in the south—ousted by his own father and mad at the world."

"Sir Halptus, you say?" *He took Edus!* Setting a coin down, the prince nodded. "Thank you kindly."

Walking out the door, William turned around as the sword came at him; blocking it and flinging it from the man's grasp, he pushed the knight against the tavern wall. "You reek of beer." The prince was forced to turn his head away from the pungent odor.

"You," the man struggled to get the one word out as he looked at the moving images of the prince before him. "You . . . made this."

"And you—" Prince William tilted his head. "I know your face." Remembering from where, he pushed the man against the wall harder. "Not only did you take my brother, but it was your throng that killed the Gemmenians!"

"They . . . helped!" Unable to resist the effects of the alcohol, the man's legs went weak. Feeling the man's weight upon him, William let go and watched the man tumble to the ground.

"Ahhh!" The intoxicated knight gasped as water splashed upon his face. Sporadically looking around, he focused on the image in front of him as he realized what a ravishing headache gripped his brain. He groaned and lay back down.

"Where is my brother?"

"Queen Camrina took him," Sir Halptus said as he shook his head in discontent.

The prince rose before him. "You need to get up. We're leaving."

"What?" The man was beginning to realize his hands were tied and that if he did not stand, he was about to be dragged by a horse. Stumbling to his feet, every step made his brain feel like it was to burst forth from his skull. "Where are you taking me?" Silence was his answer. "How far am I to walk?"

William turned his horse around to face the man. "I owe you no answers. You are a traitor to Anchony." He looked away and then turned the horse. "That is what I do: I collect traitors."

"You are the traitor! The whole lot of you! You let the Demolites come! You let the Sethelians take our people!" He stumbled as he was pulled forward.

The prince turned his horse around again. "And that gives you leave to slaughter an entire town?"

"They were helping your wretched family!"

William looked into the forest. "Do you deem what you have to say, I have not heard? Whatever words you speak, I have heard them before from my own aunt's mouth!"

The man looked at him in his hung-over state. "Who is your aunt?"

After walking south for hours, Sir Halptus rubbed his temples with his palms as he sat for a rest in the forest. "*She* took the Anchonians?" He could not consider Queen Camrina's treachery realistic. "She turned on me, but I thought it was only me."

William looked across the campfire he had built. "She used you as she has everyone. If there is someone at whom you should be angry, it is her."

"She wanted us to assault the town? She wanted us to be against one another?" A wave of disgust washed over him. Nose flaring, he looked up at the prince. "My men are dead because of her . . . and you."

"You heard the words of a malicious queen and took them to

heart. Your men wouldn't be dead if you hadn't listened to her. It's your own fault."

The knight's eyes veered away. "I wouldn't have been banished by my father if I hadn't listened to her." He shook his head. "I should have listened to him. He told me not to go, but I told him I would find victory." He looked off into the woods as he continued to speak to himself, "I shouldn't blame him. I failed. He was right to banish me. I gave him my word I would right the wrong, and all I've done is drink it away, drown my thoughts 'til I nearly forgot them." He looked back at the prince. "I must make amends with him."

William looked over the flames at him. "I'm not letting you go."

TRAVEL

Upon her horse, Cristine opened her arms for the child. Her father handed the girl over to her, then took his daughter's hand. "Godspeed, Cristine. Stay safe."

"Yes, Papá." Turning her gaze to her other family members, she could not help but smile. "Liza, don't look so sad."

The youngest princess defiantly crossed her arms. "You go and leave me here, and I'm not to be sad?"

"Liza," Isabella tried to calm her with a stroke on her back.

"This task is mine, Liza. I must do it."

Clara squeezed her daughter's hand one last time. "We will pray for your safe return."

"Thank you, Mamá."

Turning forward, she watched Samus, seated on his own horse, say his goodbyes to his sister and father. From a third horse, Bishop Dominicus waited. She took another moment to consider the wisdom of the mission that she and her two companions had set for themselves.

"Are we ready then?" Dominicus called out. "Let us be off."

Moving her horse forward, the princess glanced at Samus as all three horses began to walk. "Clare stays?"

"She doesn't want to leave Papá."

"And you go for your uncle?"

"Yes, I go for my uncle."

Bishop Dominicus looked over his shoulder with a smile. "Am I in need of your aid?"

"That is backwards—it is I in need of your company."

"Very well, then." With a smile, the uncle turned his horse to the northern path running through Aboly.

Cristine looked around, a bit bewildered. "Is this the right direction? I thought the slaves came from the south."

The bishop nodded. "That they did, but New Conlee is in the north, so that is where we should try first."

"I understand and I agree but who would spread the—" Next to his wife, King Francis halted his discussion with Sir Doey on the necessity of pages to make proper knights. His eyes had just met those of someone he never expected to see walking through the gatehouse. "I don't believe it! Silus the Steward?"

Unsheathing his sword, Michael took off in a sprint toward the man.

Clara followed her husband's gaze, and together they watched in wonder as the steward entered the bailey and knelt before the head knight, freely offering his hands to be bound. Michael eyed him suspiciously as the queen and king walked toward him. "He offers himself—or is it a feint?"

"Your Majesty." The steward bowed his head to his king. "It is no feint."

Francis looked at his wife and his friend. "You have returned," he said with great curiosity.

"I give myself to you and beg pardon for my deceit."

"Did you return to steal more gold?" Michael asked incredulously as he pulled the man to his feet and searched him for weapons.

He looked at the knight. "You know I don't have anything on me."

"There are no weapons," Michael stated after thoroughly patting the man down.

The steward looked at the king. "I returned to tell you why I stole the gold. After that, do your will with me."

The king stared at him in silence as he tried to ascertain whether deceit or truth motivated the man. At the point when the level of discomfort was about intolerable to the shamed steward, Francis finally ventured, "Why did you steal it?"

"The queen came to me," he admitted with a lowered head.

"The queen?" Michael asked.

"Camrina?" the king asked with agitation as he placed his hands upon his hips.

"Yes, Sire."

"And what did she say to get you to betray your king?" Michael asked with irritation.

The steward shook his head. "I did it to give the kingdom protection."

"You stole from Anchony for her protection?" Michael asked with a shake of his astounded head.

"Yes, sir, I did. I gave the gold to her for the protection of the people on the coast from the pillagers." With a worried face, he looked up at the king. "I return because I fear what they will do when they don't receive it."

Francis shook his head in confusion. "What does Queen Camrina have to do with pillagers?"

"She likely pays them to pillage," Michael said with disgust as he looked away.

"Who are they?" Queen Clara asked with faith in the steward's words.

"The Seafurs."

"They're a legend," Michael said adamantly.

The steward lowered his head. "I'm glad we only know them as such."

Clara tilted her head. "You fear the tales to be true?"

"Her ship, Your Majesties, was made by the Seafurs' hands!" He shook his head. "That's why it is so quick, why it can't be caught!"

The king stared at the man before him. "Camrina claims she has met these people?"

The steward shook his head. "It's far worse than that: She claims they do her bidding!"

Michael put up his hand as if he would clear through all the confusion. "So, you stole gold from your king, to give to his sister, who in return gave it to the Seafurs so they would not pillage Anchony?"

The steward nodded. "I did."

"And why did you not tell him his sister had made such a deal?"

He lowered his head. "Because I believed her to be better for Anchony—to my shame." He shook his head. "I didn't know she had killed Queen Katarina."

Clara's mouth dropped open as she became light-headed. "And this was because of me? Because King Francis married me?"

"Clara." The king pulled her close.

"My lady, I knew you as a servant before, and suddenly you were queen and . . ." He shook his head. "It was my folly."

"Yes, but that was years ago," Michael said as he stepped closer, finally making mental connections. "But Typhus the Baker, whom you recommended, that was not so long ago."

"I was afraid I would be found out if I didn't do as they asked." He swallowed with great difficulty. "I am guilty of treason and ready for my punishment. I only wish they could be stopped somehow."

Michael shook his head in distress. "Words from Camrina's mouth can't be trusted!"

The king, taking in all of the information, finally spoke. "Do you know where they are to pillage?"

"No, Sire." He shook his head. "I only know they will come from the north."

Clara looked at her husband. "The northern coast of Anchony is broad." She shook her head. "There is no way of knowing where, if it is true."

Francis looked through the bars. "How clever you think you are, Camrina."

In the near darkness, she tilted her head. "Brother, what do you want from me this time?" Her indignant eyes glanced toward the spiral staircase at the slightest sound of movement.

"We've found your spy—Silus the Steward." She sneered at the sound of the name. "How cunning of you."

"Whatever you want from me, you shall not get it!" She stepped closer to the bars. "For I know *your* spy is listening." She lifted her nose. "I shall not speak another word with that servant within hearing."

Francis grabbed the bars. "The truth, Camrina! I want the truth: Are they only a fable or do the Seafurs truly live?"

Looking into her brother's eyes, she tilted her head. "I could tell you one way or"—she tilted her head the other direction—"I could as easily tell you the other." She smiled. "Do you want to hear what I have to say?"

Disgusted, the king lowered his hands and stepped away toward the stairwell.

"Take heart in this, dear brother: I shall tell you one day." He looked back at her. "When it shall work for my good."

Francis paused and then continued up the stairwell.

When it shall work for my good. Francis shook his head as he stood outside the stairwell of the dungeon. "The fables have to be true." He shrugged his shoulders as he looked at Michael and his wife. "If they weren't, she would have no words to help her in time to come."

Clara nodded. "Indeed, Francis."

Michael shook his head. "What are we to do with this? The northern coast of Anchony might be assaulted by people we know of only in fables because of words *not* spoken by the vile queen?"

Clara released the slightest chuckle at the current situation. The two men looked at her queerly. "I deem it odd how her treachery continues though she is locked away." She shook her head. "She truly is cunning." She looked away. "If only she had used it for good."

Michael looked at his friend. "Sire, what is your will?"

Will? Where is William? The king shook his head as he looked away. "We have so little to go on."

Smile fading, Clara looked at her husband with all seriousness. "Is Cristine safe? She went north."

Trying to calm her, the king took her hand. "She is with the bishop. She'll be alright, Clara."

Looking at his friend, he ordered, "Send word to General Hoskins."

"And where are the soldiers to go?"

Francis shook his head in despair.

"Hurry up!" ordered the sheriff of Wesson County on the southern route leading to Peddleton, who Prince Thomas had charged with delivering the crew of the *Sockortale* to Aboly, taunting the men with his leather strap.

The former captain of the *Sockortale* shook his yoked neck. "If you think you can hold all of us bound, you are in error!"

The sheriff cracked the leather strap against the bare skin of his back, drawing a new trickle of blood. "Don't speak! I heard what you and your queen did to our people—taking them to be slaves." He looked at the captured man before him. "It's only fitting that you should end up one yourself!"

The captain, glancing behind him at his men and noting their secluded position on the dirt path in the forest, smirked. "Is that so?" Turning back around, he smacked the man in the face with the wooden frame holding his arms bound. The village men responded with a pounce upon the captives as every yoke, save one, was being used as a weapon.

Warinus smashed the yoke that held his hands bound upon a tree. With a cracking sound, he felt it loosen around his wrists. He hit the tree again, wincing at the pain of the wood digging into his flesh, and this time the yoke broke into several jagged pieces and fell to his feet.

The captain, breathing heavily as all the villagers lay bleeding and injured with a couple fallen mariners, looked at his remaining men. "Let's go get our queen back!" He glanced at the freed mariner. "Warinus, help free us!"

Warinus, about to step forward, heard a rustling behind him and dashed behind a tree.

The horse halted in front of the ten captured men. "Who is this before me?" Prince William asked as he stared down at the mariners.

"They're held bound," Sir Halptus stated behind him before studying the faces.

"They are traitors to the king," the sheriff gasped as he struggled to push himself up. He was quickly kicked by a mariner.

"Traitors to the king?" Riding over to the injured man, William kicked the assaulting mariner and jumped off of his horse. When the mariner recovered from the force, he advanced toward William in fury. Unsheathing his sword, William lacerated the man's yoked arm. As the mariner fell, bleeding from his appendage, the prince looked to the other captives. "Does anyone else want to meet his fate?"

The captured men looked toward the captain, who called them off with a shake of his head.

"I know these mariners!" Sir Halptus stepped closer with his own hands bound. "They were with Queen Camrina. They are her men!"

William looked at the knight in disbelief. "The mariners from her ship, you say?"

Halptus nodded. "They were the last ones to have your brother!"

William looked at the yoked prisoners. "What do you know of him?"

"They took him on to the *Sockortale*!" Sir Halptus said from behind. "If you want to know where your brother is, you need to ask them! They had him last." Sir Halptus pointed with his tied hands. "That one's the captain."

Glaring at the knight, William pushed him to the ground and rushed toward the captain. "Where is Prince Eduard? Where is my brother?! Tell me where he is!" When he received no answer, fury grew inside of him. His chest heaved in anger. "Then the king shall seal your fate!"

"How are you to take them all to Aboly? There are too many of them," Halptus asked.

William looked at the knight in contempt. "Don't forget, Sir Halptus, you are a traitor just as they!" Put in his place, the knight lowered his head as he backed away.

Hiding within the woods, Warinus stalked the prince and the captives as he patiently waited for the perfect opportunity to attack. Tilting his head, he watched a ghastly scene: One of the young mariners, desperate for freedom, used his shoe to move a flaming stick from the campfire the prince had started toward himself. As the other mariners watched him move, he intentionally leaned over to light his tunic on fire.

"What are you doing?" another captive yelled, bound next to the man with the prince's rope. "He's on fire! He's on fire!" Trying to stomp the flaming shirt out himself, he was pulled down as the one on fire rolled while screaming in pain. All connected by the prince's rope, the mariners were pulled down one-by-one by the jostling and frantic movements as the flames spread throughout the man's tunic and to the tunic of a second mariner as the other captives tried to stand back up and get away from the flames.

"Get down!" William yelled as he ran toward the second man.

"He's on fire, too!" a mariner yelled as he tried to back away from the burning man, unable to gain distance from the heat.

"Get down!" William yelled again as he ran into the man, forcing him to the forest floor. The other mariners, falling like dominos, crawled toward the prince, and soon there was a large lump of men obscured by smoke and moving appendages.

Hearing shouts and noises from within the pile, Sir Halptus realized the flailing extremities were being directed toward the prince. "No!" Sir Halptus followed the mariners into the pile with his bound hands.

"This is our time for escape! Make sure he's dead!" the captain ordered as he watched the moving pile before him. "We shall get our queen back!" Hearing someone next to him, he turned toward the forest. "Warinus, there you are! Quickly now, free us!"

Warinus looked at the pile of mariners attacking the prince and, glancing back at the captain, cut the ropes tethering the captain to the rest of the men.

"Thank you! Thank you! Now—"

Warinus grabbed the captain's arm and hurled him toward the forest.

"What are you doing?" The captain scrambled to his knees as he turned to look at the insubordinate mariner. "What are you doing?"

Warinus kicked the man farther into the thick woods.

Finding the prince's sword, Sir Halptus unsheathed it and sawed his way through his ropes.

Opening his eyes, William attempted to stand but was greeted by horrific pain from bruised and broken ribs. He could not help but cry out as he fell back to the ground.

Sitting on the ground across from him, Sir Halptus tilted his head. "Here's what you're going to get for me: my freedom."

William placed a shaking arm on the ground in a failed attempt to push himself up. Closing his eyes, he swallowed hard and pushed with all of his might until he rolled over and tried looking around.

"Five are alive, if that is what you wish to know."

"You killed them all?" the prince asked with a painful struggle.

"Two burned, and the captain seems to have run away."

The prince breathed with great pain. "Why did you help me? Why didn't you let them kill me?"

"Because I want pardon from the king, and I deem you are the best person to get it for me."

"You forget yourself!" William said, struggling to speak. "You took my brother, and that is a thousand injuries to one saving. Why would I help you?"

Halptus pointed with passion. "Because *they* took him from me! They are the last ones to have seen him alive!"

Pushing with all his might, the prince twitched in pain as he sat up, guarding both sides. "We already know where he is! Camrina admitted he is in her castle!"

The knight, cascading through the memory of the events surrounding the *Sockortale* just off the coast of Anchony, calmly asked, "How certain are you that she spoke the truth?"

William looked at him. "What do you mean?"

"I saw her ship meet with another. One headed south, the other north. I don't know which one he was on."

William lowered his head in disgust.

Sir Halptus squatted down next to the prince's head. "Give me your word that I shall have my freedom, and I'll get you back to the king."

Nostrils flaring, William stared at him, not wanting to give such a promise.

"If not . . ." Halptus stood. "I'll leave you here with her men. And I might just sit back and watch what they do to you." He shrugged his shoulders. "Will they use you to free their queen? Do you think that loving father of yours would be up for a trade? I hear that is how one gets him to do one's will."

William shook his head in discontent. "You are the lowest of beings."

"No. If I were 'the lowest of beings,' I wouldn't give you a choice, would I? So, what's it to be—my freedom or the queen's?"

Gritting his teeth, Prince William uttered a cry from pain and manipulation as he forced his body to do what he did not want to do. "Alright! Help me get the mariners to my father, and I will speak on your behalf!"

Sir Halptus smiled. "Very good."

"Where is she?" Warinus punched the already bloody nose of the captain. Gripping the man's hair, he pulled the captain's head back. "Do you not see? You will either tell me or I will kill you. Now, where is she?"

"I don't—" Another hit landed squarely on his face.

"Yes, you do! I saw you there! You can't deny it. Now, where is she?"

"Alright! Alright! I'll tell you all I know."

EMPTY CASTLE, EMPTY HOPE

Nicholaus shook his head with all disgust as he joined the other knights in the two-story Great Hall of the Sockorian Castle. The brightly-colored plasters and geometric designs on the walls throughout the castle, though cheery and festive, did not sway Nicholaus' gloomy mood. "Prince Eduard isn't anywhere! No one is here!"

"We didn't find Princess Anastacia either," Sir Frankus said.

"Pillagers from the sea," Thomas said as he walked into the hall. "The townspeople said it was pirates that overcame the castle."

"So pirates have the prince now?" Sir Nicholaus exclaimed as his disgust deepened.

"And Princess Anastacia!"

Thomas, in a calmer fashion, eyed Nicholaus and the Sethelian knights. "They saw no one bound. They took chests of gold, that's all."

"Queen Camrina said they were here. They had to have taken them!" Sir Frankus conjectured.

Thomas looked at the arching ceiling. "What if it was a lie?"

He shook his head. "We shouldn't have trusted her word—it was given under duress."

Nicholaus stepped away from the group, concluding with a mixture of agitation and sadness, "We are far worse than we were before." Thomas looked at him. "We don't have the hope of finding him in her castle. We don't have the hope of finding him anywhere."

Thomas sighed. "Where have you gone, Edus?" Shaking his head, he looked at Nicholaus. "There are yet more troubling tidings."

Nicholaus tilted his head as he turned toward his prince. "Speak them quickly."

"The crypt in the church has been robbed—the body of their prince stolen in the night."

Nicholaus's mouth dropped open. "Who would steal the body of a prince?"

"One that's been dead for years," Thomas added.

"Would it be the same person that would steal a living one?" Sir Melvon suggested.

Sir Jacobus shook his head. "I don't believe this! Princess Anastacia was stolen by grave robbers? No, they had no one bound. She has to be somewhere! Your mamá said that she saw Princess Anastacia on Camrina's ship, yes?"

Thomas nodded.

"Then where is she?"

"She's certainly not on her ship now, since we have it," Frankus observed.

Sir Melvon stared at the floor, then looked up at his fellow knights. "What if Camrina gave her to her uncle? Or, if she was stolen away, the grave robbers or pirates gave her to her uncle?"

"I pray not!" Sir Jacobus said quickly.

Sir Frankus's eyes dashed around the room. "We must get her back! How can we?"

Sir Melvon slowly smiled. "How about a trade?"

Prince Thomas shook his head. "That is only with hope that she is still alive."

Sir Jacobus looked at the prince. "Hope is all we have."

Thomas shook his head as he looked at the three Sethelian knights. "I'm sorry, sirs, but we have our own prince to find; we can't aid you."

Jacobus nodded. "We understand." He put his hand upon the prince's shoulder. "But I ask one thing—allow us to take your captive."

"If it will save Princess Anastacia's life, you may have Queen Mona."

As they left the Great Hall with their plans secured, Nakala peeked around a pillar to watch them walk out the doors.

Shaking his head as he stared at the Sockorian Castle from the *Sockortale* and watched the Sethelian knights row to the shore with the captive queen, Nicholaus pondered, "How am I to return without him?" Thomas, next to the knight, glanced at his distressed brother-in-law as he faced the water on the opposite side of the ship. Nicholaus continued, "How am I to face him with yet another failing?"

"How far is it from here?" Prince Thomas stared across the ship at the vast ocean as he spoke beside the knight.

"How far is what?" Nicholaus asked.

"Snake Island."

Nicholaus lowered his head as if he had been injured.

"I want to see it," the prince said.

"Why? Nothing of her remains," Nicholaus said with agitation.

Thomas glanced at him. "That is why I need to see it."

Nicholaus shook his head in resistance. "No. We are to search for your brother."

Thomas turned around and looked at him. "Where? We have no clues as to where he's gone. Camrina would have no reason to give him to Prince Howercus. He could be anywhere."

"Whomever took the princess could have taken Prince Eduard with her."

"If he was taken to Sethel, we will hear about it—Howercus will ransom him. He has no reason to kill him."

"Did he have any reason to take my wife?!" Nicholaus, with a stiffened jaw, stared resolutely across the sea of blueness as he bit back the bitterness within.

Thomas nodded. "He was doing Camrina's bidding. That's why he left her on Snake Island." He tapped the ledge thoughtfully, then walked off to find the captain. "We're going."

Mona looked at the knights around her as they rowed the boat toward the castle. "Did you find Anastacia?"

"Why would you care?" Melvon was the first to reply.

"No," Jacobus answered.

No? "Where is she?" Mona said with concern.

"Your friend was the one that took her; you tell us what Camrina would do with her," Sir Melvon said sharply.

She whispered to herself, "I don't want to think about Camrina. I only want to go home." With great hope, Mona watched the Sockorian beach draw ever nearer. *Home. I'm so close. I have to find out the truth.* As the knights stepped out of the boat to pull it to shore, she looked at them. "What are you going to do with me?" Swallowing with great difficulty, she spoke louder: "What are you going to do with me?"

"We're going to Sethel," Sir Jacobus finally admitted.

"Sethel?" She looked around at the land. "I don't want to go back there."

"Are you afraid of what the Sethelians will do to you when they find out you betrayed your husband?"

"I'm not afraid of the Sethelians!" she said coarsely to Sir Melvon.

Jacobus tilted his head. "Yet, you are afraid."

"If Howercus took Anastacia, he will kill her. Nothing will be in the way of the crown but me."

"What do you mean? You have no claim to the throne," Sir Frankus commented.

"Claim, no. But I have truth. I was there when King Henrard died. I was privy to Howercus's plots with Camrina."

"So, after the princess, you are first in line for him to want to kill?" Melvon could not help but smirk at the idea.

Mona turned away, disgusted. *I can't die without knowing.* Nodding her head, she looked at the two other knights as a frigid, late autumn rain began to fall. "If that is to be my fate, then there is one thing I seek to do before it comes to be."

Sir Jacobus looked at her. "What would that be?"

Nakala, watching at a distance, cautiously followed the entourage of two Sethelian knights and a woman walk through town and stop at a door. Was this the stepmother Princess Anastacia wrote about?

"Mona, dear, you're here!" A smile spread across Lady Myriad's face until she noted the two knights standing guard behind her daughter. Each of them were soaked in the cold precipitation. "Are you in trouble?"

"These men are to take me back to Sethel."

"You're leaving? Didn't you only arrive?" the middle-aged

noble woman asked as she stood in her fine green linen gown with a wimple around her head.

Mona looked at her with a stern face, dismissing her question. "I want to know if it is true."

"Is what true, my dear?" the countess asked with concern as she glanced at the knights and then moved sideways. "Come in! You all are welcome! Come in out of the weather." Mona refused to enter.

"That you aren't truly my mother?" The queen's voice was tight.

Gasping, the woman walked forward and leaned against the door; the action was confirmation enough for Mona.

"Why?" The veins within Mona's neck bulged as she whispered her discontent, hoping the knights would not hear. "Why did you not tell me you didn't give birth to me? That I was born a commoner?"

The countess looked worried as she looked to the knights and then quickly scanned the surrounding to see if any neighbors were privy to their words. "Who told you?" Finding her daughter's eyes, she took Mona's arm in an attempt to pull her inside as the knights stepped closer. But Mona resisted. Dropping her hand, the countess lowered her head and spoke softer, "We were ordered not to by the queen. She said she would give us a child only if that child never learned she didn't come from us."

Mona swallowed with stinging eyes and a lump in her throat. "So it's true? I am *common*?"

The countess shook her head. "I don't know who your parents are. She never said. Mona, you are—"

Mona, no longer trusting anyone, tilted her head. "So you used me, too?"

"Used you? Mona, you were our gift! You *are* our child—that will never change!" She reached for her; Mona pulled away.

"You've lied to me my whole life!" Mona said as she stepped backward.

"Mona, please! We didn't mean to! We were only doing what she told us."

The queen's whispered voice grew louder and louder until it ended in a yell. "Didn't mean to? Didn't mean to! Didn't mean to is when you trip over a rock—not when you plant it in front of me hoping I will fall!"

"Mona!"

Shaking her head, the queen backed farther away. "I can't trust you!" She looked around wildly as she grabbed at her wet hair. "I can't trust anyone!" Frankus and Jacobus stepped closer.

"Mona, come back!" Lady Myriad said as she stepped past the threshold.

I am nothing! It's all true. I am *nothing!* Wandering down the path, a thousand thoughts away, she was yanked into reality when Jacobus grabbed her arm.

"Where do you think you're going?"

Looking at him vacantly, a familiar voice passing by in the street perked her ears, and she suddenly struggled to peer around the knight. "Haron! Haron!"

Jacobus grabbed her by the core as the passing man turned around. "Yes?"

Not recognizing the woman that called, he walked closer. Suddenly recognition sparked in his eyes, and he asked with all incredulity, "Lady Mona?" He quickly glanced at the knights. "What are you doing here?"

Sinking into the mud, Jacobus released her for a moment. She seized the moment and scrambled to the man, her one-time love. "Haron!" She clung desperately to him.

He looked around awkwardly, with near embarrassment on his face, as he pulled her away from him. "Shouldn't you be in Sethel?"

She looked at him in confusion. "Why do you push me away? You said you loved me!" She desperately grabbed at his arms.

Frankus and Jacobus looked at each other, embarrassed for both the people standing in front of them.

"I heard you married the king of Sethel."

"He's dead! Haron, please! I don't know what to think. You are the only person who has every truly loved me." She looked desperately for any signs that he still cared for her.

"Lady Mona, I . . . I did . . . say a lot of things." He moved his head closer. "Because Queen Camrina paid me to."

Mona's mouth opened wide, unable to believe the words she heard. She shook her head in horror. "No. You said you loved me—"

He whispered into her left ear, "Queen Camrina paid me to pursue you—"

"But if it hadn't been for that servant—"

"And she paid me to break it off with you for Rosala." As he pushed her arms away, he lowered his head. "I'm truly sorry. I should not have, but what can be done when Queen Camrina comes to you?"

Sorry? He was paid? As Haron stepped away, Mona fell to her knees, finally realizing the depth of Camrina's deception. Kneeling in the mud, with the rain soaking her from every side, she watched the man—that man with whom, at one time, she was madly in love—walk away as if she were nothing to him. *I have never known love.* "I have been used my whole life," she said in despair.

"Mona!" Lady Myriad pleaded as she stood in the rain, watching her daughter cry in the mud.

The two knights, curiously looking at one another, cautiously approached the woman on her knees. "Queen Mona, we've got to go."

She felt herself rise as the two men pulled her up by her

arms. If she could have stayed there and shriveled up and died, she would have.

Watching the Sethelian knights walk past her with the lady in tow, Nakala thought about all the words that she had just heard spoken. *Given to Lady Myriad as a baby? Used her whole life?* She shook her head at the sadness.

"Father, may she rise above all Queen Camrina has subjected her to. That poor woman."

Sir Narkalus walked out of the gatehouse of the Salone castle. Turning around, he shook his head and then walked toward the forest.

"Did they throw you out of the castle?" a fellow Monakalian knight asked as he emerged from the tree line.

"Indeed they did," Sir Narkalus said with astonishment. "Prince Howercus is not right."

"Does he wish for war?"

"I don't think he knows what he wishes for." Shaking his head, he asked, "What of the sirs at the ports, have you any tidings?"

"No signs of the princess or the pirate." The knight took a deep breath. "What will you do now that you are no longer welcome in the castle?"

"That shall be up to King Marcus." He looked back toward the castle. "Truth be told, I marvel at this Captain Anguis."

"What do you mean, sir?"

"It seems he flew the Sethelian flag against the prince's knowledge. Howercus sees him as a traitor. It's as if the pirate went out of his way to make it so."

REASONS

The bishop watched Cristine swallow the little chunk of bread as if it contained all inconceivable disgust as they, along with Samus, sat around the campfire that evening, northwest of Aboly after three days of travel. As she took another handful with a heavy sigh, he could not help but ask, "Princess Cristine, why do you do that?"

She looked at him in surprise—he was present when she had promised to fast for her aunt.

"What I mean is why do you fast on bread for another?"

Her forehead crinkled as she looked at him in disbelief. "I want my prayers for my aunt to have more power."

He tilted his head.

She moved uncomfortably. "Denying myself what I truly want to eat is a form of penance. When I choose to suffer for another and add it to Christ's suffering, God sees my willingness—what I deny myself—and my prayers have more merit."

The bishop slowly nodded as his eyes turned toward the forest. "It's all about Christ, isn't it?" He took a deep breath. "It's all about Him. It's all about Him."

Cristine, believing the conversation to be over, placed

another small chunk of the bread in her mouth as she looked away.

"Princess Cristine, I ask you again—why do you do it?"

Finding his face again, she swallowed and shook her head unsure what answer he was seeking. "I . . . I do it for my aunt."

Slightly nodding, he continued his probing, "I understand, but *why* do you do it for your aunt?"

Cristine let loose. "Because I want her to change! I want her hardened, blackened heart, to feel something—*anything*—for anyone! I want her to have contrition—some kind of guilt!" Looking down, she took a quick breath.

"Why?"

Cristine stood with her agitation. "Because she shouldn't treat people like that! She needs to change!"

"So you do it so she will fit into what you believe she should be?" he said calmly as he sat in front of the fire.

Cristine turned to him. "You think she should not . . . live by the Ten Commandments? Not be moral?"

He shook his head as he made a face. "That's not what I'm saying at all."

"Then what are you saying?!"

"I think you should pray about why you are truly fasting for your aunt."

Watching him lie down, she threw up her hands. "Or you could tell me the reason you think I should be fasting for my aunt and make this a whole lot easier!"

"Good night, Princess Cristine."

She watched him turn away from the fire. In desperation she looked at Samus, who shrugged his good shoulder. "I deem he wishes you to learn this on your own." He lay down, too.

"Wh—" Looking at the two men lying down, she shook her head and sat down to stare at the fire. *Father, what does he want me to know? To understand?* Releasing a ragged breath, she, too, lay down, next to the sleeping child.

As the sun's rays broke the darkness of the horizon, Cristine slowly awakened. Pushing herself up off the ground with leaves stuck in her hair, she watched the bishop praying in the breaking of the dawn's light. She suddenly felt ashamed of yelling at him the previous night. He was only trying to help her understand.

Understand what? She did not know.

Lowering her head, she looked at the slumbering Mabel. *I am blessed to have someone who would set me right. Though I don't know what I need to be set right for. What am I doing that is wrong?*

Riding into what was left of Conlee, Cristine's mouth opened. She searched her bag for her hand-written account.

"I think the overgrown vines around the sign should have been the first telling of what was to come," Samus said as their horses walked down the fading path of the once-thriving Conlee.

Cristine looked around at the huts in disrepair, with a plethora of weeds and lack of lively noises. "I don't understand —I have written here: Conlee."

Dominicus, looking ahead, took a deep breath. "There at least is one sign of life. What was the woman's name?"

Cristine turned her attention to the stream of smoke rising from the sloping hills that appeared as if it could slide out into the sea. "Lucia. The woman is Lucia of Conlee; the child, Gavana."

They dismounted in front of the one house that seemed to be somewhat kept up and knocked upon the door. When it was opened, they found something unexpected: a white-haired man.

Dominicus quickly glanced at Cristine before addressing the

man. "We beg a bit of your time. We were searching for a Lucia of Conlee."

"I am she," a voice spoke from inside. The man stepped away to reveal the older woman.

Cristine's mouth opened in recognition. "You—yes, you were looking for your grandchild."

Lucia, recognizing the princess before her, curtsied. "Your Highness, to what do we owe this honor?" She glanced nervously at the man. "This is my husband, Lotus. Come in. Come in." As they entered, Lucia shook her head. "It was not my grandchild for whom I search, for we have none. It was my daughter. Did you find her?"

Cristine, quickly glancing around the home, spotted a bed, a table with two stools, and a firepit. Her eyes returning to the paper, she shook her head in confusion. "I have written here 'Gavana, age 5.'"

The woman nodded. "She was, when she was lost to us."

"And when was that?" Bishop Dominicus asked with a tilt of his head.

"Many years ago. Many, many," Lucia shook her head.

"Our Gavana was lost when we were out in the fields. She was playing with the other children . . . and they all vanished," Lotus revealed.

"Vanished?" Cristine repeated, trying to understand.

Samus shook his head. "What came to be?"

"We don't know for certain," the husband said as he shook his head.

"We think them taken," Lucia stated with fright as memories tumbled forward and she was forced to sit down.

"By whom?" Cristine asked as she walked closer to the woman.

Lucia looked at the princess. "My lady, that is why I came to you."

"It was during the reign of King Xavier," her husband replied.

"My grandpapá? He has been dead for over twenty years!" She looked at the bishop and Samus.

"It was toward the beginning of his reign."

Dominicus lowered his head. "Forty years would be closer."

Samus turned from looking out the window. "Did the town die on that day?"

"In a way, yes," Lucia replied.

"The people who lived moved inland, thinking Conlee cursed."

"But not you? You live out here alone?" Cristine asked with concern.

"The people live in New Conlee. We go there for Mass. They come here to work the fields, but they will not live here—not again." Lucia shook her head. "Too much sadness."

Cristine looked at the older couple in front of her. "You think Gavana will come back to you someday?"

Lucia, lowering her head, admitted, "I don't know. But if she tries, I want her to be able to find us."

It appears so calm. So peaceful. With the vast ocean before her and the twinkling stars not yet overcome by the morning's rays, Princess Cristine took a deep breath as the ocean breeze moved her hair and engulfed her with the late autumn chill as she stood on the sand just outside the reach of the lapping waves. Trying to imagine what that day would have been like—with all the village children snatched into the sea and the adults remaining in the village being slaughtered—she rubbed her arms underneath her cloak. *What did Gavana live through? What have Lucia and Lotus endured not knowing the fate of their only daughter?*

"Princess, he's ready," Samus said to her from behind.

Turning around, she was overcome with the marvelous sunrise breaking across the horizon and lighting the village in a dazzling hue of gold. *They have such love for their daughter. Father, I don't understand. I have been told that You love us richly. But why then did You allow such things to come to be? What does it all mean?* She felt herself following Samus to the stone church, frozen in time thanks to the tender efforts of the remaining couple.

"The evil wrought upon this earth can't darken Christ's greatness." She paused as the thought came into her mind. She slowly nodded in agreement. *To undo the evil—that's why He came. What is evil but the ill use of our free will? When we choose our own path and not His.*

She lowered her head as her thoughts continued, and she soon realized her prayers were being answered. *We all have free will—including my aunt. He will not take that away from us. It is what we do with it that shows the person we truly are.*

Entering the church, she pulled the hood of her cloak over her head as she looked at the painting of Christ's crucifixion behind the altar. *It is my choice to fast for my aunt, so why do I do it?* She looked to the dirt floor. *Should I ask, rather, why wouldn't I? If I didn't, it would be because of pride—proud I am not like her? If I see myself as right, she as wrong, and I want her to get what she has coming to her? Would it be a coldness in my heart because I don't care about the fate of her soul? Or would it be worse—hate?*

She looked up at the painting, the personification of love itself. *So why do I do it? I do it because I love her. And I love her only because He has loved me. The flesh in me doesn't want to—it wants to be prideful, right, cold, and hateful. But my soul wishes to do the Father's will. What He wishes for me is to love everybody as well as my aunt, even with all her evil feints and flaws. To love the person she is because she is made in His likeness. I don't have to like the things she does, but I do have to love her. What ill words have I spoken of her? And what do they do but add more vileness to this world?*

"Oh!" Samus looked at her as her hand flew to her mouth to cover her cries.

What a fool I've been with my judgements and all I avowed! She closed her eyes. *Oh, Father! Why did You make me is such a way that I speak so bluntly?*

Lowering her head, she heard a reply within herself: *"Do some not see only when told bluntly? I made you as you are, Cristine. Pray for grace so that what you say—bluntly—shall be aided by the Holy Spirit and will not degrade another in anyway."*

She felt tears trickle down her cheeks. *Yes, Father! Aid me always! I don't want to be ruled by my will but by Yours! Nothing but Your will in my life, Father! That is my* true *will!*

Wiping away her tears, she looked up to see the bishop praying at the altar. Glancing at Samus, she was struck with the realization: She was the one who needed the company of the bishop, the successor of the apostles.

Turning away from the lone couple with Mabel pressed between her arm and her body as she sat upon the horse, Cristine looked at Bishop Dominicus, sitting on his horse. "I understand now why I fast for my aunt. I fast because I'm called to love her. All things must be done out of love." She lowered her head. "But I am weak."

"When one is humble, being weak becomes your strength, because you know that's when you need God the most. Then you ask for His grace—and receive it."

Slightly nodding, she looked up at him. "Will you pray for me?"

"I always have and always will." Turning his attention to the town, he glanced around. "Let's see if we can find a family for that child in New Conlee."

Bravely wandering farther and farther from the cave with her children swaddled and secured next to her chest with straps made from the rabbit fur and warmly bundled between her body and Lina's blanket, the arrangement freed Annabelle's hands for collecting sticks and hunting, but made squatting and leaning forward much more of a challenge. Regardless of the awkwardness of bundling both babies on her chest, she knew it was the warmest way to carry her children, and the only way that would allow her outside the cave to prepare for winter. And preparing for winter would be their only chance of survival in the harsh land. As for her outings, they were timed around her children's schedules: after feedings and changings, she would venture out when they were most likely to fall asleep.

With her mind set on preparation, Annabelle found it curious how the natives seemed to have given up on their search for her. Ever vigilant for the natives footprints, she had seen none lately. She had heard no Seafurian voices upon the wind. *If they stay away from me, I will stay away from them.*

Scanning the forest floor for the perfect pieces of wood for spears, arrows, a bow, or any other weapon she could possibly craft, she awkwardly knelt down next to a tree, holding her babies in the bundle as she did so, so she could investigate the scene before her: a large area of soil, wet and darkened with what surely seemed to be blood. She glanced around her—there were no other creatures nearby that she could see. She drew closer on her knees, then reached out to touch the dark earth. The tips of her fingers came away damp and crimson. *What took place here? What died and spilled* all *of its blood?*

Looking all around, she took a deep and nervous breath. "What creature stalks this place? What creature leaves nothing of its prey?"

Annabelle glanced toward the sky. "Father, what is the true reason you brought us to the island? What could I do here?" Shaking her head, she closed her eyes. *I will not doubt the One who shines the stars at night.*

Lina gazed into the woods for any signs of the mother as she tightened the fur around her to fight off the bitter cold wind. *Annabelle, are you out there? Or did you truly die as the Seafurs—who say they found your blood poured out upon the ground—insist?* Her eyes scanned the standing skeletons of the once abundant trees, abandoned by their leaves to prepare for the onslaught of winter. Small animals scampered within the bare bones, hastily collecting their last storage of food.

As the coldest wind of the season blew through, all hope for the life of the unknown woman and the wee babes flew away with the air. It had been weeks since she last saw the woman in the woods, and she was sadly accepting the fact that this Annabelle, whom she barely knew, had perished along with her babies. "Father, I don't understand," Lina whispered.

"How can it be so?" Lowering her head, she warmed her arms as she turned back toward the village, called by shouts of the natives.

Encroaching upon the spectacle causing such chaos, she spotted, through the movement of the protective furs, a young boy. *Not another one.* Despairingly, she turned away and headed toward her cabin. *He shall be dead in a few days' time.* Exhaling heavily, she shook her head as she opened the door. *The poor lad.*

Hearing the throng of voices nearing, she turned her head to see Ecwab approaching with the boy. "You keep."

Lina looked from the Seafur down at the boy as he was pushed into her. Speaking no words to the native, she hastened the boy inside. Closing the door, she backed against it as if it would keep away the treacherous natives and protect the boy forever. *They wish for me to tend to him?* She looked at the shivering child. They had never asked her to do such a thing for a sacrifice before. Why now?

Hearing the voices fade away from the door, she finally took a breath. Straightening herself, she looked at the crying child. "They call me Lina."

The boy looked up at her with hope. "You speak my words?"

"Are you from Baltam?"

He shook his head as his neck bent, trying to hide his tears.

Grabbing a fur overthrow, she placed it around his shoulders and knelt before him. "Sethel?"

"Anchony."

Anchony? She sat back upon her legs and tilted her head. "What's your name, child?" She leaned in closer. "It's alright—you can tell me."

He looked into her eyes. "Eduard."

"Well, welcome to my home, Eduard from Anchony." She looked around the place, accommodating it for two in her mind as she stood.

"Of," he corrected.

Her eyes flew back to the boy. "Of?" Her mouth opened in shock. "Speak in haste—who are you?"

"Prince Eduard of Anchony."

"A prince?" Her heart began to pound with more vigor. *However did they take a prince? They're extending their reach!* Her worried eyes jumped all over the dark interior of the cabin.

"My brother will come for me," the boy insisted with all certitude.

"Is he the king of Anchony?" Hope began to fill her. *If he does come . . .* She almost dared not to think it. *They could take me home! I could be rid of this place!* "Does he"—her voice came out shaky—"does he know the Seafurs took you?"

All hope faded as she watched him shake his head.

"But he will come for me," he said. "He will! He gave me his word!"

Dejected, Lina turned away, unable to speak any words but the truth. "I'm sorry, Prince Eduard. But you won't be saved from these people. No one but the natives have ever found this island. It is so far north, no one would dare to venture here without a reason."

"He will!" the boy insisted, grasping her arm and pulling her back to face him. "He told me he would always find me!"

"I wish he would. Oh, how I wish he could."

Stepping beside the prince upon the swaying deck of the *Sockortale,* Nicholaus nodded toward the distant speck. "That's Snake Island. Must we go closer?"

Thomas scanned the horizon and pointed to another distant mass. "What is that?"

"That is Trader Island," the captain said. "Are we to go closer, Your Highness?"

Thomas, staring at the horizon, nodded. "Yes, much closer. I want to go around it."

Nicholaus, shaking his head, walked away in disgust.

"Prince Thomas, may we set sail yet?" The captain was growing impatient. He had already watched the prince circle Snake Island several times in a rowboat and now, with Thomas back on deck and the *Sockortale* anchored one sixth of a mile away, he waited for the prince's word to be on their way. But the prince, lost in his own thoughts, seemed not to want to give the command. He leaned against the port side, staring at the distant island.

Thomas suddenly stood straight. "Wait." He pointed out toward the horizon. "That. Right there, what's that?"

The captain stepped closer. There was something out there on the water, an object, and it was moving. It looked to be another rowboat. As they watched, it reversed its direction and increased its speed, rowing back to Trader Island.

Thomas tilted his head. "I want to go to that island."

Summoned from the hull, Nicholaus walked toward the port side. "Prince Thomas, what is this about?" he said with a tiredness that went beyond mere fatigue.

Stepping over the bulwark, Thomas looked to the knight. "What if, sir, Annie's body isn't on the island because she didn't stay on the island?"

Nicholaus's mouth dropped open as he curiously followed his prince over the bulwark. "What are these words?"

Thomas looked to the land. "Earlier, we watched a small boat going toward Snake Island. It reversed course as quickly as it came when whoever was in it saw this ship." His eyes found Nicholaus's own. "Why ever would someone take a rowboat to an island of death? Is there an angel of life?" He shook his head as he looked down. "Could she have been taken off the island before she perished?"

Nicholaus twisted around to look at the land as their boat was lowered to the sea. *Could it be true?* He did not want to dare to hope, but a spark was lit by the prince's fiery words. Turning back around, he looked at Thomas. "You think she could be on Trader Island?"

Thomas shook his head. "I don't know. But there is at least one person we can ask."

On Trader Island, Nicholaus tilted his head as he looked at the unusual footprints leading away from the poorly concealed rowboat, hidden in a hurry. Standing, he unsheathed his weapon. "He has fled into the forest."

"Don't be so quick to swing your sword. He could be friendly," Thomas said.

"Or he could as easily be foe." *Anna? Anna, are you here?* His eyes scanned the vines and greenery as he headed into the thickness, daring to hope.

Stepping into a clearing within the woods, Nicholaus's hand thrust out to stop Thomas's advance. "What is it?"

"There are many hidden ears."

Seeing nothing, Thomas looked at the knight. "How can you tell?" The knight's sword pointed downward to the path. "Are there prints?" The prince squatted down. "I don't see anything."

"Hidden in haste," Nicholaus replied as birds flew away from some shrubbery. He silently crept toward it.

"Sir Nicholaus!" Thomas called out as a warning when he spotted figures emerging—some hastily, some cautiously—from the periphery of the small valley.

"Do not harm him!" a voice rang out.

Nicholaus turned to see several men, appearing from their covert places, jogging toward them.

"Kyphosis, come here," one man, with graying hair, said.

A large, malformed man crawled away from the underpinnings to the authoritative voice.

The man, watching the cumbersome form come to him, looked back at Nicholaus. "Whatever you wish to say to him, you say to us."

Nicholaus, turning toward the lot, asked severely, "Who are you?"

"Trader Island is our home. You are the stranger here. State your claim," the man spoke defiantly.

Thomas, wanting to break the growing tension, stepped forward. "We are here in search of my sister." He pointed to Kyphosis. "We saw that man row toward Snake Island. Has he done that before?"

The men looked at one another. The one addressing them with the graying hair placed his hands upon his hips. "You are not a knight."

"I am not," Thomas answered.

"Nor a mariner. Who are you?"

Quickly glancing at Nicholaus, Thomas took a short breath. "I am one in search of my sister. She was left upon Snake Island to die."

The unknown men looked at one another. "And what did she do to warrant such a deed by Queen Camrina of the Sockor Islands?"

"She did nothing!" Sir Nicholaus stepped forward but was halted by his prince.

"You know something." Thomas studied the half-dozen men donned in attire that could be noble, if not faded and worn. "You all have felt the heavy hand of Queen Camrina?"

Another man spoke up: "We would all be dead if it weren't for Kyphosis."

"He saved each one of us." This from yet another speaker.

"And what did *you* do to warrant such a deed?" Nicholaus asked.

The unknown group silently stared at the mariners and their company until the one appearing to be the leader spoke. "There was a woman pulled off the island months ago."

Nicholaus stepped forward with a gasp. "A woman?" His heart began to rapidly beat. "Please tell me, did she have emerald eyes?"

All eyes turned toward Kyphosis. He nodded once.

Nicholaus stepped closer as did the prince. "Where is she?"

"What came to pass?" Thomas pleaded.

The man looked back and forth between the prince and the knight and then tilted his head toward Kyphosis. "We're not certain. She assaulted him before he could bring her to us."

She lived! Nicholaus looked down in shock as his legs weakened and he tried to collect himself. "Where? Where is she?"

The man shook his head. "They took her."

"Who?" Thomas demanded.

"He tried to get her away, but she hit him."

Nicholaus looked into the man's eyes with growing agitation. "Who took her?!"

"The Sethelians or Sockorians faithful to Queen Camrina—they're all working together!"

Thomas shook his head as he stepped beside his brother-in-law. "Where would they have taken her?"

"We don't know to where," another spoke up.

"To be a slave," the leader said.

"A slave?" Thomas's eyebrows furrowed as he looked to the knight. "The Anchonians that were freed . . . ?"

"She would've come to Aboly if she was with them." Nicholaus wiped his face, not quite sure what to do.

Thomas looked to the ground. "Are there more Anchonians held by my aunt's grip?"

"Your aunt?" The man placed his hands upon his hips. "Your aunt is Queen Camrina?"

Another man, who had been silent the entire time, stepped forward. "You are son of King Francis of Anchony?" He looked down as his mind sorted through all the words spoken. "The woman you seek is princess?" Glancing at the other men, he stepped forward. "Likely you can help us then."

"Help you?"

"I am Lord Bartus. I was high counselor to King Barthelmus, Queen Camrina's husband . . . until he died." His head lowered. "She did not like my counsel."

The one who had appeared to be the leader then spoke up: "I am Sir Dartel, commander of the king's knights. She didn't like any of our counsel. We were all left to die upon Snake Island." He nodded in the direction of Kyphosis. "And all saved by that man."

"All of you?" Thomas shook his head with disapproval of his aunt's actions.

"There was yet another, the first of her prey . . ." The counselor, shaking his head, changed topics. "We need your help."

The Anchonian slaves came from Oro Island! Nicholaus was so beside himself he did not know what to do. *She must be there! Anna! Anna, are you there?*

Thomas looked upon the cast-aside noblemen, counselors, and commanders, those who had once held such power, humbled by the actions of his aunt. "What help is it that you seek?"

"Prince Thomas," Nicholaus whispered with impatience, "Anna is alive and out there! And Prince Eduard is . . . somewhere. Let's go!"

Thomas put up his hand to halt the knight's speech. "I am aware, and I will not forget."

"We want to depose her," Sir Dartel spoke. "We've been waiting and contriving for years! Anchony can help us!"

Prince Thomas shook his head. "Queen Camrina isn't ruling anything anymore. She is imprisoned in the Abolian dungeon."

Sir Dartel's mouth dropped open. "She is not in her castle?" He looked to the other Sockorians. "Now is our chance to take it back!"

"Could we truly be rid of her?" said another.

Lord Bartus turned toward Thomas. "We beseech you—give us passage to the Sockorian castle."

Nicholaus shook his head as he turned toward his prince. "We must get to Oro Island!"

Thomas shook his head. "Sir Nicholaus, everyone was brought to Anchony from Oro Island."

"No!" Nicholaus turned around to look at his brother-in-law. "If she was brought to Anchony she would have found her way to Aboly! So she must still be there!"

"But if she thought Camrina had taken reign?"

Nicholaus's eyes investigated a blade of grass with intensity. "Then she would have gone to Gemmeny Castle. She would have waited there for me, but she wasn't there. I prayed that in some way, she would be, but she wasn't!" With new vigor in his decision, he looked up at Thomas. "I *need* to get to Oro Island!"

Thomas turned away from the stubborn knight to the cast-aside Sockorian advisors. "Anchony shall oblige the hurting kingdom. And if you could not paint Anchony as an enemy to the Sockorian Islands for imprisoning their queen, Anchony would be grateful."

Nicholaus, turning back toward the path they took to arrive

at the valley, shook his head in dismay as he heard Lord Bartus reply, "Enemy? You've helped us. The Sockorian Kingdom is indebted to Anchony."

Nodding his head, Thomas looked at the high counselor. "The Sockor Kingdom has more problems than its imprisoned queen. Your prince's crypt has been robbed. The Sockorians are frightful and without a leader. Leadership is needed there."

Lord Bartus glanced at his fellow Sockorians and then quickly nodded.

APPEARANCES

"How's this?" Elizabeth shoved the paper toward her sister.

"It's better, Liza," Isabella replied as she looked up from the dough she was attempting to form into a ball. "Your lines are getting straighter."

"I want them to be good as Crisa's so I can help."

Isabella smiled. "They're getting better, that's certain."

"Princess Elizabeth, do you want to help me bring more wood to the oven?" Rachel asked as she dusted flour from her hands.

Elizabeth set the paper down upon the table as her mother walked in. Glancing at it, she smiled with a nod. "Your letters are becoming more legible."

Alicia peeked at the paper, shaking her head. "I don't know how you do it. They look great to me! But to me they are markings and have no meaning."

"Do you want to be a scribe, Princess Elizabeth?" Ida asked with a grin as she followed Rachel to the door.

"No. I only want to be able to help others like Crisa did." Setting the quill down, she looked at the servants. "I'm coming!"

Clara smiled as she watched her youngest daughter run out of the door. "She always wants to be helpful." The queen looked at the table. "You're doing a fine job with that dough."

"Truly?" Isabella attempted to pull her fingers away. "Because I feel like I'm only making a mess! I think baking this bread should be part of the penance for Camrina!" Under her breath she added, "As well as taking it to her."

Not hearing the additional comment, Clara smiled as she took a handful of flour and sprinkled it over her daughter's creation. "You need more flour, that's all."

"Crisa is better at this than I." Shaking her head, she took a quick breath. "I think what we need is a baker that doesn't try to make us ill."

"That is—"

"Mamá!" They heard Elizabeth cry out outside.

Michael's voice followed. "Princess?"

Dusting off their hands, the queen and eldest princess hurried to the door. They scanned the area outside nervously. Clara found the fallen wood next to the oven with the servants standing next to it, staring down the path.

"Elizabeth?!" the queen called out.

Stepping out of the hut with a pounding heart, she heard Elizabeth crying out before she found her. "Will!"

Clara gasped when she saw her daughter running through the old, empty market to her son upon a horse. She looked to Isabella with a tear of relief in her eye. "William's back!"

Sir Michael, overcoming Elizabeth's sprint, tilted his head as he recognized the other mounted man. As the prince dismounted the horse painfully, Michael unsheathed his sword and, pulling the unbound companion off the horse, shoved Sir Halptus against a building. "Traitor!"

Elizabeth yelled out at the movement and hurried toward her brother.

"Sir Michael," William weakly raised his arm in objection.

"It's the man that took Prince Eduard!" Michael hissed as he pressed his blade next to Sir Halptus's throat.

"It is, but he has aided me."

Michael looked at the prince and then glanced at the other captives. "Who do you bring?"

"I swear, Your Majesty, there was another ship that went north." Sir Halptus pleaded for understanding with hands bound, upon his knees, in front of King Francis and the queen in the bailey. Michael stood watching warily an arm's length away, ready to strike him if need be.

The king paced in front of him. "North? One of Queen Camrina's ships?"

"Yes."

He looked to the other captives bound to the wall. "And those are her mariners?"

"Yes, Your Majesty."

"The ones that left my daughter to die?"

Sir Halptus lowered his head. "I don't know anything about that, Your Majesty."

"So you come to Aboly with Camrina's men, my injured son, and asking to be pardoned?"

William, weak, tired, and in pain, shook his head as he sat upon a boulder. "I beg of you, Papá, I gave him my word that I would speak for him. He saved me from—"

Francis raised his hand. "Your word is fulfilled. You have spoken for him." He shook his head as he looked at the man before him. "But there is no contrition in him. This could be a feint to attempt to free Camrina."

"No, Your Majesty," Sir Halptus pleaded.

He looked at his son. "You did say he worked with her?"

"He said as such." William lowered his head.

"She used me and my—"

The king raised his arm for the man to silence himself. "As you are using my son?" King Francis shook his head as his jaw stiffened. "Sir Halptus, if there was a speck of contrition in you, I would think about a pardon for saving my son's life." Walking closer, he took a deep breath. "You used my son to plead for your freedom. That shows to me that you are only sorrowful that you were caught! Not to mention that Prince Eduard is missing now because of you!" He looked at Michael. "Lock him up with the others. Make him build the castle—what he helped to destroy!"

"I never assaulted your castle!"

"My family is my castle!"

"And the other men, Sire?" Michael asked.

"Find out what they know about the other ship. I want to know where Camrina took my son!"

As the king and Sir Michael went to the other mariners, Queen Clara walked toward the prince sitting on the stone. "William, you need rest."

"Mamá," he said as he grabbed her comforting hand.

She looked around to see who could assist him. "Sir Josephus!"

Peter jogged over. "Your Majesty?"

"Will you help him to his cot?"

"Certainly." Placing the prince's arm around his shoulder, the king's knight helped the prince to stand.

"Wait," William said once he was up. "I need to speak with Clare."

"Clare?" Peter asked.

"Yes. I didn't believe her. I need to tell her of my sorrow."

"It can wait until you've rested," Peter countered.

"No, I—"

"Sir Josephus will help you to your bed and then he will go get his daughter," the queen said as she looked at her son and then glanced at the knight. Peter nodded.

Clare walked into the royal hut behind her father as Queen Clara stood next to the wall by the prince's bed. When Clare saw the prince sitting on the edge of the bed waiting for her, she lowered her eyes.

"Clare." Her father guided her forward with his hand upon her elbow. Standing before the prince with her eyes lowered, her father then touched her cheek to get her attention. "He wants to talk to you. You're going to have to look at him." He then gently pushed her forward.

"There are some stools, if she would like to sit," the queen suggested as she walked toward the first half of the hut, where the table and stools were located.

Peter brought over a stool, and gestured to his daughter.

Cautiously, she sat down and slowly brought her eyes to the prince's face.

"Clare, I'm sorry I didn't believe you. You were right about Silus the Steward. I never should have questioned your word." He looked at her in admiration. "You are the *only* reason we know he is the traitor. Thank you."

Cheeks reddening, she was not sure what to say, so she said nothing and diverted her eyes away instead.

"Please!" Although it caused him pain, he grabbed her hand. "Please, I need you to forgive me."

Seeing him wince, her brow furrowed. "Ya hart?"

"I'll be more hurt if you don't forgive me!" he pleaded.

Clare looked at her father. "Hay hart!" She stood, wanting to do something about it.

"Clare, please!" the prince cried from his heart. The queen, watching from the other side of the room, covered her mouth at her son's words.

"Manks mak salva ta tack 'way pain," she said to her father. "Ya mak far hem?"

Peter nodded. "I'll see what can be found." Glancing at the prince and then the queen, he walked toward the door.

Turning back around, Clare sat down. "Hey mak salva ta halp with pain."

William shook his head. "Clare, I don't care about the pain. Do you forgive me?" He took her hand so she would look at him. "Do you forgive me?"

Looking at his hand grasping hers, she said. "Yas, I forgave ya."

Relieved, he pressed her hand into his cheek. "Thank you." And then, letting go, he laid down to rest.

Clare stared at her hand and stood when she noticed the queen was beside her.

The queen smiled. "He can rest now."

Peter, standing next to the campfire watching the servants prepare a drink for the prince, turned toward the queen. "I've told them how to make the willow bark tea. It will help him with the pain. Samus and Stephanus are searching for the elements of the salve." He looked at the side of the cathedral. "Clare went to pray."

"Thank you." The queen looked at Rachel stripping the wood, Alicia pouring the water into the cauldron, and Ida stirring it. "Jous, would you come with me?"

"Certainly, Your Majesty. Where do you want to go?"

She pointed north between two of the huts. He followed her.

Stopping once they were out of the earshot of the servants,

she said to him, "Many years ago you asked Sir Michael to check upon your family. Do you know of when I speak? William was a boy—nine or ten at the time."

"When I was in southern Anchony, yes. Why do you ask?"

"Francis thought it would be great for William to go with him, so he could see Anchony—to see what he would rule someday. But out of all the land, all the forests, all the waterfalls, all the villages and all the people, there was only one thing he spoke of when he got back . . ."

"What was that?" he asked when she did not say it.

Looking into his eyes, she whispered, "Clare." She glanced at the royal hut. "I think a love for her was carved into his heart as a boy and it has never faded."

"*My* Clare?"

The queen shrugged her shoulders. "The ways of God, but what does He speak to her?" She stared at him for a moment and then, glancing at the fire pit with the servants around it, she added, "I thought you should know, Jous."

As she walked back toward the door of the royal hut, he said, "Thank you, Your Majesty."

SOCKORIAN SECRETS

Watching the Sockorian Castle grow closer, Anguis took a deep breath as he helped to row the small boat toward the rocky shore. Just the tip of the castle's highest tower battlements could be seen above the cliff from his position. His eyes lowered from the stone castle to the grassy cliff, to a man, hunched and moving with unease, helping to bring the rowboat to shore.

The mariners stared at the impaired movement of Kyphosis. Yet knowing they gawked at him, the man showed no malice toward the visitors. As the mariners murmured among themselves regarding Kyphosis's walk and stature, they and the captain climbed out of the boat. "Leave him be," the captain ordered as he walked toward the rocky steps built into the grassy cliff.

Anguis, the last one to step out of the wooden vessel, slowed in contemplation as his captain and the other mariners approached a set of stony steps affixed to the natural incline and ascended from the shore. When Kyphosis spotted him, he took a second glance.

Once the captain and mariners disappeared out of view, making their way to the village, a young voice yelled out from above the cliff, "There he is!" It was a dirty, young boy. "There's the beast!"

"Cripple!" another voice rang out as a small group of boys emerged from the overhang above the rocky beach. Anguis watched as the boys picked up clumps of earth from the ground around them and threw them down the hill toward Kyphosis.

The man lurched forward, battered by some of the mud, rocks, and sticks, while dodging other clumps that fell around him.

"Stop!" Anguis shouted up at the harassing boys and stepped forward for Kyphosis's defense.

The boys, spotting the mariner next to Kyphosis, scattered quickly.

Anguis turned back to Kyphosis, who was looking at him to the best of his ability with the abnormal curvature of his neck and back.

Stepping closer, the hunched man grabbed Anguis's arm as Sir Dartel's voice chastised the boys from above and became louder as he approached. "Kyphosis? Are you down there? Were those boys tormenting you again?"

Anguis lowered his head and looked away as Dartel's voice grew in volume. Kyphosis grabbed his sleeve and held tightly.

"Let me go." Pulling Kyphosis's fingers off his sleeve, Anguis stepped away. "Let me go," he whispered again and walked in the opposite direction.

Kyphosis humbly bowed his head and turned toward the stone steps up to the ledge to meet Sir Dartel.

"Are you alright?" Anguis heard the voice of the leader of the king's knights. It became gruff. "Did they throw mud at you again? I told you to stay in the bailey, so you'll be safe! These children here seem to have lost all knowledge of right and wrong." His voice faded away as he ushered the man toward the castle walls.

Climbing up the rocky terrain, Anguis's mouth dropped open as he spotted the crowd of around one hundred converged around the castle gatehouse. It appeared to be all of Callum. Lured by the shouts of the crowd, he joined the mariners and captain. *Do the people wish to storm it?*

"We want our queen!" a man's voice shouted.

So she has *forsaken the Sockorian Kingdom for Anchony?*

"And justice for our prince!" another, this time that of a woman, added.

Anguis looked at the woman who yelled out the comment as more voices joined in:

"Prince Leonardus—where did his body go?"

The prince? What is this? Anguis shook his perplexed head.

Lord Bartus, mounted upon his horse, called out, "She is evil and rightly placed in chains!"

Sir Dartel ushered Kyphosis through the gatehouse. Once through, he mounted his awaiting horse next to the high counselor. From atop his mount, he studied the faces gathered around.

"Anchony can't take our queen!" one villager yelled out from the crowd.

Captain Harmonus, at the back of the crowd, glanced at his men. "There is strife in this kingdom—let us not tarry for long." The mariners turned toward the taverns, all but Anguis.

Listening intently, Anguis slowly moved forward through the crowd of people. *She is taken? Anchony? Anchony has taken her? Can it be true?*

"Queen Camrina was never to take the throne!" Lord Bartus proclaimed boldly. "It was to go to—"

"The prince is dead!" another vociferated with passion. "And his body is missing!"

"Who took his body?" yet another called out.

"Who's to be our ruler now?"

"If there is no royal line, then the crown goes to the high counselor. *I* was high counselor to King Barthelmus! It is *my* duty to lead you." Lord Bartus glanced at Sir Dartel as the knight's eye caught a distantly familiar countenance from within the villagers, and the king's knight dismounted his horse and walked through the crowd.

Anguis, with a pounding heart, lowered his head and slowly slipped backward farther into the sea of people until he was no longer discernable.

Nakala, soaking up all the interactions, followed Sir Dartel with her astute eyes as he moved through the crowd. Seeing a man turn away from the crowd, she quickly followed after to catch a glimpse of his face.

Can it be true? She is finally imprisoned? Captivated by hope, Anguis wandered past the taverns, gaining speed with his distance. Jogging past the huts and homes, he sprinted toward an abandoned stone cottage, overtaken by weeds and the abrasion of time, a distance away from the village. Pulling open a shutter, he looked through the dust-filled darkened room to stare at the long-forgotten abode.

"Good day?" Anguis, hearing the young voice, turned around to see a boy approaching him from the direction of the village. "I am to give this to you." He held out a single sheet of paper in his hand.

"What?"

"I was told if a man came by here—by this cottage—I was to give this to him. I see no one else, so it must be for you."

Anguis hesitantly stood and took the offering. "A note? Who's it—" Looking up, he saw that the boy was already running back to Callum. Curiously opening it, he read the few words to himself: *"Into the forest—west—you will come upon a clearing. South of the clearing, you will find her."*

"Find who?" he asked to the air.

Following the directions written on the sheet of paper, Anguis tilted his head when he spotted a house emerge from the woodlands in the distance. A wattle and daub structure separated from all other structures, deep within the forest. Approaching, his mouth slowly lowered in shock as he looked upon the person sitting outside near the door. The body, slumped with age and wrinkled in time, was unfamiliar, but the face was still recognizable. "Castella?"

"Who is it that calls my name?" the older woman called out as she released the beans she was snapping and turned toward the voice. It was clear that her eyesight failed her. "A voice I do not know."

"Castella." Anguis approached slowly, attempting to figure out how she was before him. "I was one of the many babes you brought into this world."

Listening intently, she slowly nodded. "One of many, is that so?"

Utterly confused, he knelt beside her as the memory bombarded him:

"Please! Please!" a woman cried out from the poorly lit innards of the cottage.

Camrina, walking from the hut, addressed Sir Dartel outside, "No one must know."

The young Anguis, hiding next to the window, watched in horror as Sir Dartel nodded and pulled out his dagger, waiting for Castella to emerge.

The young Anguis fervently shook his head. Stepping out from behind the bushes, he screamed at the knight with all his might, "You can't! Don't kill her!"

Camrina, hearing the young voice, tilted her head as she turned around to look at the boy. "What have we here?" Her jaw stiffened as she spoke to her knight, "It seems we were followed, Sir Dartel."

Upon his knees, he stared at her in disbelief. "Castella, how is it that you live? I was there at the cottage. I heard Queen Camrina order your death!"

Finding his face, she rubbed his cheek. "There you are, child."

"Castella?"

Turning her head to the left, she stated with assurance, "Not everyone does the queen's evil bidding." She held out her hand as if she could still feel the weight of the small bag Sir Dartel had given to her, instead of a blade. "I thought he was going to cut my throat, but it was freedom that he offered me." She nodded to herself. "I've done as he told me. I've hidden away here—my daughter, her husband, and I."

"Mama, is someone there?" a woman's voice called out from inside the house.

"Dartel?" The name came from Anguis's mouth in a whisper as his eyes looked across the clearing to the trees. "He didn't kill you?"

"Yes, it was Sir Dartel that let me live." She turned her head to her right shoulder. "Yes, Janus, we have a guest."

He stood as her middle-aged daughter came out of the house. "Who are you? How did you find us?" she asked sharply.

Shaking his head, he stepped away. "I have learned . . . you don't need to fear the queen anymore. She's been imprisoned by Anchony. You can come from your hiding."

"Queen Camrina?" The daughter looked from the mariner to her mother back to the mariner. "In truth?"

He slowly nodded. "If what I heard is the truth." He stepped away. "I . . . I will take my leave."

Castella lifted her hand. "Wait!"

Anguis shook his head. "I'm sorry. I mustn't stay!" He ran back toward Callum, unsure of the meaning of all that he had learned.

Shaking his head, Anguis knelt in front of the engraved, stone tombstone in the churchyard. "Fr. Hartus, nothing is as I thought it to be. I was so certain. I'm not certain of anything now."

Anguis paused before speaking the words he never would have believed he could say. "Castella is alive. Is it true then? Is Queen Camrina truly imprisoned . . ." He slowly stood as he realized, "If she's in Anchony, it would be safe for Princess Anastacia there!" He closed his eyes. "But I took her where she needed to be. I did what was asked of me."

But who are those men? I left her with unknown men!

They weren't unknown to her brother.

She would want to go to Anchony if she knew it was safe!

But I've already done enough!

He slapped the tombstone. Her pleading face bombarded all of his thoughts. "No, I will get her to Anchony if the queen is truly imprisoned! But I have to know it for certain!"

Nakala, standing before a castle window, watched Anguis rise from before the tombstone.

That grave? Her heart began to pound. *Can it be?*

The door to the chamber—the very one that had held Princess Anastacia imprisoned in the Sockorian castle—creaked open. Light from an oil lamp slowly lit the room. Sir Dartel, taking a deep breath, entered slowly and closed the door behind him. Wandering over to the table, he placed the lamp upon the wood and sat down upon the stool. He looked across the room at the bed. "I thought I might find you here."

"And I thought you killed Castella." Anguis's voice was cold and unforgiving as Sir Dartel lowered his head. "You always did the will of the queen."

"No." The knight shook his head. "What I did for Queen Camrina was only because I was deceived by her." He stood. "Trust me!"

"I don't know if I can trust you! I don't know anything anymore!" Anguis, who was waiting on the bed for the knight to come, moved off quickly. "The one person I trusted is lying in a grave, slaughtered by a decree of Queen Camrina. A decree carried out by your men!" Shaking his head, he headed for the door. "I don't know why I came here!"

"They were my men, but it wasn't my order. They turned against me, too." Dartel stepped in front of the door as Anguis approached it. He did not want the pirate to leave. "You came because deep down, you know you can trust me." Anguis pushed past him. "So you're going to run away again?" Dartel said.

Anguis, pausing with the latch in hand, looked back at the knight. "You know good and well I did not run away to begin with!"

"You can't leave. You are—"

"*You* are the reason I became a pirate! If you think I will just willingly—" Shaking his head, he looked down at the stones of the floor. "I need to know if it's true—if the queen is truly imprisoned." He looked over his shoulder at Dartel, his face partially lit by the flames from the oil lamp.

"A pirate?" Sir Dartel asked with great incredulity and a tinge of disgust. "You're a pirate?"

"Is it true?" Anguis demanded.

The knight stared at him for a moment and then nodded, "So says Prince Thomas of Anchony."

Anguis lowered his head. "His sister lives."

"What?"

"A merchant was to take her from Oro Island."

"What?"

"I paid him gold."

Sir Dartel shook his head as he watched the pirate open the door and walk out into the hall. "You can't just leave!"

Anguis turned around. "There is work to be done! Sethel needs its true heir to the throne!"

Nakala, walking to the chamber, paused to watch the pirate walk by. She turned back to look at Sir Dartel as her heart wildly pounded.

"Wait!" Nakala called out to Anguis as he made his way closer to the stairs leading to the shoreline. "Wait, please!"

Anguis turned around. "Are you in search of me?"

"Yes!" Stopping four feet from the man, she nodded as she breathed heavily. "Was it you that took Princess Anastacia?"

He looked around cautiously. "Do I know you?"

"Sir Dartel said you are Anguis the Pirate. I am Lady Nakala of Monakala. I am cousin to the king. Monakala will help her!" she cried out desperately. "I have the king's ear! He will listen to anything I have to say!"

Anguis shook his head in irritation as he turned back toward the steps.

She followed him. "My brother, Sir Narkalus, has gone to Salone to search for her and you, Captain Anguis—"

Halting, he turned around on the steps to look at her.

"I've been told King Marcus has placed a price upon your head," she said. "But I will tell my king that you were offering the princess succor. Please, don't go!"

"If your king wants me, then he can send his men after me!" With those words spoken, he hurried down the steps.

"He will certainly come after you!" she yelled as the man jogged down the beach toward the rowboats.

"Wait!" Anguis called as he hurried down the overhang toward the rocky beach. "I'm here! I'm here!"

Captain Harmonus, shaking his head, stood in the rowboat. "We nearly left you."

"I know. I know. I'm glad you didn't. I'm here now," Anguis said as he reached the rowboat.

The captain, glancing from the belated mariner to the lady upon the steps, asked. "Who is she?"

"A servant of the castle," Anguis replied, stepping into the boat.

"I didn't see you at the tavern. Where did you go?"

"Everywhere." The captain scowled at the insufficient answer. Anguis, wanting to change topic, asked, "Where do we go next?"

"Back to Sethel."

"Western?" he asked with hope.

"Southern."

Anguis lowered his head. *Can Monakala truly be trusted when she wants me arrested?* He shook his head at his own thoughts. *I need to get the princess myself, but how will I get back to Brotherton? And, when I make it back there, how will I get the princess to Anchony? I have no ship, but if Prince Howercus doesn't know she lives, then I do have time.*

SOUTHERN SETHEL

Arriving in Port Longbrooke, Anguis and the other mariners came ashore to a town silenced by the trauma of what had befallen them. It was not until they ventured into the marketplace that they found what plagued the town: The heads of eight men were displayed on wooden stakes, standing eight feet tall for all to see.

Captain Harmonus shook his head in discontent. "What was their offense?" he asked a passerby.

"Pirates they were. No trials were they given. That Sir Arkel, he hanged them and beheaded for all to see."

Stepping closer, Anguis's face went ashen, for the faces he beheld were those of his former crewmates.

"The whole ship worth?" the captain asked.

"All save one. That knight took him; he was saying things."

"Like what?" Captain Harmonus asked.

"That our princess lives!" the man shook his head in discontent. "We don't know what to make of it!"

Anguis looked at the man as his heartrate increased. The time remaining to rescue Princess Anastacia was evaporating before him.

"That is odd indeed." Captain Harmonus said. "What strange times in which we live." He looked back at the heads, shaking his own. "The lot for thievery before our eyes, but a shame there was no trial." He looked at his crew. "Three days of rest, then we shall sail again." Finding Anguis's face, he asked, "Have you taken ill?"

"I . . ." Anguis shook his head. "I can't go. There are other things I must do."

"Of course. You have fulfilled your word. See the first mate for your pay."

Breathing deeply, Anguis walked up the steps into the church, a block away from the marketplace. Pushing open the doors, he stepped on to the stone floor and looked toward the altar. The light streaming in from the green-tinted windows, seemed to show what God was doing to his heart: allowing grace to flow through and penetrate the darkness. Realizing there was a man praying before the steps going to the sanctuary, Anguis turned around to leave.

"No, come in!" the man said as he stood and waved Anguis forward.

Anguis looked at his dark alb. "Are you the priest?"

"Yes. Do you want to be alone?"

"I . . . I want advice. You see, I must help someone, but to give the succor she truly needs, I must go back to a life I don't want."

"What is life? What is to live? What is Christ asking you to do?" He shook his head. "There is no life away from Christ. We all must do His will. Nothing for our glory, but all for Him." Looking back at the crucifix in front of the altar, he added, "In giving you this advice, I see the answer to my fight. It was only fear of what the bishop would think of me, if I were wrong, that has kept me silent."

Anguis looked at him, clueless as to his meaning.

"You have heard the talk out there," the priest said, "that the princess might live." He shook his head. "To tell the bishop or not? The truth of which I do not know. For if it is true, Prince Howercus is not the rightful heir, and the bishop should not crown him. If it is false, then I spread lies."

Anguis chortled in disbelief.

"What is it?" the priest looked at him.

"For once in my life, I deem I was meant to be here at this very moment."

"The hand of God leads us all," the priest said.

"I feared if I stepped foot in here, God would strike me down. It has been years since I've come into a church."

The priest smiled. "Well, welcome home!"

"Home?" Anguis said in perplexity. "I haven't known for a very long time where home is."

"You've run from her—the Church is our home. Christ is our King, and while we are yet on this earth, this Holy yet blemished Church ruled over by men is what He made for us. It is our home. We all sin. We all fall short. That is why He left us the Sacraments—to make amends and to come back to Him, to come back to home."

"Father, I was five when Queen Camrina decreed all the clergy leave the Sockor Kingdom. And those that did not obey were killed on her order." Closing his eyes, he thought of Fr. Hartus.

"So the only Sacrament you have known is Baptism?"

"Yes," he said as he opened his eyes.

"Do you wish to Confess?"

"I don't know how," he answered honestly.

"I will help you," the priest said assuredly.

Nodding, he looked up at the crucifix, "If this is what Christ set up, the reason He died—what He wants us to do—I am ready to *try* to do His will, and not my own."

After hearing the words of absolution for the first time in his life, Anguis rose from kneeling on the stone floor. "I feel free, yet I am still burdened with the task in front of me."

"'There is no better love than to lay one's life down for a friend.' Keep that in mind in all that is ahead."

"There are many ways to lay one's life down," Anguis said as he looked at the priest. "Write to the bishop, Father. It is all truth."

"About the princess? What do you know of it?"

"Princess Anastacia lives. I took her from the Sockorian Castle. I left her in Brotherton in Baltam. I hope to get her safely to Anchony."

Speechless, the priest watched Anguis walk out of the church. With whom had he been conversing?

DRESS OF OLD

Tilting his head, Nicholaus walked over to a folded piece of fabric. *It can't be.* Sweeping his torch toward the dress, his right fingers felt the faded fabric as it unfolded with the lifting of his hand. *It is—Anna's dress!* He looked up. *She's here?*

His gaze turned frantic and his eyes blurred. "Anna? Anna, are you here?!" he cried out, and he heard his voice echoing off the stone walls of the empty castle on Oro Island.

He ran outside toward the light, where he threw down the torch to examine the dress with all his attention. It was proof she had survived Snake Island—survived her aunt's death wish. Breathing heavily with the revelation, he looked around at the silenced bailey. *But where is she now?* Turning his gaze to the ground, he searched desperately for any signs, but anything that might have given away her location was long ago altered by the passage of time and the violence of tempests that had hammered the land.

As the excitement of finding her dress faded to the hard reality, Nicholaus's shoulders dropped. She might have made it off of Snake Island, but she was no longer on Oro. He was no closer to finding her than he was before and, wherever she might be, she was without her dress. What did that mean, anyway?

Thomas's brow crinkled as he walked closer to the knight. His eyes immediately caught sight of the fabric held within his brother-in-law's grasp. "That's Annie's dress!"

"Yes, it is," Sir Nicholaus said with a mixture of perplexity and solemnity upon his countenance.

"Where did you find it?"

"She's been here, but she's not here now."

Thomas looked at the castle in front of him. "But she didn't make it back to Anchony?" He turned around to look at the knight to find Sir Nicholaus with a downcast glance.

"If she did . . . if the Sockorians found her and . . . kept her . . . who knows where she'd be . . ."

Thomas's mouth opened a bit as he thought of the queen's words. *"He is with* her." His eyes darted around as he thought of the words until they rested upon Nicholaus's face. *What if she wasn't speaking of Princess Anastacia?*

"Do you think Queen Camrina knows?" he asked Nicholaus. "We didn't ask her about Annie because we all deemed her dead!" He watched Nicholaus touch the fabric.

"How would she have known? Did the Sockorians on Trader Island tell her?"

"They wouldn't have . . . I don't know." Thomas looked at the dress. "But I think my aunt knows much more than of what she speaks."

Nicholaus looked at his prince with a new determination. "I say we go back to Anchony and find out what Queen Camrina knows of my wife!"

"Your orders, Prince Thomas?" the captain spoke from behind him.

Thomas slightly shook his head, unsure what action to take. When he finally spoke, he did not address any of the issues at hand. "Let me see Annie's dress." As the once fine woolen dress was placed within his fingers, he tightened his grip and walked away from the probing eyes and countless questions.

What is the right course to take, Father? You gave us reason and thought, but right now it would be much easier if You told me what to do. Closing his eyes, Prince Thomas shook his head at his own thoughts. *Searching for the easy way out, am I?* Holding up the dress, he watched it tumble open before him. *What can be learned from this?*

Coming from the Great Hall back outside in the bailey, Thomas spoke in haste, "I don't think Queen Camrina knows where Annie is at all!"

Nicholaus tilted his head. "How do you—"

Thomas hurried forward with the dress tightly within his grasp. "Look here, at the seams. What do you see?"

Nicholaus looked down. "They are . . . stretched."

Thomas nodded as a smile burst across his face. "Yes! She was too large for this one." He shook his head. "If she was picked up with the Anchonians, she wouldn't have been large enough to pull at the seams by the time they had to leave Oro Island to arrive in Anchony when they did."

Nicholaus took the dress back. "I don't know whether to be joyful or saddened by these tidings. I'm glad Camrina didn't find her again, but then . . . where is she?"

Thomas's smile faded as he placed his comforting hand upon Nicholaus's shoulder. "That I can't answer."

"Prince Thomas, where do you wish to go?" the captain asked.

"Sailing around the sea has not aided us. I think our best

course is to dock and ask around." His eyes wandered back over to the captain. "Baltam is the closest kingdom, is it not?"

"It is."

"And how far are we from there?"

"The west coast? A day or so."

"Then let us set sail."

With the ship safely in the harbor of Port Cottal—a busy port city around the middle of the western coast—and a frigid air blowing in from the northwest, Thomas and Nicholaus happily entered the local tavern that was a busy and noisy as the city itself with its one dozen occupied tables.

Prince Thomas and Sir Nicholaus stepped up to the bar. "Good day to you. Does anyone go to Oro Island?" Thomas asked the tavern keeper.

The man eyed him oddly and slowly shook his head as he wiped down the bar. "Most avoid that place."

"Why?"

Lowering his gaze, he said, "There are whispers of slavery."

"They were true," Nicholaus stated bluntly. "But not anymore. No one is upon the island now."

"If someone were to go to the island—not for slaves—why would they go?" Thomas continued to question.

"The wood is strong. Some go for that, but only to the eastern side."

Turning to his brother-in-law, Nicholaus whispered, "The castle where her dress was, is on the eastern side."

"Wood?" Prince Thomas stood a bit taller. "Have you heard of anyone going lately?"

The tavern keeper shrugged his shoulders as another man, coming to the bar to get a drink, stepped up beside him. "Captain Vitalis and his mariners went to Oro Island."

"A Captain Vitalis?" Thomas asked as he turned toward the informant. "For wood?"

The man shook his head. "That's the oddity—he was a merchant. He had no reason to go there."

"Where can we find him?" Nicholaus asked quickly.

"You can't. Ship busted up, no one lived."

Thomas glanced at the knight. "How do you know he went there if no one from his ship lived?"

"The captain's journal came to the shore with pieces of the boat."

Nicholaus looked distantly across the tavern. "When was this?"

"Months ago."

Nicholaus shook his head in rejection to the news.

The man sadly nodded. "Pieces of the boat have been found up and down the coast."

Nicholaus, swallowing hard, pleaded, "Tell me, this Captain Vitalis, if he were to find a lady upon the island that needed passage, would he give it to her?"

"Vitalis? Of course he would—God rest his soul."

"Do any other ships go to Oro Island?" Thomas searched for any hope of his sister's survival.

"No." The man looked at the two, slowly nodding. "If anyone on the island needed a ride, Captain Vitalis would have given it to her. So, if he found her, she was lost at sea with the captain and his men. I'm sorry." Lowering his gaze, the man stepped away from them to give his order to the tavern keeper.

Nicholaus's face paled. Thomas gripped his shoulder. "I don't know what to think. One moment she's dead upon Snake Island, and then she is alive, and then she made it to Oro Island, and now she's lost to the sea?" Turning away from his prince, he slumped onto a stool.

❄

Thomas stared out the semi-transparent stretched-animal-horn window as the first flakes of a blizzard swirled outside the tavern. *So Annie truly is dead now? What about Edus? We are nowhere closer to finding him.* He shook his head. *Camrina knows about him.* He rubbed his face. "We must get back to Anchony. Camrina knows where Edus is."

Nicholaus stared at the packed earth beneath his boots. "I have failed in every way."

"She will know if he was at the castle or if he was taken from it." Thomas thought out loud.

"She lived through snakes and slavery, but not the sea?" Nicholaus looked despairingly at his brother-in-law. "She was alive when I thought her dead. Is there any hope she is still alive now?"

Thomas turned away from the blowing snow outside to look at the distraught knight. "I deem we don't know for certain, but it sounds as if she's perished."

Nicholaus's eyes found their way to the swirling whiteness outside. "Am I to believe this, too?" He turned back to the prince. "If she lived, that means our child could have, too." The knight released a whimper.

A niece or nephew. Thomas did not know what words he could give to the man sitting beside him. For a moment, he said nothing. "We have no tidings of Edus's death."

"We have no tidings of anything on Prince Eduard."

Thomas took a deep breath as he sat down next to the knight. "I don't want to give up, but where else are we to search?" He slowly nodded. "We have to return to Anchony. There's nothing left for us to do." Looking out the window at the howling wind and swirling snow, he shook his head. "Though I fear it shall have to wait for spring." Pulling himself away from the stool, he stood. "I will try to send a message so Mamá will not worry."

CHILL IN SALONE

Looking at the Sethelian castle in the distance, Sir Jacobus's eyes studied the outline, wishing he could see into every crevice and chamber. "What's the best way to do this?" Though he spoke to himself, his company was privy to his words.

Queen Mona sat back as she lowered her head. "Princess Anastacia won't be at the castle." The three knights turned to look at her. "Everyone would know her. If he had her and by some chance kept her alive, he wouldn't keep her *there*."

Melvon looked at her with agitation. "And where do you think she would be locked away from all people then?"

Mona glared back at the knight. "Would you even believe me if I told you?"

"We are all ears." Sir Jacobus cut in promptly before the questioning could escalate to bickering. "Where would she be?"

Glancing at the knight, Mona lowered her head. "There is an abode in Southshire. It is a desolate land. Someone could easily be taken there without anyone knowing. If he has her alive, I'd say she'd be there."

Sir Melvon shook his head. "Why are you telling us this now

that we are so close to Salone and weeks away from Southshire?"

Mona pulled her cloak closer to her as a cold winter breeze brought the promise of a bitter snow. "I only now thought of it!"

Sir Melvon, standing, looked at his brother knights. "I don't trust her. I'm going to Salone."

"She could be in either place," Sir Frankus commented as he looked between his fellow knights.

Jacobus nodded. "Indeed." Turning toward the castle, he looked back at the group. "Sirs Melvon and Frankus, you go to the castle to see if our princess is there. I'll stay here with Queen Mona. If we do not find her here, we'll go to Southshire."

When Lord Cortell entered the public chamber, Prince Howercus was sitting at a table staring across the room. Cortell saw dark circles under his eyes. "Your Highness, are you alright?"

"Her face haunts my dreams," a humble truth slipped out.

Cortell cautiously stepped closer. "Queen Camrina?"

"No! No, no, no, no, no! That princess from Anchony!" He looked at Cortell hollowly. "She was with child, you know? She was with child, and I sent her to that island. I sent them to their death!"

Cortell tilted his head. "You speak of Annabelle of Anchony?"

"Annabelle? Was that her name?" His eyes dashed around sporadically.

"I think, Your Highness, you should try to get some rest."

Staring at a parchment upon the table, Howercus shook his head. "Rest? Rest I can't find!" He looked over at the duke. "Her eyes—those emerald eyes—they burn my soul! They are there when I close my eyes!"

Cortell stared at him, unsure what to say.

"What am I to do?" He looked up at the duke with desperation plastered across his face. "Tell me what to do!" Standing, he tapped upon the proclamation. "This. This shall do it!"

It is Annabelle's death that haunts him? What of his brother, niece, and nephew? Stepping closer hesitantly, Cortell cautiously looked at the parchment, half afraid of what he might find. "What is it, Your Highness?"

Their thoughts were interrupted by a knight in the doorway. "Sire, Sirs Melvon and Frankus have arrived from Anchony."

Lord Cortell turned toward the door as Prince Howercus glanced up from the table in a half-stunned state. "Only now? So long? Why did it take them so long?"

"We've been in Aboly," Sir Frankus informed him as they stepped into the room.

"Aboly, you say?" Howercus's eyes dashed around the room. "Who rules? Does Queen Camrina rule?" He leaned upon the table as he desperately waited for the reply.

Melvon, standing next to Frankus, answered, "I vow to you, she is in Aboly."

Howercus slowly nodded. "Good. Good. That is the first tidings. Tidings from Aboly."

Lord Cortell eyed the two knights. *He didn't say she was ruling. Is she, or do they hide that she's not with purpose? Do they know King Francis lives? Did King Francis make it back to Aboly? They have not turned me in yet—they either do not know my part in what was contrived, do not know of it, or do not know me.*

"And that servant? The servant Clara? What did Camrina do with the servant?" Howercus's eyes seemed not to be able to settle on one point of focus for longer than a few seconds.

The knights glanced at one another. Sir Frankus offered, "We did not come across a servant named Clara."

"No? What became of her? What was her lot?" Howercus

spoke more to himself. "Did she kill her, too? I didn't do it. It wasn't me this time. Was she in the dungeon?"

Cortell studied the prince. *Is it the fact that he was there that haunts him? Not her death, but that he watched it take place?*

"No," Sir Melvon replied cautiously, unsure if the prince was asking them a question or speaking to himself. "I tell you she was not."

"And the others?" Howercus asked nervously.

Frankus quickly looked at Melvon. "The others, Your Highness?"

"King Francis had a large family. Did he not?"

"There were many chained," Sir Frankus revealed slowly.

"Those bound are forced to work on the castle," Sir Melvon added.

"The princes forced to work? Her own nephews?" A crooked smirk crept across the prince's face as he said quickly, "That sounds like her. Like Camrina, indeed." He glanced at Lord Cortell. "Kill them after they help your castle to rise." Nodding, his smile slowly faded. "Did they speak about her—their sister?"

"Which sister would that be, Your Highness?" Sir Frankus asked.

Howercus glanced at Lord Cortell. "Annabelle. Annabelle. That princess, Annabelle." Speaking the words frantically, the prince sat down in his chair.

Cortell glanced at the knights to speak her name with clarity: "Princess Annabelle of Anchony."

"She was left to die upon an island, Your Highness," Sir Melvon stated, unable to hide the tinge of contempt that slipped out with the words.

Lord Cortell tilted his head, attempting to discern the meaning of the knight's tone.

"Yes. Yes." Howercus dismissed them with a wave of his hand, trying desperately to forget his part in her death. "I know. I know. Leave me at once. Don't speak of it again. Be gone now."

The duke watched them exit the chamber without emotion. *Are they purposefully holding back the truth?*

"Cortell?" the prince called.

"Your Highness?" Shifting his eyes from the door, he looked down at the seated, frantic Howercus.

"Sir Arkel? Have we heard from him? About the gold."

"No, Sire."

"No tidings of Anguis at all?"

"Not a word, Sire."

Taking a deep breath, Howercus shook his head as he spoke to himself, "He has betrayed me! That pirate! He will be found. He will be found! Put a price upon his head. A high price upon his head!" His eyes lowered to the table. "They won't see me as their king. They loved their beloved King Henrard! They have to know he's dead! The word has to be spread. The time is now. Now! It is perfect. It is perfect." Pulling the parchment from the table, he looked up at the duke. "She's ruling Anchony. She got what she wanted. I can get what I want now, too! The time is perfect! It is time. It is time!"

"Time, Your Highness?" Cortell asked, not letting Howercus's frantic emotions disturb his own calm.

"Camrina got what she wanted. She won't thwart my plot. It's time everyone in Sethel knows that *I* shall be king!" Slapping the parchment back down and hastily signing his name to the decree upon the table, he melted some wax and stamped the Sethelian seal into it. Standing with a frantic pace, he quickly rolled up the scroll and slapped it at Cortell's chest. "I want you to tell all the people! You must do it. You must do it now!"

"Me, Your Highness?"

Howercus gripped his shoulder. "You, my trusted friend, are a servant of Sethel. It was to go to Sir Tratus, but he's not to be found. Not to be found at all!" He looked the opposite direction. "Where has he gone?"

"Yes, but . . . *now*, Your Highness?" Howercus looked at him strangely. "Winter is upon us." He glanced toward the window as a strong breeze pushed the heavy curtain allowing winter's undeniable signature to enter the castle. "Travel shall be harsh upon the horses."

Howercus, spotting white flakes blowing through the window from his periphery, lowered his head. "Haste, haste then when winter has passed." He quickly looked away. "And when the bishop can make it. Where is that bishop? Did he not get my letters? He must crown me king!"

Walking from the chamber, Cortell looked down the hall to see Frankus emerge from the dungeon stairwell and whisper to Sir Melvon—and Sir Melvon whisper back.

As the duke approached, they turned from their private words to face him. "Sirs, was there word of Sir Nicholaus Hunts in Aboly?"

Sir Melvon tilted his head. "Why do you ask about an Anchonian knight?"

"I . . . had heard he was the husband to Princess Annabelle."

"Is that so?"

"He must be very troubled." Cortell fished for any signs of where the two knights' allegiance really lay.

"I deem he would be." Melvon gave away no answers.

Cortell decided to be more direct. "Sirs, what did you do while in Aboly?"

"We watched over a captive," Sir Melvon answered.

"Only one?" Cortell, stiffening his jaw, stepped closer and lowered his voice. "If I were to say there were whisperings from Anchony that one from King Henrard's family lived"—he noted how Sir Frankus quickly glanced toward Melvon—"what do you have to say to that?"

Melvon's neck tensed. "What tidings that would be for Howercus."

Cortell lowered his head. "He has not heard such words."

Frankus tilted his head. "You don't tell your soon-to-be king?"

Cortell looked into the eyes of one man, then the other. "If it's true, he won't be my king, will he?"

Melvon chose his words carefully. "*If,* then means she's not here?"

Cortell lowered his head as he whispered. "No, not here."

"Your name, My Lord?" Frankus ventured.

"Lord Cortell, duke of Summerton."

Frankus took a quick breath as Sir Melvon raised his head with the revelation. "Do you know where she is? Is she in Sethel?"

Cortell lowered his voice with his head. "Her fortune I do not know." He looked for any eyes that might be watching them. "What have you heard?"

Sir Frankus tapped them on the arms and pointed to movement he saw in the shadows across the dark hall.

"You return with another?" Jacobus asked as Sirs Melvon and Frankus walked through the swirling snow with Lord Cortell behind them.

"This is Lord Cortell—the one who fooled Howercus into thinking King Francis was hanged."

"Good—" The duke stiffened when he spotted Queen Mona. "What is *she* doing here?"

"We are charged to watch her."

He stated adamantly with a pointing finger, "Prince Phillipus didn't trust her."

"We are aware."

"Neither do we," Melvon added quickly.

Mona shook her head. "I didn't want harm to come to my husband! Why won't anyone believe me?"

"Because you will say anything to get your way!" Sir Melvon answered without hesitation.

"My way? All I want now is for Howercus and Camrina to pay for using me!" Her face twitched in agitation as she held her arms close to her body in an effort to ward off the cold.

Cortell addressed Jacobus: "I need to know if Princess Anastacia lives. If she doesn't live, it doesn't matter that Howercus was behind the death of his brother—there is no one else with claim to the throne. Sethel needs a monarch. It shall fall into chaos without one." Taking a deep breath, he revealed, "Most Sethelians don't yet know King Henrard is dead. Howercus wishes me to tell of his brother's death. I wish to tell the people the truth, but I don't know the truth to tell them."

"He will kill you if he finds you betraying him," Sir Jacobus said.

"I have already betrayed him." He looked at the knight. "The truth is worth dying for. I only want to know what the truth is before I die."

"We believed she was taken to Camrina's castle, but she's not there now. We're not certain where she's gone or if she was there to begin with," Jacobus said.

"Pirates came to the castle, but they only took chests," Frankus added.

"Chests of gold?" Cortell held his breath.

"We assume. We found no gold in the castle," Sir Jacobus added.

Cortell dared to smile at the knight's words.

"You deem this good?" Jacobus asked.

"I'm not certain, but it could be." The duke slowly nodded. "If it was Captain Anguis, and we trust in Prince Phillipus's judgment, it could be very good."

"Who is this Captain Anguis?" Sir Jacobus asked.

"I don't truly know."

"Where can we find him?"

Cortell shook his head. "Monakala has a price upon his head. Howercus searches for him, too. He was to take Camrina's gold, but he has not returned with it."

The Sethelian knights looked at one another. Sir Frankus asked, "Is this a good tiding that he has not returned?"

"Did he take the princess somewhere?" Jacobus asked.

Looking into the swirling snow, Cortell suddenly lit up with an inspiration from a memory. "Brotherton in Baltam—that's where he would have taken her!"

"Why there?" Sir Frankus asked.

"It was agreed upon between Prince Phillipus and—"

"How far is it?" Sir Melvon interrupted.

"In this weather, it would be spring by the time you make it there, if you make it at all."

Mona sprang forward, hurriedly speaking her words, "I have a thought!"

Sir Melvon turned away, mumbling under his breath.

Mona looked toward the duke. "Let me go into the castle with you."

"Absolutely not!" Sir Jacobus insisted as Sir Melvon turned around with intrigue. "That is a death wish! You know the truth—"

"That's why I must!" A grin spread across her face. "You have avowed that I will say anything to get my way, and my way is for Howercus to pay!"

Sir Melvon tilted his head as he scowled. "What are you hoping to do?"

"I was there when my husband died. I will lie. I will say Anastacia died, too. It will stop him from looking for her!" She scanned the faces to see who liked her plan.

"He's not looking for her. He already deems she's dead," Cortell stated.

"There. There is no need." Sir Jacobus ended the idea. "He could find your deceit and then he would kill you."

She turned toward the knight. "If you give me your word that he will never gain the crown, that he'll lose everything he's ever wanted, it will be worth it! I shall die with joy!" When the men gave no response, the vindictive queen folded her arms and sat down in the snow vexed—she knew the meaning of their silence.

ALANA'S INFORMANT

Anguis, looking upon the castle gates of Summerton in Sethel, walked closer. "I need to speak with Lord Cortell."

"Lord Cortell is not here."

"Then Lady Alana. I must speak with her!"

"Why?" the guard insisted.

"It is for her ears alone. Please! Tell her Captain Anguis is here!" He watched one of the guards begrudgingly walk toward the castle. "Thank you!"

A few minutes later, Lady Alana stepped out of the castle, crossing her arms with a stern countenance, as the guard ran back to the gate.

"Open it at once," the guard said at the insistence of the duchess.

Watching the gates open, Anguis stepped inside. "Thank y—" He was suddenly tackled by the guard and his hands bound. "She'll only talk to you if you are behind bars." With snow upon his face, he was pulled upward and marched to the castle.

With an oil lamp in hand, Lady Alana walked down the spiral staircase to the prison, stopping on the last step. "Why you would show your face in Summerton, I cannot fathom," she said with discontent. "You are a traitor to all that is right and just." Stepping down the last step, she looked at his face and shook her head. "I can't help but wonder why you would come here, unless you were in need of something." Alana walked toward the iron bars in the dark dungeon.

He lowered his head. "I am in need, but I have amended my ways. I'm not a pirate. Not anymore. I'm trying to do what is right," Anguis said stiffly.

"Is that so?" she said with disbelief.

"I have traveled a great distance to get here."

"Here to Summerton?"

"Yes."

"Whatever for?"

"For a ship!"

Alana laughed. "A ship? You claim you have given up your days of thievery? So you come to ask for a ship?" With a serious face, she stepped closer. "Even if you are no longer a pirate, you are still a traitor."

"I am not!"

Studying him for a moment with the flickering flame, she turned a circle to look at him again. "I can't forget: It was in this very castle where you refused to help Prince Phillipus. I am wondering why you would dare—"

"His sister is alive! She's in Brotherton," he said quickly.

Silenced for a moment, Alana tilted her head. "What is it that you claim?"

"Princess Anastacia. I left her with the fishmongers in Brotherton, as he asked me to do if he and his father were dead and I came upon his sisters." She stared at him dumbfounded as he continued, "As of late I have learned that the queen of the

Sockor Islands does not rule Anchony. The princess could go there and be safe! She should get as far away from Sethel with haste! I will take her myself, but I have no ship. I have no way of getting her there."

"So you came *here* for a ship?" Alana stepped away for a moment as she thought of all of his alarming words. "I have heard tidings that Monakala, along with Sethel, have a price upon your head. Tell me, Anguis, do you try to make enemies wherever you go? Or is your manner of being so coarse that it can't be stopped from taking place?"

Anguis lowered his head; he offered no rebuttal.

"Being wanted by a multitude of kingdoms, I deem you are not the best person to aid her."

His face was made clearer from the flame of the oil lamp as he stepped forward, grabbing the bars. "I have to help her!"

Lady Alana tilted her head. "And why is that?"

He lowered his head as he admitted, "Because I lied to her brother and I am ashamed. If I could make amends—"

"Make amends?" Alana looked into his eyes. "Tell me, Captain Anguis, why did Prince Phillipus deem you, a pirate, would aid him?"

"You're letting him go, my lady?" Luna, Lady Alana's servant, asked as they both watched the one-time pirate exit the castle grounds.

"Yes."

"Why, my lady?"

"To make amends."

"You think he will, my lady?"

"Lady Alana!" a man said behind them. The duchess turned around, and he placed a letter into her hands. "It only now arrived."

"It's in Lord Cortell's hand." Seeing her husband's scripted letters, she eagerly turned it over, eyeing the wax carefully. "Was this resealed?"

"Not here, my lady," the servant said with certainty and then bowed and walked away.

Looking back at the paper, she opened it quickly and read the lines:

My dearest Alana,

Winter is setting in and the fish in Salone have begun to rot. If you go in haste, the proper fish should be in season when you arrive. Salone is in dreadful need. Will you tend to the fish at once for our sake?

My love is always yours,
Lord Cortell, Duke of Summerton

"Shall the duke be home for Christmas, my lady?" Luna asked as she looked toward the note she could not read.

The duchess took a quick breath and shook her head. "It does not say."

"Does if offer good tidings?"

Alana, briefly smiling, looked into her servant's eyes. "It was what I needed to know." Looking around at the castle, the duchess took a deeper breath, "I shall be taking a trip, Luna, after Christmas."

"Where shall we go, my lady?"

Glancing at the letter, she gave a quick smile. "It is only me this time, Luna. I will be off to Baltam."

"Baltam? And alone?" the servant said with concern.

"Yes, Luna."

"My lady, may I ask why Baltam?"

Alana glanced down at her husband's scripted hand.

"Because Baltam has the best fish for Salone." Looking back at the servant, she smiled. "Call upon my messengers. I must write some letters."

The young servant curtsied. "Yes, my lady."

TIDINGS OF A PRINCESS

Hearing his door open, Prince Howercus looked over his shoulder from his chair in front of the fireplace. He'd been sitting in the same spot, with a blanket wrapped around him, for hours, staring into the flames. The vile prince was looking more and more sickly from his sleepless nights.

He heard footsteps coming through the doorway behind him.

"Sir Arkel? Is that you? Is it truly you? Have you returned?" Howercus turned toward the door.

It was Arkel, and he was leading a bound and gagged man into the room with him. Howercus tilted his head. "Who is that?"

"One of the betraying pirates who worked with Captain Anguis. I found him in Longbrooke."

Howercus, showing signs of life for the first time in weeks, stood to scan the captured man before him. "Was he feasting with my gold?" He dashed forward. "He is a traitor!" His wild, reddened eyes looked to his knight. "Why, then, is his head still on?"

The captive moved desperately, making noises as he tried to plead his case with a gagged mouth.

"Sire, he has words about Captain Anguis. Words I think you should hear from his mouth."

Having listened to the story of how Anguis had thrown himself overboard for his captive, Howercus slumped into his chair. His mind twitched with thoughts of treachery, trickery, and regret.

"A girl that claimed to be my niece?" He slowly turned around to glance at Arkel and then the captured pirate kneeling on the stone floor. "You threw her into the water? But the captain jumped in after her?" His eyes ran unceasingly from one side of the room to the other.

"Yes, Your Highness."

Standing, Howercus burst into a forced laugh as he touched his perspiring forehead with the palms of his hands. "A story! A story it is!" Lowering his hands, his smile faded, and he cleared his throat and spoke with clarity that had eluded him for weeks. "I don't know who that girl was that Captain Anguis threw himself after, but it wasn't my niece!" He leaned over the captive. "All of my brother's children are dead; every one of them is buried in Anchony!" Standing up straight, he looked down upon the man. "Why did you bring me these tidings? What did you hope to gain?"

"I thought you should know, Your Highness."

"I should know?" Howercus stared at the man. "A lawless pirate thinks the monarch should know?"

Lowering his head, the man admitted, "I was hoping the truth would gain me my freedom."

"There it is." Howercus paced in front of the man. "You want your freedom. Freedom, freedom, freedom—for a lie? Is that it?"

The captive, in distress, shook his head. "It is not a lie, My Lord. Those are the words I heard! If it is a lie, it is not mine!"

Pausing, Howercus looked at the man. "Yet you bring false tidings to your king? Nothing but stories?" Howercus, turning to Sir Arkel, said with a tight countenance, "You already have your orders of what is to be done with this man."

"Yes, Sire." Sir Arkel bowed his head as he pulled up the man, while the prince, with hands behind his back, turned back toward his smoldering fire.

Glancing over his shoulder, he spoke quickly. "At once. No dungeon. No mercy for traitors. Anguis is mine! Monakala mustn't know."

"Is it done?" Howercus stared at the fireplace as he heard someone enter—in the exact position in which Sir Arkel had left him.

"Yes, Sire. Would you like the head to be put on show?"

Howercus spoke tightly, "Bar the door."

Arkel, moving back, closed the oak door. Howercus turned around and, losing all composure, instantly slipped into the frantic, petrified, and paranoid mood that had overtaken him for weeks.

"What if it is true? What if Rissa or Anastacia lived? What if one of them lived?!" He looked desperately at the floor. "She would have claim to the crown! This could all be for nothing."

If it is true, then Camrina had her. She knows I don't have claim to the throne. She purposefully hid her? Hid her from me. Why is Monakala here?

Who else is still alive? Do they all live? Do they all live and no one tells me? He rubbed his face with his hands. *This could be my ruin! Am I ruined already?*

His eyes found those of Sir Arkel as he spoke with fierceness, "What of the other pirates on the ship?!"

"They were all taken care of, Your Highness."

"All."

"All but Captain Anguis," Sir Arkel revealed with discontent.

"I want the knights to find that traitor, Captain Anguis! I want knights to go to Anchony to find out what Queen Camrina has plotted against me!"

Sir Arkel stiffened. "Sire, I sent knights weeks ago to Aboly."

"You did?"

"So you would know the state of the monarch in Anchony."

"Oh. Have you had word?"

"No, Sire. I will send more knights to search for Captain Anguis, Your Highness."

If the other kingdoms don't see me as king, why would the Sethelians? Prince Howercus shook his hand. "Listen here. Monakala mustn't know! Nothing! Tell them nothing!"

Sir Arkel bowed his head and left immediately.

"A secret meeting in the forest? Did you hear their words?" Sir Arkel whispered to his brother as they stood in a secluded section of the castle.

"I couldn't hear or see much—there was a blizzard at the time. But there was a mention of Prince Phillipus and a Brotherton."

"Brotherton in Baltam?" Sir Arkel's chin stiffened. *Did Lord Cortell work with the prince? Does he know where the outlaws are?*

"Arkel, Prince Phillipus is dead, isn't he?"

Arkel tilted his head as he looked at his brother. "Yes. Have you been told otherwise?"

He shook his head. "No. But how did he die?"

"He was in Anchony. King Francis claimed it his doing. Justice has already been served to Sethel."

"But is the prince alright?"

"Prince Howercus? He's nothing but health. Why would you ask?"

"I've heard the servants say he cries out in the night. That he is haunted by their ghosts."

Sir Arkel grabbed his brother behind the neck, pulling him closer. "I avow to you, brother, there is nothing wrong with Howercus's mind. Now, don't you believe me?"

Out of fear the man nodded.

CHRISTMAS

"Close the door, child, you're letting out the warmth."

Eduard, on Walva Island in the northern sea, glanced over at Lina. "Yes, but what of the mariners? They've got to be cold. They don't even have an abode."

Lina, closing the door to her hut, leaned against it. "Yes, Prince Eduard, I know. It is very cruel what they must endure, but that is why they cut the wood."

"But the Seafurs take it—I see them. They don't get to keep all that they cut. The Seafurs take most of it. The mariners keep so little."

"'Tis true—they hardly keep any. But that is why the Seafurs keep them alive. I've learned that if you want to stay alive here, you must live up to what they want you to do."

He looked up at her. "Is that why you're alive?"

"I don't know, child. I don't know at all."

"Why do you have a home while the mariners sleep out in the open? Why did they give me to you?"

Touching his face, she could not help but smile. "What a curious mind, but the answers I can't give."

Lowering his head, he walked to his cot and sat down. "I

miss Mamá. I don't know where she went. Someone took her!" He wiped away a tear as he remembered the last sight he had of his mother as she was taken away by Sethelian knights. "I tried to stop them, but I couldn't."

"Oh, child." Kneeling in front of him, she remembered Annabelle's words, *"You are the only hands of Christ they know."* Taking his hand, she squeezed it. "I've tried to help others, too, and I've only failed. But take heart: It shall be Christmas soon. If there is anything to bring us joy, it is the Christ child coming into the world." Pushing herself up, she sat down beside him. "Tell me, child, what does your family do for the Christmas season?"

Wiping away a tear, he thought back. "There's a feast for many days. For Christ's Mass we go at midnight. There are candles as far as I can see! The whole church is lit in light!"

Lina pulled him over to herself. "There is no better way to show that He is the Light of the World."

In Aboly, Queen Clara looked at the cathedral glowing in its décor as more and more candles were lit amongst the greenery. Looking at her husband, she whispered, "Eduard loved the candles." The king hugged her.

Elizabeth lowered her head at the luminosity that spoke of the transcendent Truth. "Where's Crisa and Thom?"

Isabella shook her head as she pulled the young princess to herself. "Take heart that God knows. We are always in His hands —the God who took on flesh and became one of us. Our Emmanuel—God with us! That is our well of joy!"

"Wherever they are, Princess, pray that they may feel the joy of Christmas," Symon said as he leaned over.

She looked up at the crucifix as she said to herself, "He came to show us how to live."

"What's that, Princess?" Symon asked.

Her tired eyes turned to look at him. "I pray for them, but I pray most of all for Aunt Camrina."

Annabelle looked at her children lying on the deer skins, kicking their feet and making noises. "Mary and Joseph were away from their home, too. They had to journey to Bethlehem—the House of Bread. There was no room for them at the inn, so they found a haven in a cave that was home to animals." She looked around as the firelight painted the cavern walls. "It could have been like this one."

She closed her eyes. "Thank you, Father, for tending to us. For helping us to know what it was like for You in the cave at the time of Your birth—the greatest king to ever live born among animals." She could not help but smile. "What humility. You have blessed us to share in the same humble beginnings as You lived. I know You are with us as You were with the Holy Family on that first Christmas. Your gift to the world was Your Son, and You have given me these two gifts of beauty! This would be the perfect Christmas if only Nicholaus were here. Oh, Father, can You let him know, wherever he is, that we love him so dearly?"

Opening her eyes, she looked back at her children. "And an angel appeared to the shepherds that tended the flocks, from which the Passover lamb was taken, so they would come and adore the true Paschal Lamb. And they sang, 'Glory to God in the Highest and peace to all people on earth!'"

Nicholaus, kneeling next to the prince in the church in Cottal, Baltam, looked at the flickering flame from the altar candle.

Christ is present within us; He will not leave His bride, the Church, without Him. He lowered his head. *I didn't want to leave my bride, either, or my child. Father, please let them be at peace. Let them be praising You in Paradise this Christmas morn!*

Taking a deep breath, it felt as though new life moved throughout his body, and a smile came upon his face as he was overwhelmed with the Holy Spirit—love itself.

Holding the two babes within her arms, Annabelle could not help but tell her children of the wonders of God. "The Son of God was placed in a manager—where food was held for the animals—for He came to be our food so that we might have life within us."

She suddenly realized the truth of words spoken to her upon the Forbidden Island years ago as she looked across the cave toward the large pond. "Peter once told me that he longed to return to Anchony for the Most Blessed Sacrament alone. I now know what he meant." Rocking her children, she looked down at them. "It's a marvel that I can't wait to tell you more about! You see, the Blessed Sacrament fulfills the New Covenant. There had to be a covenant because we fell. Pride made our parents turn away from what God had told them and eat forbidden fruit. It was through this disobedience of eating food we were not to eat that we fell. So, too, with the eating of food, we are brought back to life! It's like we say, 'You are our God, and we are Your people.' When we eat of the Eternal Sacrifice, it is we who go into His resurrected Body. We come alive with our King!"

Watching the sweet faces of the sleeping babes, she touched their soft skin. "And it never could have been without His Incarnation and birth. Oh, Father, how much do You love us?"

"Mass must have just ended." The bishop, walking through the streets of Aboly on his horse, pointed with his head. "There are the carolers."

Cristine watched the crowd of people dance around in a circle singing. "So we missed it?" The princess lowered her head. "It's the first time I've not been there with my family."

"You won't miss Mass," the bishop said matter-of-factly.

"Take heart, you'll be with them for the rest of the twelve days of Christmas," Samus said.

Cristine glanced at him. "This will be your first time in quite a while that you'll be with your Papá and sister?"

He nodded once as the crowd of carolers came closer and closer, singing with joy at the birth of Christ. Looking at the faces of the crowd, Cristine smiled as she dismounted her horse.

"There they are!" She ran towards the merriment. "Isa, Liza, Symon!"

Symon, first noticing the new arrival, tapped his wife on the arm. "Look who it is."

A larger smile burst forth as Princess Isabella released Elizabeth's hand and offered her own to Cristine. Elizabeth, wondering why Isabella let go, looked over to find Cristine holding her hand. She shouted in glee and hugged her sister. "You made it back! I asked God to bring you back for Christmas and He did!"

Clare ran from her father's side to her brother. "Sam-mas! Ya bac!"

Queen Clara, realizing her daughter had returned, ran down the cathedral steps to greet her as Bishop Dominicus walked to the king and his brother. "Merry Christmas, Your Majesty."

"What a Christmas blessing. You've returned Cristine to us!" The king greeted him with a pat on his arm.

"Did you find trouble along the way?" the Lion asked his brother as he hugged him. "It took you quit a while."

"We went to more than Conlee."

"Did the woman not want the child?" the king asked.

"The woman and her husband are not young."

"I thought the child was five," Francis said.

"Conlee was assaulted when your father reigned. Gavana was five when she was taken."

"Assaulted?" William looked at his father, beginning to ponder the validity of the steward's words.

"The children were taken. Adults in the town—slaughtered."

Francis's face paled. "Did they come from the sea?"

The bishop nodded. "Likely. There weren't any that lived. And it was not only there. It was at least three other places, and they were all close to the shore."

The king's eyes went to the height of the cathedral. "Is the steward right? Did the stolen gold keep the Seafurs from assailing us?" His eyes fell down the height to look at his son. *What will they do if they don't get their gold?*

Camrina held her ears in the corner of the dungeon, yelling her dismay of the carolers. "Will they ever shut up!"

"Do the praises of Christ's name cause you such pain?"

She looked through the darkness to the man in front of her. "Brother, did you come to greet me with some—"

"I don't want to hear any lies from your mouth. I want an answer to a question: How would you give the gold to the Seafurs? How would you stop them from assailing Anchony?"

Pulling herself up along the wall of the dungeon, she walked toward the bars. "Seafurs? What's a Seafur?" A sly grin slid across her face as she tilted her head.

"Camrina! Why can't you speak the truth? I was hoping for a

Christmas miracle. I know all about your plots and your work-ings. Atone for them now! Tell me how to spare Anchony from being assaulted by the heathens!"

"Francis, why ever would I do that? Don't you see? When the Seafurs attack Anchony again and again, the people will see you for what you are—weak. And they will come to see that *I* have kept them from being assaulted all these years. They shall beg for my release and beg me to reign!"

Infuriated, he stepped away from the bars about to lash out in anger, but his ears were filled with the distant sound of the carolers and some of the prisoners who joined in: "*. . . dum pax terris nuntiatur, caelis gloria. Hei hei, nova gaudia!*" He forced himself, in his anger, to dwell for a moment on the meaning: "*. . .* while peace is announced to the nations and glory to the heav-ens. Behold, new joys!"

Francis nodded his head. Nova gaudia! *New joys, indeed. Getting upset is what she wants me to do.* Taking a deep breath, he looked back at his sister. "*Nova gaudia,* Camrina. New joys! New joys."

Camrina's mouth opened is disbelief. "Did you not hear me? I said they shall beg—"

"Do you not hear them? It doesn't matter what you say, what you do. Christ came as a child to fulfill the Old Covenant —to make the New. And when He ascended into Heaven, He took rule of this world. Don't *you* see? He has already won. And behold, he was born this very day!" He nodded his head. "New joys. New joys. Camrina, I will not add any measure of hate to this world by lashing out at you in anger. Your words will not steal my joy." He lifted his hands. "Everything is in God's hands. *Hei hei, nova gaudia!*" Singing along with the carolers, he left her to her lonesome self as she grew more and more agitated.

"I will take this kingdom! It will be mine! Did you hear me? It will be mine!" She slumped down in the corner, trying to block out the voices as the carolers and prisoners seemed to grow louder and louder. "Shut up! Shut up!"

A few hours later, Isabella stepped down the stairwell. "Merry Christmas, Aunt Camrina."

Utterly drained from her angry weeping and lack of sleep, the queen dropped her hands from her head. "Not you, too."

"I brought you a special Christmas treat." Isabella searched for any kind of reaction. "Do you not want it?"

Camrina's chains rattled as she forced herself up and forward. "What is it?"

Isabella, watching the guard open the door, looked to her aunt and nearly gasped in fright at the darkness under her eyes. "It's . . . goat's milk." Handing it to the guard, the princess watched him place the clay cup upon the stone floor. "If you don't want it, I shall take it back."

Camrina stared at the cup upon the floor as her nostrils flared. "You would drink my share?"

"When I asked the goat herder for milk for you, he denied it. So, you see, it is my share I give to you." When Camrina made no movement forward, Isabella took a quick breath. "Do you not take any kind gift?" Receiving no reply, Isabella glanced at the guard. "I shall have him take it back then."

"Leave it!"

The princess watched her aunt pick up the cup and taste the milk.

"Merry Christmas, Aunt Camrina."

The queen looked at her from above her cup. "Why are you so kind to me?"

Isabella shined her radiant smile. "I don't do it for you. I do it for Jesus."

As the cup flew toward her, Isabella stepped away from the

bars. She looked at the trail of milk upon the ground before turning around to leave with a shrug of her shoulders. "You missed."

Before the princess could take two steps toward the stairwell, Camrina's voice rang out, "What do they say of me? With what vileness do they speak of me?"

Isabella turned around with light beaming from her face. "Why do you think we speak of you at all?"

Camrina's chains rattled as she stepped forward, tilting her head in amazement at her niece's words.

Isabella took a quick breath, realizing her aunt might actually be listening. "The only time your name is spoken is when it is in prayer for your soul."

Camrina's skin began to itch on the inside. "But your father—"

"Any words my papá speaks about you are for the bettering of your soul. You know that, Aunt Camrina." She turned around to leave.

The princess placed her foot upon the first step as Camrina called out, "Do you know why the Seafurs gave me their ship?"

Isabella glanced over her shoulder. "No. And I'm not certain I care to know."

"It was an exchange. I took their ship for taking a child off of their hands. Do you care to know who that child was?"

Isabella, turning around, stepped down. "No. Thomas has not come back yet, so what am I to think but you lied about Edus being at your castle? I can't trust the words that come from your mouth."

"You will not listen to what I have to say?" Camrina asked in consternation.

The princess shook her head. "No, I shan't at all!" A new smile burst forth upon her face. "Merry Christmas, Aunt Camrina!"

As she joyously ascended the steps, Camrina yelled in rejection of being so easily cast aside. "Don't walk away from me! Come back here!"

King Henricus, in his Baltamian castle, stared past the reflection of the dancing flame toward the distant land of Anchony as King Francis's words jingled in his mind, *"If it is Cristine of which you speak, you would certainly know if she did not like you."*

"Your Majesty."

"Come in." King Henricus turned away from his window for the present concern. It was Sir Novus.

"Do Ruffatus's whereabouts bother you so much you can't find rest even on this Christmas morn?"

King Henricus lowered his head. "There are many people upon my mind."

"Hopefully this will not add to it." Entering the chamber, the knight walked forward. "It only now arrived."

King Henricus reached for the note in the outstretched hand. "Thank you." He studied the man before him. "Sir Novus, what are you still doing here? I told you to spend Christmas with your family."

Novus lowered his eyes. "I heard you, Sire, but that would leave you all alone, and no one should be alone on Christmas. I was able to be with them for Mass."

Henricus looked at him with a bit of annoyance. "To your family, Sir Novus. I shall call upon you if I'm in need."

"Yes, Sire," the knight said with reluctance.

Watching the knight leave his chamber, the king walked back toward the oil lamp next to his window. Glancing eastward toward the distant Anchony, he broke the seal. Lowering his eyes toward the scripted words, his stance grew stiffer the farther he read.

Swallowing quickly, his voice rang out: "Sir Novus! Sir Novus!"

WINTER'S BITE

Queen Mona, still perfectly vexed that her plans were not even considered weeks earlier, watched Sirs Frankus and Melvon ride away to the northwest on the recently acquired horses.

"So they are off to Baltam?" Mona asked as she stood in the forest.

Sir Jacobus glanced at her, unsure whether it was good that the defrocked queen knew of their plans.

"Yet you do not go? And you are to what? Tend to me?"

"I'm to find the knights who hold fealty to King Henrard. Now go in." He pointed to the cabin they had constructed in the forest south of Salone.

The queen crossed her arms. "And how are you to do that? You are to ride all over the kingdom and drag me along with you in this bitter weather?"

"It is this weather that shall bring them in. I don't need to go to them. They are already in the town. Now go in!"

Reluctantly, she walked inside the cabin. "And you think they will believe you?"

He picked up a vine he had cut down earlier in the forest. "I suppose many already know it in their heart and only need to hear it from another."

With an irritated head, she said with disgust, "You're going to tie me up and leave me here?"

"I can't trust you." Taking her hands, he bound them. "It will only be a few hours."

Releasing an agitated sigh, she sat down upon a stool as he configured the vine around a piece of wood in the wall. "A few hours! Would if I need to go to the bathroom again?"

"Hold it." As he walked toward the door, he looked back at her. "You've already tried yelling and there was no one to hear, so save yourself the trouble. I will be back later."

She grunted as she watched him close the door. As soon as he was out of sight, she began pulling, stretching, and rubbing the vine in hopes of breaking it and gaining her freedom.

Walking into the tavern, Sir Jacobus scanned the room and found a young face he recognized from the young knight's time in training as a squire. "Sir Warcus, you look upset."

The young knight stood in astonishment. "Sir Jacobus?" He shook his head as he looked around the room. "How are you here? I thought everyone in Anchony was killed!"

In front of the castle gates, Mona—having broken the vine and found her freedom after nearly two hours of work—caught her breath from her run from the cabin in the woods. As she smoothed her dress and hair with her breath billowing out in front of her, she walked up to the gatehouse and peered through the bars. "Sir, it is I, Queen Mona. Let me in!" she said to one of the guards.

"Queen Mona?" the guard said with confusion as he glanced at his fellow guard. "You're alive? How?" He nervously fumbled with the keys as if he was seeing a ghost.

"It's her! Let her in!" the other guard called out.

As the gates closed behind her, she heard someone riding up in a fury. Turning around, she saw Sir Jacobus abruptly stop in front of the gate. When their gazes caught one another, Mona smiled in her glory. Jacobus turned away in disgust; he could do nothing now but return to his hidden location.

Sir Narkalus, the Monakalian knight watching from the woods, glanced at his brother knights from their lookout position, pondering who walked up to the gates and was let right in.

"Queen Mona?" Howercus looked toward the guard at the door as he sat in his chair. "*Here?*"

"Shall I send her in?"

He sat up straight in his chair. *She lived? Did they all? Is it true? A princess is alive? Is Phillipus alive?* Trying to control his breathing before utter panic set in, he tried to think rationally. *If he were alive, he would have come already—he would have challenged me! Is he gathering men? Is he purposefully waiting?!*

"Sire, shall I send her in?"

Jumping to his feet, he drew his dagger as he rushed toward the doorway and pushed himself against the wall. "Send her in alone."

The guard hesitantly bowed his head. "Yes . . . Your Highness."

As Mona stepped into the chamber, Howercus immediately pushed her into the wall. With her cheek forced against the cold stone, she heard the man's voice in her ear and felt the presence of the dagger a hair away from her neck, "With whom do you come?"

"No—no one, My Lord!" she managed to say through her shock.

"No one?" He grabbed her shoulder roughly, pulled her around to face him, and shoved her back against the stone wall. "You come alone? You come alone?" He nervously looked at the closed door.

"Yes, Sire," she managed to utter as the air returned to her.

"Why? Why, why, why, why? How are you alive? How are you here—before me?!"

Taking a deep breath, Mona gained composure as she straightened her stance. "Why? Howercus, dear friend, I lived through the assault upon my family."

"Assault?"

"Yes, by the Anchonians."

"Anchonians?" He stepped away.

"Yes, those . . . those Demolites." She leaned her head forward as if to share a secret. "I think they were working for King Francis! You should be glad to know your brother has gotten justice: King Francis's family no longer rules Anchony."

He looked at her with great intrigue. "So it is true? Camrina now rules?"

She forced a smile. "Isn't that what you were helping her to do? To restore the sovereign bloodline to Anchony?" She lowered her eyes. "But what a horrible cost. The cost of your family. The cost of *my* family."

He stepped away in utter shock. *She sees King Henrard as having fallen to Anchony's woes? And she was there? She was there? Did she see it all?* He shook his head in disbelief at the best tidings he had heard in quite a while.

"Camrina. Camrina. You came from Anchony? I was told she was ruling. I sent knights to confirm, but no word has reached me. No word from them at all!" Halting he turned toward her. "Tell me! Tell me all you know!" He shook his head. "How are you now here?"

"The Demolites killed King Henrard, Prince Phillipus, and the princesses, and they took me as a hostage!"

He looked at her with an urgency. "You saw this? You watched them die?"

She nodded without flinching. "I did indeed. Every one of them is dead."

He began to pace again as he thought upon her words. "But you're only now here? Why? Why did it take so long?"

"The Demolites kept me, wanting pay from Camrina. When she paid, they let me go."

"Like that? So easily?"

"Yes. They wanted pay is all."

Taking a deep breath, he calmed. "And you've only now came from Anchony?"

"Indeed." She stepped away from the wall. "I had to wait until Camrina got a ship for me. As soon as she did, I came."

"Why did it take so long?" he asked in a panic.

"Aboly fell easily, but there were still some Anchonians with fealty to the Anchonian family," she said with ease.

He chortled. "It doesn't come easy for her?" He looked at Mona with a smile. "That gives me comfort."

Mona smiled with pleasure. "I have been to Aboly. Whatever you would like to know, you may ask me."

"Will you tell them? I have sent Lord Cortell, but it would be better if they were to hear it from one who was there. Will you tell the Sethelians how the Anchonians slayed my family—slaughtered them!"

"Of course I will."

His eyes darted around the room nervously. "Why did you come back here?"

Touching her hand to her heart, she offered her most endearing voice: "You were my husband's brother. You are the only family I have left."

❄

Prince William shook his head as he stood in the royal hut in Aboly with his father, Sir Michael, and the Lion. "We're getting nothing from this one. Bring the next one in."

Michael forced the Sockorian mariner up and took him outside, where he exchanged him for another of the captive mariners.

Leading him into the room, he pushed the man down on the stool before the prince and King Francis and pointed to the map on the table. "Where would you to give the Seafurs their pay?"

The man sat stoically.

William, still healing from the mariners's attack, moved uncomfortably close. "From where do they hail? From where do the Seafurs come?"

The mariner shook his head. "I don't know."

"Don't know or won't say?" William said with disgust.

"I don't know! I've never been to their land."

Intrigued, King Francis stepped closer, for this mariner had already spoken more than any of the other mariners combined. "What can you tell us?"

The man shook his head.

"Why do you have such fealty toward a vile person?" William asked.

"I don't know toward whom I *should* have fealty. She is my queen, but did she truly kill her own mother?"

"Yes. She was our princess, but that has not stopped us from imprisoning her and doing what is right," Michael said with all seriousness.

The mariner, staring at the map, swallowed with difficulty and finally ventured for a trade. "What is right? If I tell all, and am left here and the others find out, that will be the end of me."

William stepped closer. "Are you up for a trade? The truth for freedom to the Sockor Islands?"

"You will release me?" He looked at the prince.

William looked at his father; the king quickly nodded. "When we are done with you, you shall have your freedom."

The mariner, leaning down over the map, pointed across from Baltam. "There."

William leaned in closer, reading the letters. "Oro Island?"

"The Seafurs would go there to get their pay for not assaulting Anchony?" Michael asked for clarification.

The mariner nodded and then looked at the king. "She did take your boy, but she put him on another ship. They might have gone there—I don't know."

"When?" Peter asked as he stepped forward. "When would the Seafurs come to the Island?"

"It had to be there during the Wolf Moon."

"When is that?"

The mariner shook his head. "The second full moon after the Winter Solstice. It would be in January or February."

Francis, with his hands laced around his neck, looked over his shoulder. "Could we make it to Oro Island by then?"

"The weather is fierce. That's why they go then—only they are bold enough to venture in it." The mariner shook his head. "The gold was already there. You don't need to worry about it this year."

The men all looked at one another, contemplating whether the man spoke the truth. As Michael forced the man up, William shook his head. "Whether it is lie or truth, I don't know."

Francis released a jagged breath as he unlaced his fingers. "We shall have to pray it is truth, for with the bad weather we can't make it there by the Wolf Moon."

"What of my freedom?" The mariner asked as Michael returned him to his chains.

"Time shall tell if what you speak is the truth."

"Then, please, don't tell the others I spoke to you." He swallowed nervously as he looked around.

Close to the western coast of Anchony, Eunisia, the fleeing servant from Lathrop Castle, looked up from the campfire to find two Sethelian knights before her. Recognizing the color—for it was the same black tabard to whom she had given tidings of Queen Clara—her heart rate increased. She diverted her eyes as the man looked at her. She turned her head away.

"You. You there." He pulled her up. "Yes, it was you. You aided us in finding the servant."

She shook her head. "I don't want any trouble."

"Do you know the way to Aboly?"

"I have never been there before!" she was quick to reply.

"But do you know the way?" the other knight asked.

Lowering her head, she slightly nodded and felt a pouch of coins hit her arm.

"You will take us."

She shook her head. "I . . . I don't—"

The first man grabbed her clothing at her shoulder and pulled her closer. "You will take us. Is that understood?"

She was forced to nod. When he released her, she backed away in fright as she thought about the circumstances in which she found herself. Finding strength, she stepped forward. "I'll show you the way, but I won't enter Aboly."

"You will if we say you will."

"But if Queen Camrina has taken power and she works with your king, why do you need me?"

"Because we don't know if she has the throne! You shall see for us." The man stood straighter. "She won't harm you; you helped us find the servant she was looking for."

Eunisia felt as if she had been punched in the stomach. *Queen Clara is being held by Queen Camrina?*

The other knight laughed. "Why do you look so frightful?

Eunisia moved uncomfortably. "If the queen has not taken power, then I aided your prince in taking the Queen Mother."

The knights looked at one another and chuckled. "That's your trouble, not ours."

About to turn the corner in the castle in Salone, Queen Mona, seeing Sir Arkel meeting with a castle laborer, pressed herself against the wall to try to hear the whispered words.

"Did you ask the priest to read it?" she heard Arkel say.

"I did." It was Sir Arkel's brother.

"And what did it say?"

"He said it spoke only of 'Fish for Salone.'"

"No doubt Lord Cortell has a secret meaning to his words."

"I don't like doing this, and the priest wonders why I had a letter when I can't read. I had to lie. I don't like this at all!"

"Brother! Stay the course!" She heard the knight take a deep breath. "Now what of the knights sent to Brotherton?"

"Pardon me, my lady," a servant called out as she walked past Mona.

She heard no more words spoken by Sir Arkel. Turning to walk away, she jumped as the knight stood before her. "Queen Mona, what do you do in the shadows?"

"In the shadows? Whatever do you mean. I was walking down the hall."

He stepped back to look at her nervous reaction.

"I'll be on my way now," she insisted.

"I find it curious how you are so close to the man that takes your husband's throne."

Stiffening, she looked back at him. "Sir, he is the only family

I have left." Channeling her anger lying dormant within her, she rose further still to his challenge. "And why should I be upset with Prince Howercus? It was not Howercus that killed his brother. It was those Demolites in Anchony." She tilted her head. "Do you give caution to your prince? Are you the one that does not trust him?"

"Trust?"

A servant appeared from around a corner. "My lady, Prince Howercus summons you," she said.

Mona glanced at the servant and then looked back at the knight. "He calls for me."

Walking away, Mona released a ragged breath. *Sir Arkel is too keen. He has to go. But how to rid him from the castle?*

RUMORS OF SPRING

After the harsh winter, Anastacia was happy that the fishing season had resumed. She had grown accustomed by the end of the previous fall to her unpleasant duty of dumping the discarded fish guts back into the sea, and she was quite happy now to be outside again rather than trapped inside the cramped home. She had settled with the fact that the brothers held tightly to a secret. Trusting in God, she humbled herself before His providence, knowing that all would be revealed when it was supposed to be. It was an early spring afternoon when God's providence was unveiled before her.

"Excuse me," the princess said when a man stepped into her path to the water as she carried the basket of waste. Stepping to the side, the man with reddish hair stepped in the same direction. As she looked up at him, he took the basket from her hand. "No, I—"

"Let me do it for you."

She shook her head. "No, it's my—" He dumped the contents. Noticing the Sethelian tabard for the first time, she froze.

The knight looked toward the fish market. "With whom do you stay?"

He doesn't know me? With a pounding heart, she dared to glance at his face. *Is he a king's knight? I don't know him.* She opened her shaking hands for the basket. "May I have it back, please?"

He tilted his head. "You shake?" He stepped closer. "I came to Brotherton looking for four men wanted by the crown of Sethel."

Anastacia's eyebrows furrowed. *My uncle sent him?* Shaking her head, she slowly backed away. "I . . . I don't know anything about wanted—" She jumped when he grabbed her wrist.

"The man that you stay with—who is he?"

She tried to pull her wrist away. "Please, sir, I only want my basket and I'll be on my way."

"Who is he?" he repeated with a more severe tone as she jumped in shock.

"Fulco! His name is Fulco! He's a fishmonger! Only a fishmonger! Please, release me!"

He pulled her closer against her will. "Prince Howercus, who will be crowned king soon, is looking for four outlaws—brothers they are. They stole his gold, and he wants it back! Those fishmongers are brothers, are they not?"

The weapons—were they stolen? Were they bought with stolen gold? With whom have I been staying? Who did Phillip dare to trust?

"Is it them?" He shook her. "Is it them?!"

"I . . . I . . ." Shaking, she looked up at him. "I don't know!"

"Who are you? How do you come to live with them?"

"My . . . my family's dead. I needed a place to stay. They took me in. That's all I know! That's all I know!" Tears of fear streamed down her face as her legs were losing all strength to hold herself up.

"Release her." With blurry vision, she turned toward the voice to find Fulco standing a few feet away, his knife in hand.

"The man you claim should be king does not deserve such a title."

The Sethelian knight looked at him. "There's one of the outlaws now."

"Release the girl. She has no part in our dispute." Anastacia suddenly found herself upon the ground as the knight pushed her away. "Get out of here, Stacia!" Fulco called.

Looking toward the fish seller, or outlaw, or whatever he might be, the princess somehow found her feet through her utterly frightened state. As she scrambled away, she watched five other men surround Fulco. Nervously shaking, she ran toward the fish market. "Aricus! Huebertus! Martelus!" the names came out in a squeak.

She looked around in perplexity. All the vendors were gone.

"Amana! Amana!" Bolting through the door of the wattle and daub hut, she was greeted by silence. *Where has everyone gone?* She looked to the back window that faced the forest. *The weapons!*

She ran back to the door and hurried into the yard behind the house. She dropped to her knees on the soil where the hidden lid was. She pushed it open, revealing the hidden storage hole there. It was void of its contents. With shaking hands, she touched the dirt. They were really all gone.

Looking up to the trees, she released a fresh wail. "Where have they gone, Father? Are they truly outlaws?"

Her eyes zig-zagged their way back to the empty hole. *Outlaws to my uncle.* "Are they on my side?" She shook her head. *It doesn't matter. They'll be dead now. The knights got them.* A fresh tear streamed down her face. *What of Amana and Ienna?*

Suddenly, she stood and took off in the direction of Huebertus's home.

She banged upon the door. "Ienna! Ienna! Please, are you there?"

A shutter opened the slightest bit, and then the door was unbarred. "Stacia."

The princess ran into Amana with a hug. "I was down by the water and a man came. He said he was—"

Amana held Anastacia's cheeks as she looked into her eyes. "We know. We know."

"But Fulco came and there were so many men—"

"Stacia." Amana patted the princess's hair. "You don't need to worry about him. He'll be alright."

"But there were six men."

"And there are four brothers," Ienna said with reassurance.

Anastacia looked at her. "They were all knights. Six knights!" The wives looked at one another. "What? What is it?" Swallowing back some of her tears, she took a deep breath. "That man called them outlaws. What did they do?"

Suddenly the door swung open, and the brothers, led by Huebertus, strode in. They carried the weapons that Anastacia had sought in the hidden hole. The princess backed away as she watched the fish cleaners, transformed before her eyes.

"Are they gone?" Ienna asked her husband.

"Yes," Huebertus answered back.

"We must move on. We can't stay concealed any longer here in Brotherton," Fulco stated to everyone.

They are knights? I don't know them—they aren't king's knights. Anastacia shook her head with confusion. "Who are you?"

Everyone looked at her.

"Stacia," Fulco said as he shook his head, "we must part ways. It's not safe for you to be with us now."

"We must depart at once," Martelus spoke with haste.

Everyone began gathering supplies for the road.

"You aren't king's knights. I don't know any of you,"

Anastacia said. Every one of the men ignored her. She watched them hurriedly shove the few food supplies into a bag. "How did you know Prince Phillipus?"

She spoke louder with force: "Answer me!"

Fulco looked at her. "Stacia, we are keeping true to our word when we leave you here. They are after us, not you. That man didn't know you. You are safer if you stay here." Picking up the bag, he hurried from the hut.

Anastacia shook her head as Huebertus and Martelus left to prepare the horses. "I'm not . . . I'm not a servant."

Amana glanced at her as she tied the bag. "Stacia, what are you saying?"

"Stacia isn't my full name." With more strength she stepped forward. "I must go with you. I must."

"If you weren't a servant, how did Prince Phillipus know you?" Ienna ventured.

"I am Princess Anastacia of Sethel. He was my brother."

The women froze.

Aricus walked forward. "What?"

"Prince Phillipus was my brother. He was killed in Anchony along with my father and my sister. My uncle worked with Queen Camrina of the Sockor Islands to have them killed so he could take the crown. The queen took me to her castle. I was saved by a pirate. It was he who left me with you!"

Huebertus stuck his head through the doorway. "We must leave in haste. Why do you tarry?"

Fulco looked at Aricus strangely as his brother hurried the princess out of the hut and helped her upon his horse.

Aricus eyed him back. "She's coming with us."

Fulco, watching his brother help his ward down from the horse as the last ray of sunlight faded below the horizon, asked, "Aricus, why did you bring her along again?" Having heard Aricus's reply earlier in the day, Fulco could not fathom that he heard the answer correctly. "She's a servant and you've only placed her in peril!" After riding all evening, they had finally slowed when they could no longer see the grass in front of them.

"And I told you—she is no servant." He bowed to Anastacia. "Your Highness, did you mean to say the man that dropped you off to us, Anguis, is a pirate?"

She nodded. "Yes, he is."

Fulco raised his hands in exasperation. "So I did hear correct? *She* is Princess Anastacia of Sethel?"

"Yes, Fulco," Amana addressed her husband, "and she is the true heir to the Sethelian throne!"

His eyes jumped from his wife to the princess back to his wife. "The throne? You should be queen. Why did you not tell us?"

"I didn't know you were knights. I didn't know you could give protection." She lowered her head. "Anguis was afraid my uncle had spies that might find me. He thought it was better if no one knew."

"Well, we didn't know he was a pirate," Aricus commented.

"He's a pirate?" Huebertus asked with disbelief.

Fulco shook his head. "Wait! Just wait! Princess, do you know why your brother would trust a pirate?"

"Not at all." Her few encounters with Anguis streamed through her mind. "But he didn't turn me over to my uncle even though he works for him."

Martelus threw up his arms. "Well, there you go! That's how they found us."

Anastacia shook her head. "No. He wouldn't. He gave me his word."

"What is the word of a pirate?" Ienna asked quietly.

Anastacia stepped backward. *He wouldn't, would he? What if he did?* She shook her head at her thought. "No! Phillip trusted him.

I don't know why, but he did." She pointed to her chest. "I'm going to trust my brother. He was quick and wise. Likely he knew more than we know. I will not question my brother's judgment!"

She looked to the forest floor as Aricus started a campfire and his face lit with the light from the flames. "I want to know why you were hiding. Why you were cleaning fish if you are knights." She looked at Fulco. "From what county do you all come?"

"Bartum." Fulco lowered his eyes. "You are correct when you say we are not king's knights."

"Our youngest brother," Aricus said, standing, "was the king's knight. Sir Ilum of Bartum."

She nodded in recognition of the name. "I knew him. He was a good friend to Phillip."

"Yes, he was."

She thought back. "He was killed a few months before Phillip left for Anchony." She shook her head. "I never learned how."

"We know how. That's why we're here," Martelus said as he bent down next to the fire to warm his hands.

"Prince Phillipus came to us. He told us what took place. Your uncle killed him because he found out something concerning the plotting between your uncle and the queen of the Sockor Islands."

"My uncle had him killed?" She spoke the words as though she was somewhat responsible. "I'm sorry. I'm so horribly sorry for all my uncle has done!"

"Princess, it was not your doing." Amana said, attempting to offer comfort, but she was hesitant to touch the royal person now that she knew her true station.

❄

In Aboly, a gasp escaped Elizabeth's mouth and she dropped the pot of water she was holding. Ignoring the mess at her feet, she scrambled past her sister, nearly knocking the other princess down.

Cristine, wiping away the water that had splashed her face, looked to where her sister had run.

"Liza? What on—" She held her breath as if the sight before her eyes was unreal. As she stood, tears filled her eyes. "Mamá! Mamá, come quick!" she said as she followed her sister in a sprint. "It's Thom!"

"You're alive!" Elizabeth embraced her brother, her eyes full of tears. "We hadn't heard from you. We thought you were dead!"

"Liza, no!" He bent down to look into her watery eyes. "The winter caught up to us in Baltam. We couldn't make it home, that's all."

Baltam? Cristine paused for a moment.

"Crisa!" Thomas stood to greet her. "You both have grown so much!"

"I have?" Elizabeth pondered as her eyes looked behind him. "Sir Nicholaus!" She ran to greet him, too.

"Princess Elizabeth." He wrapped his arm around her as she ran into his side with a hug.

Her eyes scanned around and then found their way upward. "You didn't find Edus?"

"Thomas! You're alive!" the queen cried in happiness as she ran to her son.

"Did you not get the note?"

"What note?"

Thomas shook his head. "I sent word that we wouldn't be back until spring. It must not have arrived."

"No, it did not." Her joyful eyes looked to the knight. "Sir Nicholaus!"

"Your Majesty." He bowed.

Looking back at her son, her smile faded. "You didn't find Eduard, did you?"

Thomas shook his head. "Camrina's castle was raided by pirates."

She gasped. "Did they take Eduard?"

He shook his head. "I don't know. We searched for signs of him but found none."

"Thomas!" the king exclaimed with great joy as he walked toward his family.

"Papá!" Thomas embraced his father and then looked at the knight. "There's something we must tell you about Annie."

His family's full attention transferred to him. "Speak in haste," his father demanded with a tinge of hesitancy, entirely unsure what tidings his son could bring.

Thomas, shaking his head, took his mother's hands. "Mamá, I'm sorry I have to tell you this . . ."

She looked at him with fright. "What?"

The prince continued, "We found that Annie didn't die on Snake Island—"

Clara's face lit in excitement. "That's—" Her smile faded into fear. "Why are you to be sorry? Where is she?" Her eyes jogged across the scenery, falling upon Nicholaus for only a moment. "Thomas, where is your sister?"

Shaking his head, he licked his lips nervously as he began again. "She was taken from Snake Island to Oro Island—"

"From where the slaves came? She was taken as a slave?" his father spoke curtly.

"She was, but that's not the worst—"

"We've already thought her dead," the king interrupted. "Tell us!"

Thomas looked into the queen's eyes. "Mamá, she—"

Staring back at her son, Clara took a jagged breath as she physically weakened. "She drowned?"

Thomas nodded as he stepped closer to her, taking his

mother's weight. As she leaned upon him, Nicholaus spoke. "She was trying to find her way back to Anchony. The ship she was on . . ." He shook his head. "It was broken into pieces in the sea west of Baltam."

The king's comforting hand landed upon the knight's shoulder. "Sir Nicholaus."

Elizabeth looked around at everyone. "Annie drowned?" She glanced at her sister for confirmation. "Like Mamá always worried?"

Staring at the flames dancing upward in agitation from the fire pit near the royal hut, Peter shook his head, wrapped in the same mood as the fiery dance. *Drowned in the sea? It can't be.* He looked away as memories of the young Annabelle, swimming upstream in the bisecting river on the Forbidden Island, flashed before him. *She was a better swimmer than I.* He released a deeply held breath.

"Papá, I'm to take watch."

He looked over his left shoulder as the happy memories faded away. "Nic."

The young knight tilted his head. "You were elsewhere?"

Peter turned toward his son. "I heard about Annabelle. I'm . . ."

Nicholaus lowered his head. "You don't need to say anything, Papá." He stepped closer as he looked at the fire. "She lived on the island. The two of them. I'm . . . I'm glad it wasn't by snake." He shook his head.

But the sea instead? Peter shook his head with great confusion. "How far was she from land?"

"It was between Oro Island and Baltam. We don't know where."

Peter held his breath for a moment. "Nic, are you . . ." As his son looked at him, he could not complete his question.

"What is it, Papá?"

Peter glanced away for a moment, just to find his son's eyes again. "Are you certain you are ready to take watch?"

"Her body was lost to the sea. There's nothing I can do now. I've thought about it all winter. I think I've come to peace with it." He took a deep breath. "It was months ago. My place is here. She would want me to help her family."

He grabbed his son's shoulder. "That she would. Indeed, she would." Dropping his hand, he walked toward his hut. *If she had lived, she would've found her way to Anchony. But how could she drown?*

Kneeling at the Communion rail, with his body and soul one with Christ, Nicholaus closed his eyes, praying that graces would wash over him. From somewhere deep within, he heard a voice: *"Nicholaus, find her."*

Heart-pounding, he stood as he looked around him, wondering if anyone else had heard a mysterious summoning. Gasping, his shook his head. *I give her to You, Father.* But the more he tried to forget what he had heard, the more the voice rang in his memory.

Standing next to her husband on the cathedral steps, Clara watched the young knight descend. *Father, there is still a restlessness about him. Why won't You calm him?* When Sir Nicholaus glanced over at her, she felt his discontent and it stirred something within her soul. Closing her eyes for a brief moment, she heard deep within her, *"It is for a reason."* Opening her eyes, she slightly gasped.

Francis looked at her. "Are you alright?"

Nodding her head, she gave him a quick smile before taking his arm and walking down the stairs. *Father, what does this mean? Does it mean she lives? If she is alive, help me to know that she—somehow and in some way—could have made it out of the sea and to the land.*

NO TIDINGS

"Didn't the fishing season start weeks ago?" Sir Frankus looked at Sir Melvon as they stood in the empty Baltamian market.

"Not one fishmonger to be found, yet there were to be four?" Melvon's perceptive eyes scanned the abandoned place. "Even if they left willingly, is it not odd that others have not taken their place?"

"You think them scared?" Frankus postulated. "Do the Brothertonians think it cursed?"

Melvon stepped toward his horse. "There is only one way to find out."

The murderous prince moved uncomfortably in the chair in his public chamber as he attempted to find rest, but the memory— as it had done time and time again—morphed into a nightmare that plagued his every slumber.

Annabelle's corpse, holding tightly to the child, lay still upon the beach. As he approached, the poisonous snakes slithered away, for they knew the truth—he was eviler than they. Coming within a foot, her eyes opened and she grabbed his leg. "Why did you let them take me?"

In a panic and enveloped in a cold perspiration, Howercus awoke abruptly. His eyes wandered wildly around the room. *The castle? The castle? I'm in the castle? In Salone? I left her. I left her there. I left her to die. And the child!*

Mona, spying through the crack in the door, took a quick breath before preceding forward.

As the door pushed open, he jumped to his feet. "Who comes?"

"It is only I, My Lord."

"My lady, Mona?"

"Yes." She quietly walked forward, speaking with the best concern her voice could muster. "Did you think I was another?"

Looking around the room, he haphazardly fell back into his chair and held out his hand. "Will you come closer?"

She hesitantly walked up to his chair. "Your Highness, what wakes you so? Too many mornings I have found you like this."

He grabbed her hand. "I . . . feel calmer when you're around."

"Something haunts your dreams?" She swallowed hard, wondering if it was the murder of her husband that caused such fret.

"Every night I see her face," he admitted in a whisper.

"Her?" She held her breath.

"The one upon the island." He looked up at her in desperation. "She was with child, you know?"

Mona, feeling the tight squeeze from his hand, knelt down next to him. "If what you want is for me to tell you what you did was right, I can't."

A tear of guilt rolled down his cheek. He pulled her hand to his face. "I know it wasn't! I know it wasn't!" Through blurry eyes he looked over at her. "You are the only one who would speak those words to me—who would tell me the truth!"

"My Lord, I wouldn't lie to you." How easily the words slipped from her mouth.

He nodded enthusiastically as the stray tears fell. "I know you wouldn't. I know you wouldn't!"

Mona looked toward the door as she heard the servants beginning to go about their day. "I should—"

Holding tightly to her hand, he interrupted her. "I rely upon you for your honesty, you know?"

Mona slightly tilted her head. "You trust no other?"

"I trust Lord Cortell and Sir Arkel. But Sir Arkel doesn't trust Lord Cortell." He looked distantly across the room. "So I don't know if I should trust either of them." He squeezed her hand. "But I trust you. You were there. Tell me again that you saw all of them die. Tell me again what you saw. How did they die?"

Swallowing with difficulty, she answered curtly as a tear rolled down her cheek, "By sword."

"And my nephew—tell me again that he has perished."

"He is no longer. I was told he died in Anchelo. His body was brought back to Aboly and buried."

"And their bodies? Where is my brother's body? And my nieces?"

Pulling her hand away, she stood and turned away. "I was taken by the Demolites. I didn't see where they were buried, but I was told they are in Aboly." She defiantly wiped away another tear before he noticed. Composing herself, she turned back toward him. "And you tell me—you tell me again how King Francis paid for murdering my husband!" She knelt back down.

Howercus nodded as he grabbed her hand again. "Yes! Yes, he did! He was hanged in Summerton."

Mona pulled her hand away as the servant entered to rekindle the fire.

"It is mine by right, you know. My brother is dead; his son is dead; his daughters are dead. And you can attest to it all. But tell me, do the people see me as their king? Do they assent to me as their king?"

"You forget—you're not king yet. The bishop has yet to arrive."

"But when he gets here, he shall crown me. Will the people see me as their king?"

Watching the glow from the fire cast away the lingering darkness from the room, she answered honestly, "It has been weeks since I've been out of the castle, My Lord; I don't know what the people think at all."

"There it is: honesty."

She turned back to his chair. "You are scared of losing your crown before you even take it?" She took a quick breath and, assured of his trust in her, she added, "My Lord, you want me to be wholly honest?"

"Yes." He looked at her with great concern, half afraid of what she might say next.

"When I was in Anchony, I heard the bound men speaking. It seems one reason Queen Camrina so easily overtook Aboly and the sovereign family was because there were so few knights left." Standing, she looked across the room at the fireplace. "I have thought about it, and it seems that is the first thing to go when one wants to take over—the traitor will rid you of your protection." Smiling from her own cunning, she nodded. "Yes. If someone wants to take over, he will take away your knights first."

"Take away protection?"

Inwardly smiling, her face turned serious as she knelt back down. "My Lord, I think there is something you should know about Sir Arkel."

"Sir Arkel? What about him?" He stiffened.

"I've heard him speaking. He sent knights away."

Howercus's heart began to frantically pound. "Why? Why? Why would he do that?"

Glancing at the door, Mona watched the knight walk past. Speaking quietly, she said as she stood, "There he is. Ask him yourself."

"Sir Arkel!" Howercus's voice boomed as he stood in agitation.

Called into the room, Arkel cautiously entered the chamber, glancing at Mona. "Your Highness?"

Howercus, attempting to control himself, took a deep breath as he leaned upon the table. "Tell me it isn't true! Tell me! Tell me it isn't true!"

Sir Arkel shook his head. "What, Sire?"

"I have heard word that you sent sirs away. Tell me it isn't true."

"Sirs?" he asked as he stepped farther into the room.

"Where did they go? Where were they sent?" His voice grew more and more agitated.

Sir Arkel looked to the increasingly frantic prince. "Sire, I don't—"

"Don't know?" Mona stepped up beside the prince. "Don't tell your prince you don't know about the knights you sent to Baltam and how they have not returned, for I heard you speaking about it only a few days ago."

Arkel glared at her with a look of death that would have frozen her if she were not already consumed by ice inside; his fears were suddenly realized before him.

Howercus's face reddened. "You sent knights to Baltam? What is this, Sir Arkel? What are these knights she speaks of?" With a growing rage enhanced by a new wave of paranoia, he charged toward the knight. "Arkel, what have you done? What have you done? You are trying to make me lose my kingdom! To usurp me!"

"No!" Arkel raised his arms, showing he would not defend himself against the rage of the royal. "I did it for you, Sire. I did it to get the outlaws!"

"Outlaws?" Howercus spoke into Arkel's face as he gripped the knight's tunic. "*The* outlaws? The brothers?" His eyes began to dance around the wall behind Arkel's head as he thought upon the words. With a moment of clarity, he looked to the knight. "How did you learn of it?" He quickly shoved him against the wall. "Why did you not tell me?"

"I heard rumors, but I did not know of the truth, My Lord. I sent sirs to check upon it, but they haven't returned."

Mona's voice covertly planted more doubt in Howercus's mind concerning Arkel's loyalties: "And what of the sirs that went to Anchony? The ones *you* sent to Anchony, Sir Arkel?"

"More knights sent away?" Releasing his grasp upon the knight, Howercus stepped away as his mind muddled with all the information. *Sir Arkel has deceived me? The deceiver! He admits to doing it himself!*

"How many knights have you sent away, Sir Arkel?" Mona abraded the prince of any remaining trust he might have in the knight before him.

"I sent them away to find the outlaws and to find the true fate of Queen Camrina!" Sir Arkel demanded, more agitated at the manipulative Mona than at the prince.

It was to get the outlaws, that's why he sent them away. But to Baltam? What will the king of Baltam do if he finds them there? Howercus slouched over the table as his maddening mind could not come to a conclusion.

"*I* have told Prince Howercus the true fate of Queen Camrina." Stepping closer to the prince, she added, "And now Prince Howercus has less knights for protection here . . . because of the order you gave without the prince's assent. Tell me, Sir Arkel, do you have credence in your prince's authority? In his right to rule?"

"Once he's crowned—of course I do! If there is anyone in this room who—"

Cutting off the man's rebuttal, she looked up from the floor and calmly posed a provoking question: "Then why do you act as if you are ruler yourself?"

Is he trying to get Baltam to assail Sethel? To make me appear weak? For me to lose the kingdom to Baltam?

"My Lord, are you alright?" She glanced at the knight as she stepped closer to the prince. "Sir Arkel upsets you."

Arkel turned toward Howercus in desperation. "Sire, you know I am true to—" His words halted when Howercus elevated his hand.

"I don't know what you are." Looking down, the prince took a quick breath and glanced back up. "The outlaws were not found?"

"I don't know, My Lord; the knights have not returned."

"So the outlaws could have been there and killed them?"

Arkel lowered his head. "Yes, Sire."

"And now the outlaws run loose in Baltam?" His eyes stared distantly across the room. "Or worse yet, Sethel?"

"It could be, Your Highness."

Howercus looked over his shoulder at Mona as he asked the question to the knight, "You wish more knights to go?"

Arkel, looking between the two, finally asked back, "You don't, Sire?"

What do I want? What do I want? I need truth. I need truth. Does he give it to me? I need him away—away from me! The prince, stumbling into his chair, looked up with a decision: "Send the soldiers from the northern region."

"Yes, Sire." Sir Arkel nodded and then glanced at Mona.

"And you are to go yourself," Howercus said.

A smirk spread across Mona's face as the knight quickly asked for clarification. "I, Your Highness?"

"Yes, you to Baltam. I want you gone from here! Gone from Salone! Gone from Sethel! Gone from me!"

Mona walked toward Howercus with a deep satisfaction written upon her countenance.

"Your Highness, I deem I could be of better service—"

Howercus slammed his hand upon the table as he stood straight. "You are not wanted here! Prove you are not a traitor—go to Baltam and don't return without those outlaws!"

Lowering his gaze, Arkel knelt upon the floor. "I will, Your Highness, but I must say something before I go."

Howercus's entire neck stiffened. "What?"

"Never forget all through which I have stood by you." Looking up, he tilted his head toward Mona. "She has poisoned your mind against me."

Mona gasped. "My Lord, I only want the best for you!"

"The best—" Arkel snarled at her.

"Be gone!" Howercus yelled before Arkel could speak another word. He grabbed the knight's tunic, pulling him to his feet, and shoved him toward the door.

Watching the man leave, Howercus looked back at Mona, shaking his head. "I can't believe this!"

"My Lord, why don't you go to your chamber and rest? Even if sleep can't find you, rest. You need to rest for Sethel. You need to be strong for Sethel."

From her chamber window, Mona watched Sir Arkel ride out of the gates. When he had passed them, he slowed his horse, allowing himself another look in the direction of the castle. Knowing he could not see her features from such a distance, a radiant smile spread across her countenance. "One step closer."

Walking through the woods in her cloak and hood, making sure she was not followed, Mona approached the cabin door, but it opened before she could touch the wood. She was immediately pulled inside.

"What is the meaning of this?" Sir Jacobus barked. "Has Howercus threatened your life and so you've returned for protection?"

Pulling her arm away, Mona defiantly stepped away from him and looked around the hut at all the knightly eyes. "Is this all you've been able to muster in the weeks I've been away?" She lowered her hood as she looked back to the leader of the rebel knights. "Prince Howercus listens to my every word. He has sent away Sir Arkel."

Jacobus looked at her curiously. "What is this? What could you say that would make him send away his head knight?"

"Howercus has a troubled mind. I simply used it to get closer to what I want."

Sir Warcus looked at his brother knights and then admitted, "His mind is troubled. He calls out in the night. We don't speak of it, but we all know it's true."

Mona rolled her eyes. "I didn't come here to speak of Howercus losing his senses. I came to tell you something. He is to send soldiers to Brotherton. And indeed, some knights left weeks ago on Sir Arkel's order."

"That is where the princess is to be, is it not?" Sir Warcus asked with great angst.

Jacobus stepped closer to Queen Mona. "Do you speak these words in truth?"

"Yes! I came in hopes that you can get there first and find Princess Anastacia so she can rip the throne from his grasp!" As the veins in her neck bulged from her internalized anger, she lowered her head. "Being around him is hard to bear."

"I have seen you there. You look as though you bear it fine," said another knight.

"I have learned how to deceive because I've been deceived all my life!"

"Your sufferings are your own doing," Jacobus stated unapologetically as he looked to his men. "These tidings change things. He can't get our princess. Our cause is lost, if he does so. We must ride at once."

"What will he do when he finds us gone?" asked one of the men.

Mona spoke, "I will tell the prince Sir Arkel sent you to Baltam."

Jacobus grabbed her arm. "Why do you think I'm going to let you go? Have you forgotten you are our captive?"

"If I do not make it back to the castle, Sir Jacobus, Howercus will certainly look for me." She stared him down. "Unlike my stepdaughter, he would know I am alive and missing." She struggled to pull her arm from his grasp. "That's why you're going to leave me here."

"She will only slow us down," Sir Warcus stated as he left the hut with the other men.

"I see now why Sir Melvon was so vexed." Shaking his head, Sir Jacobus released his grasp. "Whatever becomes of your life is not my doing. You should leave Salone. The prince can as easily turn on you as he did on Sir Arkel."

Mona glanced at him with great surprise. "Don't you understand? I can't leave. I want to be there when he loses everything!"

Sir Jacobus shook his head. "You are on a perilous ground."

"And if I were not here, what would I do? Do you not see? I have nothing else but this perilous ground!"

"You have no other ground because you choose no other ground. Forgiveness is a powerful thing, and it's not for the sake of Prince Howercus or Queen Camrina or your parents. It's for yourself." Taking a deep breath, he looked ahead. "You've lost yourself, Queen Mona. Find out who you truly are." He jogged out of the hut to the awaiting horse.

Following him out, she yelled, "Who I truly am?" As he took

off toward the north with the other knights, she screamed in agitation, "I am nothing!" She fell to her knees. "Camrina readied me my entire life to think that I am nothing!" The hole within her seemed to grow; it was so uncomfortable that she physically rubbed her core as if it would somehow fill the emptiness.

DELAYED TIDINGS

King Francis's mouth dropped open as he read the note. Clara stepped next to him with concern upon her face. "What's wrong?"

He turned the paper over as if to make sure it was real. "It's from Lady Alana. She says she received word that Annabelle was alive on Oro Island. A merchant from Baltam was paid to deliver her to Anchony—by a pirate."

Clara's eyes widened as she grabbed her husband's hand. "And that's how she ended up on the doomed ship?" Clara's heart pounded a little quicker. *Could she have lived? The note does not say if she lived or died.*

"It appears so."

Their attention transferred to Sir Nicholaus as he entered. The young knight paused mid-bow. "Your Majesties?"

Francis offered him the note. "It's true. Annabelle was saved from Oro Island by a merchant."

Hesitantly looking down at the message, Nicholaus swallowed with difficulty. The uncomfortable feeling within him seemed to grow larger, settling in a place in his soul where it could not easily be removed. He shook his head with great agitation and cleared his throat as if it could remove any discontent within him.

"Sir Nicholaus, it is only confirmation of what you already knew."

The knight shifted his weight as he shook his head. "I didn't know it was a pirate that paid for her to be returned." He looked at the king as if he could answer his questions. "Who? What pirate would do such a thing? And why?"

"Nicholaus," the queen gently spoke, "don't forget the ship was lost at sea." She held her breath. *Does he believe she could've lived?*

Swallowing hard, he nodded. "I know, Your Majesty, but . . . what pirate would pay for her to be freed from the island? Did he know she was a princess? If so, why did he not take her himself? Why did he not ransom her?"

He does not think she lived. Lowering her head, Clara spoke as she looked between the two men, "Was it the child?"

"That could be it," the king agreed with a nod.

Nicholaus, looking down at the note, shook his head. "What if it wasn't?"

Francis, taking a deep breath, looked into the eyes of his son-in-law. "Sir Nicholaus, you need to let this go."

Turning away from the king's eyes as if the idea was preposterous, he whispered, "I can't."

"We want what is best for you. There's nothing you can do for her now but pray for her soul."

Clara studied the uncomfortable knight. *Every time he prays, he only feels a stronger tug to search for her.*

Shaking his head, he lowered it and spoke in a near whisper. "Will you pray for me that I can?"

Clara nodded her head as her husband answered, "Of course. Yes."

"Thank you."

Swallowing with difficulty, Nicholaus walked away from the

couple as he took a ragged breath. Every step away from the conversation caused more of an urgency, a discomfort within him that could not be quelled by any amount of prayer—for it was a grace that provided it and wished action upon it.

"I have to find him." Peter closed his eyes when he heard his son's words inside the knights' hut. "I want to know why he would pay for her passage. What kind of pirate would do such a thing?"

Peter, opening his eyes, took a breath and shook his head. "None of which I know, though I haven't come across many pirates."

Nicholaus sat down upon the bed just to rise a moment later. "It doesn't make any sense!" He began to pace. "What did he know of her?" Pausing for a moment, he looked at his father. "Did she tell him she was a princess?"

"Likely he saw she was with child and wanted her to be safe."

Nicholaus looked back at the note. "I have to find him."

"A pirate upon the seas?" Peter said with doubt, nearly chuckling.

"It was the duchess of Summerton who wrote the note, so she should know the bearer of the tidings." His eyes enlarged as he looked across the room. "Whoever told her the tidings would've had to have known the pirate—since the ship and all aboard were lost."

Peter shook his head. "Nic, what will this do? You can't bring her back."

Sir Nicholaus was overtaken by an anger that had not been released in quite a while. "You were able to hold Mamá's body! You had the chance to say farewell! Where is my farewell? I thought it was upon Snake Island, and then Oro Island, and then upon the sea. If he—whoever he is—was the last person alive who saw *her* alive, then I want to talk to him. I want to know what she said—her last known words! Is that too much to ask?"

Peter, taking a deep breath, lowered his head. "You must get the king's consent."

"I know."

His father looked up at him. "And if he does not give it? What will you do then?"

Nicholaus sat down on the bed distraught. "I don't know."

Queen Clara, watching the young knight exit the knight's hut the following day, spoke to her husband. "He won't let her go. He can't move on." She looked at the king. "I think he feels he shouldn't."

"He needs to."

She touched his arm. "You're not listening. I've watched him. He prays for God's will. If it were not God's will, would he be so troubled? If God wanted him to find peace and let her memory rest, wouldn't he have found it by now? It's been almost a year."

"You deem he is meant to look for this pirate?"

"I think he will only be at peace if he can search him out." Nodding her head, she did not say what was truly in her heart for fear of being thought mad: *I deem he should look for our daughter.*

Nicholaus, with a nervous effort, approached the king inside the royal hut. "Sire, I know you shall not give it, but I ask for your consent to look for the pirate. I have prayed—"

"You have it."

Nicholaus looked up at him, wondering if he had heard correctly. "Sire?"

"Consent is given. You may go alone and seek out this pirate."

Nicholaus's mouth dropped open. He shook his head. "I didn't think—"

"That I would give it?" The king lowered his head. "I see that if I were in your shoes, I would want to find him, too. And my wife has shown me that it is God who pushes you forward. How can I stand in the way of the Father?" He looked around the hut. "The wards are as trained as they shall be at present. There is no better time for you to go."

"Thank you, Sire. I shall leave in haste."

Clara watched Peter enter the hut with hesitancy.

Francis looked at him from the table he sat at. "Jous, come in. Do you have tidings to speak?" Peter, glancing down for a moment, looked to the royal couple.

"Something bothers you?" Clara asked before he could respond.

Grimacing with a nod, he walked forward and gently tapped upon the table. "These are words I did not want to speak while Nic was here."

The king dropped his quill to give him his full attention. "Speak them now then."

Pulling out a stool, the Lion sat down with a certain amount of restraint as he revealed, "It's about Annabelle."

Clara and the king glanced at one another. "What about her?" the king replied.

Peter shook his head. "I can't . . . I can't get over it. Drowning in the sea?"

Clara held her breath as her husband shook his head and

began, "It is horrible—"

"You're not understanding me," Peter interrupted, raising his right hand. "She was a good swimmer. A *very good* swimmer. Even if the ship had gone down miles from the shore—she was strong, capable. She would have lived!"

Clara froze as the words came from the Lion's mouth.

Francis shook his head. "But . . . she was with child." He mirrored his friend's gesture as he raised his own right hand. "How could she—"

Clara finally spoke as she stepped forward with hope, "You think she could have made it from the sea?"

Peter, looking into her eyes, shook his head. "No. I *know* she could have made it from the sea." He turned toward the king to explain. "Being with child would only give her more will to live." Lowering his gaze, he swallowed as he revealed further, "She had—before—anyway."

"Made it from the sea?"

The knight nodded.

The king stood as Clara gasped. "What is this?"

"We were on the island. There was a bear. She ran to get away. She jumped off into the ocean."

"And she lived?" Clara said as she sat down, suddenly weak in wonder. *It's true? Annabelle is alive?*

"She swam in the sea?" the king asked for clarification.

Peter nodded. "She did. It was not the open ocean. She swam around the island. But the sea, indeed it was."

Looking down at the table, Francis shook his head. "She was not with child then."

"No, but she was younger and far more harmed." Peter swallowed hard as he recalled the wound he had tended to on Annabelle's shoulder. "The bear clawed her. I don't know how she swam at all." Shaking his head, a smile cracked across his countenance. Rubbing his face, he began to chuckle.

"The marks upon her back?" Clara asked to the air as she

was filled with more and more hope. Her eyes darted around the room as she thought of Annabelle's words when she forbade her from swimming.

"The meaning of your laughter?" the king, agitated by his friend, demanded.

Peter nodded. "I do know how she made it." He looked at Clara. "It was St. Celestria. She was there in the sea. She cheered her on to swim to the beach. She's the only reason she sought to make it back in all of her pain."

"'A good swimmer.'" Clara's eyes finally settled upon the knight before her as she stood. "She told me she was a good swimmer."

"Indeed, she was."

The king shook his head. "Why did you not tell Sir Nicholaus?"

Peter swallowed with difficulty as his smile faded. "Because I know—even if she had made it in the sea—she's not alive now. If she had made it to Baltam, she would've found her way here by now or would have sent word."

Francis released a breath that expressed exhaustion, but his despair was interrupted by his wife: "She's alive!"

The king looked at his wife. "Clara?"

The queen adamantly nodded her head. "She's alive!"

The king shook his head. "No, he said—"

Grabbing her husband's hand to silence him, she looked to the knight. "Jous, I ask you this: Why do you come to us now with this tiding? Why did you not tell us sooner?"

He lowered his head. "It has been on my heart since the moment I heard the tidings, but lately there has been a push. I had to speak the truth. I felt as if I was deceiving you."

Squeezing her husband's hand, she stepped closer as she continued to stare at the knight. "No! I'll tell you why. It is because these are words that I needed to hear!"

"Clara?"

Smiling with great joy, she looked at her husband. "Francis, I didn't tell you. I didn't believe it myself. But I prayed that if it were true, somehow someone would let me know that Annabelle could have made it in the sea!" She glanced at the knight. "And that you have spoken for me, Jous."

Francis shook his head. "Believe what?"

She looked back into her husband's eyes. "She lives! Our daughter lives!"

Francis glanced at Peter as he shifted his weight uncomfortably. "He said that she's not alive."

Clara shook her head. "That's what he believes because she hasn't come." As she thought about the knight's previous words, her smile faded as she looked downward. "What's come to pass?" She stared at her husband's chest as she spoke the words running through her mind. "Something's passed. Something hinders her from coming to us." Looking back up into her husband's eyes, fear transfixed upon her face as she pulled her hand away. "What's arrived to our daughter? Where is she, Francis?"

"Clara? Clara!" Grabbing her head, he pulled her into a hug as he glanced at the knight for aid in his wife's distress.

Peter shook his head. "I'm sorry. I didn't mean to cause such . . . fear." He awkwardly stepped back.

Closing the door, Peter leaned upon the side of the hut. *Clara thinks she's alive? How could it be? Is it true? Is it all true? She made it out of the sea only to be harmed or something worse?*

His eyes turned upward as he fell to his knees. "Oh, Father, if she's alive, I pray she makes it back to us safely." Lacing his fingers together with all his strength, he released a ragged breath. *Annabelle, my sweet child, where are you?* Closing his eyes tightly, he prayed with all intensity: "Father, if she is alive, let Nic find her! Let him bring her back to us!"

THE SHEPHERD

Turning around to hide behind the rocky cliff on Walva Island, Katara petted the albino wolf as she spoke with concern in her native tongue, "Such talk of no gold. What will become of the slaves?"

Pushing herself away, she silently slipped back toward her village while the wolf ran into the woods. Walking on the outskirts of the village, she watched a mariner pulled from the wood-cutting crew and forced into the northern fields to be the new, designated shepherd. Shaking her head, she turned away and went into the communal hut.

"Katara, where did you run to now?" The woman shook her head as she continued her questioning in their tongue. "If I did not promise your mother I would tend to you, you would have no one to stand on your behalf!"

"They take the slaves to watch the sheep."

"Yes. So?"

"Who will cut the wood when all of them are dead? Once the wolves have killed all of them?"

The woman made a face as if Katara was slow-witted. "We will get more."

With a baby strapped to her front and the other to her back, Annabelle looked up from the tracks in the disappearing snow. It had been the coldest, most bitter winter she could ever remember. Food had kept appearing out of nowhere, all winter long: hares, squirrels, beavers. Most of the winter she spent inside the warmth of the cave preparing weapons and winter wear so she could hunt. Every fur and hide was used as clothing for her babies or herself. She was grateful to the unknown girl and for her 15 years on the Forbidden Island with her teacher, Peter. If it was not for the training she had learned long ago, she and her babies would have perished months prior.

Someone's yelling. Tilting her head, she slipped closer to the valley from where the noise came. One of the mariners, with only a shepherd's staff as a weapon, was down on the ground with a wolf grabbing his leg, another going for his neck, while five others devoured a sheep. With a gasp, she pointed her arrow and released it toward the wolves attacking the mariner-turned-shepherd man. One injured wolf ran off as villagers descended upon the remaining wolves. She quickly hid behind a large tree so she would not be seen.

Yelling, growling, smacking, and whines filled the air for a solid five minutes. When all quieted, she peeked around the tree to see the villagers dragging the mariner and the dead wolves up the hill toward the village.

Walking closer to the valley amongst the scattered sheep, the princess knelt down just outside of the bloody smears. *The wolves are hungry.* She looked to the trees. *There is plenty to eat in the forest.* She gazed at the thick, wool-covered animals. "It's easier. That's why they take the sheep." She stood. "How foolish of them to think one man can tend to such a large herd."

Her eyes turned back to the saturated earth when she heard a whine and watched a young wolf pup struggle through the grass. "What's this?" Glancing toward the village, she looked back and knelt down. "You need to leave. They will kill you if they find you." The fuzzy wolf pup only whined. "You need to find your mother."

Standing to go, she turned back to the little thing. Unable to stop herself, she picked up the pup and looked into its face. Her brow furrowed in awe. One of the two eyes staring back at her was both brown and blue, the colors twisting together in the iris, while the other eye was a plain brown. She studied it for a moment, transfixed. Then, carrying the pup carefully in the crook of her elbow, she took it with her into the forest.

"Lina? What's going on?" Prince Eduard, standing outside Lina's hut, asked curiously as he watched the mauled body of one of the mariners pulled into the middle of the village as the natives began to shout at one another.

"Prey of the wolves, I'd say. They are savage." Lina shook her head as she picked up the jar of water. "Whoever thought of bringing sheep to a place known for its wolves?"

Shouting in their own tongue, two men began swinging at one another. Acwa quickly emerged from the crowd and pulled them apart, gesticulating wildly. But he stopped abruptly when his eyes landed upon the prince. A cold chill filled Eduard as he watched the leader point at him.

Lina grabbed his hand quickly. "Let's go."

Before he could take a step, Ecwab grabbed his other arm. "You wait."

Eduard nervously looked up at the approaching men. "What do you want with me?"

Acwa handed him the shepherd's stick as Ecwab answered: "You watch sheep."

Lina shook her head. "He's only a boy! You can't do that to him. He won't last a day!"

They both looked at her. "He watch. No talk."

Swallowing hard, she adamantly shook her head as she clung tightly to him. "No! No! Please, no!" Acwa gave her a jarring shove, and she fell to the ground, wincing as the back of her head hit the hard earth. "Aren't you to keep him alive as you have me all these years?" she yelled at the men.

"Nocht gilla! Lino wakalo!" Acwa declared.

Lina sat up as she rubbed the back of her head. *No gold? He has to work for his keep?* She looked up at the leader. "Nocht gilla?" *Who was paying to keep him alive?*

Kneeling upon the cold ground, Annabelle looked into the unique eyes of the pup. "Stay in the forest and you'll be safer. You need to find what's left of your pack." She shook her head. "I'm not going to do it for you. I have my babies to think of." She released the pup. The fuzzy thing looked unsure of which direction to head, standing amongst the sticks and leaves of the forest floor. "I'm sorry," she said before leaving it there.

Eduard, scared of both the men forcing him into the field and the beasts that stalked it, was shoved out into the pasture. He quickly turned around. "What am I to do?"

"Keep sheep alive," Ecwab said and then swung the stick. "Take out in light. Bring back at dark. Fight off wolf."

"Fight off the wolves?"

Ecwab laughed heartily. "Don't be food. Need wool."

Eduard nervously turned around as Ecwab walked away. Gripping the stick, he bit his lip. *Don't become food. Fight off the wolves.* He cautiously walked down the first hill to where the herd was now safely grazing. *Thom, where are you? If you are to come, come quickly! I might not be alive on the morrow! I need Sir Henricus's sling. Can I make another?*

His eyes darted toward the field. *I'll need rocks, too.*

Southeast of her cave, the princess tracked the wolf she'd shot with the extra weight of her babes in the front and back. Kneeling down next to the carcass, Annabelle removed her arrow and placed it back into the makeshift quiver, to the left of Augustine on her back. Taking a deep breath before standing, she said to her children, "You two are making me stronger as will moving this wolf." Grabbing the front paws, she dragged it a distance and added, "When I and Peter were hurt upon the Forbidden Island, he said we would have to work harder to get back to where we were. Any weakness in me, shall certainly be gone. I have to stay strong for you two." Once she dragged the wolf back toward the cave, a hefty distance, she fell to her knees, perspiring. "It would certainly be easier if your papá was here!"

The princess, her hands bloody from slicing the wolf's skin, looked around as she heard a small whine while her children, donned in furs and on their stomachs, pushed their upper bodies up off of the blanket with their arms. She watched the young pup, without much coordination, walk toward her. "You again?" She looked at the carcass and then gasped. "Oh, no. Was this your mother? Did I kill your only protection?"

She sat back upon her legs as her shoulders slumped. "I'm sorry."

Lina gasped as she pushed herself away from the male compound when she spotted the sheep coming up the hill. "There he is! Praise God, he lived!"

"The wolves already had their meal for the day. It's every day after this one that he'll have to live," Captain Vitalis said with little hope.

The next morning, Eduard looked around cautiously as the village men watched him walk to the sheep's pen. *Father, help me to not be eaten today!* Struggling with the handle, he stepped aside when a figure stepped next to him.

"Up."

He gasped in shock as he looked at Katara. "You know my words?"

"They go for weak."

"What?" Eduard looked around as they both opened the gate and the sheep slipped out.

"The wolf. They go for weak."

"The weak sheep?"

The girl nodded quickly. "Don't be self."

Thinking about her words, he looked down until he came to the meaning. "Don't be weak myself?" She was already gone by the time he looked up. "Thank you—whoever you are."

"Eduard!" It was Lina, walking briskly toward him. "I've made something for your staff." She rattled the gourd.

"What is it?"

"There are clay balls in it. To scare off the wolves," she suggested with hope.

He watched her tie it to the staff. "You think it will work?"

"I deem you should try all." Kneeling down, she hugged him.

"Thank you for caring." He wiped tears of fear away with the backs of his hands.

"Stay safe. I will check upon you if I get a chance."

Nodding, he turned toward the valley with great trepidation and glanced at the woods where the mariners, forced to labor cutting firewood for the whole village, looked at him, desperately wanting to help but unsure how.

Holding the wolf pup, Annabelle stood at the edge of the valley, both babies swaddled around her. "Alright, you little thing, let's see if we can find your pack, since you don't want to do it yourself." Hearing noises, she looked to the ridge. "They come already?" She looked into the pup's face. *How did they ever find someone willing to take the shepherd's place?* She squatted down to hide.

Seeing the young shepherd from a far distance, her mouth dropped open. "It is no man, but a boy! A young, young boy!" She shook her head in disgust. "What are they thinking?" As he neared, her head tilted and her mouth opened wider. *Edus? It can't be!* Rubbing her eyes, she looked back upon the shepherd boy. *It is! How is he here?* Her eyes wandered to the ridge. *Who else is here?*

Eduard's eyes scoured the forest line. *They will come from the trees. I need to watch the trees.* Hearing a noise, he bravely neared the arbors as a frightened tear rolled down his cheek. Arms quivering in terror, he swung the staff around, yelling wildly. "Go away! I won't let you get them!"

Watching the pup walk forward, he instinctively raised the staff, ready to strike despite the size, but when he went to swing it would not budge.

"Edus, don't."

He jumped away at the proximity of the voice and the name spoken, dropping the staff in the process. He fell onto his back, paralyzed in fear.

"Edus, it is I. Annie." She knelt down next to him.

Looking into her emerald eyes, he was too much in shock to speak. *Annie? She's dead!* He watched in fright as she grabbed his hand. *It's as if she were here. I feel her.*

"Edus! It's me! It's Annie!"

He shook his head as he backed away from the supposed apparition. "No. No. No. You can't be here! You didn't make it to Anchelo. Sir Nicholaus didn't find you!"

"He didn't find me because I wasn't dead." She tried to calm his startled mind: "Look, Edus, you're an uncle." She moved the fur away from the baby girl's head. "This is Claudia, and back here is Augustine."

Uncle? He watched Claudia yawn. He slowly stuck his finger up toward her and felt the young, warm breath upon his skin. Opening her eyes, she grabbed his finger. "Claudia?" He stood with help from his sister. "And Augustine?" He touched the head of the male babe. "I'm an uncle?"

"I call them Claudi and Auggie. Edus, what are you doing here?" Touching his face, she pulled him into a hug.

"I don't know! Someone took me. And I was put on a ship, and someone else took me, who gave me to these people!" His lip quivered. "Where's Mamá?"

Annabelle lowered her eyes. "I don't know what's become of her."

"How did you get here?" he asked, his face still pressing into her fur vest.

She shook her head. "It's a long story." Looking around at the sheep, she took his staff. "This rattling will not keep away hungry wolves."

"It's all I have."

"No. You need a spear."

He pathetically shook his head and shrugged his shoulders.

"Don't fret," she said. "I have plenty to spare. I've had all winter to make them." Dropping to her knees, she removed the bow and the quiver of arrows. "Have you ever used one of these?"

He made a face. "Michael says it is cowardly—"

"Yes, but you aren't shooting men. You are shooting wolves that are attacking what you are trying to defend."

He eyed the bow. "How do I use it?"

"I'll show you."

The bow and arrow proved too difficult for the boy. The arrows continuously fell to the ground as his right arm, quivering in use, could only pull the bow back minimally.

Annabelle looked at him with worry. *Oh, Edus! You'll not last!*

He looked at his sister in desperation. "It hurts my arm."

She rubbed his head as she pulled him close for a hug. "I know."

He suddenly looked up at her. "King Henricus showed me how to use a sling! Can a rock take out a wolf?"

She stared across the valley at the herd of sheep. "If you hit it right." Hope filling her mind, she glanced down at her brother. "Have you any leather?"

He shook his head. "No."

Nodding, she smiled. "I'll make one for you."

"Thank you, Annie!"

THE LIFE OF A LAMB

Annabelle jabbed the double-edged spear into the ground and then removed her babies from around her, sitting them next to her brother. "I will bring a couple at a time." She glanced up the hills that hid the village beyond. "That way if anyone wanders this far from the huts—"

"They won't," the prince interrupted. "Katara says they are scared of a wolfman spirit. That's why no villager serves as a shepherd." He pointed to the east. "They think it comes from that cliff. They think the cliff is evil. They call it 'dafod.'"

"Katara?" She looked at the shepherd sitting in the grass with her babies.

"She's one of them, but she's nice. Is it wrong for me to talk to her?"

Annabelle looked at him with great surprise. "You can?"

"She knows some of our words."

"How's that?" Annabelle picked up another spear and jabbed it into the soil.

"I don't know, but she's teaching me some."

"Is that so?"

"Is it wrong to learn their words?"

Pushing the spear deeper into the earth with her own weight, she grimaced and then shook her head as her feet returned to the earth. "No. I think it might be better—learn their words so you will know what they say." She studied the spear sticking out from the earth. "See if you can pull it out."

Standing, he walked toward the spiked wood and pulled upon it with a heave. It moved out of the hole, but it was too long; he fell with it to the ground.

Oh, Edus. What will become of you? Shaking her head, she held out her hand as she squatted down. "I fear it's too tall. I'll have to make some shorter ones." Forcing a smile, she pulled him up and handed him the leather. "Your sling."

"Thank you, Annie!" He hugged her in gratitude. "I'm certain I can stop them now!"

The princess looked at her brother cautiously. "You make certain to learn it well. Never forget that a stable tree is not like a moving wolf. I want you to keep trying the bow as well."

"It's hard to pull," he admitted.

She nodded. "Indeed, but you must keep trying."

"I will try," he said with exhaustion.

She retrieved the bow lying next to her children and looked at her nine-year-old brother. "Edus, you are so young, and I can't always be here." Taking a quick breath, she handed him the weapon. "You must learn. Your life depends upon it."

"My life?" Tears began to swell in his eyes as he took the bow that was nearly as tall as he. "I want to go back to Anchony, Annie!"

Kneeling down in front of him, she embraced the boy. "Edus, I do as well." Pulling back, she looked into his wet eyes. "But here is where we are, aren't we?"

He was forced to nod.

"So we must make the best of it." Shaking her head, she glanced over at her twins. "I don't know why we are here, but we must be here for a reason, right? In all things, we must do God's will."

"Yes," he said with a quivering chin. "But Thom will come for me! He vowed he would if I were ever taken."

The princess was uncertain what to say. He had the same faith in Thomas as she had in her husband. She nodded, "We must always hold to that hope. Thom or Sir Nicholaus will come when God wills it."

"I hope it's soon," the boy said sadly.

"Yes, and until then, you are to be the shepherd, so the shepherd you must be. Keep the sheep alive, and they will keep you alive. Stay alive yourself and they shall honor you more. Pray to your guardian angel that it might give you protection against the wolves."

Nodding his head with all certainty, he exclaimed, "It can!"

"Yes, our angels can." She smiled warmly. "Oh, Edus, you might think yourself alone as you stand watch upon these hills, but you never are. Your guardian is with you, and all of heaven shall hear you when you plead for intercession. Our Father always watches over us."

Looking at the weapons, a smile crested upon his face. "I shall ask it to help me aim well with the sling and to be better with the bow! I will use them well, I will!" Backing away, he awkwardly picked up the bow and pulled with all his might.

"I will try to make one smaller for you." She looked into the woods when she heard a distant sound toward the south.

"Is something wrong?"

Listening for a moment, she shook her head. "I should get going. Are you going to take them in now?"

"Soon."

"We'll watch you go over the hill."

Inside the forest, with a baby strapped to the front and one in the back, she looked back at her young brother herding the sheep up the hill. *How can they force a child to ward off wolves? They must want him to be killed.* As her brother disappeared over the hill, she looked to the canopy of trees above her. "Oh, Father, keep him alive, I beg of You!"

Eduard turned toward the forest as the sheep, bleating while they huddled together in a pack, continued on their journey up the second hill to their pen. Seeing movement, his heart began to race as he stiffened. "Who's there?"

Katara stepped out from behind a tree.

"Oh, it's you, Katara." He released his breath. Cautiously glancing back to the woods, he looked at her. "You didn't see, did you?"

"See what? Woman? Woman birthed babes and ran to woods?"

Panic overtook Eduard as his mouth dropped open and he shook his head. "Please, no! You didn't see anyone!"

"I did see. Ran to woods. Hide in cave. I help."

"Please, Katara. You only saw me!" Nervously looking down, he took a jagged breath as he whispered, "Annie told me what they did. If you want to help her, don't speak of her to anyone!"

Glancing back at him, she lowered her head toward him. "They not know. They think dead. I help them think."

"You won't say anything?" He dared to smile in relief.

Katara looked at him with confusion. "Why say? I help. I glad she live."

"Thank you!" He continued behind the sheep toward their pen. "You can't ever say."

"Why I say when I help?" she said with agitation.

He looked at the girl. "You mean you already helped her?"

Katara nodded. "I spread blood. I say it her. They not search now."

"You made it look like she was dead?" he said with astonishment as he followed the sheep toward the village.

"I say Blankentuk got her."

"Blankentuk?"

"Wolfman that live in mountain." Katara shook her head as she thought about that night. "Not right to take babe."

With complete surprise, he looked at her; a smile slowly crept across his face. "You helped Auggie and Claudi to live?"

"Auggie? Claudi? Babes?"

"Yes. My nephew and niece." His hand flew to his mouth as if he had revealed too much.

Katara tilted her head. "What mean?"

He lowered his head, unsure why he was telling her all. "The woman is my sister."

Katara's mouth opened when she finally understood the prince's attachment to the woman and twins living in the forest. "She safe in cave. She hunt now. I see. She not need help." Following beside him toward the sheep pen, she revealed in the same breath her true reason for searching him out. "Acwa mad—still no gold."

"What does that mean?"

"Gods get mad. No gold, no sun. Sacrifice must come."

He looked at her oddly; the only sacrifice he knew was that of the Mass. Thinking of all the Masses he had attended and all the times the consecrated wine and bread were held up, he pondered: *The chalice is gold. Does it have to be?* "You need a chalice?"

"Chalice? What's that?"

"The cup that holds His Blood."

"Who is 'His'?"

"You mean 'He'? It's Jesus."

"Who's He?"

His mouth dropped open in shock. "You don't know Jesus? He's God's Son."

"Son of which god?"

"What do you mean 'which god'? There's only one."

"No there's not!"

"Yes, there is," he said with utter confusion, uncertain why she had to be told.

"You mean chief god?" Katara asked as she opened the gate leading toward the village. The sheep followed one another toward the pen.

Eduard stared at her with his mouth open, not sure how to reply. "I . . . I don't know what you mean. There's only one."

She stared at him with an equal amount of confusion.

"I better get the gate," he said as he walked away.

Eating stew in Lina's hut, Eduard pushed around a piece of potato with his spoon.

"You're very quiet."

He looked up at her. "Why does Katara think there's more than one god?"

"The Seafurs don't know about Christ. They don't know about the Trinity. They don't know about His Church."

"Someone needs to tell them," he suggested.

With Annabelle's words upon her mind—that she was the only hands of Christ upon the island—Lina could not help but feel convicted. *Have I failed You, Father?*

"They are not being just to God," the young prince added.

"What's that?" Lina asked.

"My brother, Thom, says to pray, to go to Mass, it is giving God what He is due. If they don't know about His Church, how do they give Him His due?"

Lina sat back. "I suppose, in a way, they think they are, but it truly goes to creatures God created."

"What do you mean?"

"The fallen angels. Those fiends. That is who they mean when they say gods."

"No!" He stood up in disgust. "They offer sacrifice to fiends? That's not right nor just!" Moving away from the firepit, as if he could move away from the conversation, a grace fell upon him when he sat on his bed. "They don't know better? No one has taught them?" He looked over at Lina. "Who will teach them?" Sitting back on the bed, he thought about it and then came to an answer: "Bishop Dominicus should come here!"

Lina smiled at his innocence. "As they are now, I deem that would only lead to his death."

"But aren't we supposed to die for Christ?"

She picked up his bowl. "If . . . that is what one is called to do." She breathed deeply. "That's enough talk for tonight. Get some rest, dear Eduard."

Dragging two more spears through the woods, Annabelle placed them on the edge of the valley and then walked to her brother, who was sitting down pondering the Seafurs. "Edus, what's wrong?"

"These people don't know God."

Looking toward the periphery, Annabelle pointed. "Is that Katara?" Seeing her face, she recognized her as the one that helped her. "Do you want to call her over here?"

Standing up, he waved her over.

As Katara walked over, Annabelle searched around. "Where's her white wolf?"

"I've never seen a white wolf," Eduard said with confusion.

"You are Katara?"

The girl nodded.

"You know my words?"

She nodded again.

"It was you that brought me all the food?"

Katara, glancing at the baby strapped in front, nodded.

"Thank you. You helped us live."

Katara shook her head. "Not right to take babe."

"Where's your wolf?"

"Sna not mine. Sna is wild."

Suddenly Eduard gasped, and when Annabelle turned her head he had already taken off to the periphery of the valley. She quickly followed after. "What's wrong?" she called to him from behind.

Eduard tilted his head as he approached the little white mass, lying still in the grass. *Oh, no!* Falling to his knees, he picked up the animal. Fear filled him. *Please don't be dead! Please don't be dead!* He turned the creature over to look at the face. It was not breathing, and its body was stiff and cold. His stomach churned.

One is dead. What will they do to me? Will they sacrifice me now? Oh, no! Father! Breathing heavily, he wiped away the tears swelling in his eyes.

"Edus—" Annabelle was beside him now. Strange noises emerged from the trees and they both turned to look. Katara ran over.

"What wrong?" Katara asked.

"Wolves!" Annabelle yelled as she unstrapped her babes. "Katara, watch the babies!" She ran toward the bow and quickly took aim at a wolf about to attack a sheep.

Eduard—before he could see the wolves—watched his sister in wonder as the sheep desperately ran for their lives. *Annie?* Standing, he watched a pack of wolves chase after his herd.

Dropping the dead lamb to the ground, he ran towards them, pulling out his sling. "No you don't!"

Finding a rock, he loaded the leather and let it fly; it struck a wolf in the body, which did not deter its attention from the sheep, though it did yelp.

Running out of arrows, Annabelle picked up a spear and hit a wolf with such force that it splintered the spear into two and disoriented the wolf, which ran off to cower in the woods. Finding her brother, she watched a wolf run toward him.

He screamed for help. Falling to the ground, he reached for anything he could find as the wolf's snarls grew louder and he felt the hot breath descend toward him, going for his neck. A part of the broken spear was just centimeters away from his grasp. He reached with all of his might, but he was unable to grab it. "Annie! Help!"

As Annabelle retrieved an arrow, he felt the teeth graze his skin and then suddenly the hot breath was gone. Turning his head, he watched the albino wolf hold the other wolf's neck tightly in its own jaws. Moving slightly, he grabbed the spear as he heard another wolf running toward him. Smacking the animal with the wood as he stood, yet another jumped at him; the weight forced him down. Protecting his neck with the spear still in hand, it punctured the wolf, but it still continued to struggle.

Get off! Annabelle aimed the arrow in her resolve.

The wolf yelped as an arrow pierced its neck. Warm blood ran out upon the prince's arms and torso before the animal could scurry away. Annabelle, running full force, released another arrow. As a wolf set its eyes upon her, she threw down the bow and pulled up another spear.

Eduard watched in wonder as his sister beat away two wolves and, looking toward him, hurled the spear at the wolf he did not even know was on his attack. Watching the wolf fall and the others either run off or die from their injuries, his sister knelt down beside him to intrusively investigate his body. "Are you harmed? Are you harmed?"

He looked at her emerald eyes as if he did not understand.

"Edus, are you harmed?" She reached for the wolf's blood upon him; he touched his neck where the teeth nearly tore into his skin.

Pulling his hand away, there was only a trace amount of blood. "Annie?"

"Is this your blood?" She searched around the bloodstain. "Edus, are you harmed?"

He shook his head, as he sat up. "No. It's from the wolf."

"Oh, thank God!" Annabelle hugged him dearly. "Thank You, Father!"

As she released him, he watched the white wolf, with its muzzle stained red, run toward Katara, who was hiding in the trees. "I am hardly harmed at all." It suddenly hit him, and tears fell from his eyes. "Annie, I thought I was to be eaten!"

She gripped his shoulder as she nodded her head. "But you live. You live."

He hugged her tightly. "You saved me!"

"This is why you need to learn the bow." Looking toward the distant southern hills, the princess stood. "I have to go. They're coming."

Turning around, he watched her pick up her bow and run into the woods to where Katara was hiding.

Stopping against a tree, she squatted down, and took that moment to catch her breath. When she looked over at Katara, the girl slowly approached as the white wolf circled around her. "You have spirit of wolfman," she said in wonder.

Annabelle shook her head. "What is that supposed to mean?"

"You withstand wolf and man."

Annabelle shook her head as she held out her arms for her babies. "I only do what I can."

Katara looked at her cautiously as the weight of the children were unburdened from her. "I know bow."

"You know how to shoot the bow and arrow?" Annabelle looked back at her brother. "Can you help him? I can't always be here." She looked through the woods. "I don't know what I'd do if I lost him!"

"He too little."

A tear streamed down her face as she nodded. "I know! That's why he needs help!"

"Eduard! Eduard!" Lina nearly collapsed in front of him as the Seafur men investigated the battlefield. "The sheep came to the pen. I was certain the wolves had come and you were dead!" She hugged him tightly.

"You kill?" Ecwab asked with disbelief as the Seafur men looked in wonder at the bloodstains.

Lina followed the Seafur's gaze as Eduard turned toward the interpreter. "They came for the sheep. I fought them the best I could."

Ecwab's eyebrows elevated in disbelief as he turned toward the men and interpreted. Every single man looked at Eduard in astonishment.

Lina knelt down before him, investigating all the blood. "Are you harmed?"

"Only my neck a little." He pointed to the teeth marks.

"Oh, my!" Lina took his hand. "Come back quickly, I shall tend to that."

Eduard looked nervously toward the fallen lamb, not wanting the men to find it. "I can't lose any sheep. I must keep all of them alive!"

"It looks like they all made it back." Lina squeezed his hand in reassurance. "You did well. So well!"

The prince lowered his head. *They didn't all make it back.*

Annabelle, peeking around the tree, watched her brother disappear over the hill, holding Lina's hand. Looking farther north, she watched the men pick up the wolves' carcasses and follow toward the village.

Father, I understand one reason I'm here now—for my brother's protection. But what about him? For what reason is he here? He is but a boy in a wild land full of pagans. She lowered her gaze. "Likely it is not up to me to know. But Father, help Edus to know why he is here."

"You speak me?" Katara said behind her.

The princess watched them all disappear over the hill and then said over her shoulder, "No, I wasn't speaking to you."

Walking into the cabin, Eduard plopped down next to the fire. "I failed, Lina."

She shook her head in complete perplexity as she doffed her overthrow. "Child, whatever do you mean? You killed at least three wolves and the sheep all came—"

"A lamb died."

"A lamb?" She sat down beside him. "They'll have no memory of the loss of a lamb from this day. Their memories will be of the boy who saved the herd by fighting back!"

Looking at her, he wanted to reveal the truth, but his promise to Annabelle forced him to hold his tongue. "But I'll have memory of this day: I let a lamb die. It was my duty to give it protection."

"Eduard, a lamb doesn't stand a chance against a wolf."

He looked up at her. "It wasn't a wolf."

"What?"

He shook his head as he looked back at the dying fire. "I don't know what it was—it was dead. There wasn't any blood; I saw no wounds."

"That's odd."

Holding his knees, he rocked himself. "But it is my fault. I wish it had not died."

"Eduard." She grabbed his arm. "You saved the herd from a pack of wolves."

I did nothing. It was Annie and the white wolf. I would be dead if it wasn't for them!

"It's only a lamb! Eduard, be glad you're alive!"

He finally looked up at her. "I am. I am very thankful!"

With a poultice upon his neck, Eduard lay in bed thinking of the stiff lamb. *Father, why did it have to die? Why couldn't it be alive? I don't want to lose a single sheep. They are mine to look after—I want to do so rightly.*

Lina's words ran through his mind: *"It's only a lamb."*

He shook his head. *That only means it needs more protection. Why can't it still breathe?*

Closing his eyes, he turned to his side to find rest, but rest could not be found. Every time he closed his eyes, he felt the breath of the wolf upon him, ready to rip him to shreds.

Nervously standing upon the pasture hill the next morning as the sheep moved past him, he searched the land for any of his canine foes. Seeing no movements within the trees, he descended with the herd. *Hopefully the wolves are too wounded to hunt today.* His eyes were suddenly caught by some movement along the periphery—something small and white.

His mouth dropped open as he approached. "It can't be!" Shaking his head, he dropped to his knees before the lamb. "It can't be! You were dead!" he said to the lamb.

The little lamb bawled before him as he touched its head. Watching it run toward the rest of the herd, he looked to the sky. "Father, did You raise it to life? Did You raise it to life because I asked?" In amazement, he shook his head as he stood. "I don't believe it! Not that You couldn't do it, but that You did!" The lamb gaily ran around and through the legs of the other sheep. "You watch over everyone. Every creature is in Your hands! You keep everyone and everything into being!"

Hours later, his joy was still surging through him. "Lina! Lina it's back to life!"

She was bewildered as he burst through the door. "Child! Of what do you speak?"

"The lamb! The lamb is alive! I prayed God would bring it back to life, and He did!"

"It must not have been dead."

He tilted his head. "You don't think God would bring him back?"

"It's not that. It's . . . why would He want to? It's a lamb."

"Because I prayed for it!" He was taken aback.

"All I'm saying is that likely there's some other reason it was in the way it was."

"You mean like it was sick?"

"Likely. Could it be from something it ate?" Thinking, she began to nod. "I do believe I heard years ago of a bush that had that effect."

"A bush? Leaves?"

Lina shrugged her shoulders. "Who knows! The Seafurs believe so many things it's hard to know what is true and what is a tale."

Eduard, with his simple faith, looked up at her. "Does it matter? I prayed for the lamb to come back, and it did!" A smile burst forth across his face as he jumped up. "I'm going to go tell the captain!"

SUMMERTON

"In this very place, you watched a man die for the death of King Henrard." Lord Cortell looked around nervously at the crowd of 50 in the marketplace of Summerton. "That is why Prince Howercus charges me to read this message."

He lifted the proclamation and read: "'I, Howercus, Prince of Sethel, inform the good people of Sethel of the sorrowful tidings that their king, Henrard; their prince, Phillipus; and the princesses, Rissa and Anastacia, were killed while in Anchony. King Francis of Anchony was called to account for their deaths and was properly punished. I, Howercus of Sethel, humbly receive the throne of Sethel during this time of mourning.'"

Lowering the parchment, he looked at the crowd as a mixture of fright and courage stirred within him. Rolling up the decree, he nervously stuck it under his arm as he pulled a folded paper from within his tunic.

He continued, "I, Lord Cortell of Summerton, have also been charged to read another—not a decree, but a letter, written by Prince Phillipus prior to his death: 'I fear for my father's life. My uncle's want of power grows greater with each passing day. He desires the crown, and I fear what he will do to get it. As of late, I was informed of a plot to take my father's life—contrived by my own uncle, Prince Howercus—but failed due to the deeds of one knight. Signed Phillipus Henrardson, Prince of Sethel, in the year of our Lord 1202.'"

Lowering the letter, he looked at the crowd to see their reaction.

The faces turned and looked at one another in confusion as they murmured amongst themselves. One voice, shouted out above the rest, "What took place?"

Cortell, folding the paper, stuck it back inside his tunic as he answered, "The answer to that rests upon whom you ask."

"We want the truth!" another's voice yelled out.

"The truth?"

"Yes!"

He shifted his weight as he looked at the people. "Who do you think you should trust? Did you trust Prince Phillipus? He is the one that said he feared for his father's life, and now his father is dead. Phillipus is dead and the one that gives you the tidings of his death is the one that claims the crown." He shook his head. "I don't know all that came to be. I wasn't there in Anchony when they lost their lives. But I will tell you one thing I know to be true: Prince Howercus lies when he tells you Princess Anastacia died with the rest of her family."

Shouts came forth: "Is she alive?"

"Where is she?"

"He wants her dead for the crown!"

"Howercus killed them!" The shouts grew in intensity.

Cortell put up his hands to silence them. "I believe she is safe where she is. That is all I can say."

"Howercus is not our king! And never shall be!" a voice yelled out as a chant began and increased in intensity: "Not our king! Not our king!"

"Wait!" Cortell looked across the crowd. "What are you going to do about it? You can't storm a castle."

A silence fell over the crowd as they looked at one another. One voice yelled out: "What should we do about it?"

"Tell everyone you know, but do nothing yet. We must wait until most of the kingdom knows the truth. When no one sees him as rightful king, he won't be able to claim it." Many in the crowd nodded as they whispered amongst themselves. "Return to your homes and talk to those who you know were not here. I shall do the same." As the crowd began to disperse, he turned to go into his castle.

"Lord Cortell," Nicholaus called out.

Turning back around, he jogged down the steps to the speaker to whisper quickly, "Sir Hunts? What are you doing here?"

"I've come to speak to your wife. She sent a note to Anchony."

He put up his hand to halt his words. "Not here. Come in."

Safe inside the Great Hall, Lord Cortell looked at the visitor. "The duchess is not here. Can I help you?"

Nicholaus lowered his head. "I want to know what pirate paid for my wife to come to Anchony."

Cortell looked at him in complete confusion. "What? Did a pirate pick her up from Two Breath Island?"

"No. Oro."

"How did—" Cortell interrupted his own question and lowered his head. "Anguis?"

Nicholaus stepped closer. "Anguis? Who is that?"

Cortell could not help but chuckle. "A wanted man—both Sethel and Monakala have a price upon his head."

"Why would he pay for Anna to get off of Oro Island?"

"I don't know." He lowered his head. "Captain Anguis is a mystery. Prince Phillipus trusted him; I don't know why."

"Prince Phillipus trusted him? A pirate?"

Taking a quick breath, he nodded. "I'm glad Annabelle made it off of Snake Island and back to Anchony."

"She didn't."

"Didn't?"

"The ship foundered at sea. No one lived. I wish to find this Captain Anguis, because he was the last person I know of that saw her alive."

"Oh. I don't know where he is, but I do know where Lady Alana went. My wife has gone to Brotherton in Baltam. I don't know where she met Captain Anguis, but that's where you could find her."

"Brotherton? Thank you." Nicholaus, swallowing hard, looked up at the duke. "Those words you spoke out there are perilous. If you keep speaking them, they will lead to your death."

Cortell nodded. "I know. But if it leads to Princess Anastacia taking her crown, it is well worth the price."

"The princess was taken from Camrina's castle by a pi—" Nicholaus's mouth dropped open as he tilted his head. "Captain Anguis?"

"I believe that to be true."

"She is safe?"

"I'm hoping—in Brotherton."

Nicholaus smirked as he looked at the man before him. "So you are helping her to get her crown back?"

"In the best way I know how."

Nicholaus held out his arm. "God speed, Lord Cortell."

The duke took his offered arm. "And what will you do, Sir Nicholaus?"

Nicholaus shook his head. "I shall find my way to Brotherton, even if it means I have to walk there."

Kneeling in the darkness of the Sethelian church, Nicholaus stared at the tabernacle. "Father, what is Your will for me?" He shook his head in agitation. "And why is it that every time I ask to know Your will, I can only think of Anna? I pray for her, I do, but I want to do Your will here on earth. I don't want to cling to what I can't have! I cry out to You, Father! Help me to know Your will!"

Shaking his head, he only felt more agitated than before entering. He closed his eyes and listened intently for any interior voice.

He heard none. Despairingly, he signed himself and pushed himself up.

The afternoon light nearly blinded him as he pushed open the church door.

"I thought that was you I saw enter," a familiar voice called out.

Lowering his hand, he turned toward the voice, to confirm with his eyes what he knew from his ears. "Prince Thomas? What are you doing here?"

Thomas, looking down, slowly stepped toward him. "I don't know how quite to say this, Sir Nicholaus . . ." Nicholaus patiently waited as the prince, taking a deep breath, looked up at him. "I'm on my way to Baltam and was wondering if you would join me?"

"Is that the king's desire?"

Thomas slowly nodded. "By way of my mamá, yes."

Nicholaus walked closer, not understanding the prince's meaning. "What does the queen wish us to do?"

Thomas nearly cringed. "That's the thing. Sir Nicholaus, I don't know how to say this . . ."

Nicholaus tilted his head. "One word at a time, Prince Thomas."

The prince, holding his breath for a moment, finally spat out: "She wishes us to find Annie."

Nicholaus pathetically chuckled as he shook his head and walked down the rest of the steps. "We've been through—"

"Alive," Thomas added quickly.

The knight looked into his eyes as the whole world seemed to hold its breath. "What is this? What? Were there . . . tidings?" He gasped with the proclamation as his heart nearly leaped into his throat, a confirmation of all his prayers.

Thomas shook his hand. "No. Nothing like that. Mamá *believes* she's alive."

Nicholaus nearly fell down with the revelation. "She does?" He was forced to sit.

Thomas watched him in shock. "I . . . didn't think . . ."

"I believe it, too." Nicholaus nodded his head as he looked up at his prince. "I believe it, too!" Thomas slowly sat down beside him on the church steps. "Every time I pray . . . I . . . I can't let her go. It's as if God wants me not to give up." He took a quick breath. "I feared I was going mad. But the queen? The queen, too?"

Prince Thomas looked at the active village before him. "I deem you will either both be mad together or both be right." Taking a quick breath, he looked at his brother-in-law. "Let's go find my sister, Sir Nicholaus. Let's go find her!"

Watching the coast of Sethel shrink away, Nicholaus looked at his prince. "Princess Anastacia is in Brotherton," he said. "And Lady Alana and likely the pirate."

"What? Brotherton in Baltam?" Thomas looked across the distant ocean. "Where did you come upon these tidings?"

"Lord Cortell. He believes the same pirate that aided Anna freed Princess Anastacia from the castle."

"Pirates paying for princesses' passages, saving them himself? That is odd indeed." Thomas, tapping the side of the ship, curiously thought about all the words. "Could Annie somehow be with Princess Anastacia? Let us go to this Brotherton to find out!"

ALANA

Stepping onto a pier in Port Brotherton in the late spring air, Alana's eyes scanned the small fishing village, which was darkened with the sea of black tabards. Swallowing with difficulty, she bravely walked through the village, praying she would not be recognized by any of the knights.

"Lady Alana?"

Holding her breath, she slowly looked over to the voice. "Sir Marjus?"

He looked at her oddly as he approached. "Lady Alana, what are you doing here?"

As her heart began to beat with an increased swiftness, she looked around searching for the market. "I'm looking for some fish." She found it difficult to swallow. "Do you know where the market is?"

He shook his head. "There's not much of a market left."

"Oh? What do you mean?" she tried to ask without too much concern.

He gazed around. "Most of the townspeople have cleared away."

"Oh." She uncomfortably looked down. "To where have the fishmongers gone?"

He stepped closer, wanting to know the real reasons she was there. "Why would you come to Baltam to buy fish?"

Looking up, she met his eyes. "Why, sir, I've been told they have the best fish here." She pulled out her husband's note. "Lord Cortell says he can't get good fish in Salone. So I wish to bring some." She shoved the paper into his hands. "I deem the best fish with plenty of ice would keep better to make it to Salone. This far north, the ice should still be good by now." She shook her head as her heart felt as if it would burst from within her. "I wish to give it to my husband and to bring it for the sirs . . . and the prince, of course." She gazed at the empty market a distance away. "But if there are no fishmongers here . . ." She turned away. "I need to find some. Do you know where the townspeople have gone so I can buy some fish?"

Shaking his head, he handed the paper back to her. "They've scattered."

"Oh." Taking a deep breath, courage grew inside of her. "What are Sethelian knights and soldiers doing in Baltam?"

He straightened his head. "That is none of your business."

She smiled quickly. "Well, I only wanted to make certain Sethel wasn't having a problem with Baltam. I suppose I should have bought smaller fish from the Sethelian coast." With her eyes wandering over the remains of the village, she shook her head. "Well, I deem I should find another port." Nervously, she turned around and quickly walked back to her awaiting rowboat.

"Who was that?" another knight asked as he watched the lady walk away.

"Lord Cortell's wife."

"Lord Cortell? He's from the eastern coast of Sethel. What is she doing on the western side of Baltam?"

"That's what I'd like to know—her *true* reason."

Anguis, lurking in the trees, watched Alana climb back into her boat and those within it row her toward her awaiting ship. Watching the anchor rise, he looked toward the town to see Sir Marjus and a few other knights carefully watching the ship depart.

When they turned away, he rose from his concealed location and walked forward.

Riding his horse until it nearly collapsed, Sir Arkel goaded it to sprint up the last hill toward Brotherton. Seeing the overwhelming blackness of the Sethelian tabards inside the town, he jumped from the horse. "Where are they? Where are the outlaws?"

"Sir Arkel?" Sir Marjus said with great surprise. "There was no one here when we arrived, but we've found a traitor nonetheless." Stepping out of the way, Sir Arkel looked at the man upon his knees as the captive's head was forced up to reveal his face.

A smirk smeared across Arkel's face. "Captain Anguis? You escape us no more." Walking closer, he leaned over the captive. "What are you doing in Brotherton?" Briefly glancing at the knights holding him captive, he made a connection in his mind.

Arkel looked to his men. "I want to speak to him alone."

"Captain Anguis. Captain Anguis." Sir Arkel walked toward the kneeling captive, pacing amongst the old fish guts in the abandoned market, away from all other eyes and ears. "Prince Howercus has a large price upon your head."

Anguis looked up with a smirk upon his face. "How much? Certainly it's not as much as Monakala?"

Arkel's eyes turned sinister. He punched the captive. "You assaulted Monakalian merchant ships while flying the Sethelian flag on purpose! You traitor! You were trying to get Monakala to assault Sethel, weren't you?" Enraged, he forced the man to his feet. "What are you doing in Brotherton? Are you contriving with those outlaws, too? Where are they?"

Infuriated, he punched the reformed pirate several more times—until his own knuckles bleed—and then he unsheathed his sword. "I should kill you right now!"

Anguis, sprawled out upon the cold stones, spat out blood as he looked through a swelling eye. Finding strength, he pushed himself into a side-lying position with his bound hands and feet. "If I die, I shall die knowing who the true traitors to Sethel are!"

Sir Arkel, stepping away, looked around cautiously to make sure no other knights were within hearing distance. "Then it's true? Princess Anastacia lives?" He stumbled backwards. *If it is true, then Queen Mona truly is lying! She is deceiving Prince Hower-cus!* With a wild look in his eye, he pulled Anguis up. "It is true, isn't it? Princess Anastacia lives?" Fear enveloped his countenance.

Arkel released him, and Anguis, unable to stand because of the severe brutality, fell back to the ground. Arkel grabbed his arm and pulled him toward the road. "Horses! Bring me two horses at once!"

Sir Marjus watched Arkel, with great alacrity, tie the bleeding Anguis to the horse.

"I'm off to Salone!"

"Do you not want a night's rest? You only now arrived," Sir Marjus spoke with reason.

"No. There is no time to waste; I leave in haste!"

Marjus looked at the captive. "I don't think he'll be getting away from you if that is your fear."

Arkel climbed upon his horse. "That is not my fear at all. My fear is that he will die before I get to Prince Howercus!"

Marjus watched Sir Arkel take off to the south, with the second horse carrying the bound and beaten captive across its back.

A day later, King Henricus of Baltam, looking from atop his horse at the occupied Brotherton from a distance. He tilted his head, glanced at his men, and signaled them to go around to the other side.

Hearing rattling from the bushes, he took out toward a fleeing man. One of his knights cut the man off.

"Who are you?" he asked the man, dismounting from his horse. He grabbed the man's leather glove and looked at the emblem upon it. Disgust ran across his face as he violently dropped the man's hand.

"What is a Sethelian knight doing in Baltam?!" He shook his agitated head. "Does Howercus think he can overtake Baltam without a bad outcome?" He looked at his men. "Get him out of my sight. Get them all out of my sight!"

King Henricus walked through the abandoned fish market, contemplating its meaning.

"Sire, what are we to do with the bound men?"

The king knelt down to pick up a stone, examining it

silently. Tossing it aside, he rose and looked at his knight. "I want to know the whereabouts of Princess Anastacia."

"We're trying to find that out."

Henricus shook his head. "I doubt they know. If they found her, why are they still here?" Breathing heavily, King Henricus turned around toward the knight. "I want to speak to their leader."

"Sir Marjus over there claims he leads the northern soldiers."

Walking over, Henricus stopped four feet in front of the man, eyed him, and then said, "Sethel has made a horrible error by coming into Baltam." He looked at Sir Harkus from his periphery. "What shall we do with them? Shall we march them to Salone ourselves?"

"You wouldn't dare!" Marjus called out with incredulity.

Henricus tilted his head. "I wouldn't?" Backing away for a moment, he briefly smiled to himself and then looked up at the man. "Let me make something clear: I was pledged to be married to your Princess Rissa. That was until the man you wish to call king had her killed, along with her father and her brother." Stepping closer, he gripped the man's tunic and pushed him against the stone wall. "I searched long and hard for her sister in Anchony. If Howercus has harmed her in Baltam, I will bring this fight to him!" Releasing him for a moment, he shoved him back against the wall. "Where is she?!"

"You must be mad! It is known that King Henrard and all his children perished in Anchony! And King Francis of Anchony paid for the treachery!"

"You might be able to deceive Sethelians with such words, but here in Baltam they are called by what they are—lies!"

Sir Harkus and the Baltamian knights looked at one another as the king pulled out the letter written in Lady Alana's hand.

"As stated by one of your own Sethelians. 'King Henricus, I, Lady Alana of Summerton, have of late learned that Princess Anastacia resides in Baltam, but I have had no word of her safety. A few months before his death, Prince Phillipus arranged for his sisters, if something were to arrive to him or his father, to seek refuge in Brotherton with the fishmongers.'" Pulling the scroll away, he looked into the knight's eyes. "Where is she?!"

Marjus shook his head in perplexity. "I don't—"

Henricus hit him across the face; the knight fell to the ground. "You do know! You wouldn't be in Brotherton if you didn't know!"

Wiping blood from his nose, Sir Marjus looked up at the furious king. "I don't know what to think of these tidings! We came here in search of outlaws—brothers they are. Not for our princess—she died in Anchony! There is no one left but Howercus."

"So Howercus claims!" Stepping back, he folded his arms. "That is what he would need, isn't it? In order to gain the throne? For all of King Henrard's children to be dead?"

Sir Marjus shook his head. "You say Princess Anastacia lives? Where is she then?"

"Sire." Staring at the sea in Brotherton, King Henricus turned around at the sound of his knight's voice. "This is Ieofus. Go ahead, tell him what you told me."

"Your Majesty." The skinny man nervously bowed as he removed his hood and squeezed it with trembling hands. "The sir was asking if anybody had seen the lot of the fishmongers. And . . . and I told him . . . that they fought and they killed them."

Howercus looked away with devastation. "The fishmongers are dead? Did you see—"

"No, no, Your Majesty," the man interrupted and then lowered his head when the king looked back at him.

"No, what?"

"It was the fishmongers that killed the knights. And then

they took off on the horses with their wives and the ward." He shook his head. "Where they went I—"

"Ward?" Henricus stepped closer. "Of whom do you speak?"

"The girl?"

"Girl?" Henricus shook his head in near excitement. "About how old?"

"I . . . I don't know. She . . . uh. . . helped with the fish guts." The man nodded his head as he tried to recall all that he could. "They called her . . . uh . . . Stacia."

Stepping closer, Henricus looked into the man's eyes. "Which way did they go on their horses?"

"North. I watched them from the woods. I never thought them good fishmongers. They left too much with the bones. They always seemed like they were waiting for something."

Or someone. He looked at Sir Harkus. "Pay the man for his honesty." He turned to the crowd of captive Sethelians sitting along the market wall. "Divide the knights. Half stay here, the others come with me."

"And where are we to go, Sire?" Harkus asked.

"North until we find the fishmongers and their ward."

Sir Melvon and Frankus, after weeks of searching, stared at the fish market.

"There are four of them. They look much alike—they could be brothers. Do you think it's them?" Frankus asked.

Sir Melvon pushed away from the wall. "We have searched for too long not to find out."

"Wait!" Frankus grabbed his arm. "If it is the outlaws, they will see your tabard and run!" He shook his head. "Sir Melvon, I'm going with you. You have a way of making everyone bitter."

"Enough talk!"

"No!" Frankus pulled him back. "I have born your curtness

long enough! We can't forget that if they are the outlaws, they are doing what Prince Phillipus asked! And if they're not, then they're only fishmongers! There is no need to be cruel or to scare the wits out of them!"

"Are you done?"

"Are you? Sir Melvon, you are a skilled warrior, but you have no tact with people." He doffed his Sethelian tabard.

Melvon looked at him angrily. "What are you saying?"

Rolling it up, he dropped the tabard next to the wall. "I'm saying let me do the talking! You have scared too many fish-mongers already!" With that spoken, he stepped around Sir Melvon and walked into the market, weaving his way toward his destination.

"Do you want carp? Carp is here," Sir Huebertus stated as he chopped off the head of a fish.

Frankus glanced around at the market. "I'm not from around here. What is the best kind of fish in this land?"

Huebertus eyed him. "Not from around here?"

"But I do like fish." Sir Frankus glanced behind him to watch Sir Melvon, without his tabard, walk closer. "I'm looking for a certain kind of fish. Some might say it is *king* of the fish."

Huebertus, with eyebrows furrowed, tilted his head. "I don't know of what you speak."

Frankus's eyes scanned the table as he thought carefully about his words. "There was a king fish in Sethel, but it was killed. So a smaller fish must rule now. I am looking for *that* fish so that it may return to the sea and its rule."

Huebertus, standing up straight, stared at him.

Frankus shook his head. "If you are who I think you are, that will make sense. But if you are not, you likely think me mad." Looking at him, he attempted to discern what the man's countenance meant. "You see . . . I was in Anchony when the king fish was killed searching for the prince fish and I've been searching for the—"

"Who are you?"

"Sir Frankus of the Sethelian knights, with fealty to the true crown of Sethel." He leaned in closer. "I was told the smaller fish could be found with some outlaws in Baltam." Out of the corner of his eye, Frankus watched Sir Melvon step away, disappearing into the crowd.

"Is that so?" Huebertus eyed his brothers. "We'll see about that."

"If it is lies you speak, your life ends now," Sir Huebertus said as he pushed Frankus through the door of the wattle and daub home.

Forced to his knees after entering the structure blindly, the sack was pulled off of Sir Frankus's head. As his eyes focused in the dampened light, he looked through the swirling dust floating through the streams of small sunlight invading the inside of the hut by way of the shutter slots.

"Sir Frankus?" Princess Anastacia called out.

Focusing upon the face as it neared him, he bowed his head in wonder and gratitude. "Your Majesty! You *are* alive!"

Sir Melvon, across the way, tilted his head as he watched Sir Frankus open the shutter and wave him forward.

Walking into the hut, Melvon fell to his knees at the sight of the royal. "Princess Anastacia! Your Majesty, I am at your service!"

Anastacia, teary-eyed, looked at the knight. "Sir Melvon, I didn't think I would ever be so glad to see *you*!" With a grand smile, as hope began to invade her, she looked from one sir to the other. "Who of the king's knights are still with me?"

"Sir Jacobus," Melvon answered.

As her smile began to fade with the revelation of only one name, Frankus offered: "He was to see if there were any others, though, Your Majesty."

WARINUS

A mariner from the *Sockortale*, forced to work on the castle in Aboly, stopped to rub the perspiration off his brow and stole a double look as he glanced at the remains of the gatehouse. "It's the captain." He turned to a fellow Sockorian mariner. "Is that Warinus with him?"

All the mariners halted their work to watch the two men, the captain bound and submissive, walk into the bailey.

"I have a present for the king of Anchony!" Warinus exclaimed as he forced the captain closer.

William, turning away from the training area, watched Sir Michael jog over. "Who are you?" Sir Michael asked.

Warinus pointed to the other mariners. "I was once a part of them, but I am no longer."

The prince, joining the knight slowly with his healing ribs, watched the mariner kick the captain to the ground. "And who is he that you bring to the king of Anchony?"

"The captain of the *Sockortale*." Tilting his head, Warinus watched closely as Peter joined the prince. "I hear Anchony is in search of a young prince. I know where he is, and I now know how to find him."

With crossed arms, William, along with the king and the knights, stood in front of the mariner inside the hut. "Alright, we're listening. You claim you know the whereabouts of Prince Eduard. So where is he?"

"He was given to the Seafurs." Warinus answered as he wiped sweat from his forehead.

"The heathens from the sea?" Sir Michael asked in disbelief.

"I thought it was gold they seek," Peter stated as he watched the king place his hand over his mouth.

"They will hold anyone for gold," Warinus said with all disgust as he twitched his head.

William looked at his father. "How are we to find them?"

Peter, with his commanding presence, stepped closer to the mariner. "We were told Oro Island during the Wolf Moon was the place that the Seafurs come to collect the gold. Is it true?"

"It is."

"How did she give them my son?" Francis stepped closer. "How did she give away her own nephew to those heathens?"

"She placed him on another ship that went north. That's all I know."

William turned away. "What use is he—"

"But I know how to make it to their island."

William, as well as every eye, looked to the mariner. "How is that?"

"I have a map."

"And how did you come by such a thing?" Michael asked immediately.

Warinus lowered his head. "There is only one that knows the way. It's a copy of the map he drew." With his bound hands, he stepped forward. "I returned here as soon as I came upon it."

"Is it the captain?" the Lion asked. "Is he the man that knows the way?"

"No, but he knew of him. I don't know who the man is at all. I never met him, but I found the map carved into rock on Trader Island."

The king stared out the window, watching the summer rain fall with force to the ground. "Francis." The queen rubbed his shoulder. "What are you thinking?"

Glancing at her face, he looked back at the precipitation. "I have to go. I have to get him back."

Her fingers froze. "You?" She held her breath. *I just got you back. Don't go. Please, don't go!*

Taking her hand, he pulled her into a hug. "I know who has my son now, and I have someone who knows how to get there. I have to. Do you understand?" His eyes pleaded for her acceptance of his plan.

Gazing across the room, she asked, "Why you?"

"Because I'm going to take Camrina with me."

"What?!" She pushed away to look at him. "Why? Why would you take her? She works with those people! They could—"

He nodded. "That's why I'm going to take her. They know her. We will have more of a chance of them giving Eduard back if they trust us."

Trust her? Her eyes diverted to the floor as her mouth opened.

"Clara, say something, please."

Looking up into his eyes, she took a quick breath. "Would you pray about this?"

He closed his eyes in humility. "I have already."

"Already? And this is what you believe God wants you to do? To take your sister and leave to find the Seafurs? To go to their own land."

"I have prayed about it much. Knowing she had something

to do with his taking, I have been thinking about it for months, but until as of late, I didn't know who had my son. And now we know for certain it's the Seafurs, and we know how to get there." He grabbed her hand and pulled her closer. "Please, Clara, give me your blessing."

"This mariner—"

"Warinus," the king said with a nod.

"Why would he go against his queen when almost all the others have stood true to her? Told lies for her even when she's imprisoned?" She shook her head. "I think there are more reasons than that he knows she has done wrong."

"You think he can't be trusted?"

She turned away to look out the window. "I don't know about that. I deem he holds back on the truth, though. Can you get the truth from him first?"

"The truth?"

She nodded.

"Then you will not be angry when I leave?"

Releasing a breath, she leaned back against him. "How can I be angry if it is what God calls you to do?" She looked into his eyes. "Do I want you to go? No. But I understand that you feel you must." She gazed distantly past his shoulder. "Anchony needs its king."

"William shall stay here, so if I don't—"

She placed her finger on his mouth to silence him. "God's will be done in all things."

Nodding, he released a deep breath. "Thank you, Clara." She smiled; he kissed her.

"Why do you truly go against your queen?" When the rain had turned into a misty fog, Francis addressed the mariner at the fire pit, with Peter behind him as Michael walked over.

Warinus rose. "One too many times I have followed the beckoning of that mad woman. I will no longer."

Francis tilted his head. "I don't deem you understand: My wife has a sense about people. She tells me you hold back upon the truth. So I want to know what the truth is."

Warinus, swallowing hard, lowered his head. "The truth is . . . she's not my queen. I'm from Sethel."

"How did you come to work for the queen of the Sockor Islands?" Michael asked incredulously as he stepped next to the king.

"With intent. She took something dear from me. I have been searching for years to find it."

"What?" King Francis asked.

Warinus, looking down, swallowed hard. "My mother." He looked back up at the knights and the king. "It has been years. I have given up hope of finding her alive, but I wanted to make certain what was done to my mother would never be done to anyone else. The ship was already leaving with your boy before I knew he was on it, but that's when I realized she must have done the same to my mother. Where they took your boy, I deem they took my mother. I want to go to that island. I want to find out what became of her."

Francis nodded. "She killed my own mother—*her* own mother."

Warinus's mouth dropped open. "Her own mother? Is there no end to that wicked woman's deeds?"

Francis crossed his arms. "She is coming with us—Camrina. Will you be able to endure her?"

"I have been around her all these years." Warinus shook his head. "How can you stand to look at her after knowing what she has done?"

Uncrossing his arms, the king looked to the fire. "She has brought harm to the multitudes—most of all to me—but she still has dignity as a person made in God's image, no matter how much she wishes to deny it." He shook his head. "Life is too short to hate anyone. It will take your time and draw you away from your true calling in life. We *must* love everyone. We *must* forgive."

True calling? Who is this man before me? Tilting his head, he looked into the king's eyes. "Are you certain she's your sister?"

"Give me your word, Warinus, that you'll not let harm come to her. Can you do that?" Francis extended his arm.

Not let harm come to her? He looked up for a moment. *Father, give me strength!* He grabbed the king's arm and shook it. "I give you my word on all my honor."

Peter tilted his head as he watched the king and the mariner shake upon the agreement.

Distraught at finding pieces of food upon the packed-earth floor, Lina shook her head as the boy walked in. "Prince Eduard, are you trying to draw rats into our home?"

"Yes," he said as he sat on the floor.

Lina was shocked at the unexpected answer. "Why?"

"I want to find the Lazarus leaf," he said with all sincerity.

"Lazarus leaf?"

"That's what I'm calling it. If it's a true thing." He shrugged his shoulders.

"You mean the one that made the lamb appear to be dead?"

He nodded as he unfolded a piece of cloth. "I think it has to be this one. It came from the bush close to where the lamb was lying."

Intrigued, Lina sat down upon his bed as she watched him place it on the ground. "So you're going to feed it to them?"

"If they'll eat it."

She frowned. "I doubt they will. But I have a thought: We'll make a soup and put the leaf in it and see if that will entice them!"

The following morning, Eduard was awakened by an audible gasp as Lina scrambled back on to her bed. Opening his eyes, he spotted her looking at the floor in utter shock. Around the soup bowl there were what appeared to be five dead rats.

A smile broke out across his face. "Now we have to see if they come back to life!"

Walking hand-in-hand with the king toward the firepit in Aboly from the royal hut, Queen Clara watched the Lion say his farewells to his children. He seemed to hug his daughter for an extended amount of time with gratitude upon his face. Turning to Samus, the Lion hugged him and spoke a moment; Samus nodded his head in understanding.

Her attention transferred to her husband when he said, "I'm going to see how Michael fares with Camrina," Squeezing her hand, he kissed it. "My queen and my love."

"My king and my heart," she said before he turned away.

As Queen Clara watched him walk between the cathedral and the castle, Peter said, "My lady, may I speak with you?"

She turned toward him. "Jous? Yes."

Approaching, he pulled out two letters from under his tunic and offered them to her.

"What are these?" she asked as she took the papers, one sealed and the other not.

Peter glanced back at his daughter. "I vowed to Clare I would not leave her. She demands I go with Francis to find Prince Eduard. She holds me to my duty." With a saddened face, he said, "She has been through so much, but yet, she puts others before herself. She deserves much more than has been her lot." He shook his head. "I don't know when I will return or *if* I will return." Pausing for a moment, he then said, "You spoke of Prince William's one-time affection for her." He pointed to the papers. "Those are in case something comes of it."

She looked at the letters. The unsealed was written to Clare; the sealed to Prince William.

"You may read hers to know when to give it to her. And by that, when to give the prince's his."

With the upmost sincerity, she looked into the Lion's eyes and said, "Thank you. I will indeed."

Bowing his head, he turned to walk toward the market, but then looked back and, with a pleading heart, added, "And if you could *help* her to be . . . who God wants her to be."

Feeling the pain in his heart, she nodded. "Certainly I will."

"Thank you, Your Majesty."

Smiling, the queen touched her hand over her heart. "As you did for my daughter, I shall do for yours."

The Lion, initially straightening, bowed profoundly to the queen in gratitude.

The queen bowed her head in respect to the man and all he had done for her daughter.

"Why does he have to go?" Elizabeth had a downcast glance as she stood beside her eldest sister in Aboly, watching the king say his farewell to her brother and sister.

"He's going to get Edus back," Isabella tried to explain to her distraught sister.

"But didn't Thom already try?"

Isabella pulled her sister close. "Liza, you have to be strong. Do you think Papá truly wants to leave us? He goes because he feels he must. Seeing your tears will only hurt him more."

Releasing her sister as her father approached, she took a quick breath as she held back her emotion. "Isabella."

"Papá." She gladly hugged him. "I shall pray for your safe return."

"Thank you." He looked down at his youngest daughter. "Elizabeth."

Her chin quivered as she tried to hold back the tears, unsuccessfully. Wiping the rebel tears away, she shook her head. "I'm not to cry. I'm to be strong." He pulled her close to himself—a plethora of tears were released. "But I'll miss you, Papá!"

"Oh!" He could not help but lightly chuckle. "It is good to know I'll be missed."

Elizabeth pulled away to look into her father's eyes. "Bring him back, Papá. Bring Edus back with you!"

"I will do my best, Elizabeth."

Watching him embrace her mother one last time, Elizabeth leaned against her sisters and then, too soon, her father was mounting his horse and riding down the marketplace, which was slowly being brought back to life with the aid of many. She ran down the lonely lane feverishly waving. As the barred wagon with the captive inside joined the convoy, the villagers took note.

Joining in the parade of onlookers, she jumped back in surprise as a former slave hurled a rotten vegetable at the wagon, wishing to shame the queen inside. With that demonstration given, others felt freed to replicate the action and soon pieces of food and clumps of dirt were hitting the wooden wagon from all sides. Stepping out into the street as the crowd followed the captive, Elizabeth swallowed in anxiousness. What would become of her father? *Father, bring Papá back home to us and with Edus.*

"Don't fret, Princess Elizabeth. They won't follow them all the way." She looked at Michael as he stepped beside her.

She shook her head. "It's not the Anchonians of which I'm afraid. It's the Seafurs."

"Is the king here?" a voice called out.

Michael and the princess turned toward the male voice, not yet come to maturity. "That's him leaving. Why do you wish to know?"

The boy, a couple years older than Elizabeth with dusty blond hair, stepped closer. "Are you a king's knight, sir?" He looked at Sir Michael in wonder.

"I am." Michael turned to him. "Who would you be?"

"I am Nicholaus Leusson. I'm here on behalf of Duke Lancastor."

"Duke Lancastor of Castol County?" Michael's eyes transferred from the boy to Prince William as he stepped up beside him. "He is not a Demolite to my knowledge."

"What's this about?" William asked.

"I'm not certain at present." Grand Sir Doey looked back at the boy. "Why did the duke send you?"

"He heard you were in need of men."

William tilted his head. "So he sent *you*?"

The young Nicholaus smiled with a nod. "To be a knight!" He presented him with a piece of paper sealed by the duke.

William could not help but chuckle at the boy's enthusiasm. "What say you, Sir Michael Doey? Are you in want of a page?"

The boy looked up at him with every hope.

Michael, placing his hands upon his hips, thought of Peter's words. "That all comes down to the page he shall be." He tilted his head. "So, you want to be a knight, do you?"

The young Nicholaus confidently nodded and then looked around. "Where are all the others? Is the Lion's son here? I share his name!"

Elizabeth shook her head. "There are only three here now. The Lion just left."

The boy's mouth dropped open as he looked at the princess. "The Lion lives?"

❄

Watching Peter shackle her wrists to the hull of the vessel, Camrina could not help but smile. "I find it satisfying that you keep company with one from the *Sockortale*." She leaned closer to him. "You do know that he was there when Annabelle was left upon Snake Island? Left to be bitten by all those poisonous snakes! And what of the child? Oh, the child within her, too—poisoned while he stood by and did *nothing*!"

Pulling the chains to make sure they were tight, he stared at her for a moment and then, replying only with silence, walked away.

Infuriated that she did not get a response, she looked to the ladder when she heard a noise. "Oh, Francis, there you are! Would you like to know what I was speaking about to your heroic knight?"

"Is she locked tightly?" King Francis asked.

"She'll not be getting free, and if she does, where will she go?" He glanced back at her. "Unless she throws herself into the ocean, likely to be eaten by a sea creature."

She made a face at the knight, and then looked at her brother. "To where are we off?" Francis approached her as he felt the boat begin to move. "Are you to give me back to my people to be punished?" A smile slid across her face.

Silently studying her, he turned around toward Peter. "Tell everyone on board they are not to speak to her. Only guile comes from her mouth. And, if she continues to speak, silence her."

"Will do with satisfaction," Peter said before climbing up the ladder.

Stepping onto the deck, he caught Warinus's glance and spoke to all the mariners: "The queen is not to be spoken to, by the king's orders. Is that understood?"

A chorus of ayes rang forth.

Stepping aside, he helped the king out of the hull and then looked back at Warinus, who was busily attending to the ropes.

"Is something wrong, Jous?"

He looked back at his friend. "Not as of now." *But she is right. If Warinus went with Camrina to ensure what was done to his mother was not done to another, then why was Annabelle left on Two Breath Island?*

SUMMER

Thomas, with the sun hiding behind white, fluffy clouds, walked to the starboard side of the *Sockortale* where the captain stood looking at the hilly coast of Baltam. "You called for me?"

The captain pointed. "That is Brotherton, but I do not wish to anchor in port."

"Why is that?"

"There seem to be many horses, Your Highness."

"Sirs?" Thomas's gaze immediately swung to the shoreline. "We are too far to see the tabards."

"Is there trouble?" Nicholaus asked as he stepped next to his prince.

"There are knights in Brotherton."

"Baltamian?" Nicholaus looked to the coast, studying the distant, moving figures.

"We're not certain." Thomas, taking a deep breath, lowered his head. "If not Baltamian, then Sethelian. And if it's Sethelian, what has become of the princess?"

"Do you want me to go ashore?" Nicholaus quickly asked.

"I do wish we could see closer," the captain said.

Thomas, looking up at the ship's flag, shook his head. "We can't take a chance if it is Sethel. They will see us coming if we draw closer. Captain, do you know what the closest port is to this one?"

"North of here: Cottal."

Thomas nodded. "Then that is where we shall go."

"It was you, was it not, who asked, months ago, about Captain Vitalis's ship?"

Nicholaus looked over his shoulder to find the man who addressed him and the prince seven months earlier in that very tavern. "It was." He turned around completely, "And you told us the ship sank."

The man nodded. "Aye, it did indeed."

Nicholaus tilted his head as he watched Prince Thomas addressing another man from his periphery. "You have more to add?"

"Aye. There was someone that lived."

Nicholaus's full attention was thrust upon the Cottalian. "A person on the ship that lived?"

"Aye, but not for long."

Nicholaus tilted his head. "What is your meaning?" His voice was shaky.

"There was a body found. It was one of the mariners from the ship, about thirty miles north of here."

If one lived, Anna could have lived. Is it all true? Is Queen Clara correct? "He drowned?" Nicholaus held his breath.

The man shook his head as he looked to the floor. "From what we can tell, it was the Ruffatons." He looked back at the knight. "He was killed."

"He had a wound?"

The man touched his chest. "Looked to be about here, with a blunt weapon." He lowered his hand. "I helped bury him better."

"Better?" Nicholaus asked with swiftness.

"Aye. He appeared to have been buried with haste—so at least the animals couldn't get to him."

"How long ago was this?"

"He was found a couple months after you were here."

"A couple months? You couldn't have known it was him after that time." Nicholaus stated with perplexity.

"Aye, but he wore a special chain around his neck, given to him by his wife."

"You don't know who buried him?" The man shook his head. Nicholaus looked at Thomas. *If he lived, Anna could have lived, too! She's alive! She has to be alive! But where is she?* With an urgency filling him, he looked at the man. "Will you take us to where you found him buried?"

"Aye."

Thomas, catching Nicholaus's eye, walked over. "Have you come upon something?"

"Someone lived from Anna's ship."

"Oh." Thomas quickly glanced back at the man with whom he was previously conversing. "It is Baltamian soldiers in Brotherton. Princess Anastacia should be safe."

Lady Alana looked around with caution as she walked through the fish market, approaching Sir Fulco. "This is a hard market to find. It took me several weeks."

Looking up, he momentarily halted his knife from striking the fish's head. "What would you have?"

Alana stared at the pile of fish guts and then looked into the knight's eyes. "I was told a certain girl was here."

"A girl?" He stood up straight as he looked around.

"Yes, from Sethel." She swallowed with difficulty as her jaw stiffened.

The man chopped down on the head, and Alana flinched. "Sethel?" he said.

"Yes, Sethel," she whispered back.

He looked at her. "Likely my wife could help you better, my lady."

"Is that so? Where could I find her?"

He tilted his head to the right. "Up the hill, third house."

"Well." She backed away slowly, shaking her head. "I will not have fish today. Thank you kindly for your time."

At the sound of a light knock, Sir Aricus cracked the door and then opened it wide, He turned toward the women in the room. "It seems we have a guest."

Lady Alana, walking swiftly inside, curtsied at the sight of the princess. "Your Majesty."

Anastacia looked curiously from Aricus to the lady. "I don't rule anything yet. Who is it that addresses me so?"

"Princess, this is Lady Alana, Lord Cortell's wife and"—he watched the woman rise—"our sister."

Alana turned toward him and smiled. "It is good to see you, brother!"

"Is this Lady Alana who hid King Francis from Prince Howercus?" Sir Frankus asked.

Alana looked at him. "I am. Who are you?"

Sir Frankus stepped closer. "I think the pressing question is, do you come with a ship?"

"I do."

Princess Anastacia gasped with hope. "So you could take me to Anchony?"

"Indeed." Alana looked around the room at all the relieved faces.

"Oh, good!" Anastacia nearly cried. "I want to get out of Baltam! I want to get as far away from Sethel as I can go! I'm so weary of being afraid to go out because I might be seen by someone who shouldn't see me."

Nicholaus and Thomas watched the man point, waving his arm in a circle, to the area where Annabelle was grabbed by the Seafurs. "It was right here. You can still see the stones that helped to hide him."

The keen-eyed knight studied the indention in the earth and strewn stones. He squatted down. *Did the one who killed him also bury him to cover his tracks?* He turned around, searching the ground. *Why take the time?*

"If you asked me, I would say it was Ruffatus." The man looked around queerly. "That's one man I don't want to meet. Although he is one-eyed, I hear he is harsh. He fights with passion."

Thomas stood as Nicholaus continued to scour the ground. "Who is this man of whom you speak?"

"An outlaw, wanted by the king himself. He is the leader of the Ruffatons."

"Wanted by King Henricus?" Thomas continued to ask as Nicholaus looked around.

"Aye."

"Why? Who are the Ruffatons?"

The man shook his head. "They have no fealty toward the king."

"No fealty? Why?"

The man shrugged his shoulders. "They are outlaws. Do they have to have a reason?"

Thomas tilted his head. "Most men claim to have a reason for everything they do." He pulled out a coin. "I like to know the 'why.'" He presented the coin to the man. "We thank you for your time."

The man accepted the coin. "I wish I could help more. I'm sorry about your sister."

Thomas nodded. As he watched the man walk away, he looked at the knight rising from the ground. "Sir Nicholaus, what are you going to do?"

Nicholaus looked at him with all sincerity. "Find an outlaw."

Thomas grinned, but it quickly faded away. "You're in earnest."

He turned around to face his prince. "Yes."

"The Baltamians have been searching for this man for months—likely a year or two! You deem—" Thomas lowered his head as he realized, if anyone could find the outlaw, it was the man before him.

"Yes, I deem I can find him. I will find out if this mariner spoke any of Anna."

Thomas slowly nodded as he released a breath and looked around. "Alright. That's the best we have to go on. Where should we go to find this outlaw?"

Nicholaus slowly shook his head as he looked at the man before him. "Prince Thomas, you shouldn't come."

"I want to find my sister as badly as you want to find your wife—if she is, in truth, alive."

"I don't doubt it. But the Ruffatons are outlaws. If they find you, a prince of Anchony, it would not be good."

Thomas lowered his head, for he knew the knight was correct. "I will go to Brotherton and get word to King Henricus that we are here in Baltam and that there is a mad Anchonian knight single-handedly seeking out Baltam's outlaw to find his living dead wife."

Nicholaus nodded. "That is the truth, is it not?"

"Where shall we meet and when?"

"I shall bring the outlaw to the king. Wait for me there or leave me word you have gone back to Anchony."

"Back to Anchony? How long do you think this duty shall take?"

Nicholaus tilted his head. "As long as is needed." He bowed to his prince.

Thomas stuck out his arm. "Farewell then, for now, Sir Nicholaus Hunts. Godspeed."

"Godspeed, Prince Thomas."

Thomas watched Sir Nicholaus kneel upon the ground and read whatever he could from it. Then he rose, looked back at Thomas with a nod, and took off into the wilderness of Baltam. Turning back to the grave, Thomas knelt down beside it and curiously picked up one of the stones. *Someone took the time to bury you. If he was a true outlaw, why would he show such mercy?*

He studied the porous stone for a moment, then dropped it and rose. *Who is this outlaw? What makes one lose fealty to one's king in Baltam?* His eyes wandered from the grave to the trees, rustling in the wind. "Does anyone know him?"

Glancing southward, he shook his head and then looked north. "It is north where he finds his followers."

Anastacia, watching the Baltamian coast fade from her vision, looked at the duchess. "Princess Annabelle said she saw her father die—that he was hanged. How does King Francis live?"

"Another died in his stead," Alana answered.

"Who?" the princess asked with the greatest concern.

"Sir Tratus. Your uncle's right-hand man." The duchess

turned toward the fading land. "Lord Cortell didn't want to, but the man kept escaping. My husband was certain he would tell your uncle that we knew of his ploy."

"So you didn't intend to kill him?"

"No, not at first. It was to hide King Francis—to make him vanish—and to tell your uncle that he was killed. But Prince Howercus showed up and learned the king was there." Biting her lip, she shook her head. "He was so close to finding that we had Sir Tratus. All would've been lost." Alana lowered her head. "He was justly hanged, guilty of what King Francis was accused."

Anastacia stared at the sparkling sea. "It was my uncle's doing. It is always my uncle's doing." Taking a deep breath, she admitted, "He is the only family I have left." Wanting to think of other things, she glanced at the duchess. "Are you sad to leave your brothers? You've been away from them for so long."

"It was good to see them again and I will miss them, but I know what they do is pressing."

Selling fish? That can't be the pressing matter. Looking back at the shrinking coast, the princess tapped upon the wooden bulwark in front of her. "Do your brothers wait for something?"

"What do you mean?"

"Why do they stay while their wives come? Do they wait for some kind of tiding? Was my brother to help them somehow?"

"Tidings from whom?"

The princess shook her head. "I don't know. I thought you could tell me."

Alana slowly nodded. "It is true. Your brother was to search for tidings for them."

"About what?"

Alana forced a smile. "It doesn't matter anymore. I fear that with your brother gone, the tidings shall never come."

"But they don't?" Anastacia said as she turned back to the distant, fading land.

"What do you mean?"

"They stay. They must have hope."

Alana took a quick breath and revealed with all sincerity, "They stay because of an oath they took to one another. That is what holds them bound."

Standing from the barren land, Prince Thomas shook his head as he looked at the empty wattle and daub huts of Bartel. *What took place here? It is as if the whole town vanished.* Turning his head, he looked at the sea a quarter of a mile away. *Did the Ruffatons do this? Why would they? And if they did, what did they do with the people?* He released a breath. *It is close to the water; does that have any bearing?* He looked in all directions. *There are trees everywhere else.* Shaking his head, he adjusted his bag and walked farther north.

Four days later, his jaw stiffened at the sight of yet another ravished village.

"It can't be! What ills this land?" His eyes quickly scanned the surroundings. *It is near the sea like the others. Forests and valleys around the other sides.* "Something is, indeed, not right with Baltam. Does King Henricus know?"

As he turned southward toward the distant occupied Port of Brotherton, it suddenly hit him: *Could it be the Seafurs?* Shaking his head, he spoke aloud, "I must get word to King Henricus!"

SEARCHING

Watching the Baltamian knights curiously from a distance around Brotherton, Thomas searched for the one appearing to be their leader. He stiffened when he felt something poke into his back.

"State your claim."

Thomas, looking over his shoulder, saw that it was a Baltamian knight addressing him. He was pressing the tip of his sword into the small of Thomas's back. "Tell me who you are, and I will be glad to inform you of my station."

"Sir Harkus."

"Harkus? I have heard your name spoken by my brother for unlawfully holding him bound. I am Prince Thomas of Anchony, and I wish to speak with King Henricus." He felt the pressure release off of his back as the man stepped around to face him.

"Hmmm, you have a likeness to your brother." Harkus sheathed his sword. "King Henricus is not here. He is in search of . . . another."

"Another? Do you mean your outlaw? If he is, he's not alone in his search. Anchony's best tracker is after him, too." Thomas quickly scanned the surroundings. "Tell me, where is Princess Anastacia?"

Harkus studied him and then revealed, "She is the *other* of which I speak."

Thomas shook his head as he began to panic. "She's not here? What's become of her? Why did she flee?"

"Brotherton was overrun by Sethelians when we arrived. She escaped from them with some fishmongers."

"Fishmongers?" Thomas curiously placed his hands upon his hips. "They escaped from Sethelian knights?"

"Yes."

He tilted his head. "Who are they truly?" His eyes caught sight of a dozen faces over Sir Harkus's shoulder. Recognizing one, he straightened his head and approached that one particular captured Sethelian knight. "I don't believe it."

"What?"

He looked back at Sir Harkus, demanding, "Tell me how that knight came to be here."

"He and that whole group were watching us bind the others."

Thomas nodded. "And he didn't try to free the others, did he?"

Harkus, watching him walk toward the Sethelian knight, followed after. "I must say I thought it was strange."

"That's because this knight, sir, wants to give the princess protection—not to kill her or give her to her uncle." He looked at the Sethelian. "Sir Jacobus?"

Sir Jacobus looked up when he heard his name. "Prince Thomas? Your Highness, you have to find her! They say she was here, but now she's not!"

Thomas turned back to the Baltamian. "Sir Harkus, you need to let him go."

"He is to be imprisoned by Baltam. I will not let him go unless my king orders it."

"Then I wish to speak to the knight away from the other Sethelians."

In the desolate fish market, Prince Thomas and Sir Harkus turned around to look at the bound Sethelian knight. "The town was already overrun when we got here," Sir Jacobus announced.

"So they knew she was here, too?" Thomas said with concern.

Sir Jacobus shook his head. "No, they didn't. Most of Sethel thinks she's dead. They came here after four outlaws—knights —brothers of the slain Sir Ilum."

Harkus threw up his hands in frustration. "So now Baltam has Sethelian outlaws to deal with!"

"Outlaws to Prince Howercus I would deem would be on your side, since he's the one who sent his knights into Baltam," the prince observed.

Sir Jacobus nodded.

Sir Harkus shook his head as he addressed Sir Jacobus. "Well, do you know anything about Princess Anastacia's whereabouts now?"

Thomas tilted his head, nearly interrupting the knight. "Where's Queen Mona?"

MERCY

"Why do you stop?" one of the Sethelian knights, sent by Sir Arkel, asked Eunisia just outside of Aboly.

She glanced over her shoulder at him. "I heard Aboly was destroyed. It doesn't look too damaged to me."

"Queen Camrina is building it back," the other said.

"Let's take off our tabards, in case it's not so."

Eunisia watched nervously as they doffed their outer cloth. *What will I do if Camrina has taken the throne?* Her stomach suddenly rolled in fear. *What will I do if she hasn't?* She fell to her knees in fear.

"Let's go." The first knight looked at the pallid Eunisia. "What's wrong with you?"

"I—" The man pulled her up. She stumbled down the hill.

Pushing herself up, she glanced over her shoulders at the men and, turning to the bustling city, froze. Walking before her, on the other side of the road, was Queen Clara. Noting the king's knight next to her, Eunisia released a long-held breath as she sprinted forward. "They're Sethelians! They're Sethelians!"

Queen Clara and Sir Michael turned around to see a woman,

desperately sprinting through the people, grabbed by two knights not wearing any tabards.

As the knights pulled the woman down, the queen heard her cry, "Queen Clara, I beg mercy!"

William, running around the corner, joined his mother. "What's going on?"

Pulling his sword, Michael ran forward. "Get the queen back!"

Clara looked around her son's body. "Does she call for me?"

"Mamá, stay back!"

"Clara! Clara! Mercy from the king, Clara! Mercy!"

The queen looked at her son. "William, she calls for me." Stepping forward with her son at her side, Clara studied the woman crawling toward her as Michael engaged the knights. "I know that face! William, it is Eunisia! It is the woman who spoke of me to the Sethelians who then gave me to Camrina!"

Standing upon the dais in the newly risen Great Hall, William flared his nostrils as he watched the guards bring the servant forward. "Eunisia, servant of Lathrop Castle, you are a traitor to this kingdom and are more wretched than the Sethelian knights that were justly sentenced to hard labor! You gave the queen, whom you know, to Anchony's enemy so that she would be killed."

A plethora of tears joined those that had already fallen as the servant, upon her knees, looked up at the ruler, nodding her head. As her body quivered with her cries, she found the gaze of the emerald eyes. "Queen Clara, please, I beg of you, I know I've done wrong. I ask for mercy! I ask for mercy!" She lowered her head in desperation.

William began, "Eunisia, you are sentenced to—"

"Wait." Clara touched her son's arm as she looked at the

desperate woman. Descending the dais, she stepped in front of the servant and slowly knelt. Raising the woman's chin with her hand, she looked into her eyes.

"My lady, I beg mercy from your son!"

Releasing the woman's chin, the mother stood and, stepping between her son's view of the convict, approached the ruling prince. "William, my son, I beg mercy on behalf of her."

William tilted his head. "The woman that handed you over to Prince Howercus?"

"Yes, the very one."

"She doesn't deserve such mercy! What more of a slight is there than to assault one's mother?"

"I know she doesn't deserve mercy, but I request it. Will you grant it to me?"

His angered and tensed body slowly relaxed as he looked upon his mother. "Are you certain?"

Clara smiled. "I am."

William released a breath, "Mamá, you know I'll not deny anything you ask of me."

"Thank you."

Stepping down from the dais, he squeezed his mother's hand and then walked around her to stand in front of the woman. "This traitor has the protection of the queen. She is placed in Queen Clara's care."

Eunisia looked up at him with all gratitude. "Thank you!"

Glancing down at her, he whispered, "You should be thankful the queen was here to speak on your behalf."

Eunisia nodded as tears of gratitude fell down her cheeks, and she looked at the queen. "I am. I am."

As the wind blew in northern Baltam, Nicholaus spotted the dancing flames as he peered through the thick woods. Looking at the faces of the people gathered around a fire, he found one with a visibly scarred eye. "There you are Ruffatus. Long have I searched for you." Removing his fur coverings and belt, he strapped his sword to his back on top of his tunic and donned his furs so it was well hidden. Picking up his fresh forest catch, he walked toward the posse of men.

Ruffatus and the men stood as they reached for their weapons at the sound of a visitor. Nicholaus presented the hares. "I have meat. I will share if I can use your fire."

Ruffatus eyed him. "Who are you?"

"A man in search of his wife."

Ruffatus lowered his head. Nicholaus stepped forward and sat down around the fire. Ruffatus studied the man before him. "You won't find her."

Nicholaus froze. *What does he know of her?*

"They never come back once they're taken."

Taken? Nicholaus looked at Ruffatus as the outlaw threw a piece of a stick into the fire.

"Where was she?" another man spoke.

Nicholaus watched all eyes turn toward him. "South of here, near the coast."

"Which town?" Ruffatus asked for clarification.

Nicholaus shook his head. Having scoured the land in search of the man in front of him, he honestly answered, "I don't know. The town is no more." He patiently waited for any sign of confirmation from the outlaws' faces that they were responsible for the massive deaths from villages near and far. Disgusted by all the sights he had seen, he was ready to attack at a moment's notice if they would only provide a fresh reason.

Ruffatus, shaking his head, sighed deeply as he threw the rest of the stick into the fire and stood with passion. "May the Seafurs meet their fiends in hell!"

Nicholaus, taken aback by the outburst, watched the other

outlaws nod their heads in agreement. "Seafurs?" He looked up at Ruffatus.

"Yes, the Seafurs!" the man said with every agitation. "Those savage heathens from the sea!"

Nicholaus shook his head. *The ones that worked with Camrina?* Suddenly, there seemed to be a clarity out of the vileness. "What do you know of them?"

Ruffatus angrily looked back at Nicholaus. "I told you!"

"That they are savage heathens from the sea?"

"Yes!" He pointed to one of the men. "They took Gilus's two young sons and killed his eldest." The man to whom he pointed, nodded his head once. "Larius lost his sister and mother and father when he fought back. Jonus, at age ten, ran into the woods when his parents were slaughtered by them. Sarius lost his two daughters after losing his wife a year before."

Nicholaus looked up at Ruffatus. "And you? What did you lose?"

The leader lowered his head. "I lost my daughter and my wife that was with child." Nicholaus swallowed hard as the man slumped back to the earth. "And my eye when I fought back."

The knight lowered his head as he admitted, "My wife was also with child." He shook his head. "It was a year or so ago. My child could have been taking his first steps around now." He looked at the saddened faces. "You are the Ruffatons that fight against your king?"

"Yes."

Nicholaus shook his perplexed head. "Why? Why do you fight against him when he could aid you?"

Every eye turned toward him. Ruffatus stared at him. "Because he does not aid us! He does nothing!"

Nicholaus shook his head. "Does he even know?" Looking straight ahead into the woods, he thought of his imprisonment by the Baltamian knights. "I have met him before. He is a good man. If he knew, he would help."

"You met the king?" Sarius asked incredulously.

"I have."

Ruffatus looked at him curiously, remembering similar words from the princess's mouth. "Where did you meet him?"

Nicholaus lowered his head. "It wasn't in Baltam."

"Not in Baltam?" Jonus asked.

Ruffatus stood as he remembered Annabelle's words.

"Where did you see him, then?" Sarius continued questioning.

"In Anchony." Nicholaus looked up as Ruffatus gasped.

Ruffatus, nodding his head, slowly looked at Nicholaus. "Annabelle of Anchony, that is your wife?"

Nicholaus bolted to his feet. "You know her?!"

"I met her. Around a year ago."

Nicholaus, jumping across the fire, pulled out his dagger as he pushed Ruffatus against a tree. "What did you do with her?!"

Taken completely off guard, Ruffatus looked bewildered as the other men stood, unsure how the leader was suddenly captured. Ruffatus shook his head. "It wasn't me! It was the Seafurs! They took her!"

Nicholaus breathed quickly as he looked into the leader's eye. "She lived through the shipwreck at sea to be taken by savage heathens?"

Ruffatus nodded insistently. "Yes!"

Nicholaus, backing away, glanced at the group of Ruffatons just to look at the recovering leader and then lower his gaze, slightly shaking his head. "Where did they take her?"

"If we knew that, we wouldn't be here." Ruffatus eyed the man that had just nearly killed him. "I see you have passion." Stepping closer, he held out his hand. "If you want to fight them, join us."

SACRIFICE

Katara, with a dour face, walked up to Eduard as he poked at a dead rat with a stick in the fields north of the village. The sheep he was watching over were ambling toward the fence.

"What you do?" she asked curiously.

He shook his head. "All the others came back to life, but not this one. I thought I would give it time, but it hasn't come back all day!" Giving up, he threw down his stick and walked toward the sheep corral.

Following beside him, she was quiet for a moment, and then, taking a deep breath, she announced: "Still no gold. Need Give."

"Give? What do you mean?"

"I go to Give."

Eduard shook his head as he made a face. "Another sacrifice? How could you watch that? Do you like watching people die?"

She offered him something. "You keep sheep live—they keep you live." She patted him on the shoulder.

"What's this?" Taking the leather into his hand, he let it fall. "A sling? My sister gave me one."

"Not sling. It bind legs. I help you." Then, taking a deep

breath, she lowered her hand and revealed, "I go to Give. I not watch."

Looking at her strangely and momentarily forgetting about the gift, he thought about the meaning of her words as she walked away. "Wait!" Running after, he grabbed her hand. "You mean you give yourself? *You're* the one they kill?"

"I Give."

"No! You can't! Please! You can't!"

Katara pulled her arm away, unsure why he was acting in such a fashion. "My people glad. Why you not?"

"Because they're going to kill you!" He looked desperately at her as he closed the gate after the last sheep followed the herd safely inside the pen. "Please, you can't let them!"

Annabelle, relaxing her arms and lowering the bow, stood on the upper perch of rock in the growing twilight. "Edus, how did you find me? And you brought another?"

"She brought me," he said as he walked past Katara. "Annie, you have to help her!" he pleaded.

The princess looked at the girl. "Katara?"

"You have to help her see."

"See what?"

"They're going to use her as a sacrifice!"

Annabelle's eyes immediately looked toward the woods. "There's no one after her."

"No. She gives herself!"

She looked back to her brother and then to the girl as she lowered the bow. "Why would she do that?"

"She thinks she's helping her people." Eduard shook his head. "I tried to tell her that they'll kill her. She won't listen. Annie, she's my friend. You have to help her!"

Annabelle stared at the downcast head. "Katara already

knows the lot of a sacrifice." She glanced at her brother. "I will see what I can do." Lowering a rope ladder from the perch, she climbed down it and then looked at the little cave entrance. "Edus, will you go to the cave please, check upon the sleeping babes? Do you see the darker crevice? You can crawl or take the ladder." Nodding, he walked toward the rock wall.

Turning back to the girl, she took a deep breath. "You have been watching him?"

"Yocht."

Annabelle tilted her head.

"Yes," Katara said in the princess's tongue.

"How can you watch him if you give yourself?"

Katara shook her head. "I go to Give for my people."

She shook her head. "So Edus no longer matters?"

"You sister, you watch! I help my people!"

She never gave her word to me; she is not bound. Releasing a deep breath, the princess asked, "Katara, how old are you?"

"Old to give at Give."

She studied the girl: perhaps in her early teens. She closed her eyes. *Father, please. Help me to speak the words she needs to hear to understand the truth.* Opening her eyes, she pointed to the ground as she knelt down herself. "It is a noble thing that you wish to do—to give yourself to help your people." She shook her head. "But why do you do it? What is its aim?"

The girl looked at her quizzically as she sat before her. "Give life so gold come."

"Gold?" the princess asked with a tinge of disgust. "Did they nearly kill my children for gold to come?"

Katara looked up at her. "No. Kill babes stop people from come, fulfill need of gods."

Annabelle's mouth fell open. Stupefied, the princess refused to continue down the path of unreasonable reasons for the evil practices of the Seafurian people. Instead, she lowered her head.

Father, what can I say to make her see? Deep within she heard the reply: *"Tell her of My people."*

As she inhaled with a new invigoration, Annabelle looked at the girl. "Do your people spill blood because you believe life is in the blood?"

Katara nodded in agreement. "No blood, no life."

"That is one thing we see the same then." The princess briefly smiled at their common ground. "My people have a book that speaks about God and all He's done for us. In that book, the chosen people, the Israelites, used to make sacrifices, too—animal sacrifices—but they weren't done to calm God; they were done to draw closer to Him. You see, in the fallen world, in which we live, the only way to have communion with God is through sacrifice."

"No is? No more?" Katara shook her head in discontent, "Gods mad dafod here. They hold back gold. Acwa say now Give need." She cautiously looked at the princess. "You dafod."

"Me?"

Katara nodded. "Acwa say child of green-eye bring death."

"What? That doesn't . . ." There was no way of following, so Annabelle answered the girl's question instead. "There are no more blood sacrifices because the Lasting Sacrifice has already come."

"What mean?"

Annabelle turned away for a moment of prayer. Finding more strength, she faced the girl again. "Do you sacrifice people in winter for the sun to come in the spring?"

Katara nodded. "Blood make sun stronger. Give life."

The princess took the girl's hands and rubbed her cheek. "The Son has already come, and He remains with us evermore. He is the Word made Flesh, spoken of for ages, and He will never leave us." The girl looked at her oddly. Annabelle shook her head. "You don't need to give yourself; the One has already given Himself for us all!" She squeezed the girl's hands. "He came that we might have life, not to kill one another."

Katara made a face as she pulled her hand away. "Who 'He'?"

"God's only Son, Jesus the Christ."

"You speak like Edus! He not give good answer." The girl shook her head out of confusion. "Which god?"

Annabelle could not help but smile. "This is the truth of it: There is only one."

Katara shook her head as she counted upon her fingers. "No! There god sky, god fire, god water—there stone for each."

Annabelle touched her hands. "No." She held up her finger. "One. The 'I Am,' the 'Who Is'— the Creator of all those things which you worship. The Master of all, He set the sun in motion. He created the heavens and the earth, the sky and the water, the soil and the trees. He spoke and everything came into being in six days. He has the last word in everything. He loves us all richly, and He wants you to live a long life knowing, loving, and serving Him and only Him."

"Chief god?" Katara pondered.

"What?"

"He rule god sky, god fire, god water, god earth. He chief. You mean him?"

"There's a chief?" Annabelle stared at her, not sure what to say. *They are searching for God? They know there's one that rules all? They are close, yet so far away!* "What does this chief god do?"

"He need sacrifice always. We not have stone here."

"You don't worship the main god here?"

"Acwa not speak chief. He speak to less gods. Tell him what do."

Annabelle released the girl's hands as she looked down. "I don't doubt that he's told what to do, but they are not gods."

"They know what come."

The princess shook her head as she looked around. "No.

They have good understanding of things, but they are creatures. Creatures that observe keenly."

"Creatures?" The girl looked to the ground. "I never saw." Adamantly, she shook her head as she stood. "Do not speak gods this way!" She looked around nervously. "God sky strike down!"

"Katara . . ." Annabelle, rising a moment after the girl did, grabbed her hand before she could flee. "They have already lost."

The girl looked at her with all perplexity. "Lost? Lost what?"

The princess pulled her closer and together they leaned against a boulder. "Long before there were people, there were only angels with God—creatures without bodies. God gives to all of us—angels and people alike—free will to choose to love Him. A third of the angels said no and were cast out of Heaven. They roam the earth and the netherworlds trying to pull all people away from Him. The 'gods' you worship are nothing but fallen angels who want you to worship them and not the 'I Am.'"

The girl's head shook with confusion. "Edus say, but no!"

Annabelle squeezed her hand. "Don't try to believe. Talk to Him. Talk to the 'Who Is.' Talk to the Father. Talk to His Son, Jesus." Annabelle smiled again as she stroked the girl's cheek. "It's a thing of beauty: When we are baptized, we are all family, a part of the Body of Christ. God is our Father." The princess's finger moved to the young girl's sternum. "And there is a place in your heart that yearns for Him." Shaking her head, she looked to their hands. "Don't believe me—ask Him yourself to reveal Truth to you."

Letting go, Annabelle stepped away from the boulder and gave a quick smile. "I have spoken to Him, and I have asked Him to use me in any way He wishes." She turned around. "Don't you see, Katara? I think *you* are the answer to my prayers. He wanted me to speak to you. I thank you for coming."

"You talk to your god?"

"He's not *my* God. He is *the* God. He's not one amongst

many. He's not a creature amongst a creation. He . . . Is. He always has Been, and He will always Be. He does not change. He is constant and His word can be trusted."

"What word? What do He say you?" She shook her head. "Only Acwa speak gods."

"So only he is deceived by them, and then he leads you and your people astray."

Katara stood, resolute. "I not go against gods! I not go against Acwa!"

Annabelle looked her in the eyes. "Are you willing to lay down your life for gods to whom you aren't allowed to speak? Speak to the God in Heaven, that He may let you know Truth."

"I . . ." Katara looked around the darkening woods sporadically. "I not . . ." She was unable to complete her thought. Suddenly the confused girl took off in a run back toward the village as Annabelle watched.

Turning around toward the cave, the princess rubbed her head. *Did I say everything I was to say, Father?*

Prince Eduard, after halting his investigation of the bolas in the firelight, looked eagerly around as his sister entered the mouth of the cave. "Where is she?"

Annabelle petted the growing wolf pup upon the head as she looked from her brother to her children, sleeping peacefully. "I think she went back to her people."

"Back?" He stood. "Is she still going to let them kill her?"

"I don't know. That's between her and God." Taking a quick breath, she looked at her brother with a bit of concern. "There's something special about her. She is misled and deceived. She has not been taught the truth that is handed down in His Church, and now that she has heard it, it is hard to bear, but there is something about her." She knelt down next to her slumbering children. "God wants her for some purpose. I will pray for her. You should pray for her, too."

"I have been! I thought you could make her see. And, if not . . ."

She looked at him when he did not finish his thought. "If not?"

With great resistance, he shook his head. "Annie, you could stop them."

Her mouth opened as she looked at her brother's pleading face. "Edus, I am only one—"

"You were trained by the Lion! The best knight Anchony has ever known! You *have* to stop them!"

She shook her head as she looked back at Augustine and Claudia. "Edus, I have my children. What would be their fortune if I didn't return?"

He looked at her with a new resolve. "But if there's something special about her, don't you have to stop them?"

"Edus, it's not that easy."

With tears streaming down his face, he declared, "Then I will stop them!"

Her tone turned stern as she jumped up and grabbed his arm before he could run to the opening. "Edus, you are only a boy. You can't—"

"'It's not the size of the body that matters, it's what's in the heart.' That's what Papá has always told me!"

"Papá's dead, Edus! Killed by his own sister and a power-seeking prince! Do you think they had goodness in their hearts?" Gasping, she looked away as he looked at her saddened face and his world began to crumble.

"What do you mean?" He stared at his sister as his heart slowly broke. "Did you see him?"

"Yes, I saw him. He was alive after Aboly was assaulted, but the Sethelians stole him away." She closed her eyes as the image of his swinging feet bombarded her memory. "Prince Howercus got a Lord Cortell to hang him in Sethel." Opening her eyes, she looked to the cave floor as she knelt. *And then I gave Lord Cortell the seal.*

"No." He shook his head with all his being as he pulled his hands away. "Papá was hanged?" Tears began to stream down his cheeks as Annabelle pulled him into a hug against his resistance. She listened to his crying as her own tears descended. "What of Will and Thom? Are they alive? Thom has to be alive! He has to come for me—he gave his word! His word, Annie!"

"Shhh, we are alright for right now, aren't we?"

Eduard sniffled as he wiped his eyes. "Annie, if he's dead, who will come for us?"

The princess, holding her brother's wet face in her hands, looked into his eyes. "We must pray for all of them. I don't know who lives." Grimacing with new tears, she tried to gain strength. "If Nicholaus is alive, he will come for us. If Thom or Will are alive, they will come for us. If Peter or Michael are still alive, they will come for us. I have to believe someone will come for us!" Sniffling, she shook her head as she wiped away some tears and found her brother's eyes. "We've been brought here for a reason. To speak truth to Katara? I can't say for certain the reason, but we must do whatever God wishes us to do."

"You keep saying that!" he replied in distress. She pulled him into a hug. Silence filled the air for a moment until his young voice spoke forth. "Annie, what if He wants me to stop them? What if that is why he brought me here?"

"Oh, Edus!" She squeezed him harder. "You are just like Will and Thom!" She could not help but chuckle at her own admission. "You must use all gifts God has given you, as well as your mind."

He pulled away. "You don't deem I'm thinking?"

"You are one boy against a tribe of men. It's not wise!"

He shook his head. "Then what am I to do? Let them kill her? Sacrifice my friend for the fiends?"

"Edus! You are only a boy! There's nothing you can do but pray for her and all of them! You've already tried to help her by bringing her here. Take heart in that!"

His shoulders slumped. "It didn't help! I have to do more, Annie! I have to!"

"Then pray for her. Fast for her. Pray that she will change her mind!"

His face crinkled. "That's not enough!"

She grabbed his arms. "Give me your word, Edus, that you won't try to stop them if it comes down to it. Vow to me!"

His eyes lowered. "I have to get back to the huts."

She pulled him closer. "Vow to me, Edus!" She was not about to let go until she heard it from his mouth. She lifted his chin. "Look me in the eye and give me your word."

"Annie . . ." Fresh tears fell from his eyes. "I won't try to stop them."

She hugged him. "Thank you, Edus. Thank you."

"You met the elder?" Prince Eduard asked Katara as he stood guard in the valley a couple days later.

The Seafurian girl nodded.

"Was he wise?" Eduard was thinking about Bishop Dominicus and some of the friars in Anchelo, who were the oldest people he knew and also the wisest. "Did he tell you not to do it?"

She tilted her head, almost in disgust. "Why he tell me no?"

He looked at her desperately. "Someone's got to! You won't listen to me or Annie!" His head lowered. "I thought he would know killing people is not the way."

She defiantly placed her hands upon her hips. "It way! It way to make gods happy! Keep people live!"

"But it won't end with you, will it? So what's the point?"

"It needed for gold to come. It needed for sun stay and summer come. It only way."

Eduard turned toward her with all fervor. "No, it's not! We've never sacrificed a person in Anchony, and we don't worry about the sun shining or the seasons changing. They do it by themselves!"

Tilting her head, she held up her pointer finger. "You did One!"

Eduard adamantly shook his head. "No! Never!"

"You and sister speak Him—Jesus!"

Eduard's mouth dropped open, and he slowly shook his head. "He didn't die in Anchony."

"Not Anchony?" She crossed her arms. "Where then?"

"A place far, far away called Jerusalem."

"He die in Jerusalem, make sun in Anchony?" she asked with complete perplexity as she uncrossed her arms.

Eduard looked over at the sheep. "He is the light of the world."

She shook her head in confusion. "Why shine in Anchony, not here?"

Eduard looked back at her. "Nothing has to die for the sun to shine!"

She looked at him in amazement, unsure of the veracity of his words.

"The seasons come and go. It's the way it works!"

Katara shook her head. "I know not to believe you."

"Whatever you believe, your people are wrong!" Edward turned away as he crossed his own arms.

Insulted, Katara stood. "You . . . wrong!" Grimacing and adamantly shaking her head, Katara ran away more agitated than when she came.

Hearing a disturbance in the woods, Annabelle rose from the carcass as she grabbed the bow and set the arrow, pointing into the forest. *It sounds like crying.* She caught sight of someone running nearer. A girl. *Katara?*

"I want know!" The girl haphazardly moved away branches and leaves in her path as she fled toward the princess wrapped in all of her confusion. "I want know why one?"

Annabelle, lowering her bow, watched the girl fling herself against a boulder. Katara looked up at her with wet cheeks, begging for an answer. "One? One what?"

"Sacrifice! One man—why only one man? One man and enough?"

The princess nodded. "Yes, His sacrifice was enough to amend for all of our sins. He was our ransom."

Katara's neck strained as she begged for understanding. "But why?"

Setting down the bow, Annabelle took the girl's arm and guided her on to the woolen blanket where the children were happily sitting while playing with sticks. The princess sat down beside the villager. "Why was Christ's death enough?" She took a deep breath as she thought about the answer. "Because He is man *and* God Himself, and He does the perfect will of the Father. He poured out all of His Blood so we can have communion with Him."

She asked with all confusion. "He the God that die?"

Annabelle shook her head. "I know it doesn't make sense—it's a Mystery. But the one God has three Persons to Him. It's like a tree that has its roots, its trunk, and its branches. The three together are all one tree."

Katara, even more confused, looked to the forest. "God tree?"

"No!" Placing her hands upon her head, Annabelle contemplated how she could explain the Trinity simply to the girl before her. "He is not a tree. He is not a creature. He *Is*. He is outside of time, outside of everything. He made time and everything!" Dropping her hands, she turned around. "A tree comes from a seedling, which comes from a seed, which was dropped by another tree, does it not?"

Katara nodded in agreement.

"So, every created thing needs a creator, does it not?"

The girl slowly nodded.

"So, God is not a creature. He wasn't formed by anything. How He *is*, I don't know." Looking to the sky, she smiled. "Oh, Katara, what little we know of all the things of God!" Lowering her gaze, she nodded. "He is what made everything come into being. And He, for our own sake, wanted us to know Him. He became one of us—our Emmanuel—to do the perfect will of the Father."

"God will He die?" she asked with all perplexity.

"He willed that His Son give all of Himself in whatever manner was needed, and because of the hardness of our hearts, and death is the cost of sin, it was death. So He willingly gave it all. So, yes, He died only once. But since God is outside of time, and Jesus is God, it counts for all time; He is the Sacrifice of evermore."

Katara's mouth dropped open as she thought of the elder's words. "Unending sacrifice needed? Elder say so."

"And when Mass is said—when the words Christ spoke at His last meal are spoken again—His sacrifice is re-presented to the Father for our sake. We participate in His Holy Sacrifice." Annabelle smiled at the thought, as she grabbed the girl's hands. "Katara, He comes back to us through His sacred words spoken by the priest, acting in his stead."

Katara shook her head. "What priest?"

"A priest is a man that's given power to speak Christ's words, passed down from the men who followed Jesus." Annabelle shook her head. "There's so much to tell you." Taking a deep breath, she closed her eyes for a moment. "Christ, through the priest, is given back to the Father as our Sacrifice. He wants to be close to us—He wants us to come into His being—so He allows us to take Him in."

"How take in?" Katara asked with all confusion.

"Food keeps us alive. We eat for our bodies. We take in Christ—through eating—for our souls."

"What you eat?"

"His Body and—"

Katara stood up in protest. "You eat body?!"

"It is the Body and Blood, Soul and Divinity of Christ, but it's not a dead body! He resurrected! He came back to life! He is alive at this very moment in Heaven! And in all the tabernacles of the churches around the world!"

Katara shook her head in bewilderment. "He live? I not see sacrifice come back!"

"It is His Resurrected Body that He gives to us! We are filled with His Resurrected life when we eat the Most Blessed Sacrament! Don't you see? His sacrifice is not like your people's, for when there is a sacrifice, it stays dead. He brought Himself back to life and gives Himself to us because He loves us and He wants us to be with Him in Heaven for all of eternity! We eat His Flesh and drink His Blood to give us life! Like your people say: there is life in the blood!"

Katara nervously shook her head as her eyes scanned the outside of the cave, thinking of all the words. "I . . . I not know these words true." She moved uncomfortably as she whimpered.

Annabelle touched the girl's arm. "Katara . . ." She only continued once the Seafur was looking at her. "Talk to Him. He is a person. Ask Jesus to let Himself be known to you. Will you do that?"

"I . . ." Dropping her hands, Katara backed away. "I got go." She ran back toward the south.

Sitting upon her lookout position among the high cliffs to the northeast of the village, marveling at the majesty of the sea sparkling with the evening light, Katara awed in wonder of the creation with a troubled mind. Speaking in her own language, she spoke to any god who might be listening: "I don't know if Annie and Edus are right. Is there just one God who died and came back to life? Are my people so wrong?" She looked up at the sky. "Long have I praised the sun for its light, for its warmth. Was I wrong to do so?"

Her eyes descended, and she looked to the sacrificial hill in the distance as the sacrificial stone for the sun god glittered in its golden state. "Is it wrong to sacrifice people? Does the sun need the sacrifices?" Releasing a breath, she looked at her lap. "Edus says no. Annie says that there only needed to be one. Is that the truth?"

She turned her gaze to her people—appearing as ants from her distance. "She also says there is but one God but He is three. What is the truth? Acwa says he speaks to the gods, but I've never heard them speak." Taking a breath, she elevated her eyes. "Is there only one God—that I don't understand at all?" Closing her eyes, she nervously spoke, "God in the Heaven that Annie speaks about, are You there? Is what she says true? Was there a man that came into the world, died for everyone, and then came back to life? So no one but He would have to be sacrificed? And this Jesus gives Himself for His people to eat—that I don't understand at all?"

She squeezed her eyelids together tighter, as if that would force a response. "Anyone?" Shaking her head, she opened her eyes and dropped her shoulders. "I want to know if I should give myself for my people."

Standing up, an uneasiness seemed to invade her as the wind blew. In her heart, she had wanted it to be true, but she heard no voice nor saw any person. Feeling as though she was tricked by both her friend and his sister, she despairingly made her way back through the covert channel snaking its way inside the cliff to find Sna. As she walked amongst the dark cavern, she was reminded of stories she was once told of a boy that was given away. *Are there some people not good enough to be sacrificed? Why would that be true? If that is true, does that mean there is a perfect sacrifice? Was that this Jesus?*

Eduard looked through the small holes in the wood and metal fence of the cage. "Captain, I don't know what to do! I've tried to tell her not to do it. I've . . ." He lowered his head, not willing to reveal his sister's presence in the forest. "I can't help her—I gave my word, you see."

Captain Vitalis, kneeling down, looked at him through a small slit. "Prince Eduard, there is nothing you can do. You would only be killed yourself."

Lina grabbed his hand. "Be strong. They honor strength. You need to live through this place. You need to make it home. You need to tell the world of these people so they can be stopped."

Eduard shook his head. "What if Thom is dead? I'll never make it home."

Lina tilted her head. "What is this? The one that had such passion for his brother's word?"

He dropped his hand. "I know for certain my papá is dead! Thom could be dead the same as he." Lowering his head, he ran back to the hut.

Mouth dropping open, Lina looked through the slits at the

captain. "The king of Anchony died?" The hope the prince had enkindled in her heart passed out of being. "I suppose I truly shall die upon this island."

As she turned to leave, the captain placed his hand upon the fence. "Wait," he said. She turned back toward him. "What if . . .what if we could use this evil for our gain?"

She tilted her head, clueless as to his meaning.

MAKING PLANS

"Is there any reason for their assault?" Nicholaus continuously questioned the outlaws he had been following for nearly a week.

"There appears to be none," Jonus stated.

"They assault along the coast and go farther in if needed," Sarius added.

Ruffatus stopped at the foot of a hill. "There it is."

"A town?"

"It's where we send our women folk—the ones that have lived. There might be one here that you know," Ruffatus said as he looked over his shoulder at the knight.

Nicholaus followed in perplexity. "Of whom do you speak?"

"A girl." His hand pointed the way. "Go and see."

"The men are back!"

Melody looked up from the pumpkin patch as she wiped away the perspiration from her head. Slowly standing, she rubbed her hands upon her dress and, blocking the sun with her hand, looked toward the approaching crowd. Taking a deep breath, she knelt back down in the soil and cut the vine for the next vegetable.

"Melody?"

Looking toward the voice, all she saw was the glare of the sun. "Who calls?" Wiping her hands again, she stood and positioned her hand above her eyes to see a figure jogging toward her. As he neared, her mouth slowly dropped open with her recognition. "Sir Nicholaus?" She ran through the garden, no care as to what she disturbed. "Sir Nicholaus!" She immediately cried as she ran into him. "They took her! They took her—the men from the sea!" Shaking her head, tears poured from her eyes.

"Shh, Melody. I know. I know she was taken by the Seafurs." Her chin quivered as she listened to his words. "It's alright. I'm here now." Her arms squeezed him tighter.

Sitting around the fire pit, Melody watched the knight feel Annabelle's old dress within his fingers. "That's the princess's dress."

Not even realizing he was caressing it, he looked down at it. "Yes, it is."

Melody, remembering with what detail she fitted a new dress for the princess, bit her lip. "She was too large for it. I made her another."

Nicholaus, looking at the girl, smiled. "So, you are the reason I had hope?" He pulled the worn cloth out from around his belt. "Finding this dress helped me to know she made it to Oro Island."

"It helped you?" she asked with a tinge of a smile.

"It did."

Her smile faded as she remembered the last time she saw Annabelle. "I wish I could have helped her."

"Melody . . ." He swallowed hard. "Why didn't you try to find King Henricus?"

She eyed Ruffatus. "They told me he couldn't be trusted."

He shook his head. "It's not true."

"She is a princess, isn't she?" Ruffatus recalled. "Her brother has the throne."

Nicholaus looked at him. "Not her brother—her father."

Both Ruffatus and Melody responded, "She said he was dead."

The knight shook his head. "She only thought it."

"He lives?" Melody said more to herself than anybody. She slowly looked over at Nicholaus. "Can I go back to Anchony?"

"Of course."

Her hand flew to her mouth as she cried tears of joy.

Watching Melody sleep, Nicholaus looked across the fire pit at Ruffatus in the hut. "I won't be going back with her."

Ruffatus looked at him. "What?"

"They need to be stopped."

Ruffatus's eye looked around as he spoke with an irritated voice: "What do you think I've been trying to do?"

Nicholaus gently shook his head. "You've been going about it wrong."

"Then what do you think should be done?" Ruffatus asked defensively.

"I will let them take me."

"Let them?" He looked around at the darkened room. "That's a death sentence."

Nicholaus looked at him. "Are you not willing to die? Did

they not already take your life when they took your wife and two children?"

Ruffatus slowly nodded. "They did indeed. I'll come with you."

"No."

"No?" He stood in fury. "You don't want my help?"

"I have another duty for you."

"What is that?"

Nicholaus, standing, stared him down. "I want you to get her to King Henricus."

Ruffatus laughed. "What?"

"She needs to get to Anchony, and he'll get her there. His soldiers were in Brotherton along with Prince Thomas of Anchony."

Continuing to chuckle, Ruffatus looked at him as if he was batty. "Have you forgotten I am a wanted man? The king has a price upon my head!"

"Yes, I know. That is why it must be you."

"Come again?" He blinked in disbelief.

"If someone comes about you, they will get you to the king for the reward. Make certain she goes with you!"

Ruffatus smiled queerly. "You don't know what you're asking of me."

"If you are so willing to lay your life down killing the Seafurs, why are you not as willing to lay your life down for justice to your king?"

Ruffatus pointed angrily with his finger. "He has never given us protection!"

"He can't give you protection from what he does not know about!"

"He does know! I sent him word!" Ruffatus, neck twitching in fury, shook his head as he raced for the door. "I shall not! I shall not!"

Nicholaus, pulling the sword from his back, threw it across the room; it stuck into the door with a marvelous thud.

Ruffatus, stepping back in shock, looked at Nicholaus. "Have you had that sword all this time?"

"Where was your protection from the sword?" Nicholaus, walking over, pulled the weapon out of the door. "Will you listen now? If King Henricus will not help you, I know that Anchony shall." He stepped closer. "Get the girl to King Henricus. Go to Brotherton."

Melody, roused by the noise, pushed herself up and looked across the room. "Is everything alright?"

"Yes, Melody," Nicholaus turned toward her. "You'll leave on the morrow with Ruffatus to find King Henricus. He'll make certain you get to Anchony."

She tilted her head. "Are you not going?"

"No."

"What are you to do?" She pushed herself into a sitting position.

He looked at Ruffatus. "I'm going to stop the Seafurs."

She slowly nodded. "Will you find out what they did with her?"

Looking down at her, he knelt and nodded. "I give you my word, I will."

Melody smiled. "She always knew you would come to find her." She looked to the packed earth. "I wish it had been sooner —before . . ." She could not finish her sentence.

"I as well," Nicholaus said. "I as well."

"Give this to King Henricus. It's for him." Nicholaus handed Ruffatus a note. "And this is for King Francis. Make sure it gets to Prince Thomas." He handed him a thicker note.

Ruffatus, taking the letters, eyed the villagers as they murmured to themselves. "They don't understand."

Sir Nicholaus shook his head. "They don't have to."

"Will I see you again?" Melody asked as she stared at the princess's husband.

He slowly shook his head. "No, I don't think so, Melody."

She tilted her head, becoming angrier the more she spoke. "Then how shall you keep your word? I want to know what became of the princess! How will I, if you die?! You gave your word!"

He was taken off guard by the conviction in her voice. "I did give my word, didn't I?" She nodded enthusiastically. "Then I shall have to get word to you."

She stubbornly shook her head. "No! I want to hear it from you! You have to return to tell me!" He lowered his gaze. "Pledge to me you'll return! You are all I have left of the princess!" She turned away in her sorrow.

He turned her around and hugged her. "We are all a part of the Body of Christ. She will always be with us."

She spoke through a reddened face: "Pledge to me."

Taking a deep breath, he pulled her away and looked into her saddened eyes. "I pledge to you, Melody Picker, that I will try, with all my might, to tell you in person. But I don't know what lies ahead."

Taking a quick breath, realizing that was the best promise she would get from him, she hugged him again. "Thank you."

Nicholaus looked at the coastal village in the distance. *It has not been struck by the Seafurs yet.* His eyes wandered to the ocean farther away. *Yet it is close to the coast.* Taking a deep breath, he walked toward the village. "Here I shall plant myself and wait for them to come."

THE GIVE

Setting the jar of water down three weeks later, Nicholaus's eyes were drawn to a distant scream. As women and children ran in terror, a dozen husky men donned in animal skins trampled through the village. Swallowing hard as his heart rate increased, he slowly nodded. "This is it." Running toward a hut, he helped a child open the latch to the hidden door. "Hide like you were told." As the children and a couple women scrambled inside with their frightened tears, he spotted a Seafur coming around the corner. Slamming the door shut, he dumped some firewood in front of it for a hasty disguise.

"Lino!" the Seafur yelled at him. Turning around, he knelt in front of the man, resisting every urge in his body to attack. The Seafur chuckled as he spoke his dismay at how easily the man before him surrendered.

Nicholaus showed his hands. "No weapons! No weapons!"

The Seafur grabbed his arm and pulled it behind him as he took out a rope. "Te lino!"

"Lino?" He repeated with no understanding of the meaning.

The Seafur stared at him and then struck him across the

head with his hand. "Lino!" Nicholaus fell to the ground with the power of the man's hand. His head throbbed in pain. Suddenly he felt himself lifted to his feet.

"Walta lino!" the Seafur said.

"Katara, doa nocht."

Sitting up with a gasp, Katara tried to make sense of the dream she had just experienced. It had seemed so real. Lying back down, she closed her eyes but realized rest would not come to her disturbed mind. Grabbing a fur overlay, she tiptoed across the room and donned her moccasins. She rushed across the village until she reached Lina's hut and knocked desperately upon the door.

"Who is it?" Lina asked in the native tongue as she cracked the door.

"I need speak Eduard."

"He's sleeping. Come back—"

"Who is it, Lina?" the prince asked as he wiped his eyes.

"Katara," Lina said as she opened the door and stepped out of the way for the villager to enter.

"Katara? What's wrong?" Eduard pushed himself up and hung his legs over the edge of the bed.

"I have dream. Tell me what mean." She shook her head. "Never one like before."

"What was it?" Eduard asked.

"There man. He look me. He say, 'Do not.'"

Eduard glanced at Lina quickly before looking back at Katara. "Don't what?"

"Was there anything else?" Lina sat on the bed next to Eduard.

Katara shook her head.

"Well, what about the man? Did you know him?"

Katara tilted her head. "He know me." Nodding, she looked at Lina. "He look me. He know me." Turning to the prince, she asked with all sincerity. "It Him?"

"Who?" Lina asked.

"Jesus," Eduard said with a smile. He looked back at the villager. "No one knows you better than God! He knows us better than we know ourselves!"

Katara looked across the hut. "It true? He God? Only one?"

Lina watched a spark alight in the girl's eyes. "You know it to be true, don't you?"

Katara nodded as a tear rolled down her cheek.

"Don't cry!" Eduard said with confusion. "It's good to know God!"

"I know 'cause you tell. I not follow Him."

Lina took the girl's hand. "Well, now you can—now that you know Truth. You can learn about Him from us."

Katara, looking back across the hut, spoke with sadness: "My people follow sun, sky, earth. They fiends? My people kill for fiends?" Her stomach began to churn. Defiantly standing, she declared, "I not die for fiends!"

"Good!" Eduard jumped up and hugged her.

Lina, watching the two friends embrace, closed her eyes. *They won't take no as an answer, having already spoken your yes.*

"Aren't you glad, Lina?" the prince asked with a smile. "She's not going to let them kill her!"

"I am pleased." Nodding, she turned away.

"What's wrong?" the prince asked.

Looking at Katara, Lina forced a smile. Her eyes beheld the first rays of the morning's dawn. "Katara, you need to go back to your hut."

Katara, glancing at the ventilation hole, nodded and exited quickly.

❄

Katara, inside the preparation hut, shook her head with furiousness as she spoke in her native tongue: "I don't want to anymore. I've changed my mind!"

"You can't change your mind!" the preparer spoke back. "It's too late!"

"I'm not willing anymore. You can't use me for the Give!"

"They won't know if you can't speak!"

Awakened by a noise coming from the cave entrance, Annabelle looked through the darkness of the cave with the faint light that was able to reach her between the little legs of the wolf pup. A cascading noise from a whine to a howl to a screech. *Pup? What is wrong? You're going to wake the babies!*

Hearing a pattering sound, the princess could then make out the outline of the wolf pup as she came into the cave. The canine looked toward the princess and let out her best howl.

Annabelle jumped up. "No! Not in here!" But it was too late: both babies began to cry. "Pup!" she said with agitation.

The little wolf ran toward the cave opening and looked at her, releasing another little howl, which reverberated throughout the cave.

"Get out!" Annabelle yelled as she picked up her crying children.

Backing up through the opening, Pup continued to whine. When she got no response from Annabelle, her whine turned into a screech.

"Pup!" Annabelle looked through the hole. "Stop!" *What is wrong with her?* Annabelle paused for a moment. *Is something wrong? Today is the day of the Give. What if Katara decides not to give herself, and they take Edus instead?* Horror filled her as she wrapped her crying babies around herself and headed out of the cave with her bow and arrow.

Once out of the cave, she looked at Pup, who was waiting for her. "Is it Edus?" She ran toward the village; the pup followed after, taking a different path. She soon heard Pup howling again. Turning around, she went toward the wolf pup, her children calming with her movement. "What is it, girl?"

Finding the white wolf tied to a tree, Annabelle approached cautiously. "Why are you tied? Was it Katara?" Kneeling down, she undid the knot and watched Sna bolt through the woods.

Pup sat down, content now that her friend was free. Annabelle rubbed her head. "Was that it?"

But what if it is Edus? Rising, she looked toward the village, her babies had fallen back asleep. *I'm so close. I could make certain he's alright.*

Lina, watching Ecwab walk by, backed up until she was next to the male encampment. In her left ear, she heard the captain speak: "Are you ready to do your part?"

Nodding, she lowered her head until she looked to her moccasins.

She watched the razor-sharp flint axe pushed out from under the bottom bar of the fence. "Then take it and be on your way."

Moving over to hide it, she nodded as she casually squatted down and looked over her shoulder through the wood and metal to the man's figure. "I shall do my best." Rising, she stepped away as Eduard ran to her.

"Lina! They're going to go through with it! Even though she doesn't want it!" Copious tears ran down his face.

"I know, child." She squeezed him dearly as she looked at the hill. "We have to be on our way."

He pulled away. "I don't want to go! I don't want to watch. Don't they see? It's not a Give anymore!"

She grabbed his hand. "You must come. We must go!"

Squeezing the prince dearly, Lina led him up the hill. Standing along the periphery, she swallowed with great difficulty. "Now, we must stand here and watch."

"But Katara's my friend!" he wailed.

"I know, child." Leaning down, she whispered into his ear with certitude, "This is the only way. You must look as if you back their ways."

"I will never!"

"Appearing that way is what is needed." She straightened. "Here, they bring her." They both watched as Katara, tied and gagged and flailing her resistance, was laid upon the offering stone.

Lina whispered to Eduard, "Don't let them see your tears. And Eduard, no matter what takes place, they'll come back for you."

"What? Who?" He looked up at her to find her no longer beside him. *Where's she going?* His head tilted as he caught a glimpse of the flint axe lowering down out of her right sleeve and heading toward Acwa. *What's she doing?* His heart raced uncontrollably as his eyes darted between Acwa's rising dagger and Lina lurking behind him.

Lina let out a scream as she charged forward raising the axe, purposefully drawing attention to herself.

"There. She's doing it." Back at the village, Vitalis jiggled the lock open with his finagled key. The sailors, freed from their confinement, raced toward the sea.

At the sound of Lina's scream, Acwa turned around, and his arm was suddenly latched between the white wolf's teeth. Despite the leader's defense, the wolf would not release him. As he struggled in vain, Katara wiggled herself off of the offering stone.

Lina stepped back, in shock of the white wolf's action, as the Seafurs ran toward their leader and tried desperately to rescue Acwa from the clenches of the white wolf.

Crawling her way toward the forest, Katara was stopped by one woman. Pulling the gag from her mouth, Katara told her in the native language, "I'm not a willing sacrifice! It's his fault!" She pointed at the preparer who brought her against her will.

The woman, in shock, turned around and yelled with the meaning of "Not willing!"

Annabelle, stopping along the edge of the forest, watched the chaos unfold before her. *Edus? Where is Edus?*

"Not willing?" Ecwab stood from assisting Acwa. He set his eyes upon Eduard. "This is his fault!"

He charged at Eduard. "You speak to her. You make her change mind!"

"Of course I did! You're killing people and that isn't right!" Eduard said boldly with anger. As Ecwab, pulling a dagger from its sheath, bounded toward him, his confidence faltered.

The wolf, enveloped in a bolas, was pulled away from Acwa. Finally releasing her victim, San turned and ran back toward the woods, growling and barking.

Out of the forest, an arrow suddenly sliced through the air, lodging in the interpreter's arm. Struck by the piercing arrow, Ecwab dropped the dagger.

All the natives paused as they looked toward the forest and then cried out in fear: "Blankentuk!"

Ecwab, holding his bleeding arm with the spindle in it, fell to his knees before Prince Eduard. "You do this?"

Eduard, looking around at the chaos, shook his head. "I'm only the sheep herder. I'm not to do anything. I gave my word."

Lina, having followed Katara into the forest, sawed at the ropes binding the girl and then helped her to stand. "Let's go, child!" Grabbing her hand, they ran into the forest. "We must run!" Lina screamed to the girl. "We have to lead them away."

"Away from where?" They both squatted to hide from a voice they heard in the distance.

"From the ships," Lina whispered.

"Who take them?"

"The mariners. They will go for aid."

"No, they not get away! No one ever get away." Katara grabbed her hand. "Come with."

"Where to?"

Katara pointed toward the rocky beach on the southeastern side of the island. "To see."

Katara's eyes searched the disturbed seas of icy water from within the protective coverings of the fur trees along the water's edge. "There! Ship leave!" Her voice was filled with utter amazement.

"They made it?" Lina, thrilled by the tidings, stepped

forward on to the rocky coast as a smile broke forth across her face and she raised her arms with a victorious jump. "They made it!"

Katara nervously looked around and pulled the radiant woman back to the trees. "Shhh! They come for me."

Lina's excitement was shattered by the reality of what still faced them upon the island: Katara could not go back to her village now. And what of her? Had her actions set her as enemy against the tribe? *What will become of Prince Eduard?* "Oh, no." Her head lowered with the sobering thoughts. "What are we going to do?"

Katara looked toward the cliffs in the northeast. "You go huts. I go cave. I safe."

"A cave?" Lina adamantly shook her head. "No! I'm not going to leave you here!" Her thoughts dashed back to the lady and babes that disappeared from her. "Not again! I won't leave another!"

"You not leave me—you go for Edus! I be quick. They not see."

"No!" Lina grabbed her arm.

Hearing sounds in the woods behind them, Katara crouched to the ground and moved behind a trunk. "They come for me. You go now!"

Lina fell to the ground. "You forget they are in search for me, too! I can't go back to the huts."

Katara looked at her curiously. "You? Why?"

"Why do you mean 'why'? I helped you escape! I about stabbed Acwa! Did you not see me?"

"You yell. You warn about Sna."

"You think that's what they'll think?" Placing her hand on her forehead, she tried to make sense of all that had occurred. "There were arrows. Who was shooting arrows?"

"Blankentuk!"

"What?"

"They yell 'Blankentuk'—white wolf and man spirit in land. You be safe. I not. They want give me now so no more Blankentuk."

"They want you for more than the Give now?"

Katara looked nervously into the woods. Tears began to roll down her cheeks. "They see men gone. They to kill linas? They to kill Edus?"

Lina grabbed the girl's shoulders. "They can't! He's the reason they left! To get help. Help from Anchony. Help from anyone! They can't get him!"

Katara whole-heartedly nodded. "You go! You go back for Edus!"

Lina was torn. "But I—"

"You go! I go mountain!" Katara, wanting no more argument, disappeared into the woods.

Staring at the entrance to the cave before her, Annabelle turned around to peer into the woods. They were eerily silent. *They didn't follow? Not at all?* Holding the stillest she could, she closed her eyes and, when sufficiently satisfied, opened them. *They didn't at all.*

As satisfied as she was at that thought, it did not seem right to escape into her haven while Katara's fate was unknown.

Hearing noises from the woods, she pulled out an arrow and made ready.

When the white wolf, exhausted and whining with the bolas still wrapped around it, limped slowly toward her, she lowered her weapon. "Come here, girl. I will help you."

Whining, Sna lay down next to the boulder. Not wanting to get too close to a hurting wild animal, Annabelle used the arrow dowel to see how the animal would react to the bolas being touched. As the wolf looked at her in desperation, Annabelle set her babies down away from the creature and then slowly unwrapped the bolas. "This will make it feel better. You saved Katara's life, you know? I suppose you have helped her to save my life, too. Do you know where she's gone? Can I truly leave her alone out there?"

Once freed, Sna stood and moved a few feet away from Annabelle, as if relieved. Once she thought she was at a safe enough distance, she sat back down to lick her wounds.

Picking up an odor in the air, Sna's attention turned toward the forest. Walking a few feet forward, she looked back at Annabelle.

"You want me to follow you? To get to Katara?"

Sna began to whine again.

"Alright. I will. Let me get my children." Strapping them to her again, she followed the white wolf into the forest.

Hearing the sounds nearing her and unable to make it to the mountain with enough swiftness, Katara searched desperately for a place to hide from the approaching noises. Finding bushes, she squeezed her way under them, holding her legs, praying for them to not find her as she squeezed her eyes closed. The pattering was next to the shrubbery.

Hearing a whine, she immediately opened her eyes and released a relieved whine of her own. Crawling back out from under the greenery, she hugged the white wolf. "Sna!"

"Lina!" Eduard ran to her as she entered her home. "Where did you go?"

"I took Katara into the woods. You are unharmed?"

"They say it was a beast or a spirit—part man, part wolf— that saved her. They're terrified! They call it a Blankentuk."

"But you are unharmed?"

"I'm well."

"Oh, praise God! What about me?"

Eduard shook his head. "What do you mean? Are you hurt?"

"Did you not see the blade in my hand? Did you not hear me yell at Acwa?"

"I saw the blade, but you told him about Sna."

Lina looked down with relief. "You think that, too?" Glancing back at the boy, a smile graced her face. "And the men made it!"

Eduard tilted his head. "What do you mean?"

"The mariners—they took a ship."

"Without the captain?"

"No, the captain went—"

"No. I saw him a bit ago. Ecwab had—" They both looked to the door as they heard a man yelling in pain.

Approaching the door together, Lina looked toward the middle of the village. There two native was whipping the captain as others stood around to watch. "They must have caught him."

Mouth dropping open, Eduard looked at Lina. "Where did the mariners go?"

"To find aid. To get you off this island."

His eyes found the bleeding back of the captain. "He's being whipped because of me?" Shaking his head, he stepped out of the hut, until his shoulder was pulled back.

"You stay here. I'll go." She stepped out of the hut and closed the door firmly to keep Eduard from following.

Taking a deep breath, Lina approached Ecwab. "Please stop! Whatever he's done, I'm certain that is enough punishment!"

"Enough?" Ecwab, with a bandaged arm, scowled at her. "Not enough! Go way!"

She defiantly stepped closer. "I will not."

"Will not?" His left hand pointed at her.

Stung by a quick snap of the strap, pain burst forth from her side.

She fell to her side with a loud cry. Her left stung with the bite of the leather.

"Halta! Halta!" Eduard yelled as he ran forward. "Why do you hit them?" he spoke in their tongue.

"They ruin Give!"

"I thought it the Blankentuk? Certainly, this will only upset him more!" he defiantly spoke as his head shook in fright at the large man.

Ecwab approached him.

"Stop. He is right," Acwa spoke in their tongue as he sat on a chunk of wood, sweating and with his right arm in a sling. "I must speak to gods before punishment. Find out if it was Katara not being a willing sacrifice that made Blankentuk come."

The prince watched Ecwab back away as the village leader—looking pallid and sweating—signaled for them to release the captain.

"Lina." Eduard, stepping under her right shoulder, helped her up. Guiding her the best he could back to the hut, he looked to the encampment to watch the captain dragged inside.

Peering through the trees, Annabelle, with Claudia and Augustine—both awake and babbling—swaddled peacefully next to her, watched Katara disappear into the mountain wall.

With her left hand upon the side wall as she entered the cave,

Annabelle was enveloped by more of the darkness as she delved deeper inside. "Katara? I saw you enter. It's Annie. Katara?"

Far away in the darkness, a light emerged from a hidden chamber.

"It Annie?" Katara walked closer, clouded by confusion. "What you do here? How you find me?"

"I followed Sna. I wanted to make certain you were safe."

Katara lowered her head. "Not now. They see me." She shrugged her shoulders. "They may find when look for food, but not come in mountain."

Annabelle held out her hand. "Come with me then."

"Where go?"

"To my cave. Katara, you have helped me so much. I will not forsake you now that you are wanted by them, too." Nodding to herself, she added, "I think God wants it."

Katara looked at her with near excitement. "God tell you take me?"

"Not with words, but I deem it is what He wants."

"You save me?" Katara thought about the princess's words as they moved quickly over the terrain.

"No. I'm sorry. It was only when they went after Edus."

Katara's mouth slightly dropped open. "The arrows you?" She gasped with her revelation. "No Blankentuk?"

Annabelle looked at her oddly. "What does that mean?"

"It Sna."

The white wolf, from meandering behind them, suddenly growled and ran around them to get in front. Annabelle readied her bow just to hear a young yelp.

"What it, Sna?" Katara asked curiously as the wolf moved her head away from the ground.

"The wolf pup—it goes wherever my children do, whether I want it to or not."

Katara, without any hesitation, petted it. "It like you. It think family."

Annabelle frowned. "Sadly, I killed her mother."

"It think you mother now."

"I've figured that out."

Following the white wolf, they arrived at the entry point to the cave. Annabelle touched Katara's arm. "It was you, wasn't it? You gave us food when I couldn't hunt."

Katara nodded. "I help."

Annabelle, in astonishment, smiled. "Why? You're not like your people."

Katara, setting the wolf pup down, shrugged her shoulders as she watched it run to Sna wanting to play. "I learn not right kill babe, no matter what my people say."

The princess looked at her with all seriousness. "Who taught you?"

"My aunt tell story. Woman hide babe in mountain. Babe grow to child. My people find child; kill mother. It not right."

"Your people killed the woman because she kept her child alive?"

Katara nodded.

"And the child?"

Katara frowned. "I not know." Sna took off into the woods.

"Did you raise Sna?"

"Nocht." She shook her head.

"That means 'no'?"

"Yocht." Katara smiled to correct herself, "Yes."

As she unstrapped her children from around her, Annabelle asked, "How do you know my words?"

Katara shrugged her shoulders. "I hear Ecwab? Linos?"

"You learned by listening?"

"I not know."

Annabelle's face turned sullen as she thought of her brother. "What do you think they will do to Edus?"

"They think Blankentuk. Who blame? Me? Him? I not know."

"Oh, Father!" Annabelle leaned back against the wall. "Father, give him protection!"

Upon the wind, the faintest cry of the sacrificial horn reached her ears. A paralyzing shiver shot down her body, and she turned pale. "Is that what I think it is?"

Katara, turning toward the south, nodded. "It horn."

"Oh, no!" Annabelle's eyes skirted around and down as her legs followed. "I feel ill."

"It one?" Katara turned to the princess. "It one?"

"One what?" she asked, now nauseous.

"One horn call. Two horn kill."

"They blow it twice?" She stood with a new resolve. "The first is to call your people? So there's still time?" Taking a deep breath, she scrambled toward the girl, handing Katara her children. "Take them inside and wait for me."

Katara watched her swiftly pick up the bow and fly into the woods. "You go to horn?"

Halfway to the sacrificial hill, Annabelle stopped in her tracks as the second horn sounded. *No!* Falling to her knees, she shook her head. *Why did I leave him with them? Did the love for my children give them my brother?*

Gasping in emotion, she pushed herself up, wiping away her tears. Finding some consolation in the strength of a tree, she pushed herself against it. "Father, what do You want me to do?" Closing her eyes, she tried to think rationally. *I don't know for certain that he is dead. Who did they kill?*

"I don't understand. They turn against their own?" Eduard looked up at Lina in confusion as the preparer's body was placed on the fire to be burned.

"If I hear rightly, they think Katara was saved by Blankentuk because she was not a willing sacrifice and that man knew it."

Watching the body begin to burn, Eduard shook his head in disgust. Feeling Lina's grip tighten around him, he looked up and, spotting some of the young girls being led up the hill, cried out, "No!"

"Hold yourself back, or it will be you they take." Lina pulled him back with her good arm.

"They take the girls? They can't!" Tears fell from his eyes. Giving up, he leaned forward in sorrow.

"I know it's hard to watch, but you must stand and face forward. Look at the beauty of the blue sky. Hold on to that sight." Her own tears fell as her stomach churned in rejection.

Recognizing the outline of the dress of one of the girls held in captivity, Annabelle fell to her knees in utter disgust. Holding her mouth with her hands, she was unable to move at the horror of the sight. *I'm too late.* Reaching for a tree to give support, she closed her eyes and leaned upon it. *What evil is in this land?* Trying to hold back her cries, she was unsuccessful. Before bursting into an audible wail, she fled back to her place of refuge.

SEAS OF BALTAM

As the ship was violently rocked right to left in the deluge and lightning splintered across the sky, the captain yelled through the wind toward the king, "The storm is too strong! The seas are rough! We must find our way to the shores of Baltam!"

"But we must find the island! I must find my son!" King Francis yelled back into the wind.

Peter pulled him away from the edge of the boat. "We will, Francis. But we can't if the ship goes down!"

Going below deck, Francis shook off the water from his hair and turned to his friend. "Are these the same waters where they claim she perished?"

Peter's hair dripped. "If it was a tempest like that, it very well could be."

Camrina, with her gagged mouth, listened intently. *Of whom do they speak? Are we around Baltam? Who do they know that drowned in the seas around Baltam?*

Sir Harkus, along the western Baltamian coast, entered the tent quickly.

King Henricus looked at him. "What is it?"

"There is a ship, Sire." He glanced at Prince Thomas. "The flag looks to be Anchonian."

Prince Thomas, standing straight from studying a map of Baltam on the table, asked, "Do they come on to the shore?"

"They were lowering the boats."

Thomas quickly rushed outside into the storm, running to the cliff, to count the rowboats. Quickly counting, he sprinted down the massive hill toward the beach.

On the beach, Thomas's jaw dropped as he shook his drenched head. When King Henricus joined him, the prince spoke in near anger, "I don't believe it!"

"What is it?" Henricus yelled back above the noise of the thunder.

"It's my aunt—the queen of the Sockor Islands—the one who started all the trouble." Shaking his wet head, he unsheathed his sword.

"Did someone steal her away and deem they could find safety in Baltam?" King Henricus, with his knights behind him, unsheathed his weapon through the downpour as he followed the prince farther out on the rocky beach.

Charging forward with the rain pelting them in the face, Thomas halted and lowered his sword as he watched the Lion climb out of the rowboat and pull his aunt up. "Sir Josephus?" he spoke more to himself.

"That's one of the king's knights, is it not?" King Henricus yelled.

"Yes!" He yelled back at the king. Turning back, he stared for a moment in utter disbelief when he spotted the second rowboat. He sheathed his sword and ran toward it. "Papá!"

Francis looked up in great surprise as his son helped him out of the rowboat. "Thomas! What are you doing here?"

"Come to the tent! This way!" Thomas pulled him toward the camp.

"You don't agree?" Francis asked his son after speaking of their plans of rescue as water from his saturated hair dripped onto the ground inside the king's tent.

"Edus needs to be taken from the Seafurs, to that I agree." He looked back and forth between the two kings. "But if it's the same people that assault the towns . . . they are savages. I've yet to find one person that lived through their attacks."

"I brought Camrina so they will not think we are there to assail them but to trade. It shall buy us time."

"I agree to using Camrina, but—" The tent shook violently in the howling wind.

"Then what is it?"

"You, Papá!" He nodded his head as he stepped closer. "Sir Nicholaus told me Lord Cortell is spreading the truth about Prince Howercus all over Sethel. One of the lies that Prince Howercus tells is that Anchony claims the blame for killing King Henrard and that you were punished for it. But who is to say they will stop with you? Don't you see, Papá? You have to stay alive—not for Baltam or Sethel, but for the sake of Anchony! You have to be a witness for the truth!"

"*You* can be that witness as much as I, Thomas."

"But, Papá, *I* gave my word to Edus that if he was ever taken, I would find him. I *have* to go."

"No!" The king adamantly shook his head.

"And if I go, Papá, you shouldn't."

"Shouldn't? He is my son!" Francis looked desperately around the room for any that would agree with him.

"Sire."

He looked at Peter. "Not you too, Jous!"

"Sire, you are the king of Anchony. That will mean nothing to the Seafurs—just someone to kill."

"So you think I should send my son in my stead?"

"You do not send me, Papá. I go on my own accord! I'm keeping my word!"

"King Francis, what if more good can be done for all the kingdoms by you staying here?" King Henricus suggested with a calm voice.

Francis, as if to move away from the argument, stepped backward to look at the young king. "How is that?"

"These Seafurs are not the only problem Baltam is facing. Sethel has tried to overrun a town in Baltam. Sethel believes you are dead, do not give Howercus what he wants."

"Howercus has tried to overcome Baltam?"

"He has sent his knights and soldiers here in search for some men that were against him. It is only time until he learns Princess Anastacia is in Baltam. We have yet to find her." Slowly nodding, Henricus added, "Baltam beseeches you to stay here. You must live to speak the truth of who truly killed King Henrard. If the Sethelians know he lied about your death, they will question all that he says."

Thinking for a moment, Francis took a deep breath and shook his head. "What good can the king of Anchony do for Baltam?"

Henricus lowered his head. "There is fear in Baltam. The people in the north are against me, the people in the south have heard that Sethel killed the king of Anchony. Fear is gripping them, and I fear their fear will turn to yielding to whomever may try to overcome them." He nodded his head. "The greatest good you can do is to stay here and stay alive, so my people will know it is only lies the Sethelians spread. Indeed, I know the first people with whom you need to speak."

Francis, taking a deep breath, glanced at his son and friend before turning around. "I will have to pray about this."

ARRIVAL

S tepping on to Walva Island, Nicholaus's inquisitive eyes immediately searched around. *Where would they have taken her?* Forced forward up the hill toward the village, the intricacies of the village life were easily discernible: there were gardeners, animal tenders, crafters of dishes and bowls, wood cutters—people living for their own survival. As he turned his head toward the west, toward a giant hill, a sickening feeling overcame him. The sacrificial stones sat strongly in the center, glittering with gold under the stains of darkened crimson.

"Walta lino!"

They pushed him down the path. *I must learn their way of moving, to know how to best stop them.* Walking forward, he soon learned his destination: a prison yard. Shoved inside, he turned around quickly to watch them shut the gate in his face.

"Pacta lino!"

Inside, an older man lay coughing upon the ground. He hurried to his side and knelt beside him. "Are you alright?"

"Did they . . . did they make it?" the older man muttered.

"Who?" Touching him, he immediately pulled away, for the man's skin felt as if it would burn him if he stayed in contact.

"The mariners," the man said. His head was feverish, and he shook violently.

Nicholaus looked around the area. "There is no one here but us."

He pointed toward the ocean. "The ship at sea . . . is it at sea?"

Nicholaus shook his head. "The ship I came on was all that I saw."

The older man closed his eyes. "They did it for the boy."

"What boy?"

He looked to his right. "He's with her."

Nicholaus shook his head in perplexity. "Who?"

"Lina."

Nicholaus did not understand the meaning of the man's words. "How long have you been here? I want to know of my wife. Her name is Annabelle of—"

The old man raised his feverish hand. "Annabelle."

"Do you know her?" Nicholaus's voice cracked in great surprise, trying to move closer to the man.

The man swallowed with difficulty. "I was to get her to Anchony."

"Yes!" Nicholaus moved closer in excitement and astonishment. "Are you Captain Vitalis?"

Vitalis's weary eyes found their way to the knight's. "You know of me?"

"My wife! What's become of my wife?!"

He pointed his finger. "She ran into the woods. She died." His finger fell to the ground in despair. "I failed." He looked back at Nicholaus. "I was to get her home." He looked away. "I failed her."

Nicholaus shook his head as he tried to process the information. "The baby—what became of the baby she carried?"

"Babies." Vitalis closed his eyes as the mere mention caused a painful memory to be thrust upon him.

"Babies?" Nicholaus looked at him queerly. "There was more than one?"

Vitalis slowly nodded as he opened his heavy eyelids and said with despair, "Twins."

"Oh, Father!" Nicholaus fell back as he rubbed his temples in shock. "What's become of them?"

"They died." Vitalis moved his head in his febrile state. "Everyone dies."

Nicholaus swallowed with great difficulty. "Where did they bury her?" He shook his head as a tear ran down his cheek. "Where are their graves?"

"I don't know," Vitalis stated as he closed his eyes. He weakly waved him away. "Leave me so I can die. It is my turn now."

Nicholaus shook his head. "No!" Looking to the dying fire, he quickly jumped up and added more wood to it. "You need to be warmer, that's all."

"No," the captain said weakly. "I need to go home. I want . . . to go home."

Placing the final piece of wood atop the fire, Nicholaus shook his head. "Everyone in Baltam already thinks you're dead and all the mariners that were with you." Looking back at the man, Nicholaus froze as he studied the still man. Finding him not to be breathing, he rushed back to his side. "Captain? Captain! No! You have to tell me more!"

Grasping the man's tunic and raising the upper half of his body, he shook it as if he could rouse Vitalis from his final sleep. Shaking his head, he lowered the body back down and closed the man's eyes. "Rest in God's peace." He made the sign of the cross.

Standing, he walked toward the gate of the compound. "This man is dead!" When no one responded, he banged upon the gate. "This man is dead!"

✳

Called over by the Seafurs because of the yelling man, Lina stepped close to the gate. "What's wrong?"

Nicholaus looked at her oddly. "Captain Vitalis is dead." He stepped aside so she could see through the cracks.

Gasping, she made the sign of the cross.

He tilted his head, surprised by the gesture. "Who are you?"

Turning around, she explained to the Seafurs the issue. Unlocking the gate, two men came in and picked up the body. Lina looked at Nicholaus. "If you want him buried and not burned, you must do it yourself." She nodded toward the body. "Follow them."

He cautiously walked out of the fence with his fettered feet and followed. Lina walked along beside him. "Are you a slave here?" he asked her.

She nodded once.

"For how long?"

"Too many years to count."

"So, you might have met my wife. She was with—"

Lina shook her head as she waved her hand. "I don't want to talk about it."

"Please! I came here to find out what—"

Lina nervously laughed. "Came here? You say it like it was your choice!" As her eyes looked up at his face, her grin disappeared. "You gave yourself to them?" She shook her head. "You fool! No one has ever gotten off this island! I mean, the mariners tried, but I don't know what has become of them!"

"Captain Vitalis's mariners?"

"Yes." They both turned as one of the Seafurs handed him a shovel.

"Holta ac." The Seafur pointed.

Lina took a deep breath. "You are to dig right there." She looked around quickly. "I must leave you now. They'll watch closely, and they'll kill you if you try to run away or release your chains."

"Wait, please." He looked at the graves with the wooden crosses. "I'd like to know which grave belongs to my wife. Her name was Annabelle. She was with child when she came."

Lina's mouth dropped open as the Seafur pulled her away, yelling in the native tongue. Looking back at him as she walked toward the village, she shook her head. "There is no grave. She ran into the forest." Pulling her arm away from the Seafur, she turned around and walked back to the village.

She ran into the forest. She ran into the forest? His eyes wandered to the woodlands as he stepped upon the shovel. *Could she have lived?* He nodded his head as he looked at the earth. *She could've lived! Is she truly alive?* His gaze wandered upward to the trees. *Anna, are you out there?*

Each disheveled mound of earth brought a fight of hopeful thoughts mixed with rationalization from months of tethered loss. *She knows how to live in a forest! If she hasn't been seen or heard, it's because she doesn't want to be!* He shook his head as he thrust all of his strength into digging the hole. *I have been tormented for too long! Could it be? Could it be true? Oh, Father! Is this the reason You would not let me find peace? Because Anna truly is alive!* His eyes scanned the forest. *Where is she then?*

Closing the door behind him, Eduard turned around to be greeted by the news: "Captain Vitalis is dead."

He looked at Lina. "Mercy upon his soul, Father." He made the sign of the cross and then looked at Lina. "He was ill, wasn't he?"

She nodded. "I wish I could have tended to him, but they wouldn't let me."

His head swam in despair. "Did they burn his body?"

Her disposition lighted a bit. "No. There is a new slave—he buried him." She twisted the wool out. "It seems he wanted to come here."

"*Wanted* to?" Eduard said with disgust.

"He was in search of his wife."

Eduard's mouth slowly opened with hope. He spoke quickly, "What's his name?"

She shook her head. "He didn't say."

Eduard released a breath as he lowered his head and sat down upon his bed.

"But his wife died almost a year ago. Her name was Annabelle."

Eduard bolted to his feet.

Lina looked at him in shock. "Good heavens, child! What's wrong?"

"I—" Looking around the room, he was unsure how much he should reveal. "I need some air."

"Air? You've been out in the air all day!" She walked toward him to feel his forehead. "Are you feeling alright?"

Shaking his head, he rushed for the door. "No. I must go out."

Breathing heavily, Eduard crept to the back of the female compound where he hid to peer into the male's yard. He saw the figure squatting down near the fire. *Is it Sir Nicholaus? Can it truly be him?* Taking a step forward, a mass was suddenly in his way.

"What you do?" Ecwab grabbed him.

"Let me go!"

"What you do? Get to hut!" Ecwab shoved him toward Lina's hut.

Eduard, seeing he had no choice, reluctantly complied.

Nicholaus stood at the sound of the commotion and walked toward the edge of the compound, looking curiously at what he could see of the figure entering the hut.

"Did you get your air?" Lina asked as Eduard entered. She watched as he sat down defiantly on the bed and crossed his arms. "I deem it didn't help. What's wrong, Prince Eduard?"

Shaking his head, he laid down and pulled the cover over himself.

Hours later, he pushed down the blanket and, looking across the fire pit, watched Lina sleeping soundly. Tiptoeing to the door, he threw a fur around him and exited. Seeing his breath before him as the village was silenced in its frozen sleep, he ran to the male yard.

"Sir Nicholaus. Sir Nicholaus!" He whispered with more and more force.

Sleeping close to the fire, Nicholaus pushed his upper body up and looked around the yard.

"Sir Nicholaus."

"I know I heard that." Sitting up all the way, he searched desperately for the source. Seeing an image kneeling down beside the shelter, he crawled over. "I am Sir Nicholaus. Who calls?"

"Sir Nicholaus!" Little fingers reached through the woven sticks within the bars. "It's Eduard."

"Eduard?" He moved closer. "Prince Eduard?!"

"Yes!" The boy looked around, afraid he spoke too loudly.

Nicholaus looked at him in shock through a crack as he touched his fingers, shaking his head. "What are you doing here?!"

"Sir, Annie's alive!"

"She truly is?! Where is she?!" The knight grabbed at his fingers, not wanting him to get away until he revealed all.

"She lives in a cave in the woods." His attention transferred to his right. Someone carrying a torch was approaching. He gasped and ran the opposite direction.

"Wait!" Nicholaus searched desperately for signs of his prince. "Where'd you go?"

The Seafur, coming over, tilted his head. "Lino, domita!" He hit the fence and pointed over by the fire. "Domita!"

Nicholaus stared at him. "Why do you call me that—Lino?"

"Domita!" The man banged upon the fence with more force.

"I don't know what you mean!"

"You sleep!" Ecwab said as he walked over. "You work when sun come. You do work of all men who left! You sleep now!"

Nicholaus backed away a bit and then glanced back at Ecwab. "What does 'Lino' mean?"

"You slave."

Nicholaus shook his head. "I'm no one's slave." Turning around, he walked over to the fire to stare within the flames. *Anna is alive—out there in the woods? She truly lives!* Slowly nodding his head, he whispered to himself. "Prince Eduard would know his own sister."

Eyes jumping away from the heat, they darted around the compound. "He wouldn't tell me so if it was not true!" *She lives in a cave. What cave? Where? How far?* He turned toward the forest. "I have to find her!" *How can I get out? I can burn the twigs, but the bars will remain.* He looked at the height of the walls. *They are too tall to climb. They would see me climbing. I can dig but they will see the extra dirt. But if I spread it around . . . ?*

Opening her eyes, Annabelle pushed herself up as she turned toward the sliver of the mouth of the cave. Scrambling to her feet, she grabbed the quiver of arrows as she readied her bow with a pounding heart, keenly looking for the source of the sound that had roused her from her slumber.

"Annie!" Eduard called as he pulled himself inside with a rush and collapsed at her feet, panting from his exertion.

Lowering the bow, she quickly bent down to help him up, moving him deeper inside the cave. "Who's after you?"

Still catching his breath, he vehemently shook his head. "No . . . no. Annie!"

Listening to his words, she stepped toward the opening and peered into the woods. Finding no threats, she looked back at him. "I see no one."

Standing with all his air recovered, he joyfully proclaimed, "Sir Nicholaus is here!"

She stared at him for a moment as if the tidings could not possibly be true. A range of emotions from agitation to elation exploded within her mind and only left her completely perplexed. She could only speak one word: "What?"

"Sir Nicholaus is here!" Eduard repeated with even more joy than the first proclamation.

Her eyes jumped to the cave opening again, desperately seeking sight of her husband—any confirmation of the boy's words. Finding no one, she turned back to her brother. "No, he's not."

"He's a lino."

"Lino? You mean a slave?" It was spoken with the utmost dread. She shook her head with her clouded mind. "He's harmed?"

"No." Eduard stepped closer. "I mean, I don't think so."

Shaking her head, she could not believe the words she heard. "Sir Nicholaus is here? On the island? He's a slave?" As she watched her brother nod, tears descended. She looked toward the ceiling of the cave. "He is caged with Captain Vitalis?"

"No." Eduard lowered his head. "The captain is dead."

Wiping away tears, she turned around. "He's all alone?"

"Yes."

Looking to the cavern floor, she breathed quickly. "I must go to him!"

Glancing up at her brother, she bolted toward the opening and set off running toward the village miles away.

Reaching the outskirts of the village as the sun rose, she held herself back from approaching the compound, for she knew she could not go to him without the risk of being seen by the Seafurs beginning their day in the morning light.

Nicholaus? Is it you? Are you truly here?

As she watched, the gate of the compound opened and two figures emerged. It was Nicholaus and one of the Seafurs. Her hand flew to her mouth as she physically held back her cries. With watery eyes, she watched the Seafur push him toward the woods.

Shoved from behind, Nicholaus turned around to face the man. "Gols sharta!" the Seafur ordered.

Nicholaus shook his head. "Don't touch me again!"

"You cut wood." Nicholaus looked at Ecwab approaching. "You want stay warm—you cut wood." The knight watched him nod his head in the direction of the forest.

Swallowing hard, Nicholaus turned toward the destination. His eyes caught the slightest movement between trees. *Did I see something?* Listening intently, he heard nothing.

"Walta lino!"

He felt another shove upon his back. *Was there something*

there? Could it be Anna? Too distracted by his own thoughts, he paid no heed to the harassment. *Anna, are you out there?*

Resting against a tree, a distance away, the princess shook her head in rejection of the predicament. *If he runs away, they'll come looking for him. They'll find us.* She wiped away a tear as she concluded, *He can't leave the huts!*

"Here." Ecwab pointed. "You cut; you take back. Make pile."

A flock of birds suddenly taking flight somewhere in the woods ahead of him caught Nicholaus's attention. *Anna?* Though he could not see her, he had a sense that she had been around.

"You listen?" Ecwab, stepping closer, struck him across his body with a stick. "You listen!"

Rising with the throbbing pain, he spoke to Ecwab as he desperately searched between the trees with his eyes, "I heard you." Ecwab gestured toward the logs. *No one's there now. If she was there, I'll track her. I just have to get away from them.* Glancing back at the interpreter, he watched the man walk away while the other stared at him.

"Gols sharta!"

Nicholaus reluctantly picked up the flint axe. *I won't get far with these chains around me. I'll have to cut them off.* He struck the log, and chips of wood flew toward him. He gained fervor with every swing as his thoughts turned more and more toward his wife. Knowing she was upon that island—in those woods some-where—prompted a passion that pushed his muscles. Little chunks of freed arbor popped in every direction in his near madness. Without the Seafur guard noticing, he managed an occasional covert hit upon the chains.

Striking the final blow to separate a chunk of wood from the rest of the log, the crafted blade gave out, breaking in half. Picking the two pieces up, he showed them to his captor. "It broke."

The villager, walking forward, took one piece and looked at Nicholaus. "Rayata. Getma shar." He pointed to the chunk of wood. "Carito."

"You want me to take it to the huts?"

"Carita!" the man said with fierce eyes.

Picking up the pieces of wood, Nicholaus palmed the other half of the broken axe head. "I got it." As he walked to the village, he looked back at the woods. *Anna, it won't be long.*

Halfway to the cave, the princess fell to her knees. "Father, I thank You for sending him here, but why would You send him here and not have him to be with us?" Her gaze lowered to the ground as she shook with her despair and disbelief. Within her hysteric state, she heard a calm voice from deep within: *"Trust me."*

Her chin quivered. "I do, Father."

"Then stop him from coming."

She lifted her head. *Coming?* She quickly jumped to her feet and turned around. "No, he can't come!" She dashed back to where she last saw him.

Dropping the log, Nicholaus watched the captor turn his back to him to find another axe. As he did, the knight struck the last blow to the chains around his ankles with the broken axe head.

Seeing his feet freed to move full stride, he sprinted back toward the woods.

He quickly found the log he'd been chopping. Then he ran farther into the woods in the direction he'd felt the eyes staring upon him. Squatting down, he was forced to wipe away a tear. His wife's footprint was before him.

Breathing quickly, he rose. "I'm coming, Anna!" He ran hard, the air rushing past his cheeks and his body as the trees blurred around him.

Tilting his head, he rose from studying the ground and quickly turned around at the sound of another breathing.

There before him was his wife.

"Anna!"

Shaking her head as tears rolled down her cheeks, she whispered, "You have to go back!" It killed her to say it.

He rushed forward. "Anna!"

"No!" She moved backward. "No. You have to go back!"

"Anna?! What are you saying?" His heart nearly ripped in two.

Her chest heaved as she gasped for air and tried to explain. "They'll come looking for you." She felt him coming closer; she had no more strength to get away.

"Anna!" He grabbed her hand.

Feeling the pressure of his strong fingers upon her skin, she whimpered with his touch. "Nicholaus!"

He pulled her closer; she melted as his strong body enveloped her. Placing her face against his chest, for a moment, she was able to relax. But then she thought of the Seafurs.

Looking up at him, she shook her head. "Nicholaus, you have to—" She was silenced by his lips upon hers. Giving up her resistance, she kissed him back, and for a moment—for a brief moment within his arms—she felt all was right in the world.

It ended quickly with the sound of trampling in the forest; she immediately pulled away. "You have to go back, Nicholaus. They'll seek you out!"

He defiantly shook his head. "I'm not going to leave you—not again! Not ever!"

"The only reason we've lived this long is because they think we're dead! They know you are alive. They will seek you—"

"We?" His eyes enlarged. "Did a child live?"

She smiled pathetically. "They both do."

He grabbed for her; she stepped away. "No, Nicholaus."

"I can't leave you!" His eyes pleaded for understanding. "I won't!" He reached for her again.

Shaking her head as she took a stride backward, she wiped away tears. "You don't have to. Just don't follow."

He fell to his knees as he watched his long-lost wife run quickly into the forest, disappearing from his view. "Anna! Anna, come back! Anna!"

"Lino!"

Hearing the men approach, he felt a sting upon his head and the world went dark.

The princess did not stop running until she viewed the cave. Gasping for air, she tried to dry her tears, but it was to no avail —a plethora replaced the plethora wiped away.

"Mama," Augustine called out as he ventured some steps away from the rock wall. Claudia walked toward her.

Katara picked up the boy and walked to the distressed woman. "Edus said you went to huts. Why?"

Grabbing Claudia, who was trying to climb upon her,

Annabelle burst into a new wave of tears as she squeezed her daughter dearly.

"Annie?"

The princess held out her hand to the girl. Katara cautiously took it as she sat down beside her with Augustine in her arms. "He not tell me why. He had to get sheep."

With a quivering chin, Annabelle looked at the girl. She whispered, "It's my husband. He's here."

Katara's eyes bounced between the two children, up to the princess's eyes. "That good? Why cry?"

Claudia, standing up in her mother's arms, touched a tear on her mother's cheek.

Annabelle looked at her daughter and then pulled her son from the villager's arms. "I love you two so much!" She turned back to Katara. "If he comes, your people will follow." She took a deep breath. "And then we won't be safe at all!"

Katara lowered her eyes in understanding and whispered, "I sorry for what my people do."

Watching the evening hues slowly darken, Annabelle looked back to the cave. Catching Katara's eyes, she shook her head. "I have to go back to him. I have to see him again. I can't leave him like that!"

Katara nodded. "I stay here."

The princess stepped closer. "You don't understand—I could get caught."

"No matter what, they in Father's hands. We all in Father's hands. Go to see."

Annabelle hugged the girl. "Thank you for tending to them."

They have taken you away from me yet again. I will get away from them, and I will stop any who come after us! Staring at the fire, for a brief respite from ferociously digging along the fence line, Nicholaus breathed methodically as he schemed within his mind. *We will live—together. I need to get to them. They have been alone for too long.* His eyes shot to the eastern fence and then slowly returned to the flames. *My children live! They lived. How did they live all this time?* Looking to the east again, he stood, tilted his head, and dropped the half of the axe head he was using in his toil. *Anna. She is the reason they lived!*

Seeing a figure through the cracks in the fence, his mouth dropped open. He ran over and fell to his knees as he reached for the fingers slipping through the slots of sticks. "Anna?"

"It's I, Nicholaus." She gasped for air. "I couldn't leave you here by yourself. How badly I want you to be with us, but it can't be."

He shook his head. "No, it can. I will dig my way out and I will find you!"

She closed her eyes as her voice cracked. "There are too many, Nicholaus."

He gripped her fingertips passionately as he shook his head. "I will fight them 'til my death!"

Looking through a slot, she caught view of one of his eyes. "I don't want you to die!" Squeezing her hand through the cracks to the point of pain, she insisted, "They need their papá. We must be patient. Does anyone know you have come here?"

"No one but a wanted man and Melody."

The princess gasped. "Melody? Did you see her? Where was she?" She looked away. "They didn't take her."

"She was with Ruffatus."

"He is the wanted man."

He squeezed her fingers as he tried to move closer to the fence. "Anna, I can't stay like this. I can't. I will dig my way out and I will find you!"

"No!" She set her head against the fence as her tears fell. "You mustn't."

"I must!" He set his head against the fence as well. Both their positions set, nothing could be said to convince the other, but at that moment, what was to be done mattered little. At the cost of his freedom, he had found his way to his wife.

Annabelle's mind raced with memories of how she had ended up in this moment. "Lord Cortell and my mamá came to the castle," she said to Nicholaus. "I gave him the ring. I don't know what he did with it. Camrina took my mamá. The last I saw she was on Camrina's ship."

"Your mamá is safe. Cortell gave the ring to your papá, and all is as it should be."

Annabelle, holding her breath, found her husband's eye through the slot again and whispered, "My papá is dead."

"No, Anna, he's not. Lord Cortell made him look like he was, but he didn't hang him."

She gasped. "My papá lives?" she spoke in a normal voice in utter shock. "It was a guile?"

"Lino! Tam wortu?"

Annabelle gasped as the voice came closer.

"Anna, go." Kissing her fingertips, he stood and ran to the other side. "What do you want, Seafur?"

The man looked around the fence, hearing sounds in the woods.

"I'm over here. What do you want?" Nicholaus banged upon the fence, attempting to turn the villager's attention away from where his wife ran.

Hearing more noises, the man went toward the tree line. Eduard emerged.

"Dowa pappum," the boy said.

"Lima lino, dowa visto?"

The prince shook his head. "Nacht."

"Watta!"

"Yocht."

The Seafur, turning away from the woods, walked back to the village.

Walking by the compound, Eduard whispered to Nicholaus, "I told him I was relieving myself in the woods and I didn't see anyone."

"Did she get away?"

The prince looked back at the fence. "I don't know. I didn't see to where she ran."

SCHEMES AND LEAVES

Sitting on the hill overlooking the grazing sheep, Prince Eduard thought of his sister and brother-in-law. Could he do anything to help them?

Eyes moving to the periphery of the pasture, he jumped up and, running down the hill, readied his bow. Shooting as he ran, his arrow pierced a wolf in the side as it ran after a lamb, but was struck down before it could reach it. Turning to its companions, Eduard let the arrows fly until his quiver was emptied. He threw down the bow and pulled up a two-sided spear, placed in the ground months prior by Annabelle, that was half the height of the originals and launched it at the remaining wolf. It pierced the animal in the ribs. It did not get far before it collapsed in the grass.

After collecting his arrows, Eduard pulled the spear out of the wolf and dragged it into the forest. He then tied a vine rope to the end of one of the arrows and shot it over a branch of a tree. When it fell over to the other side, he fastened it around the trunk of the arbor. Tying the young wolf's hind legs with the other end of the vine, he then pulled upon the vine—using all of his weight—until he watched the young wolf's body advance toward the sky. When it was safely high enough for other animals to not get to it, he tightened the vine and watched it swing slightly as the wolf's blood dripped down to the earth.

Reaching his hand out, he let the blood fall upon his fingertips. *Blood—that is how you know something is hurt. But how do you know if it's dead?* His eyes looked along the periphery of the field until they landed upon one particular bush.

A body—or a sleeping body? It worked on some of the rats, but it did kill one. It had to be what the lamb ate, but what if he doesn't wake up? He walked toward the Lazarus leaves. *Annie will either wish me dead or be grateful.* He shook his head. "She doesn't have to know."

He picked a handful of leaves. "It will be his choice."

"Annie?" Eduard called into the woods east of the compound.

"Edus?" She looked around a tree.

He stepped closer to her. "I, uh . . ."

"What is it?"

He glanced toward the pasture. "I killed a small wolf today. It's hanging on the northwestern side, if you want it."

"I'll get it tomorrow. Thank you." She tilted her head as she removed an arrow from a fox that she shoot. "Are you well?"

"Yes." He nodded nervously.

"Were there many of them?"

"About five."

"How many sheep did they take?"

"None."

Hugging him, she paused. "Why do you look so worried?"

Returning the embrace, he could only say one thing: "I love you, Annie."

About to walk into the hut after delivering the leaves, Eduard spotted movement in the woods. Looking back to the prison yard fence from which he'd just came, he saw her figure emerge and kneel down next to the fence.

"Nicholaus," she whispered.

Turning away from the handful of leaves, he rushed toward the fence. "Anna!"

"Do they harm you?"

He shook his head. "It's nothing I can't take." Grabbing her fingers, he knelt down. "Tell me about them."

"Our children?" she said with a smile.

"Our children."

"Augustine and Claudia."

"A boy and a girl?"

She could hear happiness in his voice. "Yes," she whispered back with a smile. "They are full of life, Nicholaus. Walking and saying words." Swallowing hard, she moved as close to the fence as she could get, squeezing her hand through farther. "Nicholaus, I know you don't want to be away, but you must." She shook her head as she lowered it. "I know I shouldn't come here, but I can't help it."

Glancing at the leaves, he turned back to her. "You're right." He swallowed a huge lump. "I don't want you to come back. I don't want you to get caught. I don't want you or them to be found."

"Nicholaus!" she whispered in distress as her tears fell. "I don't think I can stay away."

"Give me your word you will."

She obstinately shook her head. "No, I don't want to!"

"Your word, Anna."

She looked through the crack. "But what of you, my love? I

don't want to leave you alone as much as you don't want to leave us."

"I pledge to you now: I will find a way for us to be together, or I will die trying to get to you. We'll be together—someday." He kissed her fingers. "I love you so much." He pressed her fingertips into his cheek and then pulled himself away. "You need to go now."

Pulling her hand out of the slot, she set it upon the fence. "I love you, Nicholaus, with all my heart." Gasping for air, she pushed herself up and forced herself to turn away. After a moment's hesitation, she dashed into the trees.

Sliding to the ground next to the fence, Nicholaus stared at the leaves over by the fire. "Father, You made those leaves. You gave them their ways of being, the changes they cause." Rising, he walked to them and knelt before them. "May they be my way back to my family." Picking the leaves up within his hand, he looked at them carefully. "Father, I know You don't want my children to be without their father, my wife without her husband. Your will in all things, Father. I trust in You." With those words spoken, he shoved the handful into his mouth and chewed.

Arising from her cot, Lina looked at the prince sitting upon his bed, slightly rocking himself. "You weren't in bed when I went to sleep last night."

"I wasn't."

"Where were you?"

Hearing screams from outside, he bolted toward the door. She watched him scamper up toward the male prison yard. "Where are you going?" Grabbing her fur, she followed behind him.

With a gasp, she watched the Seafurs pull the body out of the compound as they argued in their native tongue: "He's dead? How did he die? He was not ill yesterday!"

"I don't know, but he's dead now. We will burn him."

Eduard raced forward waving his arm, volunteering himself as he yelled in the native tongue: "I will bury him! I will bury him!"

"You must attend the sheep."

"No! Burial is more pressing. It must be done! The sheep can wait."

"You tend the sheep!"

Eduard adamantly stepped toward Acwa. "I have tended the sheep for months and not one has been lost to me. I beg of you this one thing—let me bury him and I will tend the sheep later!"

Acwa turned away waving his hand. "Let him bury him then, if it is so pressing for him."

The Seafurs dropped the body at Eduard's feet.

Lina, watching the boy trying to pick up the full-grown man, walked toward Nicholaus's upper body. "I'll get his shoulders; you get his feet." Lifting together, they slowly walked toward the cemetery as she spoke. "I have never heard you speak with such earnest to them. That was very bold. Dangerous and bold." She watched him clinch his teeth. "It's almost as if you knew him." The prince glanced at her just to look away. She then whispered, "Did you know him?"

"Yes."

"Who was he?"

"A knight. A king's knight."

"A knight? And he was taken by the Seafurs?" She looked away. "What have they come to?"

"Will you help me dig the hole?" the prince asked as they walked toward the graveyard.

"Yes, of course."

❄

Several hours later, with dirtied clothes and faces, they both stared at the empty grave. Looking at Nicholaus's body, Eduard turned toward Lina. "I will bury him."

Smiling, she shook her head. "I have helped you this far. I will help you all the way."

"No!" He stepped between her and the body as she approached.

She looked at him oddly. "No? Why ever not?"

"I want to do this part alone." Standing stoically, he looked at the empty grave. "Please don't ask me why."

Tilting her head, she stepped back. "You don't want my help now?"

"No. Not any longer. Not today."

Unsure what to say, she stepped away and looked back at him. "Are you certain?"

"Yocht," he answered in the Seafurian tongue.

"The work is upon you then," she said in the native language.

Watching her figure fade toward the village, he immediately knelt down next to the body. "Sir Nicholaus! Sir Nicholaus!" Shaking him desperately, he felt the coolness through the clothing. "No!" Moving his head by the knight's chin, he yelled at the body as if it would rouse him from his slumber. "Wake up! Wake up!" Sufficing in nothing, he slapped the pale cheeks and then fell backwards on to his bottom. "Oh, Father! Please, don't let him be dead. Please, don't let me have killed him!"

His eyes wandered from the body to the grave. *Maybe it will take him longer. I don't want to bury him—he could still be alive!* Forcing himself up, he picked up Nicholaus's upper half and dragged him toward the woods with a massive struggle.

"Annie."

"There you are, Edus. The sheep weren't in pasture today. Why weren't you there?"

Avoiding the question, he looked at the creature she pulled through the forest. "I need the dead wolf."

"This wolf? The one you told me I could have?"

He nodded his head. "Please don't ask me why, but I need the wolf."

She looked at him for a moment. "Are you alright?"

"I just need the wolf! That's all!" He grabbed at it.

"Be careful. It's heavy!" As he grabbed at the core of the wolf, the weight pushed him over. The carcass landed upon him, trapping him against the forest floor. Moving it off, she helped him up. "You mustn't forget you are only nine."

"I'll be ten someday—sometime in the spring." Bending down, he picked up the upper half of the animal. "I've got it, Annie."

She watched him struggle with the animal into the woods toward the south. "I could help you, Edus."

"I don't want your help, Annie." *That's the last thing I want!*

Lowering the wolf into the grave, he shoveled the dirt on top of it. *There at least will be something buried here.*

As the sun was starting to set, he laid the last stone on top.

"Still at it, are you?"

Looking over his shoulder, he spotted Lina. "I'm done now."

"Not yet. The cross isn't there." Stepping forward as he pushed himself away from the pile of rocks, she offered him a cross of sticks. "I made one for you, if you don't mind using it."

Taking the cross, he looked back at her. "Thank you, Lina." Crawling toward the head of the grave, he stuck it into the ground. *So they will not question.*

Staring at the stones, she found his eyes. "You know that is not my name, right?"

He tilted his head. "What do you mean?"

"Lina is what I've become—that's what I answer to."

"Who are you?"

She shook her head. "I barely have a memory of it. It seems a life ago I was called anything other." Smiling at the grave, she took a breath. "At least he will not be 'Lino.' I heard him tell them, 'I will never be a slave.'" Nodding her head, she concluded, "He is free now." She stretched out her hand. "Are you ready to go?"

Standing, he shook his head. "I can't go yet."

She dropped her hand next to her side. "I do wish I knew what is going on."

He looked into her eyes. "I . . . I wish I could tell you."

Slowly nodding, she turned toward the village and spoke over her shoulder. "I'll be waiting until you safely return."

"Sir! Sir! You have to wake up!" Shaking Nicholaus's body, Eduard laid his forehead down on the knight's side. "I killed my sister's husband! I killed my sister's husband!" Looking up, he looked through the thinning canopy toward the stars. "Father! Make him awaken! Just as you did with Lazarus, tell him to arise—and he will do it! You can! You are in control of all!" Lowering his head, his eyes jumped from one dark tree trunk to another. "What am I going to tell Annie? What am I going to say to her?" He shook his head as he looked back toward the sky. "No, I won't have to because You will make him live again!"

Throughout the night, he guarded the body, rocking himself as he hugged his legs.

When the morning light burst through the horizon, he looked back at the cold, lifeless figure; it looked exactly as it had when the sun went to bed. Dropping his legs in despair, he touched Nicholaus's arm. "I'm sorry, sir. Forgive me."

Pushing himself up, he looked to the village. "If I don't tend to the sheep, they will search for me, and they will find you here in the forest instead of in the grave. I have to leave you." Closing his eyes, he prayed with all his might: "Father, please!"

"Child, where have you been?!" Lina marched out of the hut when she found him by the gate.

Unlatching the gate that held the herd inside, Eduard looked over his shoulder at Lina with darkened circles under his eyes. "I slept in the woods."

"Why?"

He shook his head. "I didn't mean to worry you."

Stepping closer, she looked at his face. "I don't think you slept at all." Placing her hands upon her hips, she tilted her head. "Eduard, what is going on?"

He pointed to the herd. "I have to go with the sheep."

"Wait!"

He pulled his arm away as she grabbed for him. "I can't tell you anything—for your own good. Don't try to force it out of me." Shaking his head, he ran after the sheep.

Around midday, Nicholaus's cold body began to twitch sporadically as the poison slowly wore off. The twitching turned into a shiver as his body, awakening from its shutdown, began to elevate his temperature to an appropriate level. As the color returned to his skin, he slowly came to consciousness. Shaking his head with its pounding, he turned to his side and vomited the remains of the toxic leaves within his stomach—a natural reaction only delayed by the poison itself.

Laying his head upon his hand, he slowly remembered what had occurred. *How did I get here?* Weakly pushing himself up to a side-sitting position with all of the strength he could muster, he looked around cautiously. *Did it work? Do they think me dead? Am I free to go to her? Am I free to go to my children?*

Crawling to a tree, he pulled himself up with all his might. "Anna, I will find you."

WEAKENED BUT STRONG

Following his wife's tracks in his sluggish state, Nicholaus's heart beat wildly as he looked at the stone wall twenty feet away. *Anna.* Resting against a tree, he closed his eyes. *Is this where you live?*

Hearing noises, he opened his eyes and peered around the trunk. Two toddling babes were fighting over a stick. He gasped as the strength in his knees faltered for a moment. *Claudi and Auggie? Are those my children? The ones I thought I would never get to see?*

Fumbling forward in his weakness, he stopped to lean against a boulder as the toddlers turned to him and fell silent. "Good . . . good day," he managed to say.

Hearing a noise, they both turned toward the forest. Claudia's face began to quiver as she looked at him with fright.

"I mean . . . no harm." Attempting to stand straight, he pushed himself away from the rock. "Anna? Anna?" He looked back at the children. "Where is your mamá?" He briefly closed his eyes as his thunderous headache pounded within. "Anna?" Nicholaus shook his head as he, shaking and perspiring from all his struggle, stepped forward. "Anna, where are you?"

"Stop!" A voice yelled out from within the woods. As he turned toward the direction of the command, he spotted an arrow pointing at him. "Auggie, Claudi, come to me!"

The knight watched his frightened children begin toddling toward the girl as Katara moved toward them, arrow aimed at his head. He raised his right hand to chest level in objection. "I am Sir Nicholaus Hunts. I am looking for my wife, Annabelle of Anchony. Where is she?" Stepping forward, he stumbled and tumbled to the ground.

Katara, lowering the bow a bit, approached him cautiously. "The husband? You are not to be here."

"I'm thirsty. So thirsty." He rolled his head with his intolerable headache.

"How I know you are who you say?" Katara watched him keenly as she aimed the bow again.

"Prince Eduard . . ." He held his head. "Gave me leaves. They should think I'm dead."

Katara looked at the exhausted man. "Lazarus leaves?" Kneeling next to him, she looked up at the cave. "Come, if you fit." Setting the bow down, Katara struggled to lift Nicholaus's upper half and help him to the cave. "You need go in—you not fit."

Approaching the cave, Annabelle froze when she spotted small feet in the forest. "Claudi? Auggie?" Dropping the hare, she picked up her children in a panic. "What are you doing here?"

"Kata," Claudia said as she pointed toward the cave.

"Katara? Where is she?" Setting her children down next to a tree, her pointer finger extended. "Stay here."

Pulling the string back, Annabelle tilted her head as she realized Katara leaned over a man. "Katara, who is that?"

The girl immediately rose and turned around. "I try, but he not fit."

"Who?" The princess slowly approached.

"It the sir. He say my people think dead." She moved out of the view as the knight attempted to look toward the voice.

"Nicholaus!" The princess looked at Katara to make sure she heard correctly as she ran forward. "The Seafurs think him dead?" Dropping her bow, she fell next to his head.

He weakly raised his arm. "Anna."

"I'm here." A plethora of tears rolled down her cheeks as she picked up his head. "They think you're dead? How?"

"Edus give leaf," Katara said.

"A leaf?" Looking back at her husband, she kissed him as she cried.

Katara shook her head. "I try get in—he not fit."

Annabelle looked up at the girl and then to the small opening. Wiping away her tears, she smiled. "Katara, will you get Auggie and Claudi please?" Watching her walk to the tree, she looked back down at her husband. "Nicholaus, is it true? Are you free to be with us?"

He grabbed her arm. "I told you I'd come."

"Mama." Wiping away her tears, she reached for the boy. "Sir Nicholaus, this is your son, Auggie."

Augustine uncoordinatedly fell upon him. "Auggie."

"And this is Claudi." Claudia clung to the princess when he reached for her. "Claudi, this is your papá."

"Papa," Augustine said.

Annabelle touched his head. "That's right, Auggie, your papá."

"Mama." Claudia looked strangely at Nicholaus.

Nicholaus closed his eyes as if it would still his swirling head. "Anna, I'm . . . so thirsty."

Annabelle looked at the cave. "We've got to get you in the cave."

"He hungry?" Katara asked, unsure what to do. "I dress hare?"

Annabelle nodded as Nicholaus closed his eyes with his pounding head. "Yes. Thank you."

Closing the latch for the gate to hold in the sheep for the night, Eduard looked around and then sprinted into the woods where he last left the knight.

"Sir Nicholaus? Sir Nicholaus?" With only the fading light to guide him, he fell at the spot where the body had lain. *He's not here? What took place?*

He looked around the forest. *Did an animal get him and drag him away?* He stood. *Or does he live?* He looked to the awakening stars. *Father, does he live?* His eyes danced their way back to the ground. *I'll have to tell Annie.*

Eduard gasped. *What will I say if he's not there?* He fell back to his knees. *I killed her husband.* He looked around. *Should I go now?* He shook his head in rejection of the idea. *I don't want to tell her he's dead!* He swallowed with difficulty. *I will tell her if she comes for him.*

"Child, I've been worried sick about you!" Eduard peeled his eyes off of the male prison to look toward the door of the hut as Lina came out. "Where have you been? Are you ever going to come back in?"

Looking back toward the male compound, he nodded. "I will when I'm ready."

She followed his gaze. "What are you looking for? There are no more linos. Come into the warmth, child! Come in!"

"No, Lina!" He pulled his hand away.

"What is wrong with you?"

"I can't come in yet."

"Why not?"

"I have to wait for her!" He covered his mouth as his eyes bulged, realizing he divulged too much.

"For whom?" Lina asked with utter perplexity as she straightened her stance.

His eyes danced around, pondering what he could say to not reveal his sister's truth. "I can't tell you." He glanced back at the compound and toward the arbors. "There are things in the woods that the Seafurs shouldn't know about."

Turning him around with her hands upon his shoulders, she leaned down. "I'm not a Seafur. Tell me."

He shook his head. "I can't."

"Why not?"

"Because I gave my word I wouldn't."

"To whom?"

He shook his head. "I can't tell you."

Standing, she took a breath as she looked at the tree line. "So there is a person in the woods." She eyed him. "Is it Katara? I know you were friends. She was to live in the mountain, but I can't find her. I thought they got her."

Lowering his gaze, he turned away. "I can't tell you." He shook his head, refusing to speak any more.

Lowering her head, she went inside the warm hut.

WHAT MAY COME

Sitting upon the pasture hill, Eduard jerked his head back as he began to nod off. Spending most of the night waiting for his sister to come to the compound, he slept very little. Pushing himself up, he was determined not to fail in his job of protecting the sheep.

As he strolled down the hill, he heard a certain call of an Anchonian bird. He looked in the direction it seemed to have come from. *Annie!* Seeing the slightest movement as she hid back behind a tree, he ran over.

"Annie?" He shook his head. "I'm so sorry! I'm so sorry!"

She looked into his eyes. "For what?"

"Nicholaus!" He could no longer hold it inside, "I gave him leaves and I left him in the woods, and then he was gone. I don't know what became of him!"

"Edus, it's alright! He's alive. He found us!"

Eduard, taking a ragged breath, looked into his sister's eyes. "You mean I didn't kill him?"

"No." She could not help but smile. "You didn't kill him. You brought him to us." She hugged him. "Thank you, Edus!"

"I was so worried!" he confided as he hugged her back.

"No need to fret; all is well." Pulling away, she looked at his face. "Edus, are you getting enough sleep?"

He shook his head. "I was waiting for you to come last night so I could tell you why he wasn't there."

"Get some sleep tonight, Edus. Sleep well."

He nodded. "I will, Annie."

She hugged him again. "You can't face wolves if you are not fully rested." His chin quivered, not sure what to do. "I will help you today."

"Thank you, Annie!" Eduard looked around. "Is he here?"

"No. He's still sleeping." She looked across the pasture. "How is your supply of spears?"

He pulled away from her to look at the sheep. "They're holding."

Opening his eyes, Nicholaus looked at the sunlight streaming in through the upper level of the cave. Pushing himself up, he felt more himself. Climbing out of the cave from the upper opening with the concocted ladder, his children stopped playing to look at him.

"Papa." Augustine said when he saw him emerge as Claudia hung around Katara.

"You better?" Katara asked as she sat upon the boulder a few feet away.

"Much." He looked around. "Where's Anna? Where is their mamá?"

Augustine sat and pointed to the trees. "Mama."

"She's in the woods?"

"No. She went to see Edus," Katara revealed as her hands rubbed the two rocks against one another.

"Prince Eduard? She went to the huts in the middle of the day?" Nicholaus stepped forward with the greatest concern.

"No," Katara said as she rose from sharpening the arrowhead.

"To the hills north of huts keeping sheep," Katara pointed with her hand.

Nicholaus nodded and then looked back at her. "How long have I been sleeping?"

"Day and half."

He walked toward the forest and then looked back at Katara and his children. "Is it alright for me to leave you here?"

Katara tilted her head. "You not here before." Watching him lower his head, she felt sorry for him. "We flee to cave if noise. You go, find in hills."

Late in the afternoon, Annabelle pushed herself away from a tree to turn toward the forest, removing an arrow from her quiver and readying her bow as she did so. As the wood spoke its resistance to the concavity, she tilted her head as the figure emerged. "You are loud, Sir Nicholaus Hunts."

"I am not as light as some." He put up his hands. "Are you going to shoot an unarmed man?"

She tilted her head. "I deem not—not today anyway." Lowering her bow, she smiled. "You're better?"

"Not all myself, but much better." Walking to her, he was intercepted by the weight of a shorter body.

"I thought you were dead!" Eduard looked up at him as he squeezed with all his might. "I thought I killed you!"

The knight looked over at his wife as she gaily laughed. "You didn't."

"I was so scared, but the Father brought you back!"

Nicholaus looked down at the boy's head. "I wasn't dead."

Pulling away, Eduard shook his head. "I couldn't tell. You looked dead to me—that's certain!"

"I *felt* like I had been dead," Nicholaus admitted as he knelt before the boy. "Prince Eduard, how did you get here?"

"I was given to a queen I do not know, and her people gave me to them."

"Camrina," Nicholaus said with disgust.

"Aunt Camrina took him?" Annabelle turned away as if she could distance herself from the thought.

"Aunt?" Eduard looked at her sister in perplexity. "My aunt took me?"

"It is Papá's sister," the princess was forced to admit.

Prince Eduard made a face. "Well, she's not very nice."

Annabelle, walking over, knelt next to her husband. "She, too, took me and Mamá or . . ." She shook her head. "It was Prince Howercus that took us and gave us to her."

Eduard gasped. "Mamá?"

"She's safe." Both the prince and princess turned to the knight. "Queen Camrina is locked away in the dungeon in Aboly."

Annabelle's eyes stared into her husband's. "Who all lives?"

"Everyone."

A relieved gasped escaped her lips as she touched her husband's forearm and whispered with watery eyes, "Can it be true?"

He placed his hand on top of hers as he looked into her eyes. "It is." He smirked as he looked away. "Isabella and Symon wed."

Her mouth opened farther and then sprung into a smile as she squeezed his arm. "Did they?"

He looked back into the emerald hue. "Yes."

"And Liza and Crisa and Will and Thom are there?" Eduard asked with all hope.

Pulling his eyes away from his wife, he looked at the prince.

"Yes, well . . ." He slightly shook his head. "Prince Thomas went in search for you."

"I knew he would!" the prince said with sheer delight. "But you found me and you weren't even looking!"

Nicholaus watched Annabelle stand and walk over to the edge of the pasture. "I did, didn't I?"

"Edus, the sheep are getting close to the thorns."

He grumbled as he stood. "You would think they would learn!"

Nicholaus, watching the boy run past his sister and trample across the meadow, stood and stepped beside his wife. "Anna."

Pulling her eyes off of the herd, she looked at her husband as she swallowed the lump in her throat. "Edus is the sheep herder. They keep him alive because he keeps the sheep alive." Lowering her head, she looked at the ground. "That is the only way I can help my brother live."

His eyes wandered across the gently rolling hills. "The spears?"

She shook her head. "I can't be with him all the day."

"Anna, you don't have to—"

Shaking her head, she looked up at him and cut him off. "They are heathens, Nicholaus. They sacrifice children to their gods."

He moved closer. "Anna—"

She swung around to face him while continuing to shake her head. "The only reason our children are alive is because they are two!" She gasped as she remembered the night of their birth. "And the slave woman who saved them in the woods." Her chin quivered as her whole face reddened with her tears. "I needed you here, Nicholaus! I needed you!"

He pulled her into a hug as he caressed her hair. "I know. I wanted to be here with you. I can't tell you how badly I wanted to be here with you—wherever you were, I wanted to be there."

Closing her eyes, she soaked up the strength of his tight embrace. "Anna, I'm here now."

She squeezed him back as new tears were released. "I don't blame you, Nicholaus. I just want you to know how badly I wanted you here." She tried shaking her head against him, though she could move little. Closing her eyes, she rested against him.

The prince's voice interrupted them, "Thom is to come for us?"

Nicholaus lowered his head as he continued to hold his wife. "He doesn't know you are here."

"Who is to come for us then?" he asked with all concern.

Opening her eyes, Annabelle looked over her shoulder to look at her brother as Nicholaus shook his head.

"No one?" The prince lowered his head in despair.

Pushing away from her husband, Annabelle grabbed her brother's hand and knelt in front of him. "We are far better now than we were before. Sir Nicholaus is here now."

He looked up at the knight. "That is true but . . . if only he came with a ship."

"Edus!" The princess could not help but laugh. "How true are your words. How true are your words!"

"Will you stay with me until I put the sheep away?"

Annabelle nodded. "Yes, we'll stay."

Watching Eduard herd the sheep up the hill, Annabelle grabbed Nicholaus's hand as he stepped forward after the prince. He looked back at his wife. "You don't follow?"

"Not if we don't want to be seen." Spotting her brother turn around on the hill and wave to them, she waved back. "Once he goes over that hill, if the wolves come, he is close enough to the huts for them to help him."

"They would help him?"

She turned toward the forest as she took a few steps inward. "The sheep are theirs. They want to keep them alive. They need the wool."

He looked from her to the prince disappearing over the top of the hill. "Why do they have a boy watching them then, when there is such a threat as wolves?"

"Their shepherds are always killed. They don't mind if he dies, since he is only a 'lino'— a slave." Looking forward, she shook her head. "But I do."

He walked closer to her. "Do they know who he is?"

"I don't know." She looked back to the graying hills through the trees. "But they see him with honor now because he hasn't lost a single sheep—or his life."

"Not one?" He grabbed her hand. "You are to thank for that, aren't you?"

She shook her head. "Edus can hold his own now. He has his sling, the bolas, the bow, and the spears. He is devoted to his duty of protecting them."

"Anna?"

Shrugging her shoulders, she shook her head. "I helped him out a time or two." She looked into his eyes and as she spoke, tears began to fall until her voice was nearly indiscernible. "But now he has returned any favor I gave to him tenfold by returning you to me."

Stepping closer, Nicholaus touched her cheek. "I'm forever indebted to him."

Resting in his arms, she thought about all he had said. "Ruffatus knew you wanted to be taken by them?"

"Yes."

"Will he tell anyone?"

"Prince Thomas was in Baltam. He is to get a note to King Henricus and your papá."

"And this you believe he will do?"

"Yes. He gave me his word. As I did to Melody that I would tell her in person what became of you."

She looked up at him. "So now, all we have to do is wait."

Despairingly, he shook his head. "They have to find a way to an island that they don't even know of."

"I had faith that someday, when God willed it, you would find me, and here you are before me. I, too, have faith that Thom will come for Edus when God wills it." Resting her head back upon his chest as she looked up at him, she added, "Until then, we must wait."

Feeling his lips upon hers, she grabbed his hand and pulled away. "Come with me."

"Back to the cave?" His whole body tensed.

Smiling, she slightly shook her head. "No, not yet."

Prince Eduard entered the hut and closed the door behind him, leaning against it as he thought of his sister's words. *We are far better off with Sir Nicholaus here!* He nodded his head. He was so overwhelmed with happiness at the thought of a king's knight free upon Walva Island to offer more protection for everyone that he chortled in his utter exhaustion.

"Prine Eduard? You come in?" Lina said with great surprise as she walked over to him. Observing him keenly, she touched his shoulder. "Are you alright?"

And I helped to free him. Would he be free if I were not here? Is that why I was sent to Walva Island—to free my brother-in-law? To help my sister, niece, and nephew by freeing Sir Nicholaus? A smile burst across his face. *It is the hand of God at work!*

Touching Lina's arm, he looked up at her. "I deem I see, Lina!"

"See what?" she asked in perplexity. "I think you need some sleep." She guided him over toward his cot.

"I do," he acknowledged. "But Lina"—he grabbed her other arm—"I'm glad I was brought here!"

"Child, what?" She shook her head. "You need *much* more sleep than—"

"It's the Father's hand at work! Lina, I love you!" He hugged her dearly.

"I love you, too, Prince Eduard." She squeezed him back and then guided him to his cot. "Rest now, while I make some stew."

Scooping the stew into the clay pot, she brought it over to the soundly sleeping prince. "Eduard, it is ready now." Gently touching him, he still did not rouse. "The poor lad—so tired." Looking across the hut, she thought to herself: *At least he can now find rest. Whatever troubled his mind, I hope it has passed.*

As she thought about his words—being thankful for being on the island—she could not help but snicker. "He truly was tired—not thinking right."

She shook her head at herself as she stood and walked over to her cot. "The Father's hands at work? Where have the Father's hands been when child after child is taken to the sacrificial stone?" Looking up toward the ventilation hole near the roof, she spoke to God, "Help me to see, Father. Give me hope. The prince seems to have plenty."

Taking a deep breath, she sat down on the bed and ate the stew she had scooped for Eduard. Once finished, she sat the bowl down and lay down herself, drifting off to sleep.

Hearing shouts from the native people, she arose and went to the door. When she stepped outside into the darkness, it was not the native people she found but wailing parents, wanting their children. She shook her head as her heart broke for them. "I'm sorry, but they're dead." She looked to the sacrificial stones. "It was there. The Seafurs killed them all."

She found herself on the sacrificial hill, running toward the stone with Acwa and a victim present. "No!" She screamed in fury as she reached her hand out to save the girl, realizing she was too late. She fell to her knees in anguish. "There were too many I did not help! I could not help!"

Hearing a rumble out of the grayness overhead, she looked up.

And a single drop of His Blood fell from the sky onto the sacrificial stone as an immense light filled the heavens and a powerful force cleared away the darkness and death surrounding her.

Acwa was knocked off of his feet—blown away—as the grayness was overcome with color; Lina stood in shock as her hair blew in the cleansing wind of the Holy Spirit.

And children's laughter filled the air.

The girl, now robed in a white dress and cloak, arose and smiled sweetly as she pulled her hood over her head and walked to the trees.

Lina, watching her walk into the trees, followed after her. Soon, there were others. All were walking the same direction—to the East.

The trees thinned and Lina found herself in a field. A beautiful, beautiful field with vibrant colors she had never seen before. Among the wildflowers in the rolling grasses, the girls and boys walked toward the distant, bright light—brighter than the sun, but without harm to the eyes.

Looking around, Lina was surrounded by more and more children —she knew some of the faces. Some were holding hands, some were skipping, some were picking wildflowers, but all were walking toward the light, eventually forming a line.

Drawn toward the brilliant light herself, Lina heard a voice, "Even their deaths cannot defeat My loving purposes—not even for them. None are ever forgotten."

Feeling His abundant love, Lina fell to her knees while extending her arms. "Father!"

She awoke in the dark hut, still enveloped in the love of the Father with the realization: "He doesn't want all those children to suffer and die by the hand of the Seafurs, but in the end His love can't be defeated. They are all blessed now, and evermore." Scrambling out of her cot, she knelt on the floor next to the bed, squeezing her fingers together. "I'm sorry, Father! I'm sorry I ever doubted! I'm sorry I lost hope in You! Give me grace to keep this hope, for this slave is weak!" As a tear fell down her cheek, she continued, "Help me never to forget what You have shown me!"

CAPTURED BY THOUGHT

Rising from his knees inside a tent along the Baltam coast, King Francis turned around. "Jous, will you send my son to me?"

A few minutes later, Thomas's voice filled the air. "Papá?"

"Thomas." Francis looked down as he turned around. "I have been on my knees praying for advice and I know what God wants of me." He shook his head. "It calls for a humility that I'm not certain I have."

"Papá—"

"Let me speak!" Looking up, he took a quick breath. "You have a meekness I can't claim. It's from Clara, not me." Closing his eyes, it hurt him to say the next words. "It is you whom God wants to go."

Thomas grabbed his arms. "Thank you, Papá!"

Francis pulled him into a tight hug. "I know you must keep your word, but I won't leave you without protection!"

"You must do God's will. That's what you must do," Thomas assured him.

Standing before King Henricus, Francis informed him of his decision. "It is with a heavy heart that I make known that my son shall go in my stead. For Baltam's sake, the king of Anchony shall stay here, but this troubled father begs men from Baltam to join my son on his duty."

Listening intently to the words, King Henricus slowly shook his head. "I will not force any of my men away from their families to an unknown land, but I will see who will go on their own accord." Nodding his head, he placed his hands upon his hips. "How do you know where this island is, anyway?"

Entering into the royal tent in Baltam, Peter looked around as the two kings and the prince hunched around a table looking at the map copied by Warinus's hand. "Where did the mariner get this?" King Henricus asked.

"Sire . . ." Peter approached his king and friend. "I must speak of something before we leave."

King Francis turned around. "Jous?"

Peter, stepping closer, shook his head. "I do have a concern about Warinus. I think he is more than a mariner, and beyond that, he was on the *Sockortale* when Annabelle was taken to Snake Island. He could have at least tried to do something about it. If he didn't want another to go through what his mother did, why did he do nothing?"

"You think he is a knight and does not say it?" Francis asked.

Thomas looked at the Lion as he thought about the entire situation. *But she wasn't hurt. No one left on Two Breath Island ever died. Did Warinus know?*

"I deem he was at least on the path, at some point," Peter answered his king.

Straightening, King Francis glanced at King Henricus. "Do

you think he can't be trusted?" He spoke to himself, "Clara did have some doubts. Do you think this map is in error?"

"Hmm," Thomas said as his mind worked quickly. "Papá, I think we should question Warinus, not for a lack of trust, but for truth." He looked at Peter. "Sir Josephus, will you fetch him?"

Peter looked to Francis for his permission, and the king nodded at him.

When Peter left, his father looked at Thomas. "What is it, Thomas?"

"Sir Nicholaus and I went to Two Breath Island. No one has perished. Did he know?" He looked at the two kings as his mind swirled. "May I question him, Papá?"

When Warinus entered the tent with the Lion behind him, Prince Thomas wasted no time. "Warinus, I have been to both Two Breath Island and Trader Island. Tell me, do you know Sir Dartel?"

Warinus glanced at all the men and then answered, "No."

"Lord Bartus?"

He shook his head. "I don't know that name."

Thomas shook his head in confusion as his reasons were disappearing before him. "They were both on Trader Island. You mean you have never met them?"

"I haven't."

"Did you know the ones left on Two Breath Island would not perish?"

Straightening, he admitted, "I did."

Peter stepped forward. "That is why you let Queen Camrina and Prince Howercus leave Princess Annabelle of Anchony there?"

"I knew she would end up on Trader Island. She was safer on

that island than on Camrina's ship," Warinus said. "I did go back to look for her. She wasn't there."

"You went to Trader Island to find her?" Peter asked.

"I was going there anyway—to get the map—but she was gone when I got there."

Peter stepped away, finding the man's answer acceptable, although curious.

"How did you know? And how did you know the map was there?" Thomas asked.

"I knew about both because of a Captain Anguis."

"The pirate?" Thomas said with utter confusion. He looked at his father. "He is the one that paid for Annie to get off of Oro Island." Thomas stepped back as he tried to make sense of it all.

"How did the pirate know about the islands?" King Henricus asked.

King Francis shook his head pathetically at his sister's actions. "Did Camrina leave him on Snake Island, too?"

Thomas looked at Warinus to see his reaction. Warinus carefully said, "That is not for me to say."

"Not for you to say?" King Henricus asked with incredulity.

"What are you hiding?" Peter asked as he stepped closer. "We want nothing but the truth from you!"

Anguis was left on Snake Island? If so, he would have spent time on Trader Island. That's how he would have known about the map! But why would Aunt Camrina take the time to leave a pirate on Snake Island?

"*There was another.*" Thomas recalled Lord Bartus's words, and his mind began to swim. "*Your prince's body is not in its grave.*" *How they looked at one another! They knew it was empty!* His mouth opened in wonder.

"A man's choices are his own," Warinus said resolutely.

"Ah! *Anguis!*" All looked at Prince Thomas. "*Anguis* is Latin for snake." He shook his head as if he could not believe it took him so long to make all the connections. "That is not his name!"

"Thomas, would you like to fill us in?" his father asked.

He shook his head. "Papá, he took the name of the creatures that set him free."

"The pirate?" King Henricus asked. "Set him free from what?"

Warinus took a deep breath. "From Camrina, to begin with."

"From holding any account to anyone." He looked at his father. "To any kingdom."

Nodding, Warinus added, "Sir Ilum told me Prince Phillipus figured as much."

"What are you smiling about?" Sir Arkel, on his way to Salone from Brotherton, said in disgust as he threw a rock at Anguis across from the fire. "Go ahead, for you soon will be without a head, you traitor!"

"Traitor?" Bruised and beaten, Anguis could not help but chuckle. "Can I be a traitor when it is not my kingdom?"

"You have nothing to smile about! Nothing but death awaits you in Salone."

"God . . . has graced me with trust."

"Trust? Well *I* trust that Howercus shall have your head!"

Anguis, staring into the fire, whispered to himself, "I had to trust in the Father first."

"Before what?"

Anguis looked up at him from his knees. "Before I could trust in my uncle." He closed his eyes. "He will come for me; he gave me his word."

"The uncle of a pirate?" Sir Arkel said with a sneer. "Oh, I can't wait to see what will come of that!"

Opening his eyes, Anguis looked over at his captor. "You don't understand: I don't care what becomes of me." He smirked. "If you kill me, that is all the better!"

Princess Anastacia, standing on the port side of the ship taking her to Anchony, stared at the distant land and sighed.

Lady Alana stepped up beside her. She moved the ruby pendant she was wearing back and forth against the chain, observing Anastacia keenly. "You shall take your throne some-day, Your Majesty."

"I doubt I should ever rule. My uncle has plotted for so long; I fear only death shall stop him, and how many others would die beside him? How many Sethelians will perish? What of the kingdom will be left?" She shook her head. "That is if there were even enough to fight for me."

Silent for a moment, Lady Alana finally said, "Let's hope there are so many on your side, Prince Howercus will give up without bloodshed."

"Does Lord Cortell gain such numbers?" Princess Anastacia asked with hope.

Lady Alana shook her head. "My husband does work for your throne, but that was not the meaning of my words."

Anastacia turned toward her. "Then what do you mean?"

"I mean Captain Anguis—the men he will get for you."

Princess Anastacia held her breath for a moment. "The *pirate*? He brought me to Brotherton. How will he get men? Phillip trusted him, but for the life of me, I don't know why."

"He came to me once he found out Queen Camrina was not in rule in Anchony. He wants to get you there. He wants to get you your throne."

"He came to you? How did he know you?" She looked around. "Where is he? I haven't seen him on the ship."

"He went with me to Brotherton to give himself up to Sethel."

"To my uncle?" Anastacia said in distress as she stepped away from the ledge. "Why?" Shaking her head, she tried to come up with a solution. "Did he think that would ease my uncle from searching for me?"

"No," Lady Alana answered adamantly.

"Then why?"

"He wanted to be taken." Nervously, she added, "He had me write a letter to his uncle."

"His uncle? Who is the pirate's uncle that could possibly aid me?" she asked with utter confusion.

Lady Alana shook her head. "Not the pirate, but the prince."

Surrounded by the top commanders of the Monakalian army, King Marcus stared at the map upon his table, studying the outline of the Sockor Islands as he remembered:

Kneeling down, King Marcus took Prince Leonardus by the shoulders once King Barthelmus had died. "I pledge to you now: I will not leave you with Camrina!"

Disgusted with himself, he turned away. *A vow I could not keep!*

"Take him? Take the prince? I think not!" Queen Camrina insisted. "He is the heir to the throne. You can't steal him away from the Sockorian Kingdom! He is needed here!"

"He's but a boy!"

Camrina grabbed Prince Leonardus's hand. "He is my boy. I am his stepmother. He is in my care! Now leave my kingdom at once!"

"What would you have us do, Sire? If the queen is no longer in Anchony, are you still in need of your soldiers?" one of the commanders asked.

Disgruntled, King Marcus shook his head.

"Your Majesty." A knock interrupted them. "Lady Nakala to see you."

Looking at the door, his frustration with himself and Camrina's situation was replaced by astonishment. "Lady Nakala? What does she do here? Send her in!"

Glancing around at the other men as she entered, she curtsied, quickly rose, walked forward, and kissed the king on both cheeks. "Cousin, I came at once with great tidings!"

He looked at his men. "Leave me for a moment." Once they had left, he turned toward his cousin. "What is it?"

"You know you asked me years ago to go to the Sockor Islands and to keep watch over Prince Leonardus and an eye on Queen Camrina."

"Yes, and when he died, you would not yield your post."

She shook her head. "Because Queen Camrina was too vile and her lot too good to be the work of God."

"Anything from Anchony is vile," he said in agreement. "What brings you here now?"

A smile spread across her face. "I have come upon some glad tidings that I had to speak to your face." She placed her hands over her heart. "Our Leonardus yet lives!"

"What?" For a moment he could not breathe. "What do you mean?"

"This is why I came myself." Looking at the chair, she pointed. "Please, have a seat! It was hard for me, too!"

Leaning against his table, he slowly sat and looked up at her desperately. "How did you come about this?"

Reminiscing as she looked across the room, Nakala said, "I remember when Fr. Hartus died, Prince Leo would spend many hours at his grave, crying. It broke my heart to see the child in such a state." Turning back to the king, she touched his hand. "A few weeks ago. I saw a man at that same grave—"

"That doesn't mean it's him!" he objected, demanding proof.

"Of course not. Of course not, but I'm not finished. I had seen a face earlier in the crowd that made me think, 'If Leo were alive, he would look like that.'"

He looked at her desperately. "That is not enough. Give me more!"

"In the castle, I was walking to his old chamber, when that very man stepped out of it, with Sir Dartel behind him! Sir Dartel yelled, 'Sethel? What about the Sockor Islands! She needs her monarch!' And that is when I knew it was true!"

The room began to swirl with his confusion. "Sir Dartel? King Barthelmus's head knight? I thought *he* was dead?"

"Camrina tried to rid herself of all of them. Sir Dartel told me all, and he confirmed that that man was Prince Leonardus! He lives! Prince Leo lives!

"Well, where is he?!"

Her smile faded. "It seems he cares more about the Sethelian crown than the Sockorian."

King Marcus stood. "Well, I will make certain his throne is restored to him. I might not have been able to keep my vow to him when he was a boy. But here and now, in front of God, I pledge that I will right him!"

Another knock interrupted his thoughts: "A message from a Lady Alana, Your Majesty."

Nodding, Nakala said with worry, "There is one thing I have not told you: He is also the man you know as Captain Anguis."

"The pirate? I have a price upon his head! A price upon my nephew's head?"

"Your message," the servant offered.

Reluctantly, King Marcus took the letter. "Do you know a Lady Alana?"

"No, cousin."

He shook his hand. "I can't deal with it now. You open it."

Doing so, her mouth dropped open. She sat it in front of the king. "You need to read this!"

Reading the sentences, he stood and looked toward the door. "Bring the commanders in. I know where the soldiers are to go!"

Prince Thomas stared at the two kings and Peter in the tent in Baltam. "Captain Anguis is Prince Leonardus of the Sockor Islands! He is the heir to the throne." He looked at his father. "Which means Camrina rules nothing."

King Francis turned sharply toward the mariner. "And you have known this all along?"

"Not all along."

Henricus, trying to make sense of it all, asked, "The prince of the Sockor Islands? Didn't he die of illness years ago?"

"That was Camrina's claim," Thomas said.

"She took him to Snake Island wanting to rid herself of him," Warinus explained. "So she could have the throne."

"But he was rescued." Thomas shook his head. "Did he live on Trader Island until he decided he wanted nothing more to do with the Sockor Kingdom? That a pirate's life was better than fighting Camrina?"

"Forsake it all and start a new life?" King Henricus said.

"One of thievery," Peter observed.

Peter, watching Warinus's rowboat approach the *Sockortale*, glanced back at his king. "There is only one thing I do not understand about Warinus's story."

"What is that?" King Francis asked.

"Why would his mother be left alive, when Camrina killed so many and killed her own mother—your own mother?"

"I have wondered the same," Prince Thomas said as he stepped into the rowboat, having said his farewells to his father earlier. "But I see how it has led us to be able to find Edus, so I will not question that it is the hand of God."

"That is curious, indeed," King Francis said. "Will I ever

understand my sister's reasoning?" He shook his head. "God speed to both of you. My prayers go with you."

"Thank you, Papá," Thomas said with a nod as the rowboat was pushed out to the sea.

Standing stoically along the beach, King Francis watched the ship sail away.

"I know you wish you could be going with them," Henricus offered.

"I signed the decree for his life. I abolished the monarchy of Anchony for his life, and now I've sent him to die."

"But it was not sealed? Do you think you would have signed it if you had had the ring?"

Watching the boat shrink into the distance, Francis answered honestly, "Yes." Shaking his head at himself, he rubbed his face. "I don't know." Releasing a deep breath, his next words astonished Henricus. "How loving is the Father that He gave up His only Son? I am so far from Him."

Henricus, thinking of the king's words, watched the ship turn into an indiscernible speck. "You are not as far as you think. You gave up your son because you knew it was what had to be done and because it was the will of the Father."

Staring into the sea, King Francis whispered, "I trust in the Father, I trust in the Son, I trust in the Holy Spirit—three in one. I shall pray to the Father, I shall pray through the Son, I shall pray in the Holy Spirit—God's will be done." Closing his eyes, he attempted to make his heart feel what his mind knew as true: "It's not the present life that matters but how we fit into the cloth of creation."

"Cloth of creation?" Henricus asked.

"How will my deeds today change Anchonians in years to come, long after I'm gone? My father yielded to the demands of the nobles, and from that smoldering coal rose the fire of the Demolites. What would have taken place if he had not given in to them?" He looked back at the sea. "I am in Baltam now. What change can I bring forth here? Can I help your people? Can I somehow help to spread the truth of Howercus in Sethel? Is that what is God's will? I think it must be, since here is where I am." Taking a quick breath, he looked at the young king. "I need to do something to get my mind off of where I sent my son."

King Henricus nodded. "I know where you can start. The Sethelian soldiers that were in Brotherton believe the lies Prince Howercus has told them."

Nicholaus looked from Sna, sleeping next to Katara across the fire, to Pup sleeping by his children. "You've made some strange friends, Anna," he said to his wife as she rested in his arms.

With drooping eyes, she said, "Pup is here because I killed her mother, and she would not let me be. And if Katara and Sna would have left us be, we wouldn't be here. Sna has saved all of us: Edus from another wolf and Katara from being sacrificed." Tears ran down her cheek, soaking into his shirt.

"Don't cry." He squeezed her extra tight.

As she soaked up his strength, she whispered, "They're tears of wonder, truly."

"Wonder?"

"Awe—at God's hand throughout my life." As she melted into him, she said, "Of all the places I've been, He has always been there for me. And now He has sent you back to me, and our children can be properly tended to with both of us here." With that assurance in mind, she closed her eyes and fell asleep as he kissed her on her forehead. She could finally rest soundly.

AUTHOR'S NOTE

Dear Readers,

I hope you have enjoyed the fourth book in the *Annabelle of Anchony* series! As in the other books, all characters are fictional.

Although the dark and demonic practices Annabelle encounters on Walva Island are difficult to read and think about, the history of some pagan cultures, especially pre-Columbian cultures in the Americas, inspired it. I present it not only to remind readers to be grateful for the introduction of Christianity to these cultures (look into St. Juan Diego's tilma and the image of Our Lady of Guadalupe for the ultimate evangelization tool), but also to draw the parallels to how the pagan cultures knew that sacrifice was needed in our fallen world (though their practice of it was idolatrous and, often, evil). That being said, I would be remiss not to mention, in our post-Christian culture, how these sacrificial practices are carried out today: through abortion and the use of abortifacients. Though we might think ourselves more advanced than the Seafurian people, in our own culture the lives of unborn children are often sacrificed to the gods of career goals, achieving an "acceptable" standard of living, or maintaining control of a pre-planned life instead of humbly accepting God's loving and sometimes surprising plans. And some women—in an economically, mentally, or emotionally vulnerable state—are pressured into sacrificing their unborn children on the altar of fear when there is no one near to help and support them. There are also the occasions when an abortion is used as a literal sacrifice: when a satanic wizard visits an abortion clinic to get his "hands bloody." (For those pondering the meaning of this, I suggest they seek out video testimonials of Zachary King, a former satanic grand wizard.)

On a somewhat related topic, I would like to acknowledge that Nicholaus's emotions in the beginning of the book (hollowness and despair from the loss of fatherhood) were, sadly, inspired from research of what men experience when their children are aborted against their wishes. When it comes to abortion, often the man's feelings are disregarded, and he is left to cope alone. Even those who, at the time, supported the abortion may later come to regret their support of the act and feel overwhelming guilt, and suffer in silence for years, if not their lifetime. For all those—male or female—who have experienced abortions and are feeling overwhelmed, there is help. I encourage those to seek out help from such places as Rachel's Vineyard (rachelsvineyard.org), Priests for Life (.org), and/or Silent No More Awareness (.org). God's mercy is vast, and He will lead a person to healing if one is truly repentant.

On a lighter subject, in the past readers have questioned me about the whereabouts of Anchony and Annabelle's world in relation to our planet. Though initially surprised by the question—since the story is completely fictional and I, personally, see no need of an actual location—I have come to an explanation that I hope others may accept: The kingdoms and land-masses in Annabelle's world are what *could have been* after "all the foundations of the great deep were broken up, and the flood gates of heaven were opened" (Genesis 7:11, DRV). After the massive upheaval and every substance that God had made was destroyed from the face of the earth (Genesis 7:3, DRV) at the time of the Great Flood, there were cataclysmic continental changes (from the theoretical Pangea). If the resulting continental changes had been different than the formation of the continents we have today, the placement of the landmasses in Annabelle's world is one possibility of what could have been.

Regarding the sacraments presented in this book, I feel there is one situation that might need further explanation: that of Augustine and Claudia's Baptism. The typical minister of Baptism is a priest or a deacon; however, when there is a necessity of Baptism (when an unbaptized person is in danger of death), anyone is allowed to baptize as long as water is placed on the head, the correct formula is said, and the intention is to baptize (see the *Catechism of the Catholic Church* 1284 for more details). Once this is done, the baptized person is now a part of the Body of Christ.

I would, however, like to point out that Lina never said, "I baptized them." Stay tuned to the next book for that exploration!

Your sister in Christ,

Ruth Apollonia

ALL THINGS ANNABELLE

Anchony fans can now enjoy a deep dive into the Annabelle of Anchony series by visiting RuthApollonia.com. There, readers will encounter "Behind the Scenes," which explores the writing of the series; "The Rocky Road," which presents its publishing history; and "Explore, Enlighten, & Extract: Diving Deep into the Spirituality Behind the Series," which are book discussion questions to provoke thought and deepen relationships when completed with a fellow reader (often one older and one younger). The discussion questions are a work in progress and will be completed in book order.

RuthApollonia.com